STEVE PETERSON

DAYS OF TERROR, MAYHEM & MURDER

Published by

MELROSE BOOKS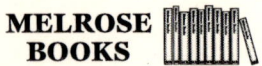

An Imprint of Melrose Press Limited
St Thomas Place, Ely
Cambridgeshire
CB7 4GG, UK
www.melrosebooks.com

FIRST EDITION

Copyright © Steven Peterson 2010

The Author asserts his moral right to
be identified as the author of this work

Cover designed by Jeremy Kay

ISBN 978 1 907040 43 6

All rights reserved. No part of this publication may be reproduced, stored in a retrieval system, or transmitted, in any form or by any means electronic, mechanical, photo-copying, recording or otherwise, without the prior permission of the publishers.

This book is sold subject to the condition that it shall not, by way of trade or otherwise, be lent, re-sold, hired out or otherwise circulated without the publisher's prior consent in any form of binding or cover other than that in which it is published and without a similar condition including this condition being imposed on the subsequent purchaser.

Printed and bound in Great Britain by:
CPI Antony Rowe. Chippenham, Wiltshire

Chapter 1

It was an hour or two past midday and nothing seemed to move in the rugged Pakistani countryside. As far as the eye could see the area was deserted, apart from an abandoned, dilapidated farmhouse which looked as though it had been empty for many years: the mud walls were crumbling and where there had been windows, glass was missing, if there had ever been any. There was a cloud of dust, far off on the horizon, and after some minutes a car appeared, driving slowly in the direction of the farmhouse. Three men could be seen inside, if anyone had been observant enough to notice. All were silent. When the car reached the farmhouse, all three men got out, stretched their legs, looked around at the barren land and then went inside the building. The tallest man, who had been driving, spoke first.

"Well, my friends, the time has come when all our planning and training is going to come to fruition. I've brought everything with me and after this meeting we'll not see each other again until we arrive at our final destination.

"First of all, I'll explain to you the details of my journey, so that we're all familiar with what each of us is going to do and how you're going to travel and what your cover stories are. My passport says I'm Dr Hamid Patel, travelling from Islamabad to Amsterdam. I'll spend four days visiting the usual tourist sites in the city, and during the evenings I'll visit the mosque, but keep to myself and not associate with anyone else. After that I'll buy an air ticket to London and make my way to a small hotel, which has been arranged." Hamid now turned to one of his associates and said, "These are all the papers you'll need. On your passport your name is Mahmoud Kamil and you're a student dental surgeon. You're on your way to Cape Town where you are to spend three days sightseeing and resting before starting your final dental training. After three days you have an open air ticket to fly to Birmingham, and when you reach the airport you're to ring the phone number in your instructions and just say 'parcel from Cape Town'. After a short time you'll be picked up and taken to a safe house. When you reach it you must burn all your instructions; nothing must ever be found."

He turned to the third man. "Here is your passport, which gives your name as Hamood Ismir, and you are a graduate of ancient history. You're going to Manchester University, hoping to enrol on a post-graduate course. You have a ticket to fly to Paris, where you'll spend three or four days sightseeing etc., then you'll use your open ticket to fly to Manchester. On your arrival at Manchester Airport, ring the number given in the folder and say 'arrived from France'. Again, you'll be picked up and taken to your safe house. And both of you; do not get picked up by the wrong vehicle. The driver will use the same words you used on the phone. What was yours, Hamood?"

For a moment there was no response and then Hamood said, "Forgive me; it was 'arrived from France'."

Turning to Mahmoud, Hamid asked, "And yours?"

"Parcel from Cape Town."

Hamid continued. "This simple example shows how absolutely vital it is to learn and remember your new identity, who you are now. One slip and our whole operation is doomed. While you are waiting to start, keep repeating your new name and the other details of your new identity.

"Today is Tuesday; I'm flying from Islamabad to Amsterdam on Thursday and I should arrive some time in the afternoon and be in my hotel by early evening. I won't be staying in a safe house like you, but I'm booked into a modest hotel, just like any tourist, which we're all posing as, and we'll behave just like them. Once you have arrived at the safe houses, I'll contact both of you. Until then, that is all we need to discuss. You'll find the dates of your flights in your instructions, and also credit cards, which you'll use for any payments and they can also be used to withdraw cash. Make a note of the PIN. Remember, the credit card has a limit and each of us will be held accountable for any money spent. We came here because this old, decrepit building is safe from prying eyes and listening devices, but we'll not meet again until all three of us reach our final destination. If something happens to me, you are to sit tight in your safe house until someone contacts you and identifies himself by the secret code you know. Are there any questions?" There was silence. "Right, my friends, we'll go back now and I'll drop you off where I picked you up."

Chapter 2

Upon his arrival at Amsterdam Airport, Hamid Patel, having collected his luggage, was directed to the non-EU passport and customs checkout. His luggage did not contain anything unusual and he went quickly on to stand in the passport control queue. The desk was busy and he had to wait. When he finally reached the head of the queue, the official looked carefully at his passport.

"From Pakistan?" he asked.

"Yes," said Hamid.

"What brings you to Amsterdam?"

"I just wanted to take a look at your famous city before I take up a position as a GP doctor in London."

"So how long are you going to stay here?"

"Three or four days."

"Seems a long way to come for such a short visit."

"I'm then going to visit London." Immediately, Hamid realised his mistake.

The official gave him a long, hard look and studied his passport again. "Please wait here," he said and went through a door into an adjacent office. While he was waiting, Hamid was fuming with rage at his own carelessness; he knew he should have realised that ever since the London bombings, words like Muslim and Pakistan spoken by an Asian and the mention of visits to London would provoke suspicion. What he should have said was that he was going to visit all of Holland and Belgium and not mention London at all. Well, it was too late now and the important thing was to bluff his way out of a difficult situation as best he could.

He did not have to wait long. The door to the office opened and the official said, "Please come through here, sir. There seems to be a small problem we need to obtain clarification about," and ushered him through the door.

On walking into the room, Hamid was struck by the appearance of a big man sitting behind the desk, with another man, of nearly equal size, standing at his side. The passport official walked out, closing the door behind him. There was complete silence.

The Inspector kept Hamid standing; he knew the technique well: try to intimidate the person by making him feel like a schoolboy facing a teacher, not knowing whether he was going to be punished or not.

Hamid kept saying in his mind, "Stay cool; don't let him unnerve you; concentrate on your cover story," over and over again.

After what seemed like a long pause, the big man said blandly, "So, you have come to Amsterdam to see our beautiful city. What particular part were you wanting to visit most?"

For a moment, Hamid was lost for words, racking his brains to remember what he had read about Amsterdam, and then he said lamely, "Well, all of it, really."

"You're a Muslim, are you not?" asked his interrogator.

"Yes, I am," Hamid responded defensively. "Is there anything wrong with that?"

"Being a Muslim, you're not allowed to drink alcohol or look at our many sex shows or our blue movie cinemas, or engage sexually with any of our numerous prostitutes or visit our drug dens. Have I missed anything out? Can you name any specific thing you're going to see?"

"Er, the museums," said Hamid finally.

"Oh yes," said the big man smoothly, "we do have one or two well-known museums which should take you a couple of hours to go round." His voice changed and became more threatening. "Or did you think you could use Amsterdam as a staging post for London, that Amsterdam would be an easy city to pass through and getting to London through here would arouse very little suspicion, coming from another EU country? Well I have to tell you, you're wrong. My colleague was not at all happy about your papers and neither am I. We're going to put your passport through some stringent checks. Meanwhile, you'll be held until we're satisfied that you are who you say you are."

"Can I have your name, sir?" asked Hamid politely.

"Certainly, sir," the man answered equally politely. "I'm Inspector Jan Stromberg, Chief of Police at this station, and my assistant is Sergeant Hans Vogel."

"I intend to take this matter up with my embassy and I wish to contact a lawyer. Where's the telephone?"

"You have a lawyer already?"

"No, I'm going to contact the Pakistan Embassy and they will appoint one for me so that I'm not deprived of any rights or privileges to which I'm entitled," said Hamid pompously, while his mind raced through the awful possibilities if his mission were discovered.

"The telephone is over there," said Jan.

"Thank you," said Hamid stiffly. He had trained his memory to recall certain vital telephone numbers, one of them being the number for the Pakistan Embassy in Holland, and he made the call, giving all his imaginary details to the clerk on duty, trying to put a note of justifiable indignation into his voice as the innocent passenger unfairly held up for no reason.

He was taken away and put in a cell, but although the time he had to wait seemed endless to him, it was only about an hour before he was escorted back to the Inspector's office. There, apart from Jan and Hans, he found a small Asian man, wearing large spectacles, sitting on a chair in front of the desk. As soon as Hamid entered the room, he quickly approached him and asked urgently, "Are you all right?"

"Yes, I'm fine, but for some reason I seem to be under arrest."

"I'm sorry, I must introduce myself. My name is Josef Mangoly and I'm a fully qualified solicitor, sent by the Pakistan Embassy to help you in this difficult situation." Having shaken Hamid's hand, he turned to Jan and said, "Why is this man being detained?"

"He's being held on suspicion of illegal entry and using falsified documents."

"You cannot hold a man in custody just because you're not happy with his documents; you're depriving him of his human rights!"

"I can and I will," said Jan.

"I'm going to contact your Advocate General and get this man released immediately," said the solicitor grandly.

Jan stood up. He must have been all of six foot three and big with it. Walking over to the little man, he leaned over him and said, "Listen to me, you little shyster; you do not come into my office and tell me what I can and cannot do. I'll tell you what I'm going to do." Turning to Hans, he pointed at Hamid and said, "Put this man back in a cell."

After Hans had taken Hamid out of the room, Jan looked at the little man and said, "I've heard a lot about you, defending all the scum of this city and using every possible loophole and any other unscrupulous method to let guilty men go. People like you are not welcome in this city or anywhere in the EU."

If Jan thought he was frightening Mangoly, he was wrong. There was a blank stare behind the glasses and the voice, when he spoke, held menace. "I'm not easily browbeaten, Inspector, and better men than you have tried to frighten and threaten me. But I have friends in this city, all sorts of friends, so don't try anything! I'm leaving now and I'll get in touch with the authorities to inform them of this matter. An innocent man is being held against his will when all he wanted to do was see some of our tourist sights. It's a disgrace that anyone should be treated like this."

"Before you go," said Jan smoothly, "I'd like proof that you are who you say you are. You've come into my office, claiming to be a lawyer, but up to now I've not seen any ID or anything to back up your story, and I'm wondering at the speed with which you landed on my doorstep. I find it very odd that you're so quick off the mark for an unknown 'tourist' who rings his embassy, without having to look up the phone number by the way, who then sends an advocate post-haste to get him released before he can be interrogated properly. Putting all the facts together, I find this suspicious."

"Come on, Inspector, you've heard that I'm a fully trained lawyer and have been practising law in this country for a number of years.

And you said yourself that I always defend scumbags and low-life villains, as you put it. Surely that makes my credentials in order."

"Nevertheless, I've not seen any documents to prove that you're certified to practise law in this country, so I'm going to have you escorted off my premises and I want to see you back here tomorrow morning with all your documents and certificates, in this office at 11 a.m., and if you don't come, then I'll have to assume that you do not have any proof of identity and I'll make it my business to arrest you on various charges of fraud."

Ignoring Mangoly's baleful glare, Jan escorted him to the outside door of the premises and closed it firmly behind him. Back to his office, he called Hans in. "I want the detained man on the earliest available plane to Pakistan – today if possible. State the reason for his deportation as that he's classed as 'a suspicious entry'. Do it right away and let me know when it's done."

Some time later, the Chief Inspector from the Advocate General's office telephoned. After a few preliminary words about home life and general information, the Chief Inspector said, "Now then, Jan, what's this complaint that's been brought to my attention from some Muslim lawyer referring to the treatment he's received at your police station?"

Jan felt a sudden premonition that there may be repercussions which he had not foreseen. He drew a deep breath. "Well, sir, I'm dealing with a case of possible illegal entry to our country. A person I've never heard of insists on seeing me, says he's a lawyer fully qualified to practise law here and has come to represent a client. He then tells me what I can or cannot do and that I must release his client immediately. Meanwhile, I'm holding the arrival from Islamabad on suspicion of using a false passport in an attempt to enter the country illegally."

"Everything looks to be in order. What are you proposing to do with the person you're holding?"

"When questioned, he let slip that he was going to London, which in the circumstances seemed to me to be a bit suspicious. Why not just go direct, unless he was thinking that flying in from Amsterdam would make him less suspicious?"

"Okay, send him back where he came from and notify MI5 with a copy of his passport. How's Helga, by the way?"

"She's fine, sir."

"Give her my best regards," the Chief Inspector said cheerfully, and the phone clicked off.

The next morning, at eleven o'clock precisely, Josef Mangoly appeared in Jan's office.

"Good morning, Inspector. Here are all my documents, my graduation certificate, the authorisation to practise law from the Inspector General and the Upper Court of Law Authority of Pakistan, and my two-year assessment certificate for my practice in Islamabad. He looked at Jan smugly, clearly enjoying what he thought was his success. "Can I now see my client?"

Jan was unmoved. "Perhaps I should point out that all this paperwork might look impressive to you, but you've missed out a vital document. To practise law in this country you need a Certificate of Authority from our Chief Justice's' Department, and I do not see it here."

The little man nearly choked, but trying to recover his composure, he gritted his teeth and said, "I'm a qualified lawyer. How many certificates do I need?"

Jan said sweetly, "This is the law of this country; all professions dealing with the public at a high level, like doctors, architects, lawyers and so on, must have the appropriate authorisation certificates to enable them to practise their profession. You don't seem to have this document, therefore you should not be practising law in this country and you've been working illegally. I'll report the matter to the highest appropriate authority, who will then make a decision about your future. In the meantime, you are not to practise in any way as a lawyer. If you do, you'll be arrested and put in jail. You're free to go and will be sent a copy of the decision and notified of what action is to be taken in due course."

The little man left the office without another word.

Chapter 3

Two days after the incident, Jan and Helga were, for once, enjoying a quiet breakfast. Helga started work at nine o'clock and Jan usually left for work soon after eight. Helga only had to walk a short distance to the primary school where she worked as a teacher. They had met and married in their early twenties and decided not to have children for a while so that they could each establish themselves in their chosen careers. But a couple of years on, Helga had the first of several miscarriages and although doctors assured them that there were no physical reasons why this should happen, they decided to wait a couple more years and enjoy each other; they were still deeply in love.

"How are things at the airport?" asked Helga lightly. "Any celebrities passing through and causing pandemonium with their huge mounds of luggage and demands for special privileges?"

Jan concentrated on his second cup of coffee and the football results in the paper – his team was not doing very well, slipping down the table. "Just the usual ups and downs," he said casually.

"I thought you seemed to be preoccupied with something. Anything in particular?"

"You know what police work is like, always dealing with something out of the ordinary. It changes from one moment to the next, which makes the job more interesting. Sorry, darling, but I have to go." He kissed his wife and said, "See you tonight."

"Will you be home at the usual time?"

"Barring disasters, yes."

As he went out to the garage, she heard the door close: the small kitchen was at the back of their ground-floor apartment. She heard the car start. The massive explosion which followed shook the whole building, shattering glass and hurling furniture. Helga was trapped against a cupboard and she could hear what sounded like an injured animal wailing. She realised it was her. In slow motion, she tried to gather her wits and struggled to open the warped door, completely disregarding the cuts on her face and hands. The horrific devastation she saw outside her home was beyond her comprehension. There were only remnants of the car, a mangled, charred and twisted mass of metal, still on fire. Other unidentifiable debris was strewn over the road. There was no sign of a body. People were coming out of their apartments, and the traffic was sliding to a stop in the road, halted by the pall of black smoke hanging over the street and the obscene wreckage.

Helga's wailing cries slowly petered out. She realised that she was looking at Jan's car. As the shock took over, her knees crumpled and she slid to the floor. The first policemen to arrive found her lying, partly on the pavement and partly on the steps, surrounded by onlookers, unable to decide what they should do for her. The policemen immediately took charge, ordering everyone back, and a policewoman, who knew Helga, came to her aid, soothing her and trying to get her to say exactly what had happened. Meanwhile, her colleagues were busy on their radio, calling for reinforcements and emergency and forensic services. Helga sat numb with shock, staring into space.

An ambulance arrived and Helga was taken to the nearest hospital emergency unit, accompanied by the policewoman. The Bomb Squad appeared on the scene and cordoned off a large area so that they could search for the slightest scrap of evidence. The official in charge of the Anti-Terrorist Unit arrived and took charge of the situation, checking to make sure nothing had been booby-trapped to catch unwary onlookers.

Helga was unable to give any information straightaway because she had been sedated. Her evidence could be crucial.

With all the preliminary work completed, there was an urgent meeting called the following day, attended by representatives of the Secret Service, the police, the Anti-Terrorist Unit and the Home Security Department. Hans was invited to update the others on the events of the previous day in the airport police station. As the meeting progressed, it became apparent that there may have been a connection between the arrest and deportation of Hamid Patel, the dismissal of his lawyer and the killing of Jan, but none of the people attending the meeting could shed any light on who had carried out the atrocity. The Secret Service had no information from their undercover agents about a new terrorist cell operating in Holland and they had checked all the known ones. The other units had also come to a dead end.

"May I make a suggestion?" said Hans.

"Sure," responded the Chief of Police.

"The evidence from the scene is being processed, but it's a slow process. Could I suggest we put a phone tap and twenty-four-hour surveillance on Hamid's so-called lawyer? We might get something quickly."

Everyone agreed to put this into place and to inform Hans of any developments on a daily basis.

As the meeting was breaking up, the Chief of Police crossed the room and told Hans that he was furious about Jan's assassination and that everything possible would be done to get whoever did it. Jan had been a good man and work colleague. "But meanwhile, you're in charge until a new inspector can be appointed, so keep on doing a good job. If anything occurs to you, let me know pronto. I have to go now and visit Helga. She's still totally shocked, but I'm hoping there might be some little thing she remembers, anything, that can help us get the bastards who did this."

Chapter 4

The first day of surveillance produced nothing. There were no phone calls and the lawyer did not appear outside his apartment. The following day was exactly the same.

At 9 p.m., the leader of the listening detail stood up, stretching and yawning. "Well, that's our shift over, and a complete waste of time, if you ask me," he said.

Around 10 p.m., they drove away with nothing to report. But about one hour later, just as Mangoly was preparing to go to bed, thinking that it would be too late for any contact, the intercom to his room rang.

"Yes," he said.

A voice said, "It's me."

"I'll come down."

A few moments later, when he stepped outside the door of his apartment block, there were two plopping sounds and Mangoly fell to the floor. A shadowy figure, blending into the background with a black balaclava over his head, quickly disappeared down a side alleyway, leaving the body to be discovered early in the morning by the shocked owner of one of the other apartments.

What followed was similar to the events following Jan's death. The crime scene was sealed off and Forensics did their work, combing the area for a weapon, but there was very little they could discover. The lawyer had been shot at close range, most likely by someone he knew, as there were no signs of a struggle or any other violence. When they had finished their work, the body was taken away for a post mortem and another meeting was held by the Police Chief and the Head of the Secret Service. Also attending the meeting was Erik van Eyck, who had been appointed Inspector of the airport police in place of Jan.

The Head of the Secret Service spoke first. "We were asked to put in place twenty-four-hour surveillance at the lawyer's address and we did just that. It was in place for two days and during that time nothing, and I repeat nothing, happened. There were no phone calls, no visits and he didn't leave the building at all during that time. But it appears that the team on duty from 10 a.m. to 10 p.m. left a little early, fractionally before their replacements took over. In that short time, somebody must have lured Mangoly downstairs to the door. It appears that the intercom might have been faulty. When he was shot, nobody saw or heard anything."

"This means they were aware of our surveillance," Erik said.

"How did they know that?" asked the Head of Security.

"They probably assumed that some kind of a watch would be kept on the person who had the most recent contact with Jan, particularly after such a suspicious death, and it doesn't take much to work out that a plain van permanently parked all day in one place might be a surveillance team," Erik suggested.

"It might have been better if the surveillance team had been placed in the building opposite, but that would have meant a large number of people would have known what was going on, and a well-meaning neighbour might have given the game away," said the Chief of Police.

"Well, that's all water under the bridge," said the Head of the Secret Service. "That particular line of inquiry is lost to us now. We have a number of terrorist cells operating in Amsterdam and probably in other parts of Holland too. We do our best to keep an eye on them through informers and undercover agents, but it appears that we have someone new active in our city we know nothing about. They appear to be well trained and very clever, so how do we go about catching them?"

There was silence. The consequences of having a completely unknown terrorist cell working underground in one of Holland's major cities posed an unquantifiable threat to the security of the whole country.

The Police Chief turned to the Head of Security and said, "There must be procedures for stopping terrorism, but at this point we have little to go on. We have two deaths, but the evidence collected so far has produced nothing positive. We know that they used plastic explosives, which can be obtained and moved around fairly easily, to blow up Jan's car, but there were no fingerprints or other forensic evidence to go on, and the only positive lead we have is that the lawyer was shot with a 0.3 calibre weapon by a professional assassin with no connection to the victim."

"But this guy has been in the country for some time," Erik interjected. "He practised law; he must have had associates, friends, people he knew. If he was part of a terrorist group he must have had some way of communicating with them."

"Forensics have carried out a fingertip search of his apartment and all his belongings and we're waiting for their report, but it seems as if our subjects have covered their tracks very successfully," said the Head of Security. "If any information comes to light, I'll inform you all immediately."

After the others had left, the Chief of Police turned to Erik. "We'll have to pursue this matter ourselves, although of course we'll co-operate with the other services. Do you have any plans for the near future?"

"Completely at your service, sir," said Erik cheerfully, pushing to the back of his mind any thoughts of leave until this problem had been resolved. He concentrated on the known facts as he saw them. "The lawyer is the best lead so far and I'd like to start by getting to know everything about him and the people he knew. I'd like to ask the sergeant who was on duty at the same time as Jan to pick a team of three other experienced police officers and dedicate them solely to this investigation."

"Okay, Inspector, you have my go ahead, but keep me fully aware of the smallest piece of solid information you get."

Hans was keen to be a part of the investigation and he and Erik decided what kind of team they needed: officers that they could work with easily, who were confident and good at their jobs and experienced in the painstaking search for facts.

"It'll take me a couple of days to come up with the right names, but I'll get on to it right away," said Hans, "and as soon as I've organised this, we can all meet and agree on our procedure."

Chapter 5

Hamid Patel, having been put on a plane by the police, arrived in Islamabad, went straight through passport control, as he had a Pakistani passport, and went out of the airport buildings without a single check. If the Dutch police had given any information to the Pakistani authorities, nothing was done there.

He took a taxi to his apartment, and having freshened up from his arduous journey, had a light meal and made a telephone call. The only contact any field operative ever had with a controller was a telephone number, which they had to memorise. The phone number was unlisted and no address would be found for it. He dialled the number and waited. Eventually, a voice said, "Yes."

He knew the rules – minimum conversation over the phone – so he just said, "0113, I'm back."

There was a pause on the other end and then the voice said, "A car will pick you up in one hour."

As Hamid was waiting, he went over and over in his mind what he was going to say. He was in a bad situation and he knew that he had failed in his mission. He must explain what had happened to show himself in the best possible light, a victim of impossible difficulties etc., because he did not want to suffer any bad consequences as a result of his failure. The company did not accept failure lightly; people usually just disappeared without any trace. There was a lot of wild mountain terrain on the borders between Pakistan and Afghanistan that was totally desolate; a body would never be found. The company did not mind if volunteers who planned and financed their own operations did not succeed, like the two London bombing failures, as this was due to the volunteers' incompetence and did not reflect on them. But if they did succeed, the company took the credit. However, this time the operation had been planned and financed by the company, and in the event of its complete failure, a scapegoat would be needed and any repercussions would rebound on Hamid, making him the first casualty.

He heard the car outside and was ready. He took a deep breath and stepped outside, taking care to lock the door behind him. The car door opened and with a fast-beating heart, he slid into the back seat. The door was closed and he heard the click of the lock. The windows were of deeply tinted glass and only while the car was under street lighting could he just see outside. With a sudden swerve, the car turned to the left, bouncing on a rough country road, and he could see nothing. The night was dark and before long he was completely disoriented, with no idea in what direction they were travelling. They evidently didn't want him to find this place in the future, supposing he had one.

The car slewed to a near halt with a squeal of brakes after passing through tall gates set in a high wall, and finally drew up at the side of a two-storey building. Hamid was told to get out. Apart from that command, the two men had said nothing, for which he was glad; the last thing he needed at that point were irrelevant remarks or small talk.

The first man rang a bell located near the door and they waited, Hamid trying not to panic and wondering if he should try to escape. Only now, outside the car, could he see the second man, who looked big and bulky. Like he had trained as a wrestler, thought Hamid. The muscle the company used when escorting a prisoner!

The door opened and Hamid was pushed inside. The spacious room had a rich carpet on the floor and the walls were hung with large tapestries, effectively covering any windows, preventing any fresh air or light getting in. But it was strangely cool and Hamid was convinced that somewhere, behind the expensive furnishings, there must be some form of air conditioning. Hamid stopped looking around, trying to concentrate on the three men he now saw sitting cross-legged on mats and holding their prayer beads. They motioned to Hamid to sit down, which he did, praying that this was not the prelude to a death sentence.

After what seemed like an interminable length of time, during which Hamid dare not speak, the man sitting in the middle of the three said in a quiet voice, "We have heard part of the story from our friend in Amsterdam, but we would like to hear what you have to say."

Hamid cleared his throat. "There is very little to tell. I got as far as passport control and the inspector there took one look at my passport and raised his eyebrows. He told me to wait and went into another office; after a few minutes I was told to follow him and then the interrogation started."

"What did they ask you?" enquired the man on the left.

"The usual type of thing: what was I going to do in Amsterdam. I said I came to visit their beautiful city. They then asked me if I was a Muslim and I said yes, but they doubted that a devout Muslim would find the drug scene, their strong beer and their sex shows and prostitutes very interesting. And when I said that I was going to look at museums and historical buildings they treated me with derision. There was nothing I could say to convince them I was just a sightseeing visitor. There must have been something wrong with the passport which put me under suspicion straight away. I don't think they would have become so interested in me if I'd flown in from somewhere like Mumbai rather than coming straight from Islamabad to Europe." He came to a halt, realising that he had criticised the organisation of the mission.

The man in the middle said, "Give us your passport. It will be of no use to us now; it will be destroyed. Have you any other papers that you took with you that were examined by the airport police?"

"No."

"Regarding your passport, the others' are exactly the same in every way. It will be interesting to see how they get on."

"It was the Pakistani passport and the destination combined that made them suspicious," said Hamid defensively.

"Yes, yes. We might be able to use you again, in which case you'll get a new passport and travel documents and continue with the operation as a leader. The driver will take you back now and you must wait for further instructions."

Hamid breathed a silent sigh of relief, glad that the meeting was over. The driver dropped him four hundred yards away from his apartment and told him to walk on that side of the road until nearly opposite his home, making sure he was not being followed or observed. When he got inside he was not to switch on any lights but go to the window and check that nobody was loitering outside and that no cars were parked in the wrong place. Hamid did as he was instructed but found nothing out of the ordinary. Exhausted, he undressed and fell into bed.

Chapter 6

When the time came for Mahmoud Kamil to make his journey, he flew to Cape Town. At passport control he was only asked his reason for coming to South Africa. He told them that he was a student dental surgeon and was taking a break from studying for a few days' holiday. The official behind the desk nodded, stamped his passport and wished him good day.

Mahmoud found his way out of the airport buildings, threading his way through all the scaffolding and hurrying workmen. At the taxi rank he asked a driver to take him to a hotel where he would not have to pay too much. The driver obliged by taking him to a hotel run by one of his many relatives and told the receptionist to look after his passenger, knowing that he could expect a favour in return for this added business. To Mahmoud he said, "There you are, sir. This is a very good hotel and they will not charge you too much. If you want to go anywhere in Cape Town or round about, they know my number, and here's my card if you want to get in touch with me direct."

Obeying his instructions, for the next three days Mahmoud spent his time like a tourist, visiting Table Mountain, Robben Island, the gardens and the beaches. When it was time to leave, he took a taxi back to the airport and tried to book a flight to Birmingham. However, he found that there were no direct flights to Birmingham, so he had to book one for Heathrow and then take a domestic flight to Birmingham.

He had no problem checking in at Cape Town, but when his flight arrived at Heathrow there was a long queue at passport control for passengers from non-EU countries and it seemed as if they were paying particular attention to Asian passport holders. He was asked to follow an official to a separate office for an interview. Mahmoud kept cool and appeared untroubled by the questions they put to him, sticking to the same story: that he had distant relatives in England and as a student dental surgeon he was hoping to take a post-graduate course at a British university. People were going to meet him at Birmingham airport, but he did not know their address; relatives in Pakistan had arranged it all for him. They might even have a suitable daughter of marriageable age for him to meet! After what seemed an age, he was ushered out and allowed to check in for his flight to Birmingham.

At the domestic flights area he was told that the next flight would not be until 17.30, so perhaps he would be better off going by rail. But he declined, as he had to meet his contacts at the airport.

When he eventually arrived at Birmingham he searched for a phone. Using the number he had memorised, Mahmoud waited on tenterhooks, repeating his message over and over in his head, until someone finally answered. As soon as the voice on the phone said, "Yes," he said, "Arrived from Cape Town."

He was told to wait just inside the main exit and that he would be picked up in about twenty minutes. Mahmoud paced up and down, trying not to appear too obvious, until a man dressed in a smart chauffeur's uniform approached him and said, "Cape Town?"

Mahmoud accompanied him to a big black Mercedes. The chauffeur opened the door and Mahmoud slid into the passenger seat. Without another word, they drove swiftly away.

Mahmoud stared out of the window at the built-up area they were travelling through, which eventually gave way to countryside, and he tried to make sense of this alien country.

The car turned off the main road and passed through some open iron gates set in a high brick wall. The gates closed electronically behind them and the driver pulled up in front of a large house. Mahmoud got out of the car and, carrying his meagre luggage, went up the shallow steps to the building. He was greeted by a man in the spacious hallway and told that this would be his safe house.

Chapter 7

Hamood Ismir flew to Paris and on arrival at De Gaulle Airport went through customs and had his luggage thoroughly searched before he got to passport control, where a police inspector interviewed him.

"And you have come to Paris, why?"

"Just to see your beautiful city."

"Any particular area?"

"I would like to see the usual tourist areas."

"But you are a Muslim, are you not?"

"Yes, sir, but I can see Notre Dame Cathedral from the outside and admire the building. I'm a graduate of ancient history so all of those old buildings are of great interest to me."

"Where are you going after you have visited Paris?"

"I would like to see some of your other interesting cities, but a lot will depend on how much money I have to spend."

"Which hotel are you staying in?"

"As I said, my money situation is not that great so I can only afford a modest pension. Do you know of any I could try?"

"You can obtain a list of hotels and accommodation at the information desk. You can go now."

Hamood tried to hide his relief as he walked away and called at the information desk to collect a brochure, although he already had instructions about where to stay.

The three days passed quickly and he was soon back at the airport. He passed swiftly through check-in and shortly afterwards he was on a plane to Manchester. Security at Manchester was very strict and he was interviewed by passport control again, with the same questions being asked: why was he there, where was he staying and for how long? They wanted to know the exact address of where he was going to reside, a question that Hamood found very difficult to answer, so he gave them the story about his relatives coming to pick him up and not being sure which family he would be staying with and not knowing the exact address of any of them.

"You'll stay in this office until your relative comes to pick you up so we can obtain the exact address where you'll be staying during your time here. Make your phone call to contact them from this office," the official said, pointing to the phone.

This was very bad, as they would probably take a note of the car registration number along with a description of whoever came to collect him. He racked his brains, desperately trying to think of a solution to his dilemma. Looking up, he saw an advert for a twenty-four-hour minicab service and private hire. Grasping at straws, Hamood dialled the number given on the advert and waited for an answer.

"City Minicabs and private hire, can I help you?" said the voice at the other end of the phone.

"Private hire," he said, trying to keep his voice low.

"Certainly, sir. How many persons and where to?"

"I'm waiting at the passport office at the airport and I have to let them know my address in Manchester while I'm staying here, but my relatives have not yet come to collect me, so I don't know where it will be. Could you give me the address of a cheap hotel and drive me there?"

"Of course, sir. I'll give you the address when I pick you up in twenty minutes."

It was nearer thirty minutes before the driver knocked on the office door.

"Come in," said the Inspector, and an Asian man walked in.

"I'm to collect someone," the man said.

"Yes," said Hamood, thankfully. "Can you give this gentleman the address of where you're taking me?"

"Yes, it's 114 Hyde Road, Manchester, M16, sir."

The Inspector wrote it down and said to the driver, "This is a private address and not a caravan or a similar sort of place?"

Hamood froze. If the driver said it was a hotel, the Inspector would want a phone number and then he could easily check if he were there at any time, but the driver said seriously, "Oh no, sir, it's a house; been there for years."

"Okay, you can take him now we've got these details. We must keep our records straight, you know."

In the car, the driver asked, "What was all that about?"

"I've just got to England and as I have a Pakistani passport they think automatically that I'm a terrorist suspect so they must know where I'm going to be staying. But I might want to go to different places and if the police are anything like the ones at home, they really cramp your style."

"Oh, we're used to the police here now. I was born in this country and they're not too bad."

For the remainder of the comparatively short journey they were both quiet, Hamood because he was tired from his journey and the taxi driver because he was wondering what the real story was about his mysterious passenger. He didn't believe for one moment the story he was giving, but hey, why should he bother? It was a good fare at this time of day and he would probably get a big tip for playing along with the story.

He pulled up to the kerb and said, "Here you are, sir. That'll be twelve pounds."

Hamood sorted out the unfamiliar currency and gave him fifteen pounds, saying, "Keep the change."

Huh, thought the driver, last of the big spenders, I don't think. But he said politely, "Can I take you anywhere else, sir?"

"No thank you. Just leave me here. I'll go in and register straight away."

Taking his suitcase, Hamood waited until the driver was out of sight, then moved away from the hotel entrance, taking out his mobile phone. He rang the memorised number.

"Yes?" said the voice at the other end of the phone.

"Arrived from Paris. Can you pick me up from outside 114 Hyde Road, M16?"

For a moment there was silence. "You're not at the airport?"

"No. The passport authorities wanted the address where I would be staying while I was in Manchester, and of course I didn't know it, so I had to..."

"Wait there for twenty minutes. You can explain later," the voice said impatiently and hung up.

A Volvo car arrived in front of the hotel exactly twenty minutes later and the driver told Hamood to get in.

"Thank God," he said. "What a dreary day this has been." He shut his eyes for what seemed only a moment. Suddenly he was wide-awake, his thoughts desperately scrambling to work out what was happening. Then he realised that the car had stopped and it was so dark that he couldn't make out where he was.

"We're here," said the driver. "This is your safe house. Better come inside."

Chapter 8

Two days later, the passport inspector rang the number he had been given to check up on Hamood Ismir, and after a short conversation put the phone down and swore long and hard.

Somewhat amused by the language, his colleague asked, "What's the matter with you?"

"The bastard deceived me. He isn't staying at the address he gave me; it's some second-rate hotel not a residential address, and he never even registered with them. He's supposed to be staying with relatives. Where's that photocopy of his passport you took?" The Inspector was annoyed, as much with himself as with Hamood, as he realised that it was probably a false passport and that the man could be anywhere by now.

"Can you remember exactly what he looked like and who else dealt with him?" asked his colleague. "Get as many people together who saw him and get an identikit picture made up; then we can release the picture to the press, nationwide. We won't say anything about him slipping through the net, just that we're looking for him and no further details can be released at this time."

"You're a pal."

All the people that had seen Hamood helped the sketch artist to make a reasonably accurate picture of him, and next morning it appeared in most of the national dailies. In some it was on the front page with varying headlines and in others it was relegated to the inner pages, but they all asked for the public's help to locate the man and gave the number of the passport inspector's office.

That same day, Hamood was just finishing his midday meal when one of his contacts walked in and threw a newspaper in front of him, saying, "You're famous; you've made the headlines in the nationals already."

Hamood looked at the sketch. "They're not that clever. I'll just have to alter my appearance a little and they'll never recognise me," he boasted.

"Don't worry," said his contact, "we'll make you look so different, even your own mother wouldn't recognise you!"

Two days later, Hamood was taken on a bus to the city centre, made up with a short beard, moustache and a long-haired wig. He wore a very expensive suit, shirt and tie and carried a long black umbrella with an expensive ivory handle hooked over his wrist. This was to be a trial run, to see if anyone would recognise him as the person pictured in the newspaper sketch. He travelled all over the city centre, with a discreet watch being kept over him, first walking, then by tram, finally by taxi and even past a police station, where an indistinct picture of him was displayed on the outside notice board. Hamood quite enjoyed himself; it was good to get to see something of a foreign city after being cooped up in the safe house for several days. But apart from some admiring female glances, nobody took any notice of him – all the passers-by were busy with their own lives – so he travelled back by bus to the safe house without any difficulty. The next few days were spent watching to see if there were any reports of him being seen, but apparently nobody had. He started to cultivate his own beard and moustache and allowed his hair to grow longer. Two weeks later still nothing had appeared in the papers.

Chapter 9

In Pakistan, in the house where Hamid had been taken, the three men were holding a discussion. The man who sat in the centre, their leader, said, "The British are being very careful and almost exposed our man who flew to Manchester. Do you think our plan of operation has been endangered in any way?"

The man on the right said, "They only have a sketch of Hamood and our operatives say that his change of appearance and subsequent outing were very successful; nobody appeared to notice anything untoward. There are a lot of Asian people in Manchester, as you know."

The man on the left said, "I agree; nothing of our operation has been revealed, so we should go on. A new passport and travel arrangements have been made and all the papers will be delivered to Hamid tonight. I don't think there is any need to alter our arrangements; after all, it has taken us a long time to get everything into place."

Hamid heard the sound of a motorbike revving its engine outside his flat and then a sharp knock on the door. A man handed a large, bulky envelope to him without taking off his helmet, so that Hamid could not see his face, and then roared away.

Hamid closed the door and looked with some trepidation at the envelope. With a sigh of relief, he found a new passport, two air tickets and a list of instructions, which he was to burn when he had committed everything to memory. The first air ticket was for a flight to Dubai from the local airport; the second was from Dubai to Heathrow, dated four days after his arrival at Dubai. He carefully lit a match and burned the paper and crushed the ashes to powder. He was now Abdul Hamis, graduate construction engineer, and he was travelling to Europe to study modern building construction, starting in Dubai. He hoped he could avoid any questions relating to technical matters, as he actually knew very little about the subject.

He set off the next morning on the first leg of his journey to London. There were no problems entering Dubai and he enjoyed his four-day stay at a so-called modest hotel, which was the equivalent of a five-star hotel in any other part of the world. He kept reminding himself that he was not there on holiday and that the worst part was waiting for him in London.

At Heathrow, he collected his luggage from the carousel and made his way to the passport-checking desk, trying to subdue his nerves. He smiled at the lady who was checking his passport and said that he hoped she had arranged some nice sunny weather for him.

She looked up and seeing a handsome face, smiled back. "Oh, yes, sir, we always try to please our visitors." She looked back at his passport and asked if he were there for business or pleasure.

"A bit of both, really."

She took another quick glance at him, noting the expensive suit and luggage, and thought what a pleasant-looking young man he was, with excellent manners; not like some of the passengers she had to deal with. Handing back his passport, she said, "Have a nice stay in England."

Thanking her, he walked away, triumph and relief washing over him: he'd made it and the authorities had let him through with no difficulty. He was so relieved that he had to stop himself shouting out, "I'm here at last." Using his mobile phone, he rang the number he had memorised so carefully.

"I'm at Heathrow."

"Wait at a taxi stand in thirty minutes and you'll be picked up," said the voice on the other end.

Abdul found the taxi stand and, looking at his expensive watch, decided he had time for a drink and a visit to the men's room to freshen up after his flight. He found a coffee bar and stretched out his legs on one of the comfortable seats, whiling away the half-hour.

Back at the taxi stand, he was just turning down an offer from an enterprising taxi driver to drive him to the centre of London for an exorbitant fare when a large black Mercedes pulled up beside him. The driver got out and said, "Waiting for me, sir?"

"Yes, I've just arrived from Dubai."

The driver opened the rear door and said smoothly, "That's right, sir, everything is arranged for you. Would you like to get in?"

Abdul had never been to London and was fascinated as they threaded their way through the busy traffic. It was totally different to what little he had seen of Amsterdam. It took over an hour's drive through London's suburbs before they turned into a quiet street lined with trees, the houses set well back from the road. The car turned into a short drive and drew up outside a detached house, the garden of which was surrounded by high brick walls. Abdul got out, picked up his suitcase and was shown into the house through the front door.

The driver said, "This is your safe house. Put your luggage down and in a few minutes someone will show you round."

Chapter 10

In Amsterdam, the police and security services were reviewing the progress made so far. After many hours of surveillance and interviews since the death of Jan and Mangoly, there were still no positive leads. Investigation of the Mangoly's friends and work colleagues made them doubt if the name he had been using was his real name, and no one could throw any light on his origins. His secretary, a local woman, did her best to be helpful, but she could only tell them about his workload since she had started to work in his office. The cases he dealt with were mostly defending immigrant workers who had fallen foul of EU regulations, and if there had been any involvement with terrorists, it was completely unknown to her. He didn't seem to have any social life outside work.

"He was a single man; he must have had some kind of sex life," Erik observed.

"We've got his photo, so if we show it round the red light area we may just get lucky," said Hans.

"Get a copy of it to every police officer in the city, with orders that each time they deal with any incidents in the red light area they must ask if anyone recognises this man and if any person has seen him at any time, no matter when or for what, and if anyone does, they must be brought to the police station at the airport."

As luck would have it, the police were investigating a theft from a client in the red light area, and when a detective showed Mangoly's picture around, one of the prostitutes recognised him and said that he was usually a regular customer but she hadn't seen him for some time. She was put in a police car, complaining that she was losing money all the time she was off her patch, and taken to the airport police station.

"Well done," Erik said effusively. "At last we seem to be getting somewhere. Please sit down," he said politely to the woman. "What can you tell me about this man?"

She shrugged and replied, "He was just a regular client; nothing particularly special about him, just straight sex. For about two years he would always ring before he turned up and then there was nothing kinky or perverted or anything like that. I offered him other services but he said he just wanted straight sex, and he was always very gentlemanly and polite."

"Did you ever talk about anything before, during or after sex?"

"No, he never said a word about himself, except 'good evening' and 'here you are' when he gave me my money."

"Did he ever mention friends, any names, any reference to anything in his life?"

"No, I told you; he seemed to be a very private person. But I did ask him once, when he first started coming, just to ease the situation like, what his job was and he said that it was just a dull, boring job like most people had and that I wouldn't be interested in what he did, even if he told me."

"So he never mentioned family or anything about his life? It must have been very boring for you."

"No, I already told you," she said patiently. "And as for boring." She gave a laugh. "Well, they all are, aren't they!"

Erik was beginning to get desperate. Here was his only lead in an apparently unsolvable crime and the woman appeared to know nothing of any use whatsoever. "Now think very carefully. This is very important. Did he ring or receive any calls while he was with you?"

She opened her mouth to give a negative answer but stopped as she remembered something. "Now, there you've reminded me." She paused with a look of concentration on her face. "I do remember," she said triumphantly. "I remember him receiving a call on his mobile and it seemed to upset him. He got very agitated but he wouldn't say why."

"Was it because it interrupted your lovemaking?"

"No, it was after we finished and he was getting dressed. He paid for two hours so that he could get undressed and have a shower and all that," she said proudly. "He was a good punter and I was sorry when he didn't ring me any more."

Erik emphasised his words as he said, "This is very important. Can you tell me the date and time he received this call?"

"Well, not really. I can't remember things like that offhand, but it would probably have been about seven weeks ago, and as he always came about six-thirty in the evening, straight after work, it would have been between eight and eight-thirty when he received the call."

At last, this could be some definite information instead of the endless theories they had been debating. Erik asked her to write down her name and address and her professional place of business, where she had met Mangoly and whether she had taken him to or met him in any other place. While she was busy writing, he arranged for a car to take her back to her patch. He then made another call to Hans, enquiring what had happened to Mangoly's mobile phone and to get it to the technical boys in the lab as quickly as possible so they could check all incoming and outgoing calls over the past ten weeks or so.

"When we get as much detail about his calls as possible, it might lead us to his contact with the terrorists. The phone call he received while he was with the prostitute apparently upset him and he was very agitated."

"I'll get on to it straightaway, sir, and let you know the outcome as soon as there are any results," said Hans.

"And when you've done that, come into my office," said Erik.

When Hans went into his office, Erik said to him, "Sit down and let's discuss the latest position regarding the two murders."

"As things stand at the moment," said Hans, "There's nothing to report on the situation which you're not already familiar with. We have no real leads. Forensics have come up with nothing about the explosion apart from the fact that it was caused by plastic explosives of a type that any criminal could obtain fairly easily from a contact in the underworld, and the detonator was set to go off when the ignition key was turned. Jan had probably been under observation for some time, being in charge of security at the airport, so they knew that his wife always walked to work and he used the car. It was made simple for the bomber: the car was left outside overnight, and in the dark, because it's a very quiet location, nobody would have noticed any unusual activity near it. It would have been easy for a skilled person to fit the device during the night and disappear without arousing any suspicion.

"In the case of Mangoly's murder, someone rang the doorbell of his flat and whatever was said to him on the intercom caused him to come all the way downstairs and open the door. He was then shot at very close range, the gun having a silencer fitted, and he died instantly; no one heard or saw a thing. His body was not found until the next morning, by another resident of the block of flats, and by that time, the killer was long gone. We can only hope that we get some information from his mobile phone records."

The following day, Hans got the details of the calls Mangoly had made and received and he went to Erik to report. "We've managed to trace the number of a caller who rang him while he was with the prostitute. He also has a landline in his office with two extensions and at home his phone is fitted with an answering machine. We have cheked all those very carefully but came up with nothing out of the ordinary; they were all to do with his business as a lawyer. This is the one call he received while he was with the prostitute and it was from a mobile. We're trying to trace the caller."

"What about any other calls he received? Has, a check has been made to trace them? We're clutching at straws here, but any information we can come up with might give us some insight into the kind of life he led and whether we can connect him with any of our known terrorist groups."

"We've checked and double-checked all the calls he made or received and all we can deduce is that he was a very methodical businessman who kept accurate, painstaking records, and in spite of the time it took to check everything, we've nothing to show for it."

"A lot of police work is like that," said Erik ruefully. "Let's hope this time we strike it lucky."

Chapter 11

Three days later, Erik had a call from Hans, who sounded jubilant. "Sir, good news. We managed to trace an address for the owner of the mobile and I drove past the place. It's a big two-storey house standing on its own in a quiet part of a residential area. All the houses round there are detached and a lot of them are surrounded with high walls: very secluded! Whoever the owner is, he must be well heeled to have a place like that!"

"Right, I want to have a look at this place. I'll collect you in a few minutes and we'll take my car so as not to arouse any suspicion if they're on watch."

An hour later they were standing outside the house. They had driven up with their story already rehearsed if anyone came out and questioned them: they were looking at properties in the neighbourhood with a view to buying and redeveloping in the area. The house had a large open area at the front for parking cars; there was a narrow garden to the left, with a concrete path to the rear on the right-hand side. There was nothing ostentatious, it was well maintained, and there were thick curtains at the windows. In fact there was nothing in the least bit suspicious about the place.

Erik and Hans walked up to the front door and rang the bell. After a long wait, a middle-aged man opened the front door, looking out cautiously.

"Can I help you?"

Erik put on his best 'estate agent' demeanour and, smiling brightly, said, "So sorry to bother you, but we were under the impression that this house was for sale."

"No, sorry," said the man, "my family has just moved in. We're renting it on a yearly basis, and to the best of my knowledge, it's always been a rented property."

"So the previous tenants also rented it?" asked Erik. The man nodded. "Did you meet them?"

"No, I just dealt with the house agent."

"Which agent was that?"

"I've got their card somewhere. I'll get it for you." He disappeared, closing the door, but soon reappeared with a grubby card giving the agent's professional address.

Erik and Hans drove straight to the agent's office. They showed their police identity cards to the receptionist and asked to see the manager. Once in the manager's office, Erik gave him the address of the property and said, "We need to know all the details about who rented the place previously."

The estate agent went straight to the filing cabinet behind him and pulled out a brown folder. "Here are all the details we have," he said nervously, wondering what had been happening at this excellent address, one of the best on his books. Erik read through the papers, trying to take in all the details. The name Kasim Ikbal Zahir, Pakistani citizen, stood out. He had been the previous tenant.

"Do you ask for any references? How do you confirm that the name they give you is correct?"

The agent said defensively, "We always check their paperwork before we let them have the keys; we ask to see passport, driving licence, identity card and bank account information. They have to agree to pay by direct debit or put up six months' rent in advance. All those details are on the file."

At a quick glance, Erik could see a photocopy of the main page of a passport, including the photograph, but there were no details of any bank account. He pointed this out to the agent.

"They paid six months' rent in advance in cash."

"You said 'they'?" Erik queried.

"I understood there were at least five people staying there. It's a big house with five bedrooms and two bathrooms."

"Were they all Asians?"

"I didn't see them all, but to the best of my knowledge they were."

"We must search the house as soon as possible."

"What about the owner?"

"Don't worry, we'll be there with an official warrant and we'll take this file with us. My sergeant will give you a receipt for it and you'll get it back as soon as we've completed our investigation. Just one other thing – when did they move out?"

"I'm not sure of the exact date, but everything should be in the file."

Outside in the car, Erik said to Hans, "We're too late to catch them here, but at least we now have some definite information to go on. Who knows, a thorough forensic search of the house may give us some further clues to follow up. At last we're beginning to get somewhere. Get a copy of that passport photo circulated to all airports, sea ports, police stations around the country and Interpol. Who knows, someone, somewhere might have seen and remembered him."

When the warrant was obtained, the house was searched intensively; every room was combed for the slightest indication that plastic explosives had been processed there or any other illegal activity. The best find was in the loft over the garage: a satellite dish capable of transmitting long-range radio signals with various plugs and lengths of cable, which somebody was going to be very sorry they had left behind. It hadn't really been hidden, so it looked as if the occupants had simply forgotten it when they left. There was no sign of any other electronic equipment and apart from the dish, very little else was discovered. The new tenants had thoroughly cleaned the rooms when they moved in a short time ago.

All they had to go on was the passport photo of a man of Pakistani origin who had signed the rental agreement. Nothing was known about who had stayed in the property, how many and what they were doing there. There was nothing illegal about using long-range communication devices. It would be some days before any forensic evidence could be assessed and in the meantime, another meeting was convened to review the progress of the investigation.

The Head of the Secret Service, the Head of Home Security, the Chief of Police and the Head of the Anti-Terrorist Unit sat round the table with Inspector van Eyck to give their own reports to the group for their assessment. The Head of the Secret Service started the meeting by telling them that they had nothing they could call a strong lead.

"Oh, come on," the Chief of Police said. "You must have some positive information!"

"Our department's mission is to observe, act only if something becomes a danger to persons or property, or both. We cannot reveal any of our ongoing investigations because it may put our agents in danger."

There was silence, eventually broken by the Head of Home Security. "We have nothing to indicate any danger to our country from any group or individual; so far, we've not discovered any suggestion of a plan of attack of any kind, but considering the world we live in, we have to be on our guard. As with all things, we can only go on events which have already happened."

"What about the Anti-Terrorist Unit?" asked the Chief of Police.

"We have no positive leads on any terrorist activity in this country, apart from the usual fanatics who preach 'Jihad' all the time. We know, from collaboration with other countries, that there are terrorist cells all over Europe. We're in close touch with Interpol and will be informed of any threats to our security."

The Police Chief then turned to Inspector Van Eyck and asked him to give his report on the situation.

"As you know, this is a very difficult investigation. We are examining two separate case of murder with a tenuous link between them, which could be significant, but possibly not. The first case, as you know, is that of my colleague Inspector Jan Stromberg, who died when his car was blown up, and the other case is that of an Asian lawyer, with whom he had a meeting two days previously in relation to a possible illegal immigrant with a false passport. These two cases might or might not be related, but on balance, the probabilities point in that direction. We think Stromberg was killed because he took a hard-line stance and sent a Pakistani national back to his country, but this was only after a heated argument with the lawyer when he threatened to start investigating his status and qualifications to practise law in this country. It appeared the lawyer might have been killed to prevent him revealing anything about his clients. We did manage to trace all incoming and outgoing calls on his mobile phone, which led us to a rented house, but unfortunately the tenants had moved on and the only tangible evidence we could find of their stay was a satellite dish, which was obviously used for long-distance contact. But we have no indication about whom they were in touch with. Forensics found fingerprints all over the house of at least four or five persons, apart from the current tenants and the estate agent staff, all unknown to us or Interpol."

"You've done very well so far, considering the difficulties," admitted the Head of Home Security, "but is it worth continuing? This is something my department will have to decide. Thank you, gentlemen, for coming. The meeting is now closed."

Chapter 12

In England, the naked body of a woman was found just outside Maidstone in Kent. A post mortem showed that she had been strangled elsewhere and then dumped in the quiet, wooded area. There was no sign of a struggle and there was no semen in her or on her body. The police were still trying to identify her. Eventually, she was identified as Molly Brody from the Maidstone area, who was known as a part-time prostitute. She also had various other part-time jobs, was a single woman with no children and had come to live in the area from Scotland but did not appear to have many friends. She was twenty-four years old and kept herself to herself, lived in a tiny flat and paid her rent regularly and on time. This was the sad death of a lonely person.

The police came to the conclusion that whoever killed her didn't like prostitutes, used them to satisfy his sexual desires and then felt guilty about it and got a bit rough, possibly killing by accident. Inspector Jack Davis was given the task of leading a team to solve the murder. After all, this bloke might feel like doing it again and that would never do. He managed to trace the next of kin. Her mother was a single woman with two younger children, living in a council flat on a south Glasgow estate. The police brought them to Maidstone to identify the body. She told them that her daughter had left Glasgow to find a job in London and had never kept in touch with her family. After identifying the body, she went straight back to Glasgow. She expressed no strong emotion about the death of her oldest child.

What a world we live in nowadays, thought Jack.

After a week, the investigation had got nowhere and other cases were piling up; the papers were put in the pending tray.

But then another woman was found strangled and dumped in rough countryside near Peterborough. The naked body had been left in a small stream, partially hidden by low bushes. The only access was a track made by farm vehicles, so it was only by chance that the body was found by someone who stopped in a lay-by on the main road to let their dog out to relieve itself. It had disappeared into the bushes and the driver had chanced on the body while looking for it.

The track was sealed off and Forensics got down to work. Time of death was estimated to have been thirty-six hours before the body was discovered, but nothing else was found to help the detectives on the case. There were no identifying marks on the body, no rings, watch or other jewellery, just the marks around her neck where she had been manually strangled. The police artist was called in to make a sketch of her face and this was circulated locally and published in national and local newspapers in the hope that she would be recognised.

Inspector Harry Melvin was appointed to lead the enquiry and he selected four detective constables to work on his team. Two days after the body had been found, and after gathering all the available information, he called a meeting of all interested parties for a review of the situation.

He started by saying, "The pathologist estimates the woman to have been around twenty-two years of age. There are no identifying marks on her body except slight bruising on her neck, no indication of a struggle, nothing under her nails, no stray hairs or semen, although there were signs that intercourse had taken place. She could well have been a prostitute but we won't know until she has been identified. There were some recent tyre marks on the track leading to the area where the body was found; these have been photographed and sent away for identification but that will only give us the make of the tyres. However, that could give us some indication of the type of vehicle that was used to carry the body. At the moment we have very little to go on."

There was a knock on the door and a policewoman came in, who said to Harry, "There's a man waiting outside who says he knows the victim."

"Put him in my office and keep an eye on him. I'll be there in a minute." Harry looked at his team. "We seem to have got a break, and hopefully we'll now find out who she is. I'll let you know as soon as I get any information, but in the meantime I want you all in here tomorrow morning, nine o'clock sharp."

In his office he found an elderly man looking somewhat bemused. After Harry had introduced himself, the man said, "How do you do. My name is Phil Gregg. I live and work in Peterborough as a driver in the food distribution industry, basically delivering to stores from various wholesale warehouses and depots."

"I was told by my sergeant that you know something about the woman in the sketch."

"I think she looks very much like a woman who used to work at one of the warehouses I drove to, and so far as I know, she was called Mary Brett or something like that. I spoke to her on several occasions and she seemed to be a very nice person, chatty and friendly, you know. Has something happened to her? I know the police don't usually circulate pictures of people unless there are suspicious circumstances or something like that."

"You're right, I'm afraid," said Harry. "I have to ask you if you would be willing to identify the body of an unknown woman who might possibly be this Mary Brett you knew. We've found no trace of any relatives and nobody has come forward to report her missing."

Gregg swallowed hard and said, "You think this body is Mary, then?"

"You'll only have to look at her face, which is quite unmarked. It would help us a great deal to know something about her, where she worked, who her friends were. Then we can go on to complete our investigation to arrest whoever it was who killed her," Harry said persuasively.

Phil nodded his acceptance reluctantly and Harry took him to the morgue. He went pale when the face was uncovered, but as he turned away from the body he said, almost inaudibly, "Yes, that's Mary."

"The last time you saw her she was working at the warehouse you made a delivery to; and when was that?"

"Well, it's some time ago. I last had a word with her when I was delivering a load there; it might even be six weeks or so ago."

Harry quietly pulled the sheet over Mary's face and took Phil back to his office, where the Sergeant brought him a strong cup of tea with plenty of sugar in it. Harry couldn't have his only witness passing out in his office when he needed to obtain every scrap of information he could get from him. After giving Phil a short time to recover and drink his tea, he began to ask for as many details as he could remember.

"Do you know the exact name of the company who owned or rented that warehouse?"

"Well, no, not exactly," said Phil, "but I know the address and I could take you there, show you the way like."

Harry called for his car and told the Sergeant that he would be driving them out to the warehouse.

When they reached their destination, Harry said to Phil, "Stay in the car. The Sergeant and I will go in to make our enquiries and then you'll be driven home, or back to work, if you wish."

Sitting at the messy desk of the office-cum-reception area was a young girl speaking on the phone. When Harry and his sergeant showed her their warrant cards, she unwillingly put the phone down and said in her best office manner, "Good morning. How can I help you?"

"I'd like a word with your manager," said Harry.

"Well, that's Mr Adams, sir, but I don't know if he can see you at the moment; he's very busy."

"So am I," said Harry gently, "but nevertheless, will you inform him that Detective Inspector Melvin is here and wants a word."

"Can I say what it's about?" asked the girl, wondering what Mr Adams had been up to.

"It's a confidential matter at the moment," responded Harry, knowing full well that if he told her why they had come, the whole building and every worker in it would be gossiping about the news before they could be interviewed.

The girl lifted the phone and pronounced importantly, "Mr Adams, two gentlemen to see you on a confidential matter."

They had to wait a few minutes and were just beginning to become impatient when a middle-aged man wearing an ill-fitting suit covered by a grubby overall came into the room.

"What's this all about, Brenda?" he asked impatiently.

"Have you anywhere a bit more private?" said Harry blandly as he showed him his warrant card. "This is a *confidential* matter."

"Come this way," said Mr Adams, searching his memory to try and remember if he had an unpaid parking ticket or had been caught speeding without knowing it. Playing for time, he said to the two policemen, "Perhaps you would like a cup of tea or coffee. Brenda will be only too pleased to make it for you."

"No thank you," said Harry cheerfully, knowing the effect their presence was having on Mr Adams. He produced the sketch of Mary and showed it to him. "I believe this woman used to work here for you."

"Not for some time," said Mr Adams, "but yes, she did work here. Has something happened to her?"

"What makes you think that?"

"I can't imagine why you would be here otherwise, Inspector."

Watching Mr Adams' face closely to see if there was any reaction to the news, Harry said baldly, "She's dead."

Mr Adams looked surprised but sad and hastened to say, "I'm very sorry about that. I didn't know her all that well. We advertised for a clerk and I interviewed her, gave her the job and she worked hard. So far as I could tell she got on fine with the other employees and she was always on time."

"What about her family?"

"I'll get her personnel file out for you, Inspector. You must know that at any one time I have about fifty people working here and the workforce is always changing, almost from week to week, so I don't really get to know them personally, only a few of the men who have worked here as long as I have."

"What about social life? Anybody seeing anybody else out of working hours?"

"I wouldn't know anything about that; the only part of their social life involved with the firm is a small Christmas party with a meal in a restaurant, that sort of thing." Mr Adams asked Brenda to get Miss Brett's personal file and while they were waiting he said, "What actually happened to her?"

"She was strangled. If you have any information, no matter how trivial or unimportant it seems to be, please get in touch. I'll let you have the file back when we've sifted through it. Depending on what we find in it, we might need to interview some of your staff at a later date."

Back at his office, Harry took the pitifully few sheets of paper out of Mary Brett's personnel file. Looking through it he found that she had called herself Joan Newman, but apart from that there was little else in the file but her address. However, this opened up a picture of her life, because the address she had given was in the red light district. Further investigation revealed that she had worked as a prostitute at weekends and had twice been arrested and charged with soliciting. She appeared to have been a bit of a loner with very few friends. It now appeared that she had met her death at the hands of one of her clients.

With this information they would be able to concentrate on questioning anyone who had known her, however slightly, and find out if there were any witnesses who might have seen her with a particular man. The post mortem established the time of death as midnight or thereabouts on the Saturday twelve days previously.

Harry put two teams onto tracing Mary's movements on that day, especially during the hours of 8 p.m. to midnight, and searching for her clothes, her handbag and its contents. Nothing tells as much about a woman as the contents of her handbag. One detective was researching Mary's phone records and another member of the team examined all the furniture and fittings in Mary's flat. Everything taken from the flat was stringently checked – mail, notes, diaries, photos, anything personal – to see if it would yield the tiniest clue. During the first meeting of the team, Harry shared his theory with them, which was that in all probability Mary had been picked up by a client in a car and driven to a secluded back street where she had met her death.

So two separate murders and two separate teams of detectives were finding similar difficulties: a total absence of positive information.

Chapter 13

Another event was to dominate the national newspaper front pages. In the Manchester football ground, the morning before a big match, a couple of the ground staff were having a last check of the seating area. A security inspection had already been done but this was a final look around in case there was anything out of place. In the eighth row from the front, six seats from the aisle, a brown paper parcel was found lying under the seat. As the man who had spotted it got closer, muttering to himself about so-called security searches that left rubbish lying around for anyone to trip over, he thought he could hear ticking. A warning bell sounded in his head as he moved nearer to the package. There was definitely a ticking sound, he was sure. He turned to run, shouting to his mate to get away. With trembling hands, he rang the special number they had been given to get straight through to the police Bomb Squad. He felt a bit of a fool, telling the operator, "Of course I'm sure. It's a brown paper package under one of the seats and I can hear it ticking."

The voice of the operator said, "Please remain calm, sir. They're on their way now and will be with you very shortly. In the meantime keep away from the suspect package and inform all persons in the vicinity not to approach it or try to touch it in any way."

Very soon, police cars screeched to a halt outside the ground and the Bomb Squad came running through the entrance on to the pitch, asking where the parcel was. The groundsmen indicated the seat under which they had seen it and were told to keep well back and to evacuate all the staff to a designated meeting point outside the ground without causing any panic. This was quite hard to do, because people were working in various sections throughout the complex, but in a very short time all the staff were answering to a roll call, shivering with nerves and cold while the Bomb Squad men got to work.

After they'd had a short discussion about how they would disable the bomb, if it were a bomb, they soon realised that they could not use their robot because of the steep steps and the closely spaced rows of seats. The three men went back to their vehicle, donned thick metal-reinforced fire-proof suits, helmets, goggles and gloves and picked up their shields, looking rather like mediaeval knights.

The team leader explained his plan to his men. "I'll move as quickly as I can, pick up this suspect package and take it to the middle of the pitch. He spoke softly to his second in command. "Are you a Catholic, Jim?"

"No."

"Okay, I'll pray for all of us!"

In his cumbersome suit he made his way carefully but quickly up the steps of the main stand, feeling a bit like a man in a spacesuit attempting to mend the outside of his ship. As he got nearer to the parcel, the sound of the ticking seemed to be louder then Big Ben and sweat began to form on his forehead. His hands were trembling slightly. With his nerves stretched to breaking point, he carefully picked up the parcel and walked as quickly as he could to the centre of the pitch. He was praying that there wouldn't be an explosion, which would ruin the even green turf for this afternoon's match. And then he tripped. He fell hard, right on top of the parcel, and waited with indrawn breath, watching his life pass before his eyes, as he anticipated the explosion. When nothing happened, he moved carefully and saw a very squashed brown paper parcel underneath him, but the ticking had stopped. Hardly daring to believe his eyes, he investigated the crumpled remains and found a battered cardboard box containing a cheap alarm clock – no wiring – and two bricks. He started to laugh, almost hysterically, at the release of tension, and soon his men were grinning too, although they were cursing the practical joker who thought this kind of prank was funny. They called their forensic department to see if anything could be gleaned on close examination of the parcel and its contents.

The Sergeant was called over to show him the 'bomb'. "Unfortunately, there has to be an extremely thorough full-scale search of the whole stadium in case this was just a distraction from a more serious attempt to plant a bomb."

The Sergeant gave his instructions to a hastily summoned search party and woe betide anyone who missed so much as a discarded gum wrapper.

Chapter 14

One morning, shortly after the alert at Manchester football ground, Inspector Erik van Eyck and Sergeant Hans Vogel were discussing their progress on the murder case.

"You know, Hans, what puzzles me most is that we didn't find the smallest sign of bomb-making in that house. Forensics and sniffer-dogs examined the whole place minutely with the proverbial fine-tooth comb and nothing, zilch, nada, a blank page. So they can't have been making bombs there. Bomb-making leaves a residue which tests reveal, no matter how careful they are to conceal their tracks, even using plastic explosives. Cellars, lock-up garages or even rented storage units are used mostly, but not private houses."

"That being the case," said Hans, "the bombers are still here. Let's concentrate on that and what we can do to catch them. At this point we still don't have any definite leads on them. In the case of say a serial killer you can set up some kind of bait. What kind of bait would an explosives expert go for? How can you set a trap for a bomber?"

They concentrated on the problem and after lengthy deliberations, Hans came up with the idea of leaking information to the news media along the lines that the police knew who the bombers were and that arrests were imminent.

"Then we would get the authorities responsible for checking the passports of people leaving the country to photocopy them so that we can compile a list of all likely suspects," he said.

"That could be very difficult. We no longer have border controls with our EU neighbours and we're surrounded by EU countries, so the bombers could just drive to Belgium or Germany."

"Yes, that is a problem. There are trains and domestic flights to think of as well."

"That's not so bad. We would have to draft in more policemen at stations which service long distance trains or coaches and check all Asian documents."

"Seeing policemen doing that may deter them from using trains, but we need the co-operation of our Home Security detachments and the Chief, sir."

"Leave that to me. Your idea is worth trying and we've nothing to lose." But he was wrong.

The following day, Erik asked to see the Chief of Police to put the plan to him. The Chief sat drumming his fingers on his expensive desk for what seemed an age before he said, "The whole scheme is very dubious, but it could just work. I need to discuss this with my other colleagues, because their commitment is crucial if the plan is to work. Leave it with me and I'll get back to you as soon as anything has been agreed."

Three interminable days passed before the Chief rang Erik to ask when he wanted the operation to start.

"As soon as all the checks can be put into place."

"What about the roads leading to our borders?"

"If a notice is erected about half a mile before the border warning of a police passport and document check, that should make a few vehicles do a U-turn!" laughed Erik.

"This is going to need a huge number of police personnel," said the Chief. "I'm just hoping that will put them off travelling by road and persuade them to use sea or air routes to leave the country. I'll let you know when everything is in place. Let's hope we don't come to regret this."

"I'm sure this is the only way to get a result, sir," said Erik, crossing his fingers and touching wood.

A week went by before there was a call from Police Headquarters. A policewoman told Erik that everything was in place and to go ahead. Erik was jubilant. Now there may be some results.

The next morning in the national press and on television there were excited announcements that a highly placed policeman had mistakenly let slip the information that the police knew who the bombers were and would be making some arrests very soon. The item was on every news programme until another story took its place.

Late at night three days later, a 4x4 vehicle drew up outside the entrance to Police Headquarters and the driver got out and started to hurry away.

"Hey, you!" shouted the armed policeman on duty. "You can't park that vehicle here." The man ignored him and continued to walk away even faster. "Stop or I'll shoot!" said the policeman, drawing his gun. A black Mercedes came screeching to a halt just beyond the man and he ran to get in the open passenger door, shouting something incomprehensible to the policeman. The armed guard opened fire, aiming for the tyres, and the car veered wildly from side to side as both rear wheels were hit. The car skidded to a halt and the two men fell out, each holding an automatic weapon, shooting almost before they reached the ground. The noise alerted others in the building and reinforcing officers, with their weapons at the ready, came surging out shouting, trying to assess the situation. The police guard shouted to them all to take cover. He crawled along the pavement a far as the abandoned 4x4 and pulled open the door. His heart almost stopped when he looked inside and saw that it was packed with explosives. There was a strong smell of petrol and there also appeared to be several gas cylinders. He turned round to find that the fight was over. One of the men was dead and the other one was severely injured.

"Get the Bomb Squad; this jeep is full of explosives," he croaked. He ran over to the badly injured man, who was desperately fumbling in a pocket for something, and had to stop himself from kicking him. "Where's the detonator?" he yelled. The man scrabbled desperately in his pocket and it suddenly dawned on the policeman that it was the detonator that the man was trying to find. He stamped on the man's foot and as he arched his back in agony, the policeman snatched the small timer from his hand.

"Nobody move!" he shouted "The smallest spark can set fire to the inside of this jalopy, even though I've got the timing mechanism. It's probably booby-trapped as well, so we have to be very careful." He was now sweating freely, wishing someone senior would come on the scene and take over full responsibility. All he wanted was to go off duty, have a beer and grope his girlfriend, but that wasn't going to happen in a hurry. He looked around at the scene of devastation. One terrorist dead, one badly wounded; two armed policemen appeared to be dead and one was sitting on the pavement being attended to by another man. Bullet holes marked the walls of Police Headquarters. It was a shambles. Strangely enough, he felt very proud of his conduct under fire. Then he remembered firing at the tyres of the car. Thank heavens he hadn't hit the petrol tank or the whole area would have been blown to smithereens and there would be several unidentifiable bodies in the morgue. Gradually, other policemen appeared on the scene, frantic phone calls were made and the whole area was sealed off so that they could photograph and scour the area for any information which may help them to identify the firearms used.

The inspector in charge phoned the Chief of Police at his home.

"Er, sorry to bother you, Chief, but there's been a terrorist attack on Police Headquarters with a number of fatalities."

"What?" The Chief was almost unable to comprehend what the Inspector was saying.

"Terrorists tried to blow up Headquarters by parking a jeep outside filled with explosives, but fortunately our guard on duty managed to stop them by shooting out the tyres of their getaway vehicle and finding the timer before they could set it off." He quickly filled in the remaining details. "I'm making a detailed report about it now and I'll have it on your desk by tomorrow."

"This is in response to those newspaper stories saying that arrests are imminent," fumed the Chief. "You say that two police officers are dead and one wounded? We've paid a high price. Is the wounded terrorist fit to be interrogated?"

"I'll have to check on that, sir. He's been taken to the nearest casualty department with two armed police officers to make sure nobody tries to finish him off."

"As soon as he's ready to be questioned, I want the most skilled interrogation officer to interview him. And Inspector, make sure he survives; that's an order. Now we'll have to inform the two officers' wives and families of their deaths. Get Inspector Erik van Eyck to go to one of the officer's family and you must tell the other widow. Assure them of my deepest sympathies in this sad situation etc., etc.; you know, the usual thing."

After the Inspector had put the phone down he started to think how near death and complete destruction they had all been. He remembered the television coverage of other terrorist explosions he had seen in the past and shuddered. But he had to pull himself together. It was up to him to rally the staff, who would no doubt be feeling exactly the same as him.

He went into the Chief's office and phoned Erik. When he had finished giving him all the details, Erik could hardly speak. He knew straight away why this had happened: it was a severe warning from the terrorists in the light of the 'leaked' newspaper and television reports that arrests were about to be made and this was how they were being made to pay for it.

"Two dead and one wounded?" said Erik, horrified. "How bad is he?"

"The injured man isn't too bad, a flesh wound in the arm, but it'll keep him out of action for quite a few weeks. And with one terrorist dead, the Chief's putting all his hopes on interrogating the other one as soon as he's fit to be questioned. Perhaps then we'll get some insight into why they're doing this and discover possible sympathisers and conspirators."

"He must be watched very carefully," said Erik. "Apart from the dead men's family and colleagues who'll want to finish him off, he might try and commit suicide so that he can go straight to heaven, or so he thinks. Which hospital has he been taken to? I'd like to make sure he's in isolation right from the start."

"Everything is being done, I'm sure, but first we should inform the widows and families of what's happened. You go and see the family of Mark Froigel. His wife is called Gerda. There are two children, a boy of six and a girl of eight. The address is 39 Rubinstrasse."

"Do I need to know anything else?"

"You can tell her that her husband was a very brave man."

"A hero, of course," said Erik.

He was soon parking his car at the rear of the apartment building. He stood at the door of No. 39 and knocked hesitantly, almost hoping that there was no one in, but there was a light on and the faint sounds of a television programme in the background. He hated this part of his job more than anything else, but the poor woman at least deserved the courtesy of a senior officer informing her of her husband's untimely death.

He heard a light footstep approaching the door and a woman in her thirties opened it.

"Can I help you?" she asked politely.

As Erik was wearing civilian clothes and she did not know him personally, he presented his warrant card and cleared his throat. "Good evening, Mrs Froigel. I'm sorry to disturb you at this time in the evening but I have some information for you. Perhaps I could come in?"

The woman knew instinctively that it was bad news and said quietly, "Please come in. Does Mark work for you?" She closed the door behind him, not even putting on the security chain, he noticed; she must have confidence in the neighbourhood she lived in.

He answered her, trying to sound sympathetic without being patronising. "Mark didn't work directly for me, no. He was on duty tonight, wasn't he? At Police Headquarters?" Gerda said nothing because she knew what he was going to say. Here goes, thought Erik, it never gets any easier. "I'm sorry to have to tell you that there has been a terrorist attack at Police Headquarters this evening and there were two fatalities."

Gerda faced him and said tautly, "You're going to tell me Mark was one of them, aren't you?"

"I'm afraid so. He was a very brave man; he and other colleagues were shot at by the terrorists as they tried to escape after planting a bomb outside the entrance." He carried on talking to give her time to adjust to his news. "By his actions he probably saved a great many lives, because one of the thugs was killed outright and the other is gravely injured."

Gerda started to cry very quietly, tears coursing down her cheeks. Almost to herself, she said, "What are we going to do? What are the kids going to do?" It was a rhetorical question.

"I can't tell you how sorry we all are. I was asked to come here by the Chief of Police himself, and please be assured that you'll be entitled to every form of assistance we can give and you will of course receive his full pension."

"Except that he won't be here to spend it, will he!" shouted Gerda.

Erik resorted to the well-tried platitudes they used at times like this and murmured quietly, "Is there anyone I can contact for you or is there a neighbour or relative you would like to be with you? There will, of course, be arrangements to be made about funerals and so forth."

"I'll ring my parents and they'll probably come over and help me when I tell the children. Oh God, what am I going to say to them? Then of course, I'll have to contact Mark's family. They'll be so upset. Although somehow you know that this could happen any time, you're never prepared for it." She found a handkerchief and tried to stem her tears.

"Here's my mobile number. If there's anything I can do for you, please give me a ring any time. I'll be in touch with you to check everything is okay with you. Also, it's a good idea to keep the chain on the door after I've gone."

"Thank you for coming to tell me personally. When will I be able to see him?"

"I'll let you know very shortly. I'm sorry, but I have to go to start the investigation into this incident."

Chapter 15

First thing next morning, Erik called Hans on his mobile. "Where are you at the moment?"

"I'm with Forensics, sir."

"Is there anything new?"

"Nothing I could call a lead."

"Okay. I want to talk to you and review our progress, if any."

"I'll be with you in an hour, sir."

As always, Hans was dead on time.

"What have we got?" Erik asked.

"Right, sir, the lab found no fingerprints. The mobile phone had no record of ever being used before and the opinion is that it was brought over here from Pakistan, as there's no record of it having been purchased in this country. It could've even been made up from a number of mobile phones, so that's a dead end. Plastic explosives – there's no record of them being bought in any European country so there's no way of tracing them, and if they've been bought illegally nobody's going to show us their records! Now the gas cylinders do have some manufacturer's numbers on them and they were made in Rotterdam. We've contacted the manufacturer and they say that the numbers on the cylinders refer to the manufacturing process and are not used on any sales documents, so we can't trace where they were sold or even where they were delivered and when, but we've not exhausted this line of enquiry yet."

"Let's pursue this further," said Erik. "At this point it's the only tangible thing we have to go on. Let's assume that someone bought them legitimately from a supplier. We might be able to find out how they were delivered and where to. Those cylinders are very heavy and a man would have to be pretty strong to lift them, never mind carry them any distance. Were they collected or did the supplier deliver them? First of all we need to find out from the plant all the customers who were supplied with this type of cylinder anywhere in Holland, and we need that list right away. Do you have their number?"

"Yes, sir. I'll get it from the lab now."

Once Hans had got the gas cylinder supplier's number from the lab, Erik asked to speak to their dispatch department. "I'm Police Inspector Erik van Eyck and my department is investigating a terrorist bomb attack. Some of your gas cylinders have been used to make a huge bomb and we're trying to trace which of your customers bought them."

"It would be very difficult for them to explode our gas cylinders," said the man firmly.

"At this moment that's not important, but we want a list of names and addresses of all the customers you supply these cylinders to in this country. This information is vital to our investigation; it could be a matter of life and death in the near future."

"Sure, sure, Inspector. I'll come back to you with that as soon as I can."

"What's your name and position in the company?" asked Erik.

"Jan Gunther, Floor Manager in the plant."

"Thank you," said Erik, making a note of the name.

"I'll get back to you as soon as I've checked our records."

While they were waiting, Erik asked Hans if there was anything else they had found, other than the cylinder numbers.

"We know the weapons they both used," said Hans. "They were short-barrelled automatic machine guns, made in China and sold all over Asia, both legally and illegally. Both weapons had fingerprints of the assailants only, so that was no help. These guns are not normally obtainable in EU countries. The shells and some bullets were retrieved from the scene but are unknown in the EU, so we have to assume that they were smuggled in with the guns."

"What about the vehicle itself?"

"Stolen locally – five days ago. The owner did report it stolen next morning and we're still trying to find out where it was kept for the intervening days, but so far nothing."

"Right," said Erik. "We want at least three photographs of the car, taken from three different angles, published in all the national newspapers, asking if anyone saw it between the two dates."

"Sir, something else just occurred to me. What if we get two of our men, roughly the same size and build as the two terrorists, and dress them in similar clothes and have a make-up artist work on them. We could publish pictures of them, asking if anyone has seen them or knows where they've been staying recently, always pointing out that they're not the real terrorists."

"That sounds to me like we might get some results. Arrange it and get the photographs published in the dailies. And get an interview on TV for a police spokesman; that should get the ball rolling nicely."

Erik and Hans went to the hospital to take possession of the wounded terrorist's clothes. There was very tight security surrounding him and it took some time, as they had to constantly produce their warrant cards, before they could collect the bag holding the prisoner's possessions. Then they went to the morgue to find out what had happened to the dead terrorist's belongings, only to be met by a junior technician who thought the clothes might have gone to the laundry because they were covered in blood!

Erik gritted his teeth and said through nearly closed lips, "Those clothes and anything the man was carrying are crucial evidence in the case of a terrorist bombing which happened yesterday, and if you want to keep your job, you'd better find them. Now. Immediately."

The young technician turned pale and began searching wildly until, breathing a sigh of relief, he found the large paper sack in a corner marked 'Unknown male, possessions' and the date of death. "Here we are," he said, trying to pass off the incident casually, as he knew perfectly well that to dump a container in a corner when it could possibly be important evidence would get him the sack for certain. Heaving a sigh of relief he said, "We were very busy in here last night. Lots of bodies…" His voice trailed away when he saw the expression on Erik's face. Two of his colleagues were occupying refrigerated containers through no fault of their own.

"Let's get out of here," he said to Hans. "This is all I need to start off my working day. Just forget about the make-up; let's leave the men's faces blank, otherwise we'll miss out on tomorrow's press deadline."

They drove straight to Police Headquarters to put their plan to the Chief. For a moment it looked as if he were going to veto the idea, but he said, "Make sure that the policemen taking part are unrecognisable as themselves, as I don't want any more of my men to die."

"Absolutely, sir. God forbid any chance of that happening," said Erik. "I'll personally check the photos to make sure of that."

"Okay, then you have my permission to go ahead."

They had no difficulty in finding two volunteers and using the police photographer, they made ten copies of the men wearing balaclavas and black gloves.

Hans looked at the prints and said to his boss, "Even their own mothers wouldn't recognise them in those outfits!"

"Let's get these to the newspapers and TV stations and get them circulated," said Erik.

They took the photographs to the press department, explained what was needed and asked them to release the information to all the relevant daily newspapers and put out a special alert on the television news programmes, emphasising how dangerous the terrorists were and that if not caught, many more people could die.

When they got back to the office, an email from the gas container supplier was waiting for them. It gave a list of all customers who had been supplied with the bottled gas containers throughout the country from more than a hundred different outlets. Erik made a mental note to start checking first thing the following morning; he had to get additional help to shorten the time it took to work through the list. He locked it carefully in his desk and pocketed the key. "Let's go for a beer," he said to Hans. "I'm buying."

"There's a good place about a mile from the airport," said Hans. "The quality of beer in the airport is only fit for passengers."

"Good beer – just what we need to lubricate our brains after a day like today," Erik agreed.

Chapter 16

The following day, Erik was at his desk by eight o'clock, hoping that he could get some assistance to check the list of customers. Hans came rushing into the office, a bit annoyed with himself, because he had wanted to get there before Erik to show how keen he was to make headway in this case.

"Good morning, sir; you beat me to it," he said cheerfully. "I feel there's going to be a breakthrough today; perhaps someone will recognise the pictures or know where the car's been hidden."

"Well," said Erik, "we'll start by checking who bought the gas canisters in or near Amsterdam."

"Right, sir, but let's put ourselves in their position; would they feel confident enough to assume one hundred per cent that their bomb would explode? Even if it did, some parts of the containers would be spread around and could give some sort of clue to Forensics."

"Hans," said Erik patiently, "we have the whole containers here and Forensics still can't identify anything."

"Yes, sir, but so far they've been very careful, very clever, not taking the slightest chance, so let's compromise; we check the first customer in Amsterdam and the next one in the most unlikely place, somewhere out in the sticks."

"And how do we guess which one that is?"

"That would be a customer in some obscure village."

They studied the list and picked an address in Amsterdam and one in a rural area. The Amsterdam address was only ten minutes' drive away and turned out to be a garage-cum-shop.

The manager did not seem too happy to see two police officers in his office but he put on a falsely cheerful tone and asked what he could do to help them. Erik debated whether to be tough or very polite and decided to appeal to his better nature by asking for his help.

"We're hoping you'll be able to help us in a case we're working on at the moment. Did you read in your newspaper about the terrorist bombing of our headquarters recently?"

The man visibly relaxed and said immediately, "Of course. I'll help you if I can. Didn't you have some casualties?"

"I'm afraid I can't give you any information at the moment but we would like to ask you about the gas cylinders you sell. They're each marked with a number and we'd like to see your records of who you sold each numbered canister to."

The manager looked uneasy again and said, rather defensively, "Er, I'm afraid I can't. We don't keep any records of who buys them; we just get deliveries when we need to stock up, count them and sell them."

Erik had been expecting this but he persevered. "Does everybody take them away immediately or do you deliver?"

"If it's just one or two canisters, they take 'em straight away, but more than that we usually have to deliver. They weigh quite a bit, you know."

Erik held his breath. "So in that case, you'll have their name and address?"

"Of course."

"And you keep records of all your transactions?"

"On our computer. Head Office is very keen on that type of thing: records and so on."

"In that case," said Erik smoothly, "I'd like a printout of all the names and addresses of people you've delivered to. How long will that take?"

"Twenty minutes to half an hour. Do you want to wait for it or shall I send it on to you?" It was always best to co-operate with the police; you never knew when it might come in helpful.

"We'll call back in half an hour."

Erik and Hans walked a short distance until they came to a bar and ordered two coffees.

"I wonder if we're wasting our time." Hans sipped his coffee and tried to sort out his ideas. "Logically, they'd pick up the canisters themselves. They wouldn't want anyone to know a delivery address, but I can't imagine them making four different journeys to collect one at a time; that wouldn't make sense. It's probably more likely that someone would remember the driver, the vehicle or perhaps both, so we have to check who bought four canisters at the same time but with at least two men to carry them away. The trouble is that we'll not know the name unless they paid with a credit card, and that seems unlikely."

"Most unlikely; in fact probably impossible," agreed Erik. "Our only hope is that there's something on the till records, or the cashier remembered them or their vehicle for some reason."

But when they got back to the garage they had no luck: the only multiple order of gas canisters was for two.

When they got back to the car, Erik said, "I don't know if it's worth pursuing this line of enquiry."

"At this point, sir, we don't really have anything else to go on. How about publishing photographs of both terrorists with a caption underneath saying something like have you seen either of these two men in the last six months; if you have, contact us."

"Do you mean the one who's dead as well?"

"We could get a make-up artist to work on his face. Then we can photograph him and make some alterations on the computer to make him look presentable."

"Okay," said Erik reluctantly, "it might get some sort of a response; anyway, it can't do any harm."

Chapter 17

Looking at the final result in the newspapers, Hans said, "They've done a really good job with these; even the dead man looks alive. Let's hope this jogs somebody's memory."

Three days passed with no response whatsoever, but then they got a call about the 4x4. The woman who rang said that until recently she had seen it every day being used by the man who lives next door to her for work. Erik banged down the phone and said impatiently, "I wish people would read the papers properly; evidently she took no notice of the dates quoted; it just didn't register with her." He was about to say stupid woman, but thought better of it.

"I think she was only trying to help, sir," Hans said soothingly. "After all, she wouldn't realise that it was probably stolen after dark. We know they'd only have driven it out on the day they planned to bomb Headquarters, so it's quite unlikely that anyone would remember having seen it."

With resignation, Erik remarked, "You're right, Hans. Do you always have to be right?"

"Sorry, sir, but we're dealing with some very dedicated people, however misguided they are, and they seem to be extremely clever at covering their tracks."

On the fourth day there was a call from the hospital where the wounded terrorist was being kept. The police officer on guard outside his door had to visit the men's room urgently because he had a bad stomach upset, and when he got back to his post he saw a man dressed in a doctor's white overall coming out of the room. He knew that a doctor had visited the room earlier in the day and unless there had been an emergency, it was most unusual for there to be a later visit now that the patient's condition had stabilised. He asked the 'doctor' what had happened and was told that he had forgotten to write up the patient's notes in the morning. Then the man tried to walk quickly away. The officer grabbed at his coat but was punched in the face and knocked down. Before he could raise the alarm, the intruder had disappeared. Despite being dizzy from the blow, he staggered to the stairs and leapt down them two at a time. Bursting through the door at the bottom, he saw the man running towards a parked car. "I'm a police officer; stop or I'll shoot!" he shouted. The man didn't even glance back but continued running towards the car. The officer knelt down, steadied his gun with both hands and aimed for the largest target, the running man's back, and fired one shot. The man slumped to the floor and lay completely still. With his gun still pointing at him, the officer moved cautiously towards the body and turned it over with his foot. He could see blood on the front of the man's shirt and was puzzled: had the bullet gone right through? He heard a groan and the man's eyes opened. The officer standing over him was one of those who had been wounded slightly in the shoot-out at Headquarters, and he could still envision his three dead colleagues and the other wounded officers. He put his foot on the man's chest, over the bloodstain, and pressed very slightly. The man winced with pain and sweat appeared on his face.

"I want to know where your friends are hiding," the officer said. The man was in agony but he maintained the pressure. With exaggerated politeness, he continued, "You seem to be in pain, but perhaps not enough. Shall I lift my foot?" The man groaned. He pressed a little more, hardly aware of what he was doing, intent on getting the information he needed. "You bastard, do you think this is pain? If you do, just imagine what it'll feel like when I shoot you through the stomach. It'll take hours for you to die. I've heard that the pain is excruciating and it goes on and on before you finally expire." He carefully aimed his gun at the man's belly.

"29 Ruben Strasse East," whispered the man, who then collapsed unconscious. Nobody seemed to have heard the shot, perhaps mistaking it for a backfiring car, because not a single person had appeared.

Muttering, "29 Ruben Strasse East," over and over to himself while fumbling for his phone, the police officer dialled Police Headquarters. As soon as he got through he said urgently, "I must speak to the Chief straight away, immediately." He was nearly incoherent with excitement.

The voice on the other end of the line said calmly, "Now, what's so urgent? What's it about? I'll have to tell the Chief what the subject of your call is, so give me the details."

"Just put me through or the terrorists will get away, you stupid fool. I've got the address of where they're hiding and unless you put me through immediately, they could be getting away at this moment."

"All right, all right, don't get so excited," said the voice and put him through.

He started talking straight away, desperately trying to get the urgency of his information over. "Sir, there's been an incident at the hospital. I'm one of the officers on guard over the terrorist and just now I stopped an unknown man coming out of the suspect's private room. When I asked him who he was, he punched me in the face and ran away. I chased after him to the car park and told him to stop or I'd shoot him, but he ignored me so I shot him in the back. I've got him here now, on the ground. When I caught up with him he was nearly unconscious but he managed to tell me where his friends are living and I thought I had to get it to you straightaway so that you can take some armed men and arrest them. It's 29 Ruben Strasse East."

"That's great work. Thank you, officer," said the Chief. "We'll send other officers to take your statement and reorganise the schedules. Is the other officer on guard okay? And the terrorist?"

There was a short silence. "I'll get this bastard looked after and then go and check the situation in the hospital, sir. I didn't have time to do that before."

"Okay, we'll get everything organised and send support staff to back you up, but try and make sure you have everything straight in your mind; you know what it's like when someone's been shot. Was he armed?"

"I don't know, sir. I'll search him now."

There was a sudden feeling of unease; the hairs on the back of his neck were bristling as he considered his colleague in the hospital. He sprinted for the door he had burst through only minutes before and raced for the private room, all the time anticipating what he would find. The first thing he saw was the blood, on the floor, on the bed, even splashed on the wall, but there was no sign of the other officer and the terrorist was obviously dead, lying in the blood-stained bedding. He put his hand out to feel if there was any discernable pulse on the body but there was none. Touching nothing else, he carefully backed out of the door into the corridor. He rang Reception and told them that there was a wounded man in the car park who needed urgent medical attention but was technically under arrest and should be detained. He also asked what had happened to the police guard in Room 104, as he was not at his post. The receptionist promised to make immediate inquiries and would let him know. He glanced out of the window and saw three men, two of them pushing a trolley and the third man walking beside them, heading towards the man lying on the ground. He turned his head from the window to see a porter pushing another trolley towards him.

"We were told to collect a body from Room 104," the porter said.

"Oh no you don't," said the officer. "Nothing leaves that room until Forensics have gone over it with a fine-tooth comb. What happened to my mate who was keeping an eye on the wounded man?"

"I think he's on the operating table; they're trying to save his life, but he's been seriously wounded and I think it might be a bit dodgy. That's all I know."

"Get me a key to this room; I want it locked so nothing can be disturbed until it's been processed."

"You'll have to get on to Reception about that," said the porter vaguely. "It's not my job to provide keys and things."

The officer rang Forensics and asked them to send a team to the hospital room where the terrorist suspect had been kept, giving them brief details of the situation, and then got on to the Chief to tell him the details of the morning's events. "It looks as if the other guard was attacked and left for dead, then the terrorist was killed so he couldn't give any information to us if he recovered. The officer's in a bad way, so they've said. He's in the operating theatre. It's touch and go whether or not he'll come through the operation."

"What about the other terrorist?"

"He's in the hospital. I had to shoot him, sir, to prevent him getting away in his car. I shouted at him to stop but he ignored me, so I shot him just once. When I caught up with him I asked where his friends were hiding and he gave me that address." He felt he had to justify why he had left his post and started to explain. "I'm very sorry I had to leave the other officer on his own, sir, but I was only gone for a very short time. It's this stomach bug which caused the problem and now I feel very guilty about what's happened to him."

The Chief reassured him that in racing after the other man and capturing him, he had done the best possible thing in the circumstances. The most puzzling thing was how they knew that their colleague was alive and where he was being kept.

"If they were alive and uninjured they would have been kept in prison for interrogation," said the Chief, "but somehow they knew that at least one of them was in hospital. Maybe they picked up on casual gossip, or maybe there was an informant. This has to be looked into."

A nursing orderly approached the police officer and handed him a key. "The receptionist told me that you wanted a key to Room 104," she said.

"Thank you."

"Who was that?" asked the Chief.

"It was someone with a key; I wanted to lock the door so that nobody could go in and disturb anything until Forensics have had a chance to go over it."

"What's your name, officer?"

"Henryk Latten, sir."

"You're one of the officers wounded during the terrorist attack, aren't you? Have you fully recovered in such a short time?"

"Yes, sir, thank you."

"How did you manage to persuade the terrorist to give you the address so quickly?"

"I'd rather you didn't ask me that, sir."

"Right; I understand."

"I hope the Armed Response Unit has arrived there already," said Henryk.

"I've set everything in motion and am now waiting for someone to report back to me," said the Chief. "You've done extremely well. Stay there and let me know how your colleague is when they've finished operating on him."

"I will, sir, thank you."

Chapter 18

Erik van Eyck was in his office writing a detailed report of his investigation, which he did every week. It helped him to clarify his thoughts on where the case was heading. Hans was following up a passport enquiry. The phone rang and Erik was surprised to hear the voice of the Chief saying, "We've received an address where it's possible the terrorists have been living. It's 29 Ruben Strasse East. Can you see it on your wall map?"

Erik scrambled round the side of his desk to his detailed street map of Amsterdam and followed the Chief's directions. He found the street and heard the Chief say, "The Armed Response Unit is on its way there now and I've ordered them to surround the place and wait for you. I'm putting you in charge of the operation, so get there as soon as you can."

"Yes, sir, on my way."

He called Hans as he was driving through the city traffic and told him to get his backside to 29 Ruben Street East pronto. Hans was amazed and wanted to know where the tip-off had come from while he was racing to his car. He kept up a constant barrage of questions until Erik told him to shut up and concentrate on his driving or else he would have another funeral to attend!

Ruben Strasse was in a quiet area and No. 29 was a detached, two-storey house surrounded by a high wall on all sides with a wrought iron gate, through which they could see the house.

Very impressive, thought Erik. Where the hell do these people get the money from to live in a property like that? On my salary I'd be lucky to afford just one of their rooms.

He parked his car well away from the house and waited for the Armed Response Unit to arrive. When two personnel transport lorries arrived, he jumped out of his car and waving his warrant card, and indicated to them to keep well back from the house.

"Who's in charge of your unit?" he asked the driver. "I'm Inspector Erik van Eyck and I have overall control of this operation."

A man in the passenger seat jumped down and said, "I'm Inspector Daniel Grubben, in charge of the ARU." They shook hands.

"The Chief has put me in charge of this operation," said Erik, "because I've been chasing these people since the start, and most of the time we've been up against a brick wall."

"Okay," said Daniel, "how do you want to play it?"

"The important thing is not to arouse any suspicion until we're all in position, so keep the lorries here, out of sight, while we surround the place outside the walls. If they're in there, we don't know how many of them there are. They'll have many different weapons and explosives in their possession. If we go inside the walls we'll be slaughtered; we've lost two officers already. Do you have a loudhailer?"

"Yes, we do."

"Once your men have got their equipment, they should spread themselves quietly around the walls. When they're in position I'll speak to whoever's in the house through the loudhailer."

Daniel told his men the situation and the need for absolute quiet and indicated where they should position themselves. There were twenty-four men altogether and they swiftly surrounded the walls.

"Here, put this on," said Daniel, giving Erik a bulletproof waistcoat. "Can't have the bloke in charge of the operation getting killed before we've got them surrounded!"

Erik put the waistcoat on and took up the loudhailer. Looking over the wall he noticed that there was a long garage or storage shed either side of the house, each about three metres wide but appearing to be the full length of the building. He switched the microphone on and keeping his head low, announced, "The house is totally surrounded by armed police. All the occupants must come out with their arms raised above their heads."

In this quiet area it sounded loud enough to wake the dead. In the deathly silence that followed, everybody was waiting for some reaction from the occupants. Erik repeated his words and another two minutes went by, very slowly. Erik repeated his words once more, but still there was no response. The tension was unbearable, nerves stretched to breaking point.

"I suppose this is the right address?" Hans whispered in his ear.

"This is the address I was given," said Erik tersely. "They're probably sitting it out quietly, hoping we'll think we've got the wrong house and go away! This is just the sort of property that would make an ideal safe house for terrorists. Two big garages for making bombs and storing a stolen vehicle in, surrounding high walls to give them absolute privacy and a very select area where people mind their own business and there are no close neighbours wanting to borrow the lawn mower or something and prying into their affairs." He picked up the loudhailer again. "We know you're in there and we're not going to go away." Still no response.

Erik rang the Chief. "Sir, we're in position surrounding 29 Ruben Strasse. I've called on the occupants to come out but there's been absolutely no response; the house appears to be empty. How did we obtain this address?"

"I didn't have time to put you in the picture before, but the man under guard in hospital has been killed. One of the police guards was badly wounded and is still in the operating theatre where they're trying to save his life; the other guard chased after the attacker and wounded him. He said that the wounded man told him the address while lying on the ground, nearly unconscious."

"That sounds a bit dubious, sir," said Erik.

"I asked him how he managed to persuade the wounded man to tell him the address but he said that he'd rather not say. You and I can probably guess by what means he extracted the information," said the Chief.

"I'm not going to ask any more, sir," said Erik and put his phone away. He picked up the loudhailer again and announced, "If you're wondering how we discovered your address, the man you sent to kill your colleague was wounded by one of our officers; he was in agony and gave up your address with no difficulty, so you can forget any hope of us going away. We'll be quite happy to cut off your water, electricity and gas supplies and prevent any food being delivered."

Still there was no response from anyone in the house.

Erik walked over to Daniel to discuss tactics.

"The stupid thing is we don't know if there's anyone inside the property," said Daniel, "because there's been no observation at this address. Perhaps if we had more information about their comings and goings we could formulate a plan. Tell you what, I'll call on some of the other properties in the street and see if we can get any details from other residents."

"Good idea," said Erik, and Daniel went off to use his charm on some of the neighbours.

Erik was quietly cursing to himself, wondering how they'd got into this situation in the first place: surrounding a house with twenty-four armed men, shouting at what might well be an empty property and hanging around wasting time. There would be some grinning faces in the rest of the force when this got out! He asked the nearest officer if any of them carried binoculars and was told that perhaps Daniel had some.

Daniel reappeared before long and told them what he had found out about the tenants of the house. "I found one man who told me he thought the occupants were very secretive, only seldom appearing outside the house, and that there are no women or children. They appear to do all their own cooking and cleaning and he's only seen men of Asian appearance living there. There have been lights on in the garage very late at night."

"I'm sure we've got the right place," said Erik exultantly, his optimism returning. "We just have to be patient."

Sure enough, after a short time, one of the garage doors opened automatically. The surrounding men could see a jeep-type 4x4 with a heavy bull bar on the front.

"They're going to try and crash out of here!" shouted Erik. "Shoot through the windscreen and at the tyres."

They could see the door of the 4x4 open and some movement, but it was difficult to make out any targets: the men were keeping low.

"As soon as the engine starts, commence firing!" Erik shouted, but for a few agonising moments nothing happened as the driver hesitated. But then came the sound of the engine roaring into life. The marksmen opened fire and as they did so, machine guns began firing from two upstairs windows of the house, causing the men to duck for cover behind the wall as the bullets ricocheted over the top.

The vehicle was now hurtling towards the gates. Erik raised his automatic pistol and fired through the windscreen, aiming for the driver's head. The bullets bounced off the bulletproof windscreen, so Erik, in a split second, changed his aim and went for the tyres. The jeep hurtled towards him but careered off the drive and hit the wall. In the confusion, the occupants of the jeep jumped out and ran towards the house, zigzagging to avoid the bullets. The machine-gun fire from the upper windows sprayed the police marksmen, trying to cover the escape of the terrorists. Of the six men who had jumped from the jeep, five managed to get through the house door, one man falling to the ground as a police bullet hit him.

The machine-gun fire ceased and it suddenly became eerily quiet. Muttering to himself, Erik said to Daniel and the others, "Now we've got them. Don't worry; we'll soon pick them up."

"That's true," Daniel said wryly, "but just think of all the trouble and time the government will need to protect the bastards and bring them to trial. Then more time and money will be spent while they're serving their sentences."

"It's a pity we couldn't have used hand grenades on that jeep," said Erik.

"Well, we have got RPGs in our back-up vehicles," said Daniel.

"You've got tear-gas grenades?" asked Erik.

"Of course we have."

"Well, lob one through the window!"

Daniel instructed one of his men to fire tear-gas grenades through two of the ground-floor windows. The reply was another burst of machine-gun fire. They seemed to be at stalemate. Should they call for reinforcements or make a direct assault on the building, even though they didn't know exactly how many men they would have to deal with or what weapons and amounts of ammunition they had? Some sort of decision had to be made.

Erik and Daniel decided that it was too risky to make a full-scale frontal assault on the building because his men could be picked off as they approached the house. If there were going to be a concerted attack it would have to be by Special Forces, who were trained for a situation like this. Erik decided that now would be the time to put their expertise into practice.

"Daniel, get your men to fire some more tear-gas grenades through the windows. They seem to be far too comfortable in there. I'm going to contact my chief about calling in Special Forces to storm the building."

Three more grenades went in, but this time there was no reply from the machine guns. An explosion cut short their conversation, as they were nearly knocked off their feet by the force of the blast. It was as if a huge bomb had hit the building. The policemen sheltering beside the wall felt their eardrums vibrate with the pressure of the impact.

Erik could see that the house was in ruins, with parts of it on fire. After making sure that no one had been harmed, he left a message for the Chief and then called the fire service and the Bomb Squad; they may find something of use for his investigation in the wreckage. There probably wouldn't be any recognisable bodies, but the fire service would deal with that. He wiped a weary hand over his face and looked over to where Daniel was checking his men. "It's not really been our day, has it, Hans?" he said ruefully.

His phone rang. It was the Chief. "It looks as though the terrorists decided to blow themselves up rather than surrender," he explained, "which they knew was inevitable in the long run. It was only a matter of time and they knew it. The building is a complete ruin; parts of it are on fire and I've called the fire service and the Bomb Squad. There's the possibility that they've booby-trapped the place." Erik's despondency was apparent to everybody. Just when he thought they were getting somewhere, the terrorists were one jump ahead and they were back to square one.

"Is everyone all right?" asked the Chief. "Nobody cut by flying glass or anything of that sort?"

"Apart from a few short-term ear problems, no, sir."

"Good, good. You stay there until the Bomb Squad arrives and put them in the picture. Tell them what they're dealing with and then you and the Armed Response Unit can go. But I'll need your report on the situation tomorrow, but not too early." He laughed ponderously at his little joke.

When the Bomb Squad arrived, Erik spoke to the team leader, explaining that they had surrounded the house because it was a suspected terrorist hideout. "We exchanged shots, they tried to escape in a 4x4 and crashed it into the gates. Then they ran back into the house and machine guns were fired. It all went very quiet for about twenty minutes and suddenly there was this big explosion, leaving the house in its present state. We think they might have booby-trapped the entrance or possibly the windows, so I warn you: take great care. There could be about seven bodies in there, as far as I can judge. Your final report could be invaluable to our investigation. After you've made the building safe, Forensics would like to examine everything – you never know what they might be able to find out – so if you could liaise with them I'd be most grateful. We're going off duty now but here's my number. Get in touch with me any time. Be careful: those bastards are capable of anything. You're armed – shoot to kill."

Chapter 19

Erik and Hans decided to go for a drink to help them unwind after the taxing day they had just experienced.

"I wouldn't like to go through another day like that," said Erik. "At least, not tomorrow. I have to write up a detailed report for the Chief in the morning and whatever I put down, it's going to make me look a complete idiot in the way I ran the operation. But tonight we drink and drink, and if we're still standing after that, we can drink some more."

"Are you married, sir?" asked Hans.

"No need to call me sir when we're off duty. It's Erik."

"Okay, are you married, Erik?"

"I'm glad to say no. Are you?"

"I was, sir, but the wife couldn't get used to life with a policeman so we parted, amicably, before we had any children. That's one thing I'll always be thankful for. A lot of policemen get married and have kids and when they decide to separate it's heartbreaking for the children; they don't know where they are." The beer was beginning to have an effect. "What about you, Erik?"

"I came very close to being married once, but for various reasons it never came to fruition."

"And now?"

"And now, Hans, it's difficult to find time for a regular relationship. I go for so long between making love to a woman that when it happens my passion overwhelms me; frightens them off."

"I thought women liked a man to be a bit of an animal."

"But not if the animal devours them," said Erik, somewhat dramatically.

Hans grinned. "I must get to study your technique a bit. Most of my girlfriends complain I don't show enough passion!"

"What we need to do is get two women and swap them after the first go," said Erik.

The beer was definitely taking effect now. "You're on," said Hans. "Shall we do it tonight?"

"Tonight? If I walk out of this bar I'll only fall down. Let's make it another night."

Nursing a headache the size of an overgrown elephant the following morning, Erik groaned as he checked his mail and messages. He was summoned by the Chief to his office to give a full account of the previous day's events, but when he arrived at Headquarters, the Chief had gone to lunch.

While he was waiting, Erik rang Forensics. He didn't recognise the voice of the person on the other end.

"And who might you be?" he asked, not very happy to be talking to a complete stranger.

"I'm Chief Inspector Hendryk Durrell, Head of Field Operations," said the gritty voice.

Erik wondered to himself why such a senior officer was answering the phone. "Sorry, sir; I was expecting a junior officer to answer the phone."

"Obviously. Now what do you want, Inspector?"

"I'm trying to find out what was found on the site of the bomb explosion."

"So far, eight bodies, or rather the remains of them, and my men are still searching."

"Thank you, sir."

The call was terminated abruptly. Seems like a real charmer, thought Erik. He rang Hans and discovered that he was at the bombsite. He asked him how he was holding up after their convivial evening.

"I'm fine, sir. I thought I should be here to see if anything interesting turns up."

"Good man. I'm waiting while the Chief finishes his lunch, probably with a nice bottle of wine." As soon as he said this he knew it was the wrong thing to say. Out of the corner of his eye he saw the Chief standing waiting for him.

"Actually, it was a salad and a bottle of mineral water," said the Chief.

"Got to go," said Erik, putting away his phone. "Sorry, sir; that didn't come out quite the way I meant it."

"Obviously. Come into my office and give me a rundown on everything that happened; how the operation went from start to finish."

Erik related the events from the time he received the call telling him of the terrorists' possible address. The Chief asked if he thought that would be the end of the matter.

"For this particular group – yes," said Erik. "Eight bodies have been found and I can't imagine that this group would have any more members. It looks like the building was their HQ and the whole operation was conducted from there. It's a great pity everything was blown up, as it would have provided us with an enormous amount of information. They knew that and were prepared to die so that we would obtain little or no help from them. But Forensics will be ferreting about there for weeks. They might turn up something useful. I've just spoken to Chief Inspector Durrell; well, I spoke, he grunted. He simply told me about the eight bodies and hung up."

The Chief laughed. "So you spoke to the famous Hendryk, did you? He's very good at his job and gets excellent results, but he never went to charm school and doesn't suffer fools gladly."

"Well, sir, I didn't expect him to be answering the phone."

The Chief laughed again. "He does have a secretary-cum-receptionist-cum-coffee maker-cum-general dogsbody, but she must have been out at lunch so he had to answer the phone himself."

"Can't they get another person to cover when she has to be out of the office?"

"Unfortunately, we all have budgets we must stick to and Hendryk uses his money where he thinks he gets the best value, i.e. field operatives. He's of the opinion that he spends his money wisely and as head of the department he has the last word about who gets what."

"That must be what makes him so grumpy."

"No, he's exactly like that at home."

"I wouldn't like to be his wife."

"No, I don't think he would either." They both laughed. "I'd better get back and do the work I'm paid to do; I've a mountain of paperwork."

Two days later, Erik was sitting in his office when the Chief called to inform him that there had been another bomb explosion at 59 Ludwig Strasse, only a mile away from Ruben Strasse. The fire service had already been called and the Bomb Squad was on its way there.

"Get your sergeant and get down there as quickly as you can to find out what the background of the situation is."

"Right away, sir. I'll keep you in touch and report back when I get some details." Erik rang Hans and told him to meet him at 59 Ludwig Strasse, checked the map to find it and almost ran out of his office.

It took over twenty minutes to drive there through heavy traffic. He didn't want to use his flashing light and siren, so he fumed quietly behind the wheel while he cursed every driver. When he got there he saw that the end house of a terrace was all but obliterated. The small fire had been put out and the Bomb Squad had examined the wreckage and judged it safe to search.

"Who's the team leader?" asked Erik.

"I am," said a man who looked to be in his early thirties. "Alberto Monza."

"I take it you're from Italy?" said Erik. "How did you manage to get into the Dutch Bomb Squad?"

"Not exactly from Italy, sir. My parents were from Italy but they've lived here since the Second World War. I was brought up and educated in Amsterdam. After college I joined the police force and finished up in the Bomb Squad." He sounded as if he had told this story quite a few times.

Erik looked around at the damage. "What can you tell me about the explosives used to blow up the house?"

"Well, I think someone was making a bomb, perhaps in the cellar, and I'd guess he was a bit of an amateur, probably using information he'd seen on the Internet, and then boom, it went off. The technical guys are already in there doing their usual fingertip search, so perhaps they'll come up with something. We're waiting for the authorities to post guards around the site so that no one gets to interfere with any evidence. Then we can all go home," Alberto said cheerfully.

"How many bodies were found?"

"We've only found one so far, sir."

"Thank you, Alberto." Erik walked over to the fire truck to repeat his question. "How many bodies have been found so far?"

"Only one," replied one of the firemen.

Hans arrived and looked at the smoking ruins of the house. "Surely this can't be another terrorist cell?"

"At this point, until they've finished their preliminary investigation, it's too early to tell. Nothing we can do here. I'm going to ring the Chief and put him in the picture. You'd better listen in to get up to speed."

Erik explained to the Chief where the search was taking them and the results produced so far. "At this point it looks as if an amateur supporter of the terrorists' cause was trying to make a bomb in his cellar using information taken from the Internet and the thing detonated and blew up the house, killing him and anyone else who might have been there at the time. We're not completely clear if there was anyone else in the house, but after a cursory examination of the ruins, it doesn't look like it. Sergeant Vogel and I are going to try house-to-house enquiries to ask the neighbours if they can help in any way. That's it for now, sir."

The Chief thanked him and said that he was going to release this information to the press.

"What I told you, sir, has not been officially confirmed by anybody."

"He's dead, isn't he?"

"Oh yes, sir, he's dead all right, but there may be more bodies and he's not been identified yet. Forensics are already swarming over the place so they might come up with a lot more details."

"That doesn't matter. We're not announcing this as if it's local gossip. We have to reassure people that this explosion is not a new terrorist campaign, but just an idiot meddling with some chemicals. It should serve as a warning to others who might be thinking of experimenting with or trying to make anything they've seen a recipe for on the infernal Internet!"

Erik quietly agreed. "Come on, Sergeant Vogel," he said to Hans, "let's get started on our enquiries. You take that side of the street and I'll take this side."

Erik knocked on the door of the house next to the ruined one. A woman in her early thirties opened the door. "And who might you be?" she asked.

Erik showed her his warrant card and explained that he was making enquiries into what had happened next door.

Her expression changed and she shuddered. "Am I glad to see you. That explosion shook my house to its foundations and I don't know what the insurance company will say about any damage caused. Is there any damage outside?"

Erik pretended to look at the exterior of the house and told her that he couldn't see any.

"I've checked my windows and doors but none of the glass has shattered."

"That's good," said Erik. "Could you tell me how many people lived next door?"

"To the best of my knowledge, there was only one person living there." She was beginning to get quite chatty and Erik tried to keep her to the point. He was just about to thank her and go on to the next house when she said, "Apart from some young men who came round from time to time, just visiting."

Erik thanked her and asked if she would be all right.

"Oh yes; my husband will be back from work later. Wait till I tell him what's been going on here today. I always thought it was a bit funny that only one person lived next door, and he wasn't in the least bit friendly. Just put his head down and scuttled passed whenever I saw him, which wasn't very often. Seemed to go out more at night than daytime and he didn't appear to have a job."

Erik made a note of this and turned to look where Hans was. He was two houses down on the opposite side of the road, so Erik waved him over and asked him what information he had gleaned.

"The two neighbours I asked said much the same thing: they thought he was Asian, hardly spoke a word to anyone, seemed to live on his own but had some Asian-looking friends visiting from time to time."

"That tallies exactly with what I got, so I don't think there's any need to visit the other houses. We've enough information for now and can make further enquiries from the office."

Once back in his office, Erik rang the local council. "This is Inspector van Eyck. I'm trying to find out the names of all persons living at 59 Ludwig Strasse."

"You want the Housing Department, Inspector. I'll put you through."

After a short wait, a voice said, "Housing Department; Art Gruebber speaking."

"This is Police Inspector Erik van Eyck. I want to know the names of all the people living at 59 Ludwig Strasse, as quickly as possible."

"That could take a little time, Inspector," said Gruebber. "There are several lists we would have to consult. If you want to find the owner of the property, the quickest way is to go to your PC and consult the telephone list. If you key in the house number, this will tell you the name listed in the phone records, so logically, this has to be the name of the owner or the current occupant. I'll try to get back to you with the names of anybody who is living in the property at this time, but it may take several days."

Erik told him to leave it for the moment and hung up.

He went to his office computer, found the telephone enquiry page and typed in the address. A name – Lahore Renting – a telephone number and an email address came up. Erik rang the number.

"Lahore Renting. How can I help you?"

"This is Inspector van Eyck of the Amsterdam Police Department. What is your name?"

"I'm sorry, sir, but it's company policy not to give out names over the telephone."

"I'm a police inspector."

"You may well be, sir, but from where I'm sitting it's not possible to tell."

"You sound very cautious!"

"Nowadays we have to be very careful, but if there's anything I can help you with, I'll be only too happy to do so."

"Very well. As you may know, there's been an explosion at 59 Ludwig Strasse and I understand this property is rented out by you."

"I'll just check, sir, if you'll wait a moment."

Erik could hear drawers opening and papers being shuffled. Then the voice said, "Yes, sir, it is our property."

"The police have started an investigation into the explosion and I want to know the names of every person living at that address."

"The name of the person paying the rent is Waseem Kebal and he lives alone."

"Are you quite sure?"

"That's the agreement he signed, but we don't normally check unless we suspect something or someone brings us information that that is not the case."

"How long has he lived there?"

"Three years and four months. Can you tell me anything about the explosion you mentioned?"

"Oh yes, the house is in ruins after what looks like a bomb went off by mistake. Perhaps you'd better get your insurance assessor round there; there's not much of it left!"

Chapter 20

In the local Manchester paper, a story headline read: 'It's three weeks since the bomb hoax at the football ground and all that the intelligence services in the United Kingdom have found out is nothing.' It continued: 'Was it really a hoax or was it perhaps a dummy run for the real thing? Are we due for a calamity now that the terrorists know it can be done?'

This was immediately picked up by all the national newspapers and was brought up in Parliament, much to the discomfort of the Home Secretary. A directive was issued for someone – anyone – to come up with an answer in the shortest time possible; in other words yesterday! Extreme pressure was put on the chief investigating officer to come up with an answer. In near desperation, a theory put forward by a rookie detective was re-examined. At the time he first suggested it, the Chief Inspector laughed it off, but now the detective was called in and told to put together a demonstration of his theory, which would be filmed and watched by all concerned, and if everybody agreed, it would be shown to the Home Office.

The plan was this: three members of the terrorist cell would be represented; one would carry a flat cardboard box under a long jacket or raincoat. The box would be the exact size as the one used for the actual event. The second man would carry wrapping paper, the same amount as there had been in the original hoax bomb, again hidden round his body. The third person would carry a new alarm clock, exactly the same make and size but without any batteries in it so that it would not tick, again hidden under a coat or jacket. The three men would purchase tickets to enter the stadium in the same way as the other spectators but keep a very low profile and go in separately, not as a group. They would watch the match, but ten minutes before the final whistle, the person with the cardboard box would make his way to the public toilets, go into the end cubicle and lock the door. Once inside the cubicle, the first man would take out his flat cardboard box and, using sticking tape, form a square container. The second man would then come in, see that all but one of the cubicles were empty and knock on the door with a pre-arranged signal. The door would open and the first man would come out and the second man would go in and lock the door. The first man would then go back into the crowd of football fans and disappear. The third man would come along minutes later, carry out the same procedure, find the box ready for him and put in the alarm clock, which he would not set, as that would be done later when everyone had gone. When the stadium was empty, he would put the batteries in the clock, set it and seal the box before hiding it between two rows of seats, some way back from the pitch. He would then leave the ground.

There was silence for a short time amongst the audience.

"May I," asked the head of the investigation, "put in a few negative points? The last man walking out would stand out like a sore thumb, wouldn't he?"

Although the junior detective had put the whole presentation together, his Chief Inspector, who had previously dismissed the idea completely, now took over. "There are always some stragglers walking out after everybody else has left the ground. He might pretend to have lost or forgotten something if anyone asked him why he was still there. No one pays any attention to anyone leaving after all the rest because all the checks are made when they enter the ground, not when they're leaving."

"Would they not be filmed as they're walking out?" asked the head of the investigation. "What about when these men went to the toilets?"

"There are no cameras in the vicinity of the toilet areas, since you cannot enter or exit the stadium that way."

"So we're saying that this plan could work?"

"It would require a lot of nerve, but terrorists take risks all the time."

"One other thing: if they were actually going to explode the bomb, how would they carry the box back into the crowd without anybody noticing, or perhaps remembering when questioned later?"

There was silence while the Chief Inspector looked at his junior detective for inspiration. If that were the chief drawback, the whole idea was no good and disappointment showed on the faces of the onlookers. But the junior detective cleared his throat and said firmly, "They wouldn't need to carry the box back into the crowd; they'd simply set the detonator to go off a few minutes after they'd made their way to the exit. The toilets are under the main seating area and the blast would be positioned so that it would explode where it could do the most damage. Hundreds would be killed and probably thousands injured and maimed, plus the complete panic of crowded gangways as fans were leaving the match after the final whistle."

"Yes, they only carried the box back into the seating area to prove their point. If it were an actual bombing, they wouldn't have to do that; their only concern would be to get away quickly without being noticed. You've put this plan together extremely succinctly; it makes sense and the efforts you've made to present it will not be forgotten. We now need a first-class, professionally made video presentation, including shots of the cardboard box and everything found inside it, to be finished as quickly as possible. I want to present it to the Home Secretary the day after tomorrow."

The meeting ended with a close examination of the box and its contents.

The Police Commander in charge of the investigation had everything ready to present to the Home Secretary when he was driven to London. As his driver was threading his way through the heavy traffic in the centre of London, he went over the presentation in his mind, trying to think of any awkward questions which might be asked and how to answer any points which could arise, and thinking to himself about the 'gold stars' he would get, improving his promotion prospects immeasurably. He was still a comparatively young policeman at forty-five years old, and he could get a lot higher up the promotion ladder. Who knew where this might lead?

He was given an identity tag at Home Office reception and asked to wait a few minutes. Just as he was about to take a seat, the receptionist's phone rang.

"I'm so sorry," she said to the Commander, "the Home Secretary has been called away to an urgent, unexpected meeting and he sends his apologies. Because of the importance of your presentation, he'd like his junior minister to see it and then provide him with a detailed report."

"A junior minister," said the Commander, trying not to be sarcastic. "Has he left school yet?"

The receptionist laughed dutifully and said, "Oh yes; Mr Bowen-Smith is forty-five and the word 'junior' is only used because his rank is below that of the Home Secretary. If you'll go with the clerk, she'll take you to a demonstration room and set up your video and any other equipment you might need."

A young woman appeared and asked the Commander to follow her along the corridor to Demonstration Room A. "Can I get you a cup of tea or coffee?" she asked when she had finished setting up the screen and had put the video in the machine. "Mr Bowen-Smith will be here in a moment."

Just as she said this, a portly man came in, looking a little flustered, and introduced himself as James Bowen-Smith. "Have you offered the Commander some refreshments?" he asked. "I could do with something a lot stronger than tea or coffee at the moment. It seems as if all hell's broken loose; people are doing all sorts of weird things and expecting us to cope. I'll be lucky to get home before midnight, and I don't get paid overtime, you know."

The Commander waited until Mr Bowen-Smith stopped talking to draw breath and introduced himself as Commander Tony Wells from the Manchester police force. "Actually, I would like some coffee," he said. "We didn't stop anywhere on the way down and if I'm going to talk you through the video we made, I'll need something!"

The clerk went to get their refreshments and the Commander started setting out the main points of the situation. When the coffee arrived he asked if anyone else would be coming to watch the presentation, but Mr Bowen-Smith shook his head and murmured that it was best to keep the facts on a need-to-know basis; perhaps afterwards they would be able to inform others when the Home Secretary had been apprised of the details.

The Commander commenced by explaining about the hoax bomb found at the football stadium. After describing the events of that day, he opened the box and took out its contents. Bowen-Smith examined them and announced, "Well, this is definitely a hoax, but how did they manage to get it into the football ground and leave it there? I assume someone would stop a person carrying a box and asked him what was inside."

"This has been puzzling us for some time. Security at the entrance is very strict and spectators are not allowed to bring in anything which cannot be carried in the hand; no alcohol or containers of any sort. Nobody could walk in with a box, particularly one which appeared to be ticking."

"Go on; I'm intrigued. Tell me; how was it done?"

"I'll just start the video and you'll see how we think it was done."

When the video ended, Bowen-Smith said softly, "What a Machiavellian plan. Why go to all that trouble? Why do they want to see such unspeakable carnage? Who gives them the right to take other peoples' lives like that, if such a device were to be detonated?"

Commander Wells agreed, but with a slight shrug of his shoulders he indicated his opinion. "There are some perverted minds around in the world today and they take considerable risks to achieve their aims. They know if they're caught they will probably spend the rest of their lives in prison. Up to now they've got away with it; we've been through every scrap of evidence, the smallest clue, but have found nothing. Several times we've seen camera footage of that day but could not see anything in the least bit suspicious."

"What about cameras near the toilets?"

"There are none. Nobody can exit the ground there and you're not allowed to place cameras in the toilet areas, for obvious reasons. Whoever these people are, they will have checked to make sure there are no surveillance cameras before making any move. We have no chance of catching them unless someone comes forward and tells us who they are."

"What worries me," said Bowen-Smith, "is that if these were terrorists, it will give them encouragement to go ahead with the real thing."

"Well, Minister, the 'real thing', as you call it, would mean the suicide of at least one of them."

"Not necessarily. They could make the bomb in the toilet cubicle in a similar way, set the timer and walk out at half-time. The bomb would explode say twenty minutes after the re-start of the match and they would be well away by then."

Tony Wells decided that Bowen-Smith was not as daft as he looked! Aloud he said, "Carrying in the explosives would be a bit tricky, but as there's no check for explosives on entering the football ground, if there were three or four of them, between them they could bring in sufficient explosives. To make the bomb they don't even need to have a box, just some tape to fasten the detonator to whatever type of material they're using and an electronic timer, which wouldn't tick. To prevent anybody going into the toilet cubicle they would just hang an 'out of order' sign on the door."

"Unfortunately, these are clever and resourceful people," said Bowen-Smith, "and we must be more intelligent, and lucky, to catch them. Can you tell me what you're planning to do now, Commander?"

"We've done all we can at the moment; my men have been spending hours on this case and they must be sent back to their units, where they're badly needed. We'll leave a few experienced men to form the core of a small team, led by a police inspector, to report any new information to the Chief of Police. I'm going to return to my job at the Yard."

"Very well," said Bowen-Smith, "before you hand over the reins, so to speak, instruct the whole of your current team that not a word must be leaked to anyone about the investigation, not even their nearest and dearest. Tell 'em they could be facing a charge for disclosing evidence that could be vital to the terrorists if they don't keep quiet. Now, Commander, this is something we must agree on here and now. I'm going to release a story to the national newspapers that the police have important evidence about the incident at a premier league football ground where a hoax was perpetrated by some sick individuals who thought it would be a great joke, and that they're confident they're going to catch the perpetrators, and when they do they'll be imprisoned for a very long time. In the meantime, we want to reassure the public that we're working to that end and arrests are imminent; this will hopefully reassure the public that there's no imminent danger. Before you return to your unit, I want a list of recommendations from you on how to improve the security at football stadiums and similar sports gatherings."

"I'll do that, Minister. Is that all?"

"Apart from you leaving this box of tricks; the Home Secretary will want to see it."

Commander Wells stood up, shook hands with Bowen-Smith and said, "It's been a pleasure to meet you, sir, and to know that someone has been apprised of the situation and understands the urgency about dealing with the matter."

Chapter 21

The following morning, Commander Wells scanned the newspaper headlines and was very pleased with what he read. He had started drawing up a list of recommendations to improve security in places where large crowds of people gathered regularly during his drive back to Manchester, and he had tried to pinpoint the most important factors. There had been so many man-hours spent on this one investigation, without much to show for it. He wondered how much all this work had cost the taxpayer. All because some fanatics were hell-bent on killing innocent people, and for what?

Having finished his recommendations, he looked at the list of people involved in the investigation and picked out those who were to remain in situ. Then he made an appointment to see the Chief Constable that afternoon.

After lunch, he went to Police Headquarters and waited an interminable ten minutes for the Chief Constable to appear. Settled in his office, the Chief said, "How did the meeting with the Home Secretary go?"

"Well, actually the Home Secretary had been called away to an urgent meeting so I talked to a junior minister instead. Fortunately, he was clever enough to understand our explanation of the circumstances."

"So, we can stop wasting any more police time?"

"No, but he agreed to scale it down to a small team with an inspector in charge. I've looked through the list of people involved and have highlighted those I recommend to stay on the team. He also asked me to come up with a number of recommendations to improve security at all major sporting events."

The Chief took both lists, glanced at them briefly and put them aside without comment.

"I don't think this should present much of a problem to you, Chief," the Commander went on.

"What about the cost? Who's going to pay for it?"

"Sorry, Chief, I can't answer that. I suppose it'll have to come out of your budget."

The Chief drummed his fingers on his desk and did not look very pleased.

"I'm sure you'll be able to put most of them into effect without any extra cost; just additional attention to small details and such things. I'm going back to my own job tomorrow."

As if the Chief had not heard him, he said abruptly, "Do you think that this box was left there as a hoax?"

"Do you want to hear my honest answer or the official line?"

"I want your completely honest comments."

Commander Wells drew a deep breath. "I'm sure it was not a hoax; people who make practical jokes like that are a) not clever enough and b) wouldn't take that kind of risk. Several people have been put in jail for hoax telephone calls and a joke on this scale would probably carry a jail sentence of at least five years."

"So you're convinced it was a trial run? God forbid that they ever actually manage to carry out their plan; it would be carnage on a grand scale."

Chapter 22

In the house on the outskirts of Islamabad, the three men were having a meeting. "We lost many good men in Amsterdam. I would like to strangle the traitor who gave them away," said the man on the left.

"Allah be blessed," said the man on the right. "We hope they are with him in his house now. Are we arranging a visit to the traitor?"

"The man who was taken to the hospital had to be silenced to protect the others," said the man in the centre. "But now they're all gone, there's no one left to protect. But the other one, he knows very little and is of no value to them. Let them have him – it will keep them occupied for weeks, interrogating him, and it will allow us time to replace our men."

"What about the policeman who tortured our brother?" said the man on the left. "Perhaps we should kidnap him and subject him to the same treatment!"

The man in the centre said calmly, "Brothers, brothers, remember it was the killing of the police inspector which started this chain of events and ended up with us losing some of our best-trained and experienced men in Amsterdam." Turning to the man on his right, he said, "You will be responsible for recruiting and training new members. How is the situation at present?"

"We have nearly one hundred new recruits, currently being trained at our special camp. All are volunteers and are very keen to serve the cause. As you know, we've stopped training them on the Afghan-Pakistan border because the American bombing was getting too close and our friends in the Taliban wanted to incorporate our men in their force. Of course, that would have meant being under their command, which we cannot allow. We're now using training facilities in Yemen, where there is plenty of suitable terrain, away from everybody's eyes, but where there are instructors sympathetic to our cause. I'm told it will not be long before we are ready to set up a working unit in Amsterdam. We'll do this by sending men in one by one at irregular intervals with well-forged documents, entering via Germany or Hungary, for example, at rural airports where security is not so keen. Because of the EU agreement, there are no real border checks and they will travel by car, which will make it easier to get them into Holland."

"It sounds as if progress is being made," said the man in the centre, "but we must not forget that the most important operation is to take place in Britain. We must do everything in our power to maintain support to this end and supply manpower and resources. As we know, all other operations are minor and have no significance compared to this one. When we're successful, we'll have avenged all other setbacks. If it fails, brothers, no one will be safe, including us."

Chapter 23

A week after Commander Wells returned to London, a prostitute was found murdered in Manchester. She was found by some teenagers playing on a building site. They had rung the police but had disappeared before they could get to the scene.

While the investigation into the murders of the other two prostitutes, one in Peterborough and the other in Maidstone, had made very little headway with hardly any press coverage, the one in Manchester was going to be different. The two experienced officers who were first at the scene were filled with horror at what they saw and one of them was physically sick. The woman was lying on her back, naked except for the remnants of a blouse, which was in shreds. The rest of her clothing was scattered around the body. Her breasts had been cut, her genital area was also mutilated and the whole body was covered in blood. On closer inspection, it was found that her throat had also been cut. The officers guarded the site, preventing anyone from getting near, to await the medical examiner and forensic crew.

One policeman turned to the other and shuddered. "It's a bit like Jack the Ripper's come back, isn't it?" he said.

It was not long before other police cars pulled up and disgorged numerous police officers and the forensic team, who, after a cursory glance at the situation, started their usual measuring, photographing and minutely searching the immediate area around the body. The ambulance crew was told to return to their station, as it would be hours before the body could be taken to the morgue. Temporary lights were set up to illuminate the immediate area and a tent was erected over the body so that nothing could be disturbed by wind or rain while everybody worked throughout the night. It was 11 a.m. the following morning before the weary experts released the body for a detailed post mortem. Although every effort was made to keep the story from the press, the teenagers who had found the body leaked it to them. They were interviewed on television and enjoyed having their pictures in the papers. To their friends they were heroes and they basked in their fifteen minutes of notoriety as the ones who had discovered what had been dubbed 'The Jack the Ripper Slaying'. The press had begun to connect the other two murdered prostitutes with this latest case, and the headlines screamed that another serial killer was on the loose. The fact that the other two murders were by strangulation, with no knife injuries, did not seem to worry the media; they were competing for additional readership in a tough market and this increased their sales. Each morning the stories became more lurid and bizarre.

One story claimed that their reporter had interviewed a person who had seen a man in the vicinity of the killing brandishing a sword, and details of the murdered woman's family and relations were published with little regard for their privacy and dignity.

When it appeared that no progress was being made by the police, the press expanded their stories to vilify the police forces in other parts of the country, asking why it had taken so long to discover any details in the other two cases and why they had not identified the murderer months ago. There were some crude cartoons showing a man running away holding a knife and a piece of rope, with a detective standing over the body of a dead woman saying, 'Why do I always get unsolvable crimes to work on?'

The Home Secretary, Arthur Case, a very experienced politician, was sitting in his office, his elbows on his desk, wishing he were playing a round of golf or perhaps enjoying a night at the theatre; anywhere but here and now. Opposite him sat the Head of the Civil Service, Roger Cutler, who had been in the Service all his working life. They were discussing the present crime figures when somebody knocked on the door.

"Come," said Arthur.

His secretary peered round the door and said, "You wanted to see some of today's papers, sir. I've got them here for you."

"Thank you, Betty. Just put them here on my desk, please." The Home Secretary looked at the first set of headlines and scowled. "The same bloody rubbish, as usual." He pushed the papers to one side and said to Roger, "Action has to be taken and now. What do you know about the Chief Constable of Kent?"

"In the good old days, we in the Civil Service used to know all about appointments of that sort; we used to recommend names of suitable appointees. But since your party were voted in, you changed all that and we now have very little to do with it," said Roger cheerfully.

The Home Secretary's face hardened and he gave Roger a long look. "Well, it's about time you earned some of the money the Government pays you, so find out all you can about the Chief Constable of Kent and let me have it, pronto."

Roger phoned his office to set the wheels in motion and a short time later a messenger arrived with a package containing a personnel file headed 'Chief Constable of Kent' followed by a reference number. The Home Secretary started to go through the papers contained therein, and as he read he started to make comments and observations. "James Noble, educated at grammar school and Greenwich University; fifty-three years old; married; two children; extensive police experience." Putting the file down, he said, "Seems to be a good man."

"Yes, Home Secretary. I've never heard anything to his detriment."

"Make an appointment for him to come to my office with the file on the investigation into the prostitute's murder as soon as possible."

The following day, James Noble was shown into the Home Secretary's office, a large, pleasantly furnished room with one or two interesting pictures in gold frames hanging on the walls.

"Thank you for coming so quickly," said the Home Secretary, standing up to shake hands with his visitor. "I need your help in dealing with the adverse press reaction about these prostitute murders. Do sit down. Can I get you some tea or coffee?"

"Perhaps later, Home Secretary." The Chief Constable placed his file of papers on the desk and waited to be told what was wanted of him.

The Home Secretary asked him to fill in the details of the current state of play with regard to the murder of the prostitute.

"If you would like to quickly look through the current file, perhaps you can judge for yourself where the investigation has got to, although, of course, not everything could be condensed into just one file. If I'd brought all the papers relating to the investigation, I'd have needed a furniture removal van to carry it all."

The Home Secretary, using his excellent memory and speed-reading technique, went through the papers as quickly as he could. Putting down the file, he started to question the senior policeman. "How long has your team been investigating this case?"

"About two months."

"There doesn't seem to be much here relating to any conclusion you may have reached."

"Well, Home Secretary, everything in that file is directly related to the case; there wouldn't be much point in filling it with remote theories or irrelevant fancies."

"So we're still at base one. Perhaps you should make some changes to the team to prevent them getting bogged down; a fresh approach might be needed."

"I'm sorry, sir, but I cannot see how that would help. I've reviewed the case regularly and as far as I can see, there are no other possible leads we can follow. A total stranger arranges over the phone to meet a prostitute, tells her where to meet him, takes her home, strangles her, takes her miles out into the country and dumps her body. The body was found a long way from the main road in a lane only used by farm vehicles; no signs of a struggle, no bruising, no fingerprints; tyre marks were found to be from a common make used on countless economy-type cars. The girl was a part-time prostitute, a loner with few friends, who had moved down from the north and very little is known about her. Taking the team off the inquiry would negatively affect the investigating officer's career, sacrificing a reliable officer for no good cause."

"Nevertheless," said the Home Secretary blandly, "the present team needs help. I'm willing to send you one of Scotland Yard's best detectives, not to replace any one man, but who could bring in a different slant with a fresh mind, which could lead to further fruitful enquiries."

"Thank you, sir, that sound like a good idea," conceded the Chief Constable, bowing to a superior force. "The inspector working on the case thinks it was someone prominent in the community, someone who regularly made use of prostitutes, or might even have been having an affair with the girl, and then got scared with the thought it might come out or he could be blackmailed and so he hired a professional killer to get rid of her."

"So you think it might have been an assassination, in fact?"

"The first two prostitutes seem to have both been killed in a rage by a client. They were similar in that the man, having had intercourse, probably felt he had degraded himself by paying to have sex with a prostitute. Perhaps he was married or had a regular girlfriend and felt he had let himself down by paying for sex; he became furious with himself and turned his anger on the prostitute, thinking that if she were not there, he would not be in this humiliating position, so he kills her and tries to cover up the crime. In a case like that they always make some sort of mistake, but here there's absolutely nothing to even point to a suspect, no matter how hard we search."

"You may well be correct in your assumption," said the Home Secretary, "but we have three murders of prostitutes hundreds of miles apart – Maidstone, Peterborough and Manchester – and we have to ask ourselves, have we got a serial killer on our streets or are these killings just random occurrences? While one could say that the first two cases were unplanned murders, this last one seems to have been planned, bearing in mind the hideous wounding of the torso of the girl, and if any more of these killings were to take place we'd have the public and the press up in arms, wanting to know why no arrests have been made."

"I totally agree with you, sir. One has to wonder at the mental state of the perpetrator. But I still think we should investigate the cases separately, otherwise we'll just get bogged down."

"Your people are already bogged down, as you put it," said the Home Secretary waspishly.

Noble tried to placate him by saying, "We'll have to pursue the theory of a professional hit man being hired, who made it look like the client had killed the woman and counted on the fact that he had covered his tracks successfully."

"What about the Peterborough murder? They've also come up with nothing."

"As I said, sir, I can only talk about the case in my area."

"Very well. What will your next move be?"

"We'll start searching for someone who has a lot to lose if that kind of information came to be known, but who has a weakness for prostitutes. We'll concentrate on the secret lives of our rich and famous. Someone must know where the dirt is hidden and all it takes is one small hint to put us on track."

Reluctantly, the Home Secretary stood up to shake hands with his guest, indicating that the interview was over. "I can't tell you at the moment who's going to be seconded to your force to help you, as I've not yet been given a list of possible men, but rest assured he'll be one of London's finest and should be with you in no more than three days. I hope you'll make him welcome and arrange for his accommodation etc."

In Manchester, the post mortem had been carried out on the victim and death was pronounced to be due to severe trauma; in other words, she died of her injuries. The Chief Constable had all the reports on his desk and was trying to decide on a chief detective inspector to head a team of eight detectives. He picked up the phone and asked for Chief Inspector Derek Young to come and see him. He told him that he wanted him to head the investigative team into the murder of unidentified Woman A, found on a derelict building site the previous day.

"This is turning out to be a very high-profile case and it needs someone with a good head on his shoulders to find the killer. Would you like to take on the case? There might be promotion if you're successful. In any case, it would be a feather in your cap and would look good on your CV if you managed to arrest the murderer."

"You don't have to tempt me with promises of promotion, welcome though that would be. It looks a very challenging case and I'd be very interested to get my teeth into it, so to speak."

"That's very encouraging. Good man. Choose your own team, one sergeant and seven constables, one of whom should be responsible for filing and correlating the work. We all know how important that is after the balls-up in Yorkshire when they were trying to catch The Ripper! It would've saved them thousands of man-hours if they'd had a computer in those days, but thankfully, nowadays we're all up to scratch. Me, I can't tell my email from my Internet. I'd like you to start immediately, so clear your desk, pick your team and go ahead straight away."

"Yes, sir. Is there anything else?"

"It would be nice if you could name the killer and arrest him in the next few days," he said with a smile. "That would put some noses out of joint in other police forces, but I suppose that's asking too much. Keep me up to date with your progress."

"I'll do my best, sir."

Derek carried the relevant files under his arm and began to plan his first moves. He knew that some of the people he'd like to ask to join his team would be unavailable for various reasons, but he started his recruitment drive immediately. By the end of a day of prolonged telephoning he had his team assembled with Detective Sergeant George Green as his assistant. He told all the members of his new team to report to Conference Room One at 8.30 the next morning for a briefing, when he would put them in the picture and outline the enormous task they had ahead of them.

He worked late into the evening at his desk, studying every available scrap of information contained in the files. The woman had been killed at about 11 p.m. in the evening but not found by the teenagers until nine o'clock the following evening. How odd that no one had noticed her during daylight hours. The killer must have known that the building site had very few visitors, because he had made no attempt to hide the body. He didn't want to look at the photographs but forced himself to study them. Realising he was hungry, he went to the canteen to get a sandwich. Being divorced, he didn't have to worry about a wife nagging him because a cooked dinner had dried out in the oven or he was late home and the rubbish needed putting out. Those were some of the positive elements of living alone, not that there were many.

Back at his desk, he studied the evidence further and decided on the way he was going to present it to his team the following day. Deciding that he would not risk a fry-up in the canteen, he left his office and went to get a takeaway meal to eat in the relatively comfortable flat he was now renting.

While he ate, he searched for the key points in the reports in front of him. Why all the brutality? Prostitutes normally did as the client asked, providing he paid them in advance, and would not usually struggle. What had driven him into such a rage? And why the severed throat? Was it some kind of a ritual killing? There was nothing in the details that was any help. Even the area around the body had been swept to prevent shoe prints being discovered. No weapon, no fingerprints, no witnesses. A complete dead end. She had been killed where she lay, that was for sure, but at the moment that was the only thing they were completely certain of.

The following morning, after introducing himself to the members of the team who didn't known him, Derek outlined the case, the implications and the methods they would use to track the killer.

"A person who can do this to a helpless woman is a brutal and sadistic killer and extremely dangerous, more so because if he thinks he's got away with his crime on this occasion, he'll try it again. You can imagine what Joe Public will be saying if we don't catch him in the very near future and the newspapers will have a field day with headlines about police incompetence etc., etc. My second in command is Detective Sergeant George Green. He'll assign the usual tasks to you and you'll liaise with him on a day-to-day basis. This woman has not yet been formally identified, so that's our first job. When we've identified her, a member of her family, preferably a parent, can confirm her ID. Everyone should read the copy of what information we have so far and if any of you have a brilliant idea, don't hide your light under the proverbial bushel; let us all in on it!"

A voice whispered in the background, "How much overtime can we claim, guv?"

When the laughter had died down, Derek said, "Keep it reasonable and the Chief Constable himself will sign your expenses sheets! Now, here's the procedure we're going to follow: as there appear to be no obvious suspects and information is pretty scarce, we'll follow the tried and tested routine of house-to-house calls. Get in touch with your informants and check all missing persons, first in the immediate area and if that doesn't produce anything, widen the search area. Now, any questions? If not, I'll see you tomorrow morning here, prompt at eight-thirty. You've all got my mobile number haven't you? If not, ask George for it and then you can contact me if you turn anything up."

Back in his office, Derek rang the Chief Constable of the Cambridgeshire force but was told that he was out at an urgent meeting. He asked to speak to the detective in charge of the prostitute murder in Peterborough but was told that he was also out.

"Could I help you, sir? I'm the IT officer on this job and I have all the latest information on my computer; so perhaps if you tell me what you want to know, I'll be able to put you in the picture."

Derek told him that he was the Chief Inspector investigating the murder of a prostitute in the Manchester area and was wondering what evidence they had found on their case."

"Apart from tyre marks, nothing," the officer told him.

"You mean that even now you still don't have any leads, anything at all, to help solve the crime?"

"Yes, that's about it, sir."

"What about the tyre tracks?"

"They're of a make that could be fitted to just about any car and unless we find a car which we suspect was used to carry the body, there's no chance of matching them up."

"So whereabouts are you in the enquiry at the moment?"

"We're still working very hard, but the results don't seem very promising."

"Thank you," said Derek and rang off. He wondered if it were worth contacting the Maidstone Police HQ. Not much point, he thought, and decided to concentrate on his present case.

With no positive leads, they followed the usual tried and tested procedures. They established that the victim's name was Rose Murphy, who came originally from Belfast to train as a nurse. She was twenty-six years old and records showed that she had been arrested twice for prostitution, cautioned and released. Her father had been killed during 'The Troubles' and her mother died three years later. Police were now trying to locate her brother so that he could officially confirm her identification, but he was proving somewhat elusive. The team continued questioning all the people who had known Rose, especially the other prostitutes she had been friendly with, and searched her flat. But there was nothing of any help to them. No little black book with a list of regular clients, no diary. They did find £245 in a little tin chocolate box, which she had kept on the mantelpiece. No savings or bankbooks; just a few personal papers were all there was to show for her life.

The other working girls said that she had been friendly but not very forthcoming or chatty, and that as far as they knew, she did not have any special clients or regulars. A blonde girl said that on the night Rose was killed she had been standing next to her on a corner about seven o'clock in the evening, on the lookout for clients, when a car had pulled up at the kerb and the driver had opened the passenger door and said, "Hello, Blondie; are you looking for a ride?"

"So I told him I might be, if we could agree on the price. I got in and went with him, but when he brought me back to that same corner, Rose was gone and I never saw her again."

The police managed to trace Rose's brother, who confirmed that the body was that of his sister. He did not appear to be upset or surprised when he was told that she was dead. He said that he had strongly condemned her way of life and when she would not change, he never saw her again. The last time they met he had told her that she would finish up a drug addict or get killed by a maniac. He could contribute nothing to their investigation, and as time went on, the team was not getting any further.

Derek went back over what little information they had collected. He sat in his office after the others had gone to the pub, cudgelling his brains as to why Rose had been killed. Why pick on her? Had she been chosen at random or did the killer stalk her for some time? Come on, he said to himself, get back to basics. You don't stalk a prostitute unless you're a regular client of hers – in which case there would have been some record of him in Rose's flat. He knew that regular punters are bread and butter for street girls and regarded as safe, sometimes being a little more generous with their money. The women tended to keep some record of them.

Supposing he picked her up by chance and took her to a place he had already picked out; or did she tell him that she knew a place where they could go to do the business? If he knew where to take her, he must live locally, because it's not the sort of place anyone would get to know if you lived even a few miles away. Apart from local kids playing, no one else would go there. The kids had been interviewed but nothing positive had been garnered from their statements. No cars were seen parked in the vicinity; no screams or shouts were heard. If she had been picked up between seven and eight o'clock but did not die until approximately eleven o'clock, where was she in the meantime? They really needed to get help from the public and the best way to appeal to them would be to publish a notice in the local papers, accompanied by a photograph, asking if anyone had seen Rose after seven o'clock on the evening of her murder. He called Roy, a photographer he had worked with before, and asked him to take a photo of Rose but to enhance the pictures so that she didn't look like she was lying on a slab in the morgue.

"Sure, I can do that," said Roy. "I've got this software on my PC that can work miracles; take you from being a baby to looking as if you were ninety years old in seconds."

"That sounds just what we want, Roy. Make her look as if she's still alive, one full-face and one profile, and get them round here so that I can have the story printed immediately. Oh, and by the way, send me your bill and I'll make sure you get paid right away. I'll ring the morgue and tell them you have my permission to take the photos, so there'll be no difficulty there."

A few days later, his appeal appeared on the front pages of both local papers. This should do the trick, thought Derek, and he phoned the Chief Constable at Maidstone.

"What can I do for you?" he asked.

Derek explained that he was in charge of the team set up to investigate the murder of Rose Murphy, a prostitute in Manchester, and had been told that the Maidstone force was investigating a similar case.

"Yes, Chief Inspector, we are."

"I was wondering, sir, if we could compare notes, because we could possibly help each other by exchanging information."

"That seems like a very good idea. What stage has your force reached? We're in the position of having to accept one of the key detectives from Scotland Yard CID to help us out, as per the Home Secretary's instructions."

"How long has he been with you?"

"Getting on for two weeks now."

"Can you tell me what sort of progress he's made in that time, sir?"

"If you mean are we any closer to arresting the murderer, the answer is no. We're taking the line that the victim was killed not by a client during the time he was with her, but by a professional man who was afraid she might blow the whistle on him, expose his identity and the fact that he regularly used prostitutes. A man in a position where he could lose everything, perhaps with a jealous wife who threatened to divorce him and claim large amounts of his income, or business colleagues who could use the information against him in some way. So he hired a hit man whose decision it was to make the incident look as if an angry client killed her in a moment of fury; he strangled her, removed all her clothing and any jewellery and dumped her body in the countryside off a secluded lane, making sure there was nothing left which could be connected to him. The only lead we found was tyre marks in the soft soil, but they were identified as being the type of tyres sold everywhere, used on countless economy-type cars, so that was not much help."

"There are similarities between the three murders, Maidstone, Peterborough and ours, sir. The first two are almost identical; if you take away the actual method of killing our victim, all three cases show signs of being alike. Apart from the tyre marks, all three deaths show a certain degree of professionalism, almost as if the killer or killers are familiar with crime investigation."

"So what do you suggest, Chief Inspector Young?" asked the Chief Constable.

"Well, sir, it seems at this point as if the three cases are connected in some way. I think we should keep close contact between the three police forces and review our investigations as they progress."

"You've just appointed yourself as liaison officer."

"That's fine with me, sir; I'll be happy to do that. My thinking at the moment is that a gang of villains, unknown to us at the moment, are planning something big and the three murders are a prelude to this as a way of demonstrating what they'll do if there's not the response they're looking for."

"And what do you think that might be?"

"At this point, sir, I can only think it's some kind of financial blackmail – give us a billion pounds, or euros or maybe diamonds – but whatever it is, it's going to be a huge amount."

"Your theory is interesting and in some ways close to our thinking. Only we thought it was someone covering up his misdeeds and hiring a professional killer because he didn't want to be involved in the actual carrying out of the crime."

"I'm not saying, sir, that your team should not pursue their present lines of inquiry, but we have to keep a very open mind. The Maidstone and Peterborough murders are virtually identical and the idea that there are two people covering their indiscretions, so close in time but a hundred miles apart, is stretching a coincidence too far."

"If we look at it like that, then I agree with you. But why brutalise your victim so cruelly? They're making their point as it is."

"If you look back, sir, the two murders hardly rippled the surface; in terms of publicity, both investigations have sunk out of sight, so they made sure our murder attracted a lot more publicity due to the horrific wounds the poor girl suffered. Nothing like a bloodstained corpse to attract the media!"

"You make a lot of sense, Chief Inspector Young, but what can we do about it?"

"Well, sir, at this point I'm still working on the idea. If I'm right, there's going to be a lot more action from this group of villains."

"You've managed to depress me greatly. Now please tell me something that will improve my feelings and cheer me up a bit."

"When we catch them, sir, we'll all be celebrating. There's just one thing that might be worth trying. The amount of brutality used on our victim was so bad that there can be few people capable of it. I've seen bodies, I've seen murders committed by the mentally ill, but nothing compares to our victim. This was a barbaric disregard for human pain and suffering and I'm inclined to think that a member of an East European Mafia gang must have done it. I know their members are responsible for some terrible atrocities in their own countries."

"If that's the case, how did they get into our country?"

"Perhaps they were smuggled in illegally and then got out of the country immediately their job was done. We can start to work on that line."

"It's certainly a point worth pursuing," said the Chief Constable. "I'll keep that in mind and have a word with the DI in charge of the investigation here."

"Thank you, sir, I'll go and check on the progress of my team. Nice talking to you, sir. Goodbye."

Chapter 24

At Frankfurt Airport passport check-in for non-EU countries, a smartly dressed young man awaited his turn. He appeared confident as he approached the desk, handing over his passport, which had an unusually flattering picture of himself, and smiled at the official. The passport official looked at the passport and noted the details quickly and then looked up at the smartly dressed traveller who had flown in from Dubai. Blandly, with hardly a muscle in his face moving, he asked, "What is the purpose of your visit to Frankfurt?"

"Oh, I'm just visiting."

"Do you have any relatives here?"

"I have some friends in Hamburg but I'm here on holiday and hope to see a lot of Germany."

"Starting with Frankfurt?" said the passport officer with the lift of an eyebrow.

"I will be leaving Frankfurt tomorrow."

"And where would you be going then?"

"Berlin."

"Let me see; your name is Imran Wassim. Would you wait here for a moment, please?" Taking the passport, the official went into the office.

His supervisor looked up from his lunchtime sandwich. "What's the problem?" he asked.

"I've got an Asian guy at my desk; here's his passport. He's the third young Asian man to arrive here recently; well dressed, confident, says he's here on holiday, just flown in from Dubai, looks just like the other two."

"So what's wrong with that?"

"First of all, he says he's going to Berlin in the morning. Why would he fly to Frankfurt, which just happens to be near an American air force base, when he could have flown direct to Berlin?"

"Maybe he didn't know about it and money isn't an issue. Don't you trust your own judgement?"

"Yes, but two heads are better than one."

"Okay," said his supervisor resignedly, "let's go and have a look."

As they came out of the office together, the supervisor said, "Isn't that your desk? Where's your man?"

"I told him to wait; perhaps he's just gone to the loo."

"Get Security looking for him right away," said the supervisor.

"I've still got his passport, so he can't have gone far."

"Except all round the EU countries," said the supervisor sarcastically. "I expect his passport was forged anyway. Give it to me and I'll get the photograph enlarged and put on TV and in the newspapers. Go with Security and keep searching for him. Make sure they cover all possible exits from the airport. You should have told a security officer to keep an eye on him when you came to consult me."

"Sorry. I never thought he'd try to run off without his passport."

"Too late for that. You'd better get on trying to find him; he can't have got very far."

Security all round the airport was put on immediate alert to look for a young Asian man dressed in a dark suit and tie with black shoes. The passport inspector and two security men searched the whole of the airport building, but with no success. The man had vanished into thin air and at seven o'clock in the evening the search was called off. The supervisor had informed the police and circulated an enlarged copy of the man's passport photograph. The evening TV news included the photo with a message that the authorities were searching for this man who could be armed and dangerous. The next morning, a police inspector, Laurie Mueller, and his sergeant, Hugo Kalman, questioned the supervisor and the passport inspector closely.

"What made you suspicious of the man in the first place?" asked Laurie.

"He was the third Asian man to fly in from Dubai in the last two weeks; all three were dressed in similar suits, very smart, nicely polished shoes, and their passports were also new, as though they'd just been obtained. Something about this man was not quite right, a gut feeling. When he said he was going to Berlin in the morning, I wondered why he didn't fly straight to Berlin in the first place. I went to the supervisor's office to ask him to take a quick look at the man. We were not many minutes in conversation but by the time we came out, he'd disappeared. We immediately instigated a security alert on all airport exits and I went with two security guards and searched the whole of the airport building but with no luck; he had vanished. I had to check on him because with a large American airbase nearby, we have to be extra careful."

"You were quite right to suspect him, but you should have got someone to keep an eye on him while you went away from your desk. The fact that he disappeared proves that he's here with something in mind. When the other two went through, were their passports copied and put on record?"

"They didn't actually go through my passport control desk, but somehow, I don't know why, I noticed them going past."

Laurie sat thinking for a while and then said, "Is it possible to check your records to see if their passports were copied?"

"That might be a bit difficult because we don't have the date they came through; and have you any idea how many passengers come through here on an average weekend? But we'll try our best."

"Good. I'd appreciate it if you can come up with the information and let me know straight away. Here's my extension number and my mobile number; ring that first when you want to contact me."

"Am I going to be in trouble for allowing this man to get through passport control?"

"No," said his supervisor. "In fact you've alerted the authorities by drawing attention to him. He could well be a terrorist. He's definitely acted in a suspicious way. Hopefully we'll catch him before he can put any plan into action."

The photograph of the vanishing man had plenty of news coverage and the police awaited reports of sightings, but nothing materialised. Not one person came forward, which was very unusual, as normally the police would be inundated with crackpot suggestions about where a suspect could be found. But on this occasion, no one called. Perhaps people were worried that if the man were a terrorist or a criminal he might exact revenge on them or their families if they informed on his whereabouts. Whatever the reason, no one came forward and the Passport Records Department could not find any copies of the previous two suspects' documents, so the police had very little to go on. The case was almost put on the back burner except for making US military personnel aware of possible danger to their men and property. However, something else brought it to the foreground. The escapee turned up – dead. His body was found on a rubbish tip, with shots through the chest and head; someone wanted to make quite sure he was dead.

Laurie and his boss sat in the office, discussing this latest occurrence. "Is this the end or the beginning?" pondered the Chief Inspector.

"I'm sure this is not the end, sir. I think to a certain extent it may almost depend on our reactions; if we just treat this as an unexplained death of someone we have no record of entering this country, it may just end here. He was obviously killed by his own people because his photograph had appeared everywhere and he became a liability to the group. They were probably worried that sooner or later he'd be caught with the chance he might talk and give away their plans and, perhaps, where they could be found."

"So you're convinced they're here as part of a plan to carry out some kind of crime?"

"Let's face it, sir, people who are quite prepared to kill one of their own operatives to prevent any information leaking out are not here to commit a bank robbery or something similar; they're planning to commit a much bigger, terrorist outrage. That's my thinking, sir. But it might not be in our country; nowadays there are no borders to speak of between some EU countries, which gives free access to all.

Now that the man we have a photo of is dead, they can move around without arousing suspicion."

"Yes," said his boss, "that seems probable. So what do we do?"

"We can do nothing and hope that what they're planning is not in this country, or we can go after them with all we've got."

"This is a very difficult decision and not one I can take by myself. Leave it with me, Inspector, and I'll have a word with my superiors and get their backing."

He made an appointment with his superior officer to explain the situation to the Commissioner, who was a very busy man and did not suffer fools gladly. They filled him in with all the current details of the case and put forward Laurie's suggestions.

"If we ignore this situation and don't take any action and there's a serious terrorist outrage, questions will be asked at the highest levels and we'll be castigated by the public for doing nothing. We thought you should be aware, Commissioner, of the present situation."

The Commissioner looked at them in amazement and finally said, "At my level, I don't get involved in field operations; that's the responsibility of others. I think you should consult them!"

"Well, sir, that being the case, we're sorry to have bothered you."

Fuming, they left his office, each thinking to himself what a right bastard the Commissioner was and how they'd love to drop him right in it!

"The bloody fool thinks things like this are beneath him," said the Chief. "He's far too superior to become involved in field activities, so if people get blown up, it's apparently not his concern."

"What are we going to do?" asked Laurie.

"I'm only responsible for airport security," said the Chief Inspector. "Anything outside that, I have to call in other police units, and since they found the body, I assume they already know. At the moment we've gone as far as we possibly can."

"The difficulty is that the man eluded us in the first place."

"We were not involved in that, Inspector; the passport control officer neglected to put a guard on him in the first place after suspecting him of illegal entry. They didn't ask any of our men to keep an eye on him."

Laurie told the Chief that he had friends in the local police force who would keep him informed of any developments, and there the matter had to rest.

That same morning, a car containing two young men wearing casual clothes was travelling towards the Dutch border. Because of the previous terrorist incidents, the police still had checkpoints on most of their border crossings, although they were told only to stop cars with a male driver and one male passenger or if anything seemed suspicious to them. They were not to stop any other traffic or commercial vehicles. Two armed police officers with field binoculars stood at the side of the road and studied the passing vehicles. If they saw a car driven by a man with one male passenger they were to signal to it to pull over to the side of the road and ask to see their ID and driver's license. If they were not satisfied, they were to ask them to step out of the car, confiscate the ignition keys and call for backup.

One of the police officers trained his binoculars on the vehicle approaching from Germany and could see that both the male occupants appeared to be Asian. He decided to make a routine check – they hadn't been doing very much that morning – and he signalled to them to pull over. They came to a halt about ten metres away. Both sides watched each other as though waiting to see who would make the first move.

The officer who had waved the car to a halt said to his colleague, "Watch out; there's something funny here." He took a step forward and as he did so there was a roar as the car shot backwards, going into reverse at full speed. Both policemen drew their pistols but did not fire because, technically, the vehicle was still on German soil. They both spoke good German and one of them, using his mobile, rang the nearest German police station.

"This is the Dutch border control. We just tried to stop a car containing two young men of Asian appearance, casually dressed. The car is a silver BMW. We haven't got the registration number, but when asked to stop they turned round and headed back into Germany."

The voice on the other end of the phone said, "Thank you; I'll inform our road patrol vehicle immediately."

By the time the patrol vehicle had arrived in position to intercept the BMW, there was no sign of the car.

A few kilometres from the border control there was a country lane leading to a small village. A silver car sped into the central square and came to a halt in a scurry of gravel in front of a small chapel. A couple, walking to the village shop, watched the car disappear behind the chapel towards the stream which ran there, and looked at each other in amazement. It was not very often cars pulled up in such a hurry and then accelerated toward the rear of the chapel; they were used to more sedentary tourists alighting from coaches. As they continued towards the shop there was a huge explosion and a pall of black smoke rose into the air. They were looking at each other in consternation, wondering what they should do, when two young men ran past them towards the main road. A black Mercedes was coming towards them. It slowed a little to allow them to jump into the passenger seats before turning round in a tight circle and speeding off towards the main road.

There was a tailback of traffic from the border, still held up by the police, and at a major roundabout four kilometres away a German patrol car was parked across the road to prevent anyone reaching it. The Mercedes roared along the road towards the roundabout and the driver could see the police car blocking the road, with a policeman standing at each end. As the speeding car approached the roadblock, a prolonged burst of automatic fire was heard. The policemen barely had time to aim their weapons before they died in a hail of bullets. The driver of the Mercedes manoeuvred around the police car and accelerated out of sight.

The driver of the first car to come onto the scene rang the emergency services. There was nothing the medics could do but prepare the bodies to be taken away. A sergeant started questioning the witness, who kept saying, "I'm not a witness; I just happened to be driving along when I saw the police car and two bodies and I rang you lot. I didn't see or hear anything. The road was otherwise empty, apart from the police car."

They allowed him to go after taking his name and address. The road was sealed off and Forensics took over. The Sergeant summed up the scene: "The police car was being used as a roadblock to prevent suspected terrorists getting away. The car approached at speed and the occupants opened fire with automatic weapons. The poor buggers on duty didn't even have time to point their guns at the car before they were hit. There seems to be a lot of shell cases in two different rows, which to me indicates they were shot at from both sides of the car. If they were aware that they were armed and dangerous, they would have been sheltering behind the car. Not enough information was given to them and they paid for it with their lives."

At the police station, a call came in reporting a burned-out car.

"Where are you calling from?" asked the sergeant on duty.

"I'll give you directions," was the response. "If you drive towards the Dutch border, about six kilometres out, you come to the last big roundabout. We're first on the right."

"Okay, I know where you mean. What happened there?"

"A silver BMW came speeding through our village; the driver didn't appear to know where to go so he turned left when he got to the chapel and carried on towards the stream which runs at the back of there. A few moments later there was a loud explosion, a cloud of black smoke went up and two guys ran back into the village square from behind the chapel. They went on running in the direction of the main road and a black Merc drove towards them, picked them up, turned round and disappeared, going like a bat out of hell towards the main road."

The Sergeant told the caller that the police would want to speak to him when they came to examine the car, but the man said that he had already told him all he knew. The officers would find him and his wife at No. 7 on the opposite side of the square to the chapel. The Sergeant entered all this information in the Daily Events book and then called the Police Road Patrol office.

In the Patrol office, the duty officer looked at his deployment chart and noted that the nearest patrol was attending the scene of a double shooting but had already been there some time, so he rang the officer on the scene and asked him, if he were finished there, if he could attend the discovery of a burned-out car no more than a couple of kilometres away from where they were.

"Well, Forensics are still busy and will be here for some time. Where is it?"

"The witness said to drive towards the Dutch border and when you get to the roundabout, turn first right and this little village is a short way along. The burned-out car is behind a chapel, but the people you want to see are the couple at No. 7, facing the chapel. They saw the whole thing."

The Sergeant drove to the village and found the house, having no difficulty following the concise directions, and knocked on the door. An elderly man opened it. Seeing the uniformed officer, he asked him to come in and told him the full story.

"You actually saw the two men?"

"Yes, they were just as we described them. Young, Asian-looking, wearing casual clothes and running fast. They either didn't notice us or just ignored us."

"Were they armed?"

"One of them was carrying a kind of backpacker's bag."

"What about the Mercedes car which picked them up?"

"It was all black, medium size, not one of those really big ones you see sometimes; only one occupant, who was driving; no other passengers. Sorry we didn't get the registration number, but it all happened so quickly. It screeched around and disappeared in a cloud of dust!" He was beginning to feel very important, giving all these details to a police officer, who was writing down everything he said very carefully.

"What about the two men's clothing? Did you notice exactly what they were wearing?"

"Well, let me see." He turned to his wife for her confirmation. "Both were wearing black shoes, dark blue jeans, and what do you call 'em? Sweatshirts, one in grey and one in fawn, or was it brown, do you think?" His wife nodded. "The sweatshirts had collars; they weren't those crew-neck ones, you know; open-necked they were."

"Thank you, you've been most helpful," said the Sergeant, although the woman hadn't said a word. "You'll get a visit from CID and possibly a sketch artist in case we have to put out a warning about them and need a rough idea of what they look like. Now, can you show me where the explosion was?"

They took him round to the rear of the chapel to see the burned-out car and he made a note to call the experts to examine it closely. But in the meantime, he had to get back to where the shooting had taken place. Things were coming to a conclusion and the forensic team were ready to leave. They said that they had all the evidence they could obtain from the site. The police car would be taken to their laboratory to be minutely examined so see if anything further could be discovered.

The police car was still sitting forlornly in the middle of the road. The traffic had been snarled up for too long and it was time it started moving smoothly again. The key was in the ignition, so the Sergeant told one of his men to get in and start the engine. The motor was running smoothly and the engine didn't appear to have been hit by any of the bullets, so he told him to drive it back to the patrol garage.

Back at the police station, the desk sergeant told him that the Inspector wanted to see him. He groaned inwardly, but knew it was inevitable that the Inspector would want a detailed report of the day's events. When he finished, the Inspector asked him to put everything down in writing in case any of the minor details were missed out. When the report was finished he wanted two copies to go the Commissioner's office. The Sergeant knew that it was going to take him quite a long time into the evening; still, a bit more overtime would always come in useful.

When he took the reports to the Commissioner the following day, he asked him to tell him everything that had happened from the time he arrived at the scene. It took over an hour before all the questions had been answered. The Commissioner thanked him and said how much he regretted losing two good men. It went without saying that he would urge his men to make every effort to arrest those responsible for the killings.

The Chief Inspector of CID was told to spare no effort or expense to find the three suspects and the Assistant Police Commissioner took overall command of the investigation; he wanted quick results, but the three men had disappeared into thin air and no trace of them could be found.

At the airport, Laurie and Hugo were discussing the subject; Laurie asked Hugo what he thought about it and he replied that he thought there were two possibilities. One, they had already left the country, perhaps changing their clothes and appearance, dumping the car and catching a train. There were not many checks made on train passengers and they could already be in Paris or Brussels.

"If that's the case, what can be done?" asked Hugo.

"In Germany, very little; we do have sketches of the general appearance of the two men driving the silver BMW. We could notify Interpol and the Belgian and French police, informing them of the dangers."

"What about the second possibility?"

"If they're still in our country they may have gone to ground. Me, I would be long gone by this time, but they might have been told to remain hidden until the furore dies down."

"In that case, they must feel confident that they'll not be discovered, so wherever they're hidden, the chances of our finding them are nil. The passport official stopped this man because he thought he might possibly be connected with two other men of similar appearance who passed through Frankfurt in previous weeks; some sort of gut feeling or instinct that you sometimes get in this job."

"Sergeant, can you find him and bring him here?"

"Yes, sir." said Hugo and hurried off. He was back in a few minutes saying, "He's off duty and has gone home now, sir. He'll be back first thing in the morning."

"For heaven's sake, man, we're not asking him to work; we just need to talk to him and time is of the essence. It's urgent; even a day can make a difference!"

"Right, sir, I'll go and get him." He returned an hour later accompanied by the passport official in question.

"Sorry to drag you back, but this is urgent. Please tell us exactly why you stopped that Asian man. What caused you to feel suspicious about him?"

The man thought carefully and finally said, "He was the third young man in two weeks with that kind of look to him. You know, rather like the FBI in American films – young, fit, confident, well dressed in quite expensive suits – and all three flew in from Dubai. Just as though they had all graduated from a training school with their entry separated by time so as not to draw too much attention to themselves."

"You did well to spot those things; not many people are so observant when carrying out their everyday job."

"We're paid to pick out suspicious persons."

"Yes, but the first two did not even come through your desk."

"But you notice them when they're standing in the queue, waiting to have their passports inspected, and I must be unusually nosy." He laughed.

"I would say observant is a better word than nosy, and thank God for that. At least one of them has been taken out of circulation. We're thinking, my sergeant and I, that we can use your keen eye to catch the two men still out there. Do we have camera footage of the queues waiting for the non-EU passport desks?"

"I believe our security people do record throughout the day, but I'm not sure if they film all night."

"Well, the two we're looking for came in daylight hours and we're only interested in daytime footage. Sergeant, will you go and get the tapes for the past two weeks from whoever's in charge of them and bring them here?"

Hugo disappeared and while he was searching for the right tapes the passport inspector said, "Let's go get something to eat in the airport restaurant while we're waiting; the food's not too bad and you deserve it for having come back to help us. We'll have a bottle of wine as well but perhaps you would choose that because I'm a lager man myself."

The passport official did not have expensive tastes and after pasta and a light dessert, they finished with coffee, having decided it would not be a good idea to have any alcohol while at least one of them was working.

When they returned to the office, Hugo was already there, setting up the equipment to view pictures from the security cameras. Everything was neatly labelled and filed in date order for the whole of the previous year and then transferred to computer so the tapes could be reused.

"I've got the tapes for the past three weeks," said Hugo. "I don't suppose you remember exactly which days those two fellers went through control?"

"Let me see the footage; something might hit a nerve."

"Perhaps we could check the times of flights arriving from Islamabad via Dubai; there can't be all that many," said Hugo. "I'll get the list."

They played the film on the computer, trying to go through it very fast at first, soon realising that they would miss something unless they went through it slowly, which could take hours. Hugo returned with the flight arrival times. There were only two per day Monday to Saturday and none on Sundays. One was at 14.15 and the other at 16.50, so the suspects would be queuing at passport control from about 14.30 and 17.00. Now they had narrowed down the crucial times it was easier to concentrate on certain men standing in the queues. A sudden shout from the passport officer confirmed the first one. It was still going to be a slow process, but eventually, with bleary eyes, they located the second young man.

They carefully re-ran the sequences and watched the men handing over their passports and then passing through the control desk with no apparent hold-ups.

"Who's that on the desk?" asked Laurie. "He doesn't appear to be taking a lot of notice of anyone."

"His name is Ulrich de Wytt. You can't blame him. Just because the man has an Asian appearance isn't really a positive reason for suspecting him to be a terrorist. We get thousands passing through passport control and if we detained even ten per cent of them, the government would need to employ hundreds of officers to interrogate them!"

"Slight exaggeration, I think," said Laurie, "but I get your point. We now have to decide what our next action should be. If we give this information to the Assistant Commissioner, the blame will probably fall on you; a scapegoat must be found and poor old Ulrich will probably get the sack for not being vigilant enough and spotting the false passports. They'll overhaul the whole department, shuffle some of the personnel around and the man at the top will get a slapped wrist."

"We could say that because one of the men was killed, we were conscientiously going over the security tapes and eureka, we noticed the two similar types and thought we ought to have a talk with them in case they're connected," said Hugo. "Then we could get the press and TV to put out a newscast saying something like 'Have you seen these two men, if you have, please get in touch with the Passport Control Office at Frankfurt Airport', which will make it look as if it's something to do with illegal passports."

"We must be very careful here. If these two are terrorists, they're extremely dangerous and if they thought that someone had recognised them and was going to inform the police, they'd probably have no compunction in killing them," said Laurie. "Why don't we just give these two videos to whoever's in charge of the investigation? I mean the police, not the Assistant Commissioner."

"I like that, I like it very much; then it looks as though we're trying our best to help catch the two men. There may even be some advantages for us. As airport officials, our brief is to welcome visitors to our city and not to harass them if their documents are in order and there's nothing suspicious about them. In none of the three cases was there anything unusual or suspect about them – Asian males, smartly dressed with a single suitcase; everything about them looking completely normal."

"Okay," said Laurie, "we stick to our story and do as you suggested. Make sure the other officials in the Passport Control Department – you can see in the videos who they are – are made aware that they'll be questioned so must confirm what we've agreed. Emphasise our solidarity or their jobs could be in limbo. Is there anything else we haven't thought of? No, then you might as well carry on as usual. You know where I am and you can contact me immediately if you're concerned about the way things turn out."

Hugo turned to go but stopped to ask who had been put in charge of the investigation.

"They've put Commander Hugo Haas in charge, reporting directly to the Assistant Commissioner."

"Why does the Commissioner need an assistant, sir?"

"Another layer of responsibility, protection for his back, taking the blame, as in this case – if all hell breaks loose, the Assistant Commissioner will take the flak, not him. I'll take these videos to Hugo Haas, but first, Sergeant, make two copies and return the originals to Security. Tell 'em they've been a great help. Never hurts to butter 'em up a bit; you never know when you might need them again."

"Why do we need two copies of the videos, sir?"

"We're going to keep one copy of each video as a record for ourselves, just in case some fool screws up the other copies. It's our safeguard."

Laurie picked up the phone and rang the Commissioner's office to make an appointment. After being kept on hold for several minutes, he was told that the Commissioner could see him at 8.30 the following day if that was convenient. No, he thought, it's not bloody convenient, but I suppose it'll have to do. Politely, he replied, "Yes, that would be fine." Putting the phone down, he said to Hugo, who was still standing with the tapes in his hand, "If you can get the copies back to me before the end of today, I'll be very grateful. By the way, how can I access the exact place I want on the tape without having to go through the whole thing?"

"There is a way, sir, but I'm not quite sure how, but they'll be some computer nerds in the airport IT Department who'll know how to do it. I'll go have a word now."

"Thanks, Sergeant, I'd appreciate that."

When Hugo returned with the copies, he told Laurie that the IT Department had made him a CD of the parts in the videos where the two men had joined the queue to the time they walked away after passing through passport control. This was the only part the Commissioner would want to see and obviated the need to go through all the tapes, thereby not wasting any time.

"That's very good. Now the investigating team will know exactly what these two men look like; let's hope the Commissioner sees it that way."

The following morning he arrived early for his appointment with the Commissioner and as a result sat about waiting for more than half an hour. Eventually, an attractive young woman came up to him and said, "The Commissioner will see you now if you'd like to follow me."

Having seen her from both front and back as she led the way to the office, he thought that it was worth waiting for, just to see her walk away from him. Why can't I have a secretary like that instead of Hugo? he thought.

"Thank you, Zelda," said the Commissioner. "Please sit down, Inspector. Now, what did you wish to see me about?"

"When the sketches of the two men who shot the policemen appeared in the papers, we decided to see if they came through our airport passport check. The security people record everybody going through and the films are dated and marked with the time. It took us a long time, watching all the records, gradually working backwards; it was a tedious and very boring process but eventually we found them and the IT Department have made us a short CD showing the dates, times and appearances of the two men."

He looked round the office and asked if he could play the CD on the Commissioner's computer and very soon they were watching the first man standing in the queue with his passport in his hand.

Laurie spread out the newspaper sketches of the men and said, "You can see, Commissioner, this is one of the men wanted for questioning about the shooting of the policemen at the road block and this is the second one."

"Yes, yes, I can see these are the ones wanted for questioning, but it's a little late isn't it? They'll be out of the country by now. All it does is point out the accuracy of our sketch artists, but it's too little too late."

"Well, sir, wherever they're caught, they'll be tried in this country. And can we assume for certain that they've escaped? If we knew that we'd be on their trail by now, but as you know, sir, we don't have any border controls with other EU countries, so travelling by car or train could take them anywhere within the EU. They wouldn't need much of a disguise, if any. A change of clothing, different hairstyle or even dressing as a woman in a hijab, no one would pay much attention. We did introduce tighter security measures at airports, bus terminals and railway stations, but that was not implemented until three days after the shooting. From what I know about terrorists, once your cover is blown you only have two choices – run or stay hidden in a safe house until everything goes quiet again, which could be quite a long time."

"Leave the CD and video tapes here, Inspector. I'll make sure the images are fully circulated," said the Commissioner.

"Thank you, sir. Let's hope we get a break."

As he left the Commissioner's office, Laurie paused to say goodbye to Zelda, wishing he could hang around a little longer to get to know her and thinking what a pessimist the Commissioner was. Surely his attitude was not appropriate for a man in charge of such an important investigation?

Back in his own office, Hugo greeted him with, "How did it go? Was he impressed by our finding the two men out of all the faces on the tapes?"

"If you mean did he praise our hard work and dedication to duty, no he didn't. Nothing was mentioned about the department. He gave me the idea that we were too late and they would be well away from this area. He's sure they've left the country and by now they could be anywhere in the EU. He thinks they most likely used the rail network, with small changes to their appearance, and our contribution was, if not really unhelpful, not exactly mind blowing. Still, at least I got to meet his lovely secretary Zelda." He smacked his lips appreciatively.

Hugo thought for a moment before saying, "When you look at it like that, it actually makes sense; that's what I'd do in their shoes. Every day that passes there'll be more people searching for them; their organisation is clever, totally ruthless and they'll kill on sight, so the sooner they get away, the better for them."

"Are you on their side or something?"

"No, sir, but we're only going to catch them if we get into their minds and understand how they work. It's no good thinking that sooner or later they might make a slip and give themselves away; we have to put ourselves in their situation and decide what we would do faced with the same state of affairs."

"I can see what you mean, so here goes: let's think ourselves into their minds. What would be the next step they might take on seeing the roadblock?"

"If I saw the road half blocked by a police car with two police officers standing next to it, I'd probably think that all I have to do is kill them, riddle their car with bullets and hope it blows up and then drive round it and disappear. It worked in their favour that the traffic on that road had been stopped a long way back so there were no witnesses. The two policemen would have done much better if they'd parked out of sight, waited for the suspect car to drive past, radioed for assistance and given chase. Even had they been shot at, they would have been able to give an exact description of the men and the car and it's unlikely they would have been hit in the heat of the moment because the terrorists would have had to lean out of the car and their aim would have been unsteady to say the least. Then other police cars, who had been forewarned, would have joined the chase and they would have been cornered and shot instead of the other way around."

"It's always easy with hindsight, Sergeant."

"I still think that the police force should change their procedures for setting up roadblocks. One car can't completely block a road; it needs three vehicles, two nose to nose and one facing in the direction the car is travelling. If the car crashes into the roadblock and gets through somehow, the third car can pursue it. Those two men died needlessly."

"You're right, Sergeant. You put forward the suggestion and I'll sign it and put it to them for consideration. We have a department for reviewing police procedures to reduce danger and be more efficient with the use of manpower. Now, what about our two killers? I've been told they were driving a silver BMW on the road to Holland. Dutch policemen stopped them and they turned and fled when the two officers drew their weapons. To me that means they were going to Holland for a specific purpose, perhaps a special mission that had been planned, because the car must have contained explosives of some sort, probably carefully disguised in their luggage. We have to find out what this specific purpose was. Do you speak Dutch, Sergeant?"

"Unfortunately not, sir, but I'll go and find someone who does!"

While Laurie was waiting for Hugo to return, he wondered what he was thinking of doing. The lad was very bright and probably on his way up the promotion ladder.

Hugo returned half an hour later with a young man from the Security Department. "This is Phillip Bergen, sir. He speaks Dutch very well."

"Now, Sergeant," said Laurie, "as it's your idea, how about explaining your theory to Phillip and putting him in the picture, so to speak."

Hugo explained the details of what had happened and finished by saying, "What we would like you to do is ring the Chief of Police in Amsterdam and ask him if he knows why two terrorists, who had flown into Frankfurt Airport, would then hire a car to travel to Holland. Here's the number of the Amsterdam police headquarters."

Phillip nodded and picked up the phone. He spoke for quite a long time and then picked up pen and paper to make notes. When he put the phone down he turned to Laurie. "The man I spoke to at HQ really likes to talk; he must feel lonely in his office! This is what he told me. A short while ago they stopped a man travelling from Islamabad heading for a British airport, as they were suspicious about his passport, and they were going to send him back. Quick as a flash, he contacted a lawyer. The inspector at the airport police station who handled the case was then killed by a bomb explosion shortly afterwards." He relayed to them all the information he had been given regarding the events in Holland and finished by saying, "Police thinking is that the two men who shot our policemen are direct replacements to try and rebuild the group."

"That probably makes sense," said Laurie. "Thank you, Phillip, you've been a fantastic help to us." He turned to Hugo and began to assimilate the information that Phillip had given them, trying to put things in order of importance and coming to various conclusions. It would appear that the Amsterdam terrorists were intending to go to Britain eventually, but had been delayed in Amsterdam by the keen eyes and gut feelings of the passport officials and ever-watchful police. It would have been comparatively easy to get to an English destination, and once there they would have disappeared into the large Muslim population of any one of the big cities until they were ready to put their plan into action, whatever it may be. What was it they were going to do?

Hans was following his reasoning closely. "We can rule out trying to escape by flying, and they wouldn't attempt another car journey so soon after being stopped, which leaves buses and trains. I don't even know if there is a bus service to Amsterdam."

"Will you check up on that for me?" asked Laurie.

Hugo made a short phone call. "You could just about make it, sir, with four changes, but it would take you nearly three days! I guess we can leave that out. That leaves us with the railway."

"We mustn't forget that they can travel to any large city in Holland by rail and then divert into France, Belgium or Denmark. But one thing's for sure: they had to get out in a hurry; I would think the same night. Okay, Sergeant, let's put ourselves in their position. We've just killed two policemen, we phone for help while we're escaping by car, driven by another terrorist, so what happens next?"

"We have to lose the car and quickly, then change our appearance."

"Why's that? There were no witnesses."

"Yes there were; that old couple on their way to the shop. They saw them clearly – running away from the explosion and being picked up in the black Mercedes."

"You're right, of course; they would need to alter their appearance very quickly."

"It strikes me, sir, that wherever that black car came from, it can't have been very far away because it didn't take him very long to pick them up, and he couldn't have come along the road to Holland, because the police car was already trying to block it."

"You're on to something now, Sergeant. That being the case, he must have come from the Holland side of the road. Is there a side road between the Dutch border and the road block?" They searched the wall map and found a country lane which petered out at a small village of probably only a few houses. "We'll take your car, Sergeant. I have a feeling in my bones that this is going to bear fruit. Let's get going."

They drove in silence, knowing that it was going to be a long day. And they both realised that they should have told others where they were going and why. If they discovered another terrorist safe house, they could be in danger, as they knew they would think nothing of shooting two unknown men. "We are here," said Hugo.

They turned off the main road and drove slowly along the narrow lane, noting every building as they came to it.

"Turn round, Sergeant," said Laurie. "We've seen all we need to see. Let's compare notes. First, there's a big farm complex, roughly half a kilometre from the road. It might be a bit big for a terrorist hideout. Second, there's a small row of cottages nearly one kilometre away, which we must take a closer look at. And finally, I could just see a large house in the distance with its own short road leading to it, but it was a dead end so anyone driving there would be seen if someone was on the lookout. We must be very careful not to approach too closely."

"Right, sir, it's the cottages first then?"

As they drove along the narrow lane, they soon came to the cottages, seven in all, and stopped, wondering if anyone was going to come past. Nothing happened.

"We'll have to knock on one of the doors," said Laurie. "Get your warrant card out, Sergeant. We don't want them to think we're door-to-door salesmen!"

They knocked on the door of the first cottage. A middle-aged lady answered and looked at them enquiringly. Laurie put on his most winning smile and Hugo said, "We're very sorry to disturb you, madam. I'm a police sergeant and this is my inspector; here's my ID card."

She examined the card carefully before she said, "We don't see many policemen here."

"You're very lucky, madam; it must mean you don't have much criminal activity in your lovely little community. Would it be all right if we came in for a moment?" said Laurie.

"Yes, of course. Please come in." They wiped their feet carefully on the mat and looked around her immaculately clean kitchen; they could tell she was very house-proud. "Come through into the sitting room," she directed them. "Please sit down. Would you like a cup of coffee?"

Reluctantly, they declined politely. Laurie began questioning her by asking if she knew everybody else in the neighbourhood.

"Oh yes," she said. "We all know each other quite well."

"No changes recently, nobody selling up and moving away?"

"I've lived here for more than ten years and in that time only two properties have changed hands; No. 5 was bought by a young couple with a small baby and a retired couple moved into No. 7. They came here because it was so quiet," she said proudly.

Nothing here, thought Laurie. Casually, he said, "We noticed a big house up the road a bit; very nice property. I've always thought I might like somewhere like that when I retire."

She considered for a moment, frowning slightly. "I know the one you mean but I don't know anything about the people who have it now. Originally it was built for a rich family; he was a successful financier and they had two children, a girl and a boy, but as they got older there was nothing here for them and I understand that after they'd been to university they went to live in Cologne. The parents put up the house for rent and bought an apartment in Cologne to be near them. There's somebody living there because cars keep driving past, but I haven't seen them."

"What sort of cars would they be then?"

"Oh, don't ask me," she said, laughing. "One car's pretty much the same as another to me."

"Thank you very much; you've been very helpful."

"Always glad to help the police; you never know when you're going to need them. By the way, what's the matter with your assistant? Can't he talk?"

Laurie smiled and said, "As it happens, he has a very talkative wife and after years of being married he's lost the ability to speak!"

"That's a pity, and him such a good-looking lad!"

"He might have lost the ability to speak but he's more than active in other ways," Laurie said, winking.

Back in the car, Hugo said indignantly, "She was a bit cheeky."

"I think she fancied you a bit," said Laurie. "Now, I want to go and look at that big house before we go back to HQ. We'll tell them that we heard it was up for rent and we're thinking of opening a nursing home or something like that so would it be possible to look round. If they get funny with us we can always apologise profusely for causing them any inconvenience and back off. At least we'll get a close look at the house and anybody who answers the door."

"That sounds quite plausible," said Hugo.

Seen close to, the house was quite imposing. It was set well back from the lane, was flanked by outbuildings and garages and had parking space for several vehicles at the front. They rang the bell and waited – and waited.

"Either there's nobody in or they're refusing to answer the doorbell," said Hugo.

"Let's go round the back," suggested Laurie.

While they waited for some response to their banging on the back door, Laurie peered through one of the windows. He could see no signs of any occupants, so he went round to the front and did the same. Although the house was fully and expensively furnished, it appeared to be vacant. "I wonder what you'd have to pay to rent a place like this?" he mused.

"More than you and I get in a year," Hugo responded dryly.

"The place looks empty, so either they're out at work, gone for the day, or they've left for good. Let's look in the garage."

The garage was wide enough to hold two cars parked side by side with plenty of room to walk around them. The windows were dirty and difficult to see through clearly.

"I'm sure I can see something in the far corner," Hugo said with satisfaction. "Looks like a car covered with a tarpaulin. Look, sir, there."

Laurie pressed his nose to the glass with his hands cupped around his face and peered in. It was a car, sure enough. But underneath the tarpaulin, oozing out onto the concrete floor, was some white foamy substance, very difficult to see in the dim light.

"The crafty buggers," said Laurie. "They've covered it with some sort of foam, perhaps from a fire extinguisher, which will have destroyed fingerprints or any other forensic evidence we might have found. They wouldn't want to set fire to it because someone might have seen it and there could have been an explosion, which would have set the locals wondering what was going on." He swore long and quietly to himself; after all their efforts this was all they could come up with. He was itching to get into that garage to see if his suspicions were confirmed, but when he looked closely at the doors he thought he could see something behind the lock. Better be safe than sorry. "Sorry, Sergeant; if you had a date for tonight or you think anyone might be worried by your absence, phone 'em now and tell 'em you won't be home in the foreseeable future! We have to get a warrant to search this place, and as quickly as possible."

The nearest police station turned out to be very small and there was no one there who could issue a warrant. Laurie rang the Commander's office and explained their dilemma.

"Where are you exactly?" the Commander asked.

"About eight kilometres from the Dutch border."

"It's going to take a while to arrange for a warrant and a search detail so I'm afraid we won't get there tonight. If you ring in the morning, about 10 a.m., we should be able to make all the arrangements by then. In the meantime stay away from the place; it might be booby-trapped or they may come back. You mustn't put yourself and your sergeant in any danger."

Something was niggling the back of Laurie's mind, but he was forced to acknowledge that this made good sense. The idea of asking Hugo to drive all the way back to his home and then to his own apartment seemed a bit unfair, so he suggested that after Hugo had rung whoever it was who was going to miss him if he didn't appear that night, perhaps they should book in at a small hotel nearby, get a meal and a good night's sleep, also saving themselves the drive through the morning rush-hour traffic to get back in time for the raid. Besides, they could charge it to expenses quite legitimately.

After a few more phone calls, they discovered a small hotel just a few kilometres distant, and although they had no idea what to expect, drove off to find it. As they walked through the open door, they were pleasantly surprised to find a comfortable dining room with delicious smells wafting their way, a well-stocked bar and, although the hotel was only on two floors, there was also a lift. The receptionist was a smart young lady who asked if she could help them. When Laurie told her that they needed two rooms for the night because they were working on an important case in the neighbourhood, she said, "Certainly, sir. Will you require adjoining rooms?"

"No, that's not necessary," said Laurie. "However, we shall need two of those little packets you make up – you know; toothpaste, brush, razor, etc. – as we have no luggage with us."

"Certainly, sir; these things will be put in your rooms. How will you be paying?"

"By card, of course."

The rooms looked comfortable and in no time at all they were relaxing in the bar, sipping beer and wondering what to talk about that didn't involve work.

"Are you married, sir?" asked Hugo.

"No, too busy chasing villains."

"What about ladies, sir?"

"There's nothing wrong with my liking the ladies. One way or another I've always been lucky in finding them but when they find out I'm a policeman, it tends to put them off, particularly if they know anyone married to a policeman."

"Do you think it's true that being a policeman puts most women off?"

"Most of the women I meet are quite happy to be out with a policeman, but when it comes to marriage and settling down, that's when it becomes more difficult. Unsociable hours, the danger involved, low pay in the case of lower ranks; it makes them think again. You're obviously married?"

"Yes, sir, with two children, both boys."

"So what does your wife think?"
"I keep telling her my job is a piece of cake, just office work."
"Keep telling her that and you'll keep her happy."

Chapter 25

The next morning, Laurie was first down for breakfast. When Hugo joined him they both said very little. Afterwards, on the phone to the Commander's office, they were told that the support team had already started out and they were to meet them at the big roundabout to guide them to the house.

"I've been told that the team is in two vans, the first one carrying the Anti-Terrorist Tactical Response Unit and the second one the Bomb Disposal Unit. We've been told to observe but not to participate in the operation. Come on, Sergeant; things are starting to move at last. We'd better get going."

They hadn't been waiting at the roundabout for long before the two vans appeared. Laurie hailed the driver of the first van.

"Are you the team leader?" asked the driver.

"I'm the inspector who called you out here and this is my sergeant. We've found this large, secluded house, which looks empty, but in one of their garages we discovered a car, which we think was used to help two murderers escape. We think the house has been used as a terrorist hideout. The car is concealed with a tarpaulin but underneath it's been sprayed with foam from a fire extinguisher. We think they did this to destroy fingerprints and forensic evidence. As far as you're concerned, carry out the operation as though they were still there. For one thing, they may have come back and for another, I don't want you to lose a single man from your team – it's that dangerous," he emphasised. "It's all yours now. We'll keep out of sight after we've shown you where the place is."

The two vans followed their car past the cottages until they were in sight of the house. There the team deployed its manpower, spreading round all sides of the house, and waited for a signal from their leader. Keeping low, Laurie used a loudhailer to announce, "This is a special police unit. We're armed and fully authorised to use our weapons if we're fired upon. All occupants in the house, please come out with your hands raised." There was no response. Laurie repeated his message, but there was still no response.

The assault team leader gave orders to fire tear-gas grenades through the windows, but Laurie asked him to wait because he and Hugo desperately wanted to look in the garage at the abandoned car. He also knew it had to be checked out before they went in.

"It looks to me like they've been gone for some time now, but they may have left some nasty surprises for us. Let's examine the garage first. If you could have the area checked for hardware before we go in, I'll feel a lot happier."

"If that's the way you want it," said the team leader cheerfully, "that's what we'll do." He spoke to his men and they went forward to check for any signs of explosives. Their caution was rewarded: they examined the garage doors minutely and found a small device, which had they just pushed the doors open would have exploded, making rather a mess of someone's hands and chest. They dealt with it and Laurie and Hugo could get in easily through the garage doors, which were hanging off their hinges. They pulled the tarpaulin off the car and found, as they suspected, that the exterior and interior had been sprayed with foam. Everything inside the car was a sticky mess and would probably be of no help to them whatsoever.

"I'll call on the forensic guys and have the car taken to the lab; maybe they'll get something from it." He asked the team leader to open the house door without damaging the locks.

"You mean like a burglar?"

"Yes," said Laurie, "something like that."

The team leader walked over to his men and asked, "Which of you guys can open a lock without damaging it?"

A man stepped forward and said, "What, one of these house doors? It'll be a doddle." He disappeared round the side of the house and a few moments later opened the front door. "Back door opened like a dream," he boasted.

"You idiot. You took a chance coming through the house like that!" fumed the team leader. "What if there'd been a tripwire or some sort of booby trap? You might have ruined the whole operation!"

"Thanks, boss. So nice to know you care about me," he responded sarcastically, "but I was very aware of the danger. Anyway, the house appears to be deserted."

They then began a systematic search, carefully working through each room, checking for anything they could find to indicate danger. After an exhaustive search from attic to cellar, they found precisely nothing. Forensic officers arrived with a tow truck to take away the car and then started trying to find fingerprints or anything to indicate who had been living in the house: a stray hair, a used cup or glass. But whoever had been living there had either worn rubber gloves the whole time or had wiped every surface clean. There were no clothes in the wardrobes and all sheets and blankets were clean and neatly folded in a cupboard.

"Real professionals," grunted Laurie. "It's going to take our men days to unearth anything, and even if they do, it's not going to be of much help to us. We'll have to inform the owner of the property what's happened. You never know, he might be on first-name terms with our three terrorists – I don't think! I suppose I'd better give the Commander a call to keep him in the picture."

When he was eventually put through, he said, "Just like to update you, sir, about how the case is going regarding the two men suspected of being terrorists."

"Ah, I was hoping to hear that you've apprehended them, but I suppose that's too much to hope for just yet."

"We discovered a car in the garage covered by a tarpaulin. It was the getaway car but it had been sprayed with foam to eliminate anything which would be of any help to us. Nothing of any use to us was found in the house. Forensics are going over it with a fine-tooth comb, but we're not very hopeful."

"Hmm. Where do you go next?" asked the Commander.

"I'll keep you informed, sir."

After putting the phone down, he asked Hugo if he had managed to get in touch with the owner of the house.

"No, sir, but I have spoken to the man at the agency who rents it out. I told him we obtained a warrant to inspect the inside of the house but that the search showed it to be empty, so perhaps he could get in touch with the owner to tell him what's happening. The agent has keys for the place, so when Forensics have finished, he can come and inspect the premises and secure them. So what do we do now, sir?"

"It's been a very long day, Sergeant. I think we've done enough for the time being. If you can drop me off at HQ I can pick up my car. Make sure you claim for all that extra mileage when you put in your expenses claim." And with that he put his head back on the headrest and fell asleep.

Chapter 26

The following morning, they were both in the office at eight o'clock, not too bleary eyed, debating how many strong cups of coffee it would take to kick-start their brains into action.

"Let's go for some of that stuff they call coffee in the bar downstairs," suggested Laurie, "and you can inspire me with your brilliant theories about how to catch criminals!"

Starting on his third mug of coffee, Hugo said, "I think, in fact I'm certain, that our three terrorists will be heading for Holland, if they're not there already."

Laurie interrupted. "Whether they're in Holland or not, we want them tried for murder here and to do that we have to find them and bring them back."

"Of course, sir, but we have to keep putting ourselves in their shoes, so to speak, and planning what our next move will be. They'd think that sooner or later the police would find them here so would move and quickly. There might have been more than three of them and they must have had some kind of communication equipment."

"Depends on how long they planned to stay in the house," said Laurie. "That house was rented, so must have been a temporary safe house. If they were planning a long stay they would've bought a property."

"Where do they get the money from, sir?" asked Hugo.

"Don't forget they have some very rich supporters; look at the amount of oil they have in the Middle East, plus the fact that there are many rich people who support the unrest, whether for religious reasons or because there's a lot of money to be made during times of trouble."

"That's all very well, but what about those killed or maimed in these attacks?"

"They probably think that people are dying all the time from poverty, hunger, disease, road, rail and plane crashes, and this is just another way of going to heaven! Let's work on the principle that they're sitting in their safe house and have to leave in a hurry. Whatever luggage or possessions they have can be put in a suitcase, so that's not a problem."

"I've thought about this, sir, and it occurs to me that it'd be a lot easier all round if they hired a van, depending on how many of them there are. How many do you think would be in a group of terrorists, roughly?"

"I've not had had any experience of this sort of case before but I'd guess a minimum of eight, perhaps ten if those two were new members, plus their luggage."

"Next, sir, how many journeys do they make? One or two? Two journeys multiply the danger, but think of the feelings of those left behind, waiting for someone to come back and pick them up!"

"You're right; it has to be done in one trip in one large vehicle which can take at least ten men and their luggage, with perhaps two of them sitting in the cab dressed in overalls to look like workmen and the others in the back with those darkened windows so no one can see the interior. Let's assume this was their plan. So what route would they take? Do they go along the same road or do they try going via Belgium? I think you should contact that guy who speaks Dutch and ask him to question the border police and find out if they searched all the vehicles they stopped."

Hugo returned a while later somewhat annoyed, as it was the officer's day off.

"Damn," said Laurie, "just when we thought we were getting somewhere. Do you have his home phone number? I'll phone him." A woman's voice answered. Laurie put on his most charming voice and after introducing himself said, "I'm trying to get in touch with Phillip. May I have a word with him? He knows me." After a short delay,

Phillip came to the phone. "I'm sorry to disturb you on your day off, but we need your help again. If I give you the phone number of the Dutch border police, could you ring them and ask just one question. Do their police at the border crossing check all vehicles, including vans and lorries, or just suspect vehicles?"

"I'll do that for you now, sir," said Phillip and put the phone down. Ten minutes later he was back with the reply. "The police were instructed in this case to only stop cars with Asian-looking drivers and passengers. They were not to disrupt commercial traffic in any way."

"Thank you very much, Phillip. I owe you lunch. Sorry for interrupting your day off." He put the phone down and turned to Hugo. "Now we have to discover if they hired a van and who from. There were no other vehicles in the garage so they either hired a van over the phone and asked to have it delivered to the house, or risked using the Mercedes to take another driver to collect a hired vehicle from a car lot."

"I should think they asked for the van to be delivered to the house, sir."

"I agree with you, Sergeant. By that time the police had been alerted to look out for a black Mercedes car, so it had to be hired over the phone and dropped off at the house. It would have to be a large van or perhaps a medium-sized removal van. Now what we have to do is check all van and car hirers who advertise in the trade directory. There appear to be eight. I'll take four and you take four, and when we get a promising answer we can ask for details, check the story they gave and perhaps get an inkling as to what their plans were." But they drew a blank.

"What's the next step?" asked Hugo. "Have we missed one somewhere, an agent who isn't listed or perhaps someone from another district?"

"Here," said Laurie, handing Hugo some cash, "go and get us some lunch. I'll have two ham and cheese baguettes and a carton of milk and you get whatever you want for yourself. I think better with some food in my stomach. And while you're gone, I'll decide what the next step will be." He got up from his desk and walked over to the window. The phone rang. He answered it reluctantly, but as he listened, he started to smile. Eureka! This was the answer they had been searching for. Someone, who wished to remain anonymous, obviously an employee who didn't want to get on the wrong side of the police, had overheard Laurie asking questions about the hire of a large van. She had a boyfriend who, apparently, had a little sideline and rented out his own vehicle to 'special friends' who might need transport, but he didn't put any transactions through his books. A 'friend of a friend' had asked her if he would take cash for hiring out his van if he delivered it to a certain address very quickly. When he went to the address he had been told he could collect it from, there was no sign of his vehicle, and so far he had been unable to trace it. Because it had been a dodgy transaction he hadn't wanted to go to the police to report it stolen, but she had persuaded him to let her tell the story in the hope that there would be no prosecution.

When Hugo returned with the food he found Laurie grinning like a Cheshire cat.

"Just had a phone call with a very positive lead. As soon as we've polished off our lunch, we're going to interview someone who hired out his own van to a very suspicious character and then had it stolen! I'll fill you in as we drive there."

The girl had given him the address of her boyfriend's small vehicle repair shop. After making quite sure that there would be no comeback from his transaction, the young man explained everything that had happened, giving full details of where he delivered the van, the address he was supposed to collect it from and the story he was given about removing some furniture from his wife's house as they were getting divorced.

"Think very carefully," said Laurie. "The man who paid you, what exactly did he look like?"

"He was a young Asian guy, very well dressed, you know: suit, shirt, tie, polished shoes, very smart. I suppose some women would think he was good-looking. He spoke very little German but his money was good."

"What were the arrangements for getting the van back?"

"I was told it would be parked on an industrial estate nearby because he didn't want to leave it in front of his house, but when I went to pick it up there was no sign of it. I was debating how to tell the police it'd been stolen, but I thought it would turn up."

"Did you see anyone else at the house? Is there anything you can add to what you've told me?"

"No, sorry. What's all this about? Why are the police interested in my old van?"

"It might have been used by terrorists to escape from Germany after shooting two policemen at a roadblock, but apart from that, I can't tell you anything more. Better keep quiet and then you can read in the newspapers what happens."

Laurie rang the Commander, giving him all the details, who in turn rang his opposite number in the Dutch police force. When he rang back it was to inform Laurie that he and Hugo would be welcomed by their opposite numbers in the Dutch police force, who spoke German, to pool their expertise – fresh ideas etc. "After all, we did let the terrorists escape to Holland and we have a duty to the two murdered policemen's families to do all we can to ensure the criminals are brought to justice."

"I agree with you, sir. My sergeant and I have done everything we could to catch those responsible. But despite all our efforts, we seem to have come to a dead end."

"For the next two weeks, you and your sergeant are relieved from your normal duties here to go on an intensive course to learn Dutch. Then you'll both be seconded to the Dutch police force," the Commander informed him.

Laurie turned to Hugo to tell him the news. "How do you feel about that?" he asked.

"It's all right for you, sir; you're not married. How am I going to tell my wife that I've got to learn Dutch and then go off to swinging Amsterdam for the foreseeable future, chasing dangerous terrorists and risking being blown up or shot, when I've always told her I do a desk job and it's as safe as houses?" he said indignantly.

"Well, you'll just have to do your diplomatic best – tell her how important you are to this investigation and your inspector recommended you because – well, because – tell her I can't do without you or something and that way you can keep the peace. Think how happy she'll be to see you home safe and sound and what a reunion that will be! Use your initiative, Sergeant, use your initiative!"

With all the speed Laurie could muster, he started the ball rolling by contacting the head of the language department at the college and booked an intensive training course for himself and Hugo. He used the Commander's name and rank to ensure there were no difficulties put in their way. They were to start the next day.

It felt like going back to school, what with all the exercise books, dictionaries, textbooks and audiotapes. Their tutor was a revelation – her name was Liza Petrova, probably of Eastern European origin, and she was slim, attractive and wore a tight-fitting black trouser suit.

"We might find it difficult to concentrate on our lessons," murmured Laurie. But at the end of two weeks, after a lot of hard work, they both had a rough working knowledge of Dutch and were ready to set off for Amsterdam.

On their last day, Laurie bought Liza a large box of expensive Belgian chocolates and asked her if she would like to go out with them for a drink to celebrate how well they had worked together. Hugo looked at his watch and apologised, saying he had to rush off because he had promised to take his wife to the supermarket.

"Well, that leaves us," said Laurie. "Where shall we go? Is there anywhere pleasant around here?"

She took him a short distance to a café/bar with comfortable seats. They sat down and Laurie looked around for a waiter to order their drinks, but she said to him, "There's no waiter service here; that's why it's a bit cheaper. The people from college like it because it's not quite so expensive."

"I can see that; the place seems to be full of them. Anyway, what would you like to drink?"

"A vodka martini, please."

When he got back to their table with their drinks there were two students talking to Liza. He put the drinks down on the table. "Thanks, lads, for looking after my young lady, but you can go now."

They looked at him in amazement, but his height and air of authority meant there was no trouble: they left without a word. She laughed at his expression 'my young lady'. "I want to ask you a question," she said. "Why do you always call your workmate 'Sergeant' instead of his name? You work so closely together, I'd have thought you'd be on first-name terms by this time."

Laurie took a sip of his beer and tried to explain to her that it was a police rule that you address each other by their rank and not get too familiar with each other, otherwise you could be accused of favouritism or reported for not showing respect. "Something to do with human rights," he said and lifted an eyebrow in his best James Bond imitation.

"What a stupid rule," said Liza. "I bet some man made that one up. So that was pulling rank, making those two lads leave?"

"Well, I've dealt with large numbers of young men about their age and they can be earnest, hard-working people or a pain in the neck."

"Don't worry," said Liza, "I can look after myself."

"I just didn't want to exchange silly conversation with those grown-up children and waste valuable time getting to know more about you."

She smiled and said, "It was just a couple of students that I used to teach English to."

"You speak English as well as Dutch?"

"I'm a linguist and to qualify as a linguist you have to be able to teach four languages. I speak, read and write Dutch, English, Russian and Danish as well as German."

"You are clever! What's the difference between a foreign language teacher and a linguist?"

"Being a linguist is the equivalent of being a professor in other subjects."

"Does it pay more?"

"Of course; it requires a lot more study to achieve that level and the pay reflects that. Is your pay good?" she asked him mockingly.

He smiled. "Okay, let's leave that subject. Tell me more about yourself. I'll go and get some more drinks, and when I come back, you won't be surrounded by men, will you?"

"Only four or five!"

She was still alone when he returned, so he asked where all the admirers were. "I think your dismissal of the two previous admirers frightened everyone away."

"Good. Now let's hear something about you; where you're from and what makes you tick."

"A long, long time ago," she started as if she were telling a small child a fairy story, "my grandfather was called up into the Russian army, after the Germans attacked Russia in 1941. His family came from a village near Moscow and he was only seventeen at the time. He was ordered with his unit to defend the city of Minsk and the battle raged for two weeks until thousands of Russians had died, not just the soldiers, but civilians as well. In those days the Germans were better trained and equipped than the Russian troops and they captured not only the city but also thousands of Russian soldiers. Because my grandfather was very young, they moved him to Germany and used him as slave labour. In a way, that was good because most of the people left in Minsk were never heard of again. He was made to work in various German factories for the rest of the war, but luckily for him, it was the Americans who liberated that part of Germany and he had the choice of being repatriated to Russia or staying where he was, under American occupation. He'd heard stories about how communism was treating some of the Russian people, so he decided to stay here, as he'd learned to speak German while working in the factory and was able eventually to get a job and marry another Russian, a girl called Tania. They had two children, a boy called Andrej and a girl called Katusia. Andrej is my father. He married a German girl called Magda, who is my mother, so I'm half Russian, half German."

"You're a German citizen?"

"Yes, I was born in Germany, and so were my parents."

"Were you the only child?"

"I had a little brother but he died of pneumonia when he was three. What about you?"

"Nothing very interesting; my parents always lived in this area; I was born in Frankfurt Hospital long after the war so I don't really know very much about it. I'm the only son and totally spoiled. After college I wanted to get away from the area and have some life-enhancing experiences, so I went to university in Cologne!" Liza was not sure whether he was being amusing or sarcastic. "I lived in a small room in a hostel, which, of course, I never cleaned, my mother having tidied up after me all my life, but in a way it was fun. After graduating in psychology and business studies I came back to live with my parents, and my first job was as an accountant in a small factory. It was so unbelievably dull. I wanted some excitement in my life, so I joined the police force; no two days are alike and I enjoy the job."

"How old are you?"

"Sadly, I'm aging rapidly. I'm thirty-three next birthday."

"You're far too old for me," said Liza, with a smile.

"Why, how old are you?"

"I'm twenty-eight."

"There are only four years between us; that's just right."

"How do you make that out?" she asked suspiciously.

"My father always used to say that women mature faster than men, so you need this time for them to catch you up."

"That's just men wanting to get younger women."

"Why, don't you agree with that?"

"No, I'm afraid not," said Liza, trying to keep a straight face.

"Liza, do you realise we're having our first row; that's a good sign, isn't it? My mother always used to say—"

"Not another of your parents' wise sayings, is it?"

"As I was saying," he said with a very hurt expression on his face, "my mother used to say that a good argument kept a marriage alive."

"Now just a minute. I always thought it was love that kept a marriage alive, Inspector Mueller. By the way, what is your name, I mean your first name? I only know you as Inspector Mueller."

"Actually, it's Albert but I can't stand being called Al or Bert, so in my university days I used to call myself Laurence after that British actor who was so well known, and my friends call me Laurie. So if it's love that keeps a marriage alive, we have no problems because I already love you." She looked at him in amazement, wondering if he'd been drinking earlier in the day. "I'm being serious and I'm not drunk, if that's what you're thinking. You're a clever lady, you have a good sense of humour, you're a very interesting person and—"

"I suppose you want to take me home with you," said Liza.

"Well, that would be fantastic! Come on!"

"That figures," said Liza. "I think the alcohol has gone to what you call a brain. If we have another drink perhaps you'll propose to me."

"Would you like me to go down on one knee and propose to you?"

"Will you please stop this," she said. "Are your parents still alive?"

"Yes, they live not far from here. They're both still working."

"So are mine."

"Where do they live?"

"In Dresden. I have to go now; I'm going out this evening."

"He's a lucky man, whoever he is. Can I give you a lift?"

"No, thank you. I have my car in the college car park so I don't have to get lifts from strange men!"

"It's the same with me," said Laurie, making a face, trying to get her to laugh. "I gave up accepting lifts from men a long time ago after I found out they expected a reward afterwards. Too high a price to pay." He succeeded in making her laugh and offered to walk her to her car.

As they were walking, he said, "Were those men a real nuisance?"

"What men?"

"The ones who took you home in their cars."

"Not for long; you don't know me very well yet, but I can look after myself. I'm not a weak, helpless female."

"I didn't think you would be, but I'm ashamed to admit that some of my kind are real pigs when it comes to women. Being a policeman, I come across quite a lot of that in my job and have to deal with the aftermath of attacks, rapes and even murders, but I hope I've made a difference in some way."

"I guess that's the sort of world where the police have to operate. Thank goodness I don't have to live among those people. Here's my car," she indicated.

Laurie looked at her and said, "You know I want to see you again, don't you?"

"Well, you know that old Russian proverb, don't you – 'Faint heart never won fair lady' or some such rubbish." She stood with her back to the car and he leaned forward swiftly and kissed her mouth, but when he tried to take her in his arms, she put her hand on his chest and stopped him. That surprised him. He knew he wasn't the handsomest man in the world, but women usually found him attractive and he hadn't been stopped like that for a very long time, since being a callow teenager in fact. Most of them ended up in bed with him and he didn't think there had been any complaints about his technique! He took a deep breath and asked her if it was because she was going out with her boyfriend. "I thought you had an open relationship," he said pettishly.

"I don't remember saying anything like that," she said, "and besides, Inspector, I hardly know you."

"I've told you I'd like to see you again. Give me your phone number at least."

"You can contact me at the college; that's my place of work."

"You've not given me very much encouragement," he said, but she only smiled and inserted her key in the ignition and closed the car door. "You're a big boy now, Inspector." With a wave of her hand she drove out of the car park.

He stood there, watching her drive away and wondered if it had been a tease or a real turn down. Walking towards his own car, he told himself he would forget her soon enough, but in the back of his mind the thought lingered and he was not so sure.

Chapter 27

Laurie was at his desk by ten to eight the following morning, dealing with all the items that had landed on his desk in the two weeks he had been at college. He looked up as Hugo came in. "I thought you wanted to spend as much time with your family as possible," he said. "You could have had at least ten more minutes; you didn't have to be here so early."

Hugo grinned to himself and replied, "I take it our Russian miss was not very co-operative last night?"

"She wouldn't even let me kiss her properly."

"You mean appropriately or inappropriately?"

"Both. She gave me no encouragement at all."

"Well, it's worked with you, hasn't it? Show a little interest, and promise more, let the man do all the running about by not saying yes or no. That'll keep you hanging on until she decides whether or not to continue flirting or drop you like a hot stone."

"How come you know so much about women; you, a happily married man?"

"I courted quite a few in my time as a lovesick teenager, sir."

"Do you think she might just be a normal young woman, the sort that doesn't want to fall into bed with every man she meets for the first time?"

"Yes, sir, she could well be, but women have a different philosophy on life nowadays. They seem to think why not enjoy life while you're still young, before you settle down to a humdrum married life and kids. Virginity is no longer an asset or a requirement for a happy married life."

"This discussion is getting far too philosophical for me," said Laurie. "All I know is that I like her very much and I was disappointed when she didn't respond."

"Never mind, sir, our new assignment will soon put her out of your mind."

"Let's hope so."

The phone rang. It was the Commander asking if they were ready to go on their new assignment.

"We're both ready and awaiting your instructions, sir," said Laurie.

"I'll fax you the details of what's been arranged for you," said the Commander. "You're booked on the three o'clock flight to Amsterdam. Rooms are reserved for you at the airport hotel for an indefinite stay and the bills will be sent directly to us. Any other expenses will go on credit cards for you to claim expenses in the usual way. You'll get special cards, contained in the information packs, which you can collect from this office in an hour's time. In the morning you should report to Inspector Erik van Eyck if he's not got in touch with you when you arrive. Everything you need to know is in the pack. From now on your job is to work with Inspector van Eyck and his sergeant, Hans Vogel, until you bring those three murderous bastards back here for trial or see their dead bodies in the morgue. I don't think I've missed anything. Oh, your reports from the college – Miss Petrova says that your Dutch is now very good. I hope she's right."

Laurie looked at Hugo. "I should hope so, after the effort we put into learning it. Better go and collect those information packs and make sure our bags are packed with everything we need. Who knows; it might be quite a long stay."

They landed at four o'clock and shortly afterwards were signing the register at the hotel. After the usual formalities, the receptionist told them that they would have to sign their bills before they were sent to Frankfurt Police HQ and asked them if they wanted adjoining or separate rooms.

"Better have adjoining rooms, I suppose," said Laurie. "No point in being allocated rooms on separate floors, because we might need to get in touch quickly in an emergency."

Their rooms were comfortable without being luxurious, and after an initial difficulty getting the key card to open the lock and remembering to place it in the small slot at the side of the door so that the lights went on, everything went smoothly for Laurie.

He and Hugo went down to the bar to get acclimatised and to practise their Dutch. It was too early to eat so they ordered two glasses of lager. Laurie grumbled to Hugo about the key cards; how was he supposed to find the slot to put his card in at night when it was too dark to see? Hugo was patiently explaining that there should be enough light from the corridor to see where to put it when they became aware of two young women, heavily made up and wearing very tight skirts. The women made quite sure that everybody in the bar, all of whom happened to be men, could see their shapely figures, and after casually looking around, saw the two policemen and sat at a table a short distance away.

"Not bad, Sergeant," Laurie said, indicating them with a slight movement of his head.

"Very professional," grinned Hugo.

"Of course, I didn't realise for a moment that they were prostitutes. I'm a bit surprised the hotel allows them to come in here looking for customers."

"Well, sir, it is Amsterdam and it is renowned for its sex industry – porno cinemas, gay bars, places where they smoke cannabis. A friend of mine bought a box of chocolates here and gave it to his wife; she said they tasted a bit funny and he found out they had cannabis in them. I've heard there's a street where they all sit in the windows wearing next to nothing, and the men go to look at them. If they fancy a particular one, they go into the house. There are theatres where couples have sex on the stage."

"How do you know all this?"

"Oh, not from personal experience, sir. I've just got to hear about 'things'. It's a good laugh really. They'll all be asking me in the squad room when I get back if I saw any of this."

"When you get back, Sergeant, you'll be a hero and you can exaggerate about how brave you've been, but I bet you won't be telling your wife about your sexual adventures. Now of course it's different for me. I'm a free agent and I might want to put some of these procedures under scrutiny in case I'm ever asked to produce a report on the Amsterdam underworld! We'd better discuss what we should do tomorrow. I've brought the videos of the three men who went through our passport control so they'll know who we're looking for."

"Is that such a good idea, sir? It's like we're admitting we made a big mistake letting them get through."

"We just can't take that attitude," said Laurie. "It wasn't our fault; we weren't expecting trouble from apparently decent passengers, and we've got to catch them before any more lives are lost."

"The chances of that happening," said Hugo, "are virtually nil. They've shown themselves to be totally without conscience and they'll kill without mercy."

One of the two women sitting at the adjacent table sauntered over to them. Business appeared to be slow and they had decided to check whether it was worth their while to sit here or whether they should move on to another of their haunts. The redhead leaned over Laurie and said politely, "May I sit down?"

He decided to have a laugh at the woman's expense and said innocently, "Oh, I thought you were sitting quite comfortably over there."

She sat down on one of the chairs anyway and said brightly, "You two seem to be very serious tonight. How about joining us two for some fun?"

"How about it, Hugo; do we want some fun?"

"Yes, I think we do. But how should we go about that?"

The redhead laughed a little uncomfortably and said, "We could make you very happy."

Laurie glanced at Hugo and said, "Amsterdam must be such a friendly place. Back home you have to work your butt off to get a date with a lady, but here they come right out and ask you for a date."

"You don't have to waste time dating, darling. We can do what you want right away," responded the woman.

Laurie turned to Hugo. "Did you hear that? We could take these two ladies to meet our mothers straight away without any hesitation!"

The redhead was getting impatient, realising she was being made a fool of. "Are you two being funny? What I'm saying is you can shag us straight away if that's what you want."

Laurie considered the tempting offer and said regretfully, "I don't think our mothers would like that, do you?"

"No, my mother always told me not to go out with strange women, sir, especially as we're both policemen."

The woman drew back from them as though she had touched a stinging nettle, swore at them under her breath and indicated to her companion that they would do better plying their trade somewhere else. Luckily, neither of the policemen heard what was being said about their recent ancestry.

During their evening meal, they discussed what their attitude should be towards their future workmates and decided it would be in their best interests to hold back a little until they knew whether their presence was welcomed and full co-operation would be offered, or if they would want to emphasise that the Dutch police had overall precedence and the Germans were only there under sufferance.

Chapter 28

The following morning, the hotel receptionist phoned Laurie to say that there was a policeman waiting to see him. He and Hugo hurried down to meet him, and their concerns about how they were going to be treated soon disappeared when Sergeant Vogel introduced himself cheerfully and took them to the office. Inspector van Eyck immediately stood up and greeted them warmly.

"Shall we agree to call each other by our first names?" said Inspector van Eyck. "I'm Erik and my sergeant is Hans."

"Yes, of course," said Laurie. "My name is actually Albert, but I prefer to be called Laurie; a hangover from my student days. My sergeant is Hugo."

"Right, let's get started on briefing each other with all the facts we know; talking turkey, as the Americans would put it!" said Erik.

"This will take some time," said Laurie, "but here goes." He went through all the details, starting with the arrival of the terrorists at Frankfurt Airport and finishing with their disappearance in the removal van. "We feel sure there are more than three men involved, but after this we lost their trail and every effort is being made to find out if they crossed into Holland. And that's where you come in. Our Commander felt that we might come up with something if we picked your brains and you picked ours and we all worked together on this. It looks as if their final destination might possibly be Great Britain, and I'm sure their police would welcome any information we can give them. The situation over there is very serious."

Erik and Hans listened very carefully to all this.

"The reason they used your airport was because they knew Amsterdam security had been stepped up after we discovered one of their hideouts," explained Erik. "It looks as if they're replacing the men they've lost in their terrorist cell." He told his guests about the expulsion of one suspect to his own country and the events which followed, right up to the whole cell blowing themselves to pieces when they realised they were trapped.

"It's hard to believe such fanaticism, the unbelievable lengths to which they'll go to achieve their objective," said Laurie, "and for what? To kill more innocent people."

"It's partly brought on by the wars in Iraq and Afghanistan. They see it as occupation of Muslim land and the killing of their people," said Erik. "Casualties of war mean nothing if it means achieving their main objective, which is the withdrawal of foreign troops in both countries. We now have to formulate a plan of how to catch them before they can kill any more of our people."

"We could publish photographs of the three men and the van they hired and ask if anyone has seen them. The van might have been abandoned or wrecked in the same way as their car was," suggested Laurie.

"I'm a bit wary of doing that," said Erik. "We've tried to obtain help from the public several times before now and it's provoked a violent response. I told you how they killed one of our police inspectors and tried to blow up Police HQ, and we got no help at all from the law-abiding public. I suggest we circulate the photos of the three men amongst police stations, with a warning that under no circumstances are they to be approached because they're armed and dangerous."

"Who would they contact?"

"We have a twenty-four-hour terrorist response unit. They're fully armed and can be alerted at a moment's notice."

"What's our strategy going to be?" asked Laurie. "We don't have any leads at the moment, so we have to try and put ourselves into their minds. We'll assume they're now in Amsterdam and the first thing they need to do is to settle into their new property and familiarise themselves with their surroundings. They have to provide themselves with basics, like food and ammunition; they have to pay their bills so that they look like model citizens, and communicate with their leaders for orders as to how they should proceed.

"I suggest we start by finding their safe house," said Erik. "It'll probably be rented, so we can start with the usual rental agencies. It would have to be a large detached place in a secluded area where they won't have any nosy neighbours. The previous house, which they blew up, had a high wall all around it, so that would be another factor to consider. What sort of house was it where you found the abandoned Merc?"

"It was totally isolated; the road was a dead end so there wasn't even any passing traffic. The nearest houses were nearly two kilometres away," said Hugo.

"Okay, that's the sort of property they'll be renting, so we check with the four or five agencies who specialise in that kind of property. We can start with the Internet. It's amazing what you can find on the lists of houses for sale and rent; they even include pictures of the rooms and gardens in some cases!" said Erik. "You can set up your computers on those two desks over there – sorry we all have to share an office, but it means information is kept strictly to ourselves – and we can get started, but only after I've had a cup of coffee! By the way, you two learning to speak Dutch to come on this job is really good and we do appreciate it. We'll have you speaking like natives in no time!"

After studying the agents' lists of properties, they narrowed the possibilities down to seventeen houses. After contacting the agents, they learned that five houses were now occupied after being vacant for several months. However, they were all rented on short-term leases, so it was possible that the present occupiers would let them view the houses if they were told that they were thinking of renting it.

"This afternoon after lunch," said Erik, "we'll visit the agents and find out as much information places as possible, with perhaps a discreet drive past the addresses in question." He turned to Laurie. "I suggest you and Hugo take the first two agents. I'll leave it to you to make up a plausible explanation seeking information about these occupants. No whiff of police interest in these houses must get out, otherwise the terrorists would disappear completely. and they would have to see a reason for wanting to rent a large house, but your foreign accents will probably go a long way to convince them you're totally unhinged! Hans and I will tackle the other three agents. Again, we'll have to pretend to be rich, eccentric millionaires who want a secluded luxurious house to rent. Who knows; they might think we're gay!"

Erik arranged for Laurie and Hugo to have an unmarked car from the pool, drew them a map to compare with the street map they had been given, and gave them the computer printouts of the various properties they would be enquiring about.

They came up with nothing at the first agency, but the girl sitting behind the reception desk at the second one proved to be a mine of information.

"I don't think she's had anyone to talk to all day," said Hugo when they were finally able to get away. This call had definitely been more fruitful. They consulted their street map and drove to the most promising of the addresses, parking a discreet distance away, out of sight of any possible watchers in the house. It was everything they thought the terrorists would want: large, detached, probably with at least six bedrooms. But it did not have too much privacy. It did stand on its own bit of land but only had a low stone wall surrounding it. There was no garage or gate, only a gap in the wall, and there were other houses nearby. They decided that on balance, this house was not a probability and made their way back to the office to report their findings.

Erik and Hans had not yet returned from their investigations, so Laurie went onto the Internet again to see if there was an agency which specialised in renting properties on flexible terms, such as paying monthly or on short-term leases. He found one called 'Short-Term Quick Rental Agency', and when he accessed their website, their publicity slogan was 'We specialise in all sizes of property – total discretion guaranteed'. They further promised that immediately after payment, you could collect, or they would deliver, the keys. "This is just the type of agency which would suit them perfectly," said Laurie, and he looked at their list of large private houses still available for rent. "Some are very suitable for what they want and one in particular stands out." He debated whether to contact Erik before he rang the agency; he knew he had to be careful in the way he approached them so as not to arouse suspicion, but if it turned out to be a dead end, he could tell him when he returned to the office. The house he had spotted on the agent's list was of particular interest: it stood in its own grounds, had a large garage that would hold at least two cars, had a high surrounding wall, going by the picture, and appeared not to have any near neighbours.

He rang the number and told the agency he was going to be staying in the city for a number of months. He was not quite sure how big a job it was going to be and he needed a large, comfortable house in a select area with perhaps eight to ten bedrooms: they had to consider the children and their friends coming to stay and, of course, the au pair who looked after the baby. His wife was very fussy about the kind of accommodation she would stay in; it must not be overlooked, as she was very fond of sunbathing in the garden and didn't want neighbours able to see her etc., etc. Did they have anything on their books which fitted his description? He also told them that some friends who were in the same position had recommended this agency to him because they had found the perfect house only a few weeks ago and were highly satisfied, and it would be nice to be near them because being strangers in a new city, they would miss their friends at home in Germany. By this time, Laurie's Dutch vocabulary was exhausted and he waited expectantly for an answer.

"Oh yes, sir, we're very pleased to have been recommended by someone. What's the name of your friends?"

"They came originally from India or Pakistan," he hedged. "Now let me see. I'm afraid I can't spell their name; it's rather long and complicated, but I'm sure you'd have it written down somewhere, wouldn't you? They would have rented the property, perhaps even paying in cash…" His voice trailed off.

The person at the other end of the telephone said in a superior voice, "I'm afraid this is confidential information, sir, and we cannot disclose it to any unauthorised person."

It was on the tip of Laurie's tongue to scream down the phone that he was authorised and if he wasn't given the information immediately, he would arrest him, but just in time he clamped his mouth shut and took a deep breath.

"The best thing we can do, sir, would be to offer you a suitable property, as you've described, which would be roughly two kilometres away." The agent could hardly believe his luck: renting two such large and expensive properties, which had become vacant quite unexpectedly, to two business colleagues and at very high rents.

"That's a good idea, but of course we'd like to view the property to make quite sure it's suitable for our purpose. If you could give me the address of the house you have in mind, we can go round and have a quick glance at the surroundings and then get back to you so that we can have a more leisurely look at the interior."

"If you can give me your mobile number, I'll get back to you as soon as I've checked our list of properties available," the agent said smoothly.

Laurie gave him his number and said, "I would emphasise to you that it's really rather urgent, because we have to move quite unexpectedly soon, and if you're unable to help me, I have other agencies I can contact." He hoped to galvanise the agent into action. He put the phone down and slumped back in his chair, grimacing at Hugo. "How was I?"

"Very good, sir; extremely convincing. Let's hope he comes back to us very shortly."

Erik and Hans, balancing four large cartons of coffee and some doughnuts on a tray, returned and asked how they had managed during their first day on foreign territory. Laurie explained what they had done and said they were waiting for a call, but on the whole it seemed quite promising.

"Did he actually say that they'd rented a house like that recently?" queried Erik.

"He told me the information was confidential and he couldn't discuss it with anybody, so I think he probably has rented somewhere and maybe charged something extra, maybe insisted on a very large deposit and perhaps pocketed it and only credited the agency with the usual fee. I'm only suggesting this, not accusing him of anything, but I think he wanted to check with someone else that what he's done is not illegal. When he's made sure of his position, he'll tell us of any vacant properties available."

"Make a report about this," said Erik, "but keep it quiet for the present. We must know what steps we've taken and in what order, in case we're challenged in the future. I think the best thing we can do now is meet up here in the morning and check on any addresses which we think might be promising and take it from there."

Chapter 29

The next morning, Laurie and Hugo, still awaiting a call from the agent, spent time trawling the Internet again. The morning drew on but still they heard nothing, so Laurie decided to ring the agency.

A different person answered and when asked if a suitable house was available for rent, replied, "The only property we have on the lines you described is not going to be available for about a month, as it's still occupied. The tenants particularly dislike their privacy being disturbed and do not want us to show anybody round, but you could drive past to see if it's the sort of place you have in mind."

The agent gave Laurie the address and after he had ended the call, he turned to Erik. "What's the best way to approach this? Shall we all go to look or would it be better if just Hugo and I drive there?"

Erik thought for a moment. "I think it would arouse less suspicion if just the two of you went past; a car with four men in it would immediately ring a bell with anybody on the lookout and they're bound to be nervous after what's gone wrong in the past few weeks. Keep in touch by phone and Hans and I will back you up if you need it. At the moment, it would be great if we could just track down their whereabouts. We can decide what to do after that. We'll carry on checking other addresses and wait for you to call."

It took twenty minutes of careful driving and checking the street map before they realised that they had driven past the house they were looking for. Hugo drove to the end of the road and parked, hardly daring to breathe. What they could see of the house confirmed everything they thought the terrorists would want in a safe house. It was large with two storeys and dormer windows in the attics; it was surrounded by spacious lawns and a high stone wall with a wide gate surmounted with iron spikes.

"Whew!" exclaimed Laurie. "Whoever built this place certainly didn't want any unexpected visitors dropping in; raiding this one's going to take some organisation, if it's where they're hiding. What we should do is drive round the neighbourhood and look for any suitable places we could rent, say within one kilometre of here, where we could establish a base and plan how we're going to catch them."

Hugo was careful not to drive past the suspected house again and they combed the avenues and streets, making a note of one or two properties which might fulfil their criteria. They marked the properties on their street map so that they could judge which location came nearest to what they wanted, checked bus and train routes and any local shops and bars, plus access and possible escape routes, trying to think of everything to ensure a successful outcome.

"We'll go and find a café and work out what their daily routine might be. Who knows, they might even go to the mosque on Friday!"

Laurie rang Erik to tell him of his findings and they discussed how to set up surveillance with the few officers they could rely on.

"It's a long, long time since I've been on surveillance duty," grumbled Hugo.

"It's even longer since I had to watch people's comings and goings, but boring it ain't going to be, because at the end of it, we're going to get those bastards before they can harm anybody else. Just think how heroic that will be. Who knows, you can tell your wife how brave you were and you might even get a medal," said Laurie mockingly.

Hugo sighed; he hadn't realised he would miss his wife and kids quite so much, even though they were usually a pain in the arse. He would phone her again tonight before they went down for their evening meal and tell her – what could he tell her? Not very much, really. He had better keep quiet about this job or else the nagging would start about a job change when he least wanted it.

They went through all the addresses they had highlighted as being suitable safe houses, gradually eliminating all but the one they had seen earlier in the morning. Because of its unique position on a quiet road behind a high wall of its own, faced by a large college, the house had no windows directly facing it on either side or across the road.

They went back there, parked the car and decided to risk walking past, not together but individually, and pool their observations, never thinking that eyes could be watching anyone who passed along the road. They were in their car discussing their plan, when a dark green VW Passat drove past them and up to the gates, which were electronically controlled and swung open to let them pass. Laurie and Hugo strained to see if anyone left the car, but the angle of the wall obscured their view. Nothing more could be done then, so they decided to check out the nearest address given to them by the agent, which, they decided, would form an ideal base for reconnaissance, as it was not very far from the end of the road where they had parked.

Laurie conferred with Erik about a cover story, and they decided that Laurie should tell the agent that he was staying in Amsterdam on his own, as his wife had decided she didn't want to move for the short time he was going to be here, so he would take this smaller place for the time being.

Back at the hotel, Hugo rang his wife, trying to convince her that he was not enjoying himself on an all-expenses-paid trip; he didn't succeed. Over dinner, he and Laurie compared notes, but there was little enough to talk about. They hadn't been able to see into the car because of the tinted windows and they hadn't been in direct line of sight when anyone had got out. After a couple of brandies, Hugo came up with the idea that they could be famous film stars who wanted complete privacy.

"Very amusing," said Laurie, but it gave him the glimmer of an idea.

The following day, he and Erik agreed on the watch rota and he won an Oscar at the housing agent's office for his performance as a hen-pecked husband whose wife refused to move from her comfortable mansion in Germany to live in sinful Amsterdam. He paid the first instalment of rent and took the keys and went to open up their new base. Not bad, considering. As soon as they had bought a decent coffee percolator and put a few cans of lager in the fridge, it would be a positive home from home. One of the front bedrooms proved to be the best place to observe the end of the road, and when he and Hugo had settled in, they saw the green Passat again. As it drove past they filmed it, but were once again unable to see who was driving or if there were any passengers.

"I've got an idea," said Laurie. "I'm going to try their nearest neighbours, even if they are some distance away. I'll ask them if they think the people who've moved into the big house are famous and have they been bothered by any photographers hanging around; that will be a good reason for enquiring about the occupants and nobody will be suspicious."

Out on the street, he turned left towards the house and, as luck would have it, a car came driving out of the adjacent drive. Before it could pick up speed, he waved the driver down. When the car came to a halt, he put on his most winning smile and apologised for asking her to stop. It happened to be a very attractive young lady.

"Good afternoon, miss. I don't want to hold you up or anything, but the people who've moved in next door to you, would they be those famous television stars from that super programme on Friday nights – you know, the one where they have all that money but they're trying to give it away, you know the one I mean. I thought I just saw them driving down the road, and although I know I shouldn't intrude, I'd love to get their autographs or even interview them, if they were willing!" What a load of rubbish; he hoped she didn't think he was a complete idiot.

She looked up at him in surprise and, trying not to laugh, said, "I don't know where you got that idea from, but you mean my nearest neighbours?"

"Yes."

"They're a married couple with two children, who happen to go to boarding school, and at this time of day they'll both be out at work!"

Laurie cursed himself but apologised again and asked her for her name and address because he wanted to send her some flowers.

"Is that one of your come-on lines? I'm sorry to disappoint you but I'm a happily married woman with a jealous husband who might be suspicious if I received flowers from a complete stranger. Still, it's nice to be propositioned when you're going to pick up the kids from school!"

Laurie hurried back to Hugo and told him what he had learned and rang Erik to tell him the same thing.

"That's great," said Erik. "At least I don't have to spend endless hours waiting for something to happen. What shall we do about this place you've rented? Will we still need it?"

Laurie and Hugo gathered up their gear and got into the car.

"I think it was a very good idea, spinning that yarn to the neighbours about the people in the house being famous. It will probably cut down on the time we have to spend narrowing down and eliminating the various houses it could be, even if we do look like idiots," said Laurie, warming to his subject. "There are all sorts of stories we can tell, posing as photographers, paparazzi, press men, reporters."

"Yes, it's worth a try, but we still have to be very careful; don't want people comparing stories at the supermarket checkout or somewhere – it's amazing how these things get about," cautioned Hugo.

They drove in silence to another of the addresses the agent had given them and parked nearby. It fitted the bill to a certain extent but the surrounding wall was only about three feet tall, leaving it fairly exposed to passers-by on the pavement. They sat around for an hour or so before Laurie said, "It's time for you to go to the neighbours and try your hand at storytelling. See if you can get to know anything. If a car comes down the drive I'll expect you to jump in front of it and ask the driver who lives next door!"

"Doing something like that is less tedious than sitting in a car or a room somewhere bored out of my mind," Hugo responded.

As he wriggled out of the car, a vehicle stopped outside a house twenty metres away. He hurried towards it to speak to the driver. Laurie watched them having a long, animated conversation.

Back in the car with Laurie, and keeping a very straight face, Hugo said, "An old couple live on their own in that house and he told me that he was a close friend of theirs; they told him just now that they're frightened to come out of their house as there are two suspicious men parked outside watching them and he told them to call the police."

Laurie nearly choked. "What did you say to him?"

"I said we were private detectives who had been hired to do a confidential job for a client and it was just coincidence that we happened to be parked outside their house; I apologised about causing them anxiety and told him we are going to move, straight away."

As they drove off, Laurie said, "You can certainly think quickly on your feet, Sergeant. You must have had an ill-spent youth to come out with barefaced lies like that!"

"Well, that story seemed to convince the man and he could reassure them that it was perfectly safe for them to come out."

"I suppose we must be more careful in future or we'll end up getting arrested for suspicious behaviour. Better head back to the office and see if Erik and Hans have had more luck than we have." As they negotiated their way out of the leafy avenue, he added, "Let's look at the other large house the agent told us about before we head back."

They found the place, parked a little way away and looked for any sign of movement. Nothing stirred; everything was still and quiet.

"What is it about this place, sir?" asked Hugo.

"I don't know. I can't put my finger on it, but I have a feeling; something's making the hairs on the back of my neck stand up, a sense of foreboding."

"You mean like when you're watching a horror film with dead bodies and monsters appearing?"

"Not quite like that, but I have this feeling that evil is nearby and it makes me nervous."

This spooked Hugo and when he saw movement, which he only just caught out of the corner of his eye, he wondered whether he was imagining it. He cleared his throat and said very quietly, "Sir, I think I saw a slight movement at one the windows. It's gone now but I could swear I saw a man looking through a pair of binoculars from one of the windows on the top floor." Laurie came down to earth with a bump and asked which window. "Third window from the right, sir, but of course there's nothing to see now. It's probably my imagination; all your talk of evil and premonitions and things."

"Okay, Sergeant, I think we'd better get back to the office now and you can have a lay down with a cold towel on your forehead! This is obviously all getting a bit too much for you," said Laurie sarcastically.

Chapter 30

Erik and Hans had returned to the police station just before them and were feeling dejected that their enquiries had led nowhere.

"How are you two getting on?" enquired Erik, not holding out much hope that the two newcomers would have succeeded where they had failed on home turf.

"We've ruled out two possibilities," said Laurie, "which appears to leave us without a single indication of where we should try next, but I can't help feeling that we're looking the solution in the face and not seeing it. It's very frustrating, because I don't know what the next step is! Leaving my frustrations aside, let me ask this question. We know we have a terrorist cell in this city somewhere. What can be done to flush them out? What should we do now?"

"The only way to flush them out is by provoking them into some act of terrorism and hope they make a mistake that will lead us to capture them," Hans suggested.

"That's a very dangerous strategy, and the last time we did that we know what happened; we were very lucky more people weren't killed. If we do that again, we might not be so lucky," said Erik. "They could start a bombing campaign against soft targets which could result in hundreds of civilian casualties."

"What I fail to understand," said Laurie, "is what they're doing in this city. They're obviously not here to take advantage of your hospitality."

Erik sighed. "They obviously have a plan, because just staying here is costing them a lot of money. God knows how much they're paying in rent alone, to say nothing of other bills."

"How about looking into how they pay their bills, checking on who delivers their food and how the delivery people are paid?" Hugo suggested. "If only we knew where they're holed up..."

"If we knew that we wouldn't be having this conversation, would we," snapped Erik.

"What we need is a bit of luck, but then again, a good detective makes his own luck. What we should do tonight is go out on a real bender, blow away all the cobwebs. It's amazing what thoughts pop into your head when you're not looking," asserted Laurie.

"Excuse me, sir, but I'm catching the three o'clock flight to Frankfurt tomorrow," Hugo reminded his boss.

"That's tomorrow, but for now, a few drinks and a good meal won't harm any of us. Do we all agree?" They all nodded. "Right, Erik, as you know all the drinking dens in this city, we'll let you organise the event."

Erik shrugged his shoulders in resignation and said he would go and organise some poor unsuspecting driver to take them to one of the dens of iniquity he knew. Ten minutes later he was back with a young man in uniform, who was going to drive them to their destination.

In light-hearted mood, they were driven to a bar that Erik often frequented.

"What are we all drinking?" asked Laurie.

Hugo was looking a little embarrassed. "Are you going to be all right, sir, being on your own this weekend?"

"Of course," said Laurie, looking rather amused. "I live on my own all the time."

"Yes, I know, but this is a foreign city and..." He hesitated. "It's not quite the same, is it, sir."

"He's not going to be on his own," chipped in Erik. "I'm a bachelor as well, so there'll be two bachelors together. I'm sure we can find something to keep us amused for a couple of days. You can stay in my apartment, if you like. There's plenty of space. I have two bedrooms, state of the art sound system and a plasma television to watch sports on."

"Thanks, that's a great offer, but I think I'd better remain at the hotel. Tell you what. You won't mind, will you, Hugo, if Erik borrows your room at the hotel for a couple of nights?"

"No, sir, of course not."

"After all, the rooms are paid for until further notice and that includes all meals, so why not take advantage of it. The manager can't say anything against it."

"That sounds like a pretty good offer and I've never turned down a gift horse yet," said Erik.

They enjoyed their meal and finished with a brandy. While they were savouring it, Erik told them about his first days as a rookie cop when the powers-that-be put him in the Vice Squad.

"I was totally green, just out of college, and the other guys told me that they had an initiation ceremony for each new entrant and you weren't one of the team until you'd completed it. They said that as I was going to be dealing with 'working girls', I had to get to know them really well, so I had to be intimate with one of them, otherwise I'd never know how to treat them. 'Don't worry, we'll make sure she's nice looking and has a clean bill of health; you may even get to like her!' they said. 'What do you mean, intimate?' I said. The sergeant raised his eyebrows and said, 'it means you've got to shag her, Erik.' 'But I've got a girlfriend,' I said. 'Don't worry about that,' said the sergeant, we're not asking you to fall in love with her; it's just lust. Otherwise you'll never be one of the team. We've all done it!' Okay, I thought, what the hell. I don't want to start off on the wrong foot and make the rest of the team think I've got no bottle. So it was all arranged, and when she came in, she looked gorgeous. We went into a spare office and I thought to myself, this is going to be a pleasure. So we started to get to grips and I began to get excited when she said, 'I find it's much easier with the lights off,' so she gets up and switches off the lights and we started again. I worked on upstairs, and she had a nice pair of tits, I can tell you, so I think it's time to move downstairs. As I reach out, I can't believe it, it's a feller. I tried to get out of the room double quick but in the darkness I tripped and fell flat on my face, banged my head on the corner of a desk and knocked myself out. When I came to, the lights were on and the whole team was stood round grinning from ear to ear. The sergeant said, 'You must have had a real good time, if you passed out in ecstasy.' Those bastards. It took me weeks to forgive them and after three months I managed to wangle a transfer."

"Where did they move you to?" asked Hugo.

Keeping a very straight face, Erik said, "Traffic."

When they had all stopped laughing, Laurie said, "Well, it's all good experience!"

"Certainly was. It made me work like hell for my promotion and I was a sergeant two years later."

"That's good going," said Laurie with a grin on his face, "but we all know promotion is easy in the Dutch police force!"

"Perhaps if you'd screwed that feller they fixed you up with, you could have been a sergeant much sooner," said Hugo.

"Just listen to them," said Erik to Hans. "I heard a rumour that German policemen start out as sergeants and only demoted men are ordinary policemen!"

"Why waste time on the beat?" said Hugo. "Besides, you can only join our police force if you have a degree in maths and science."

"What, only maths and science? With those you can only work as a civilian clerk in Holland!" exclaimed Hans.

"To become a sergeant in the German force, you have to be a professor in mathematics and have at least two other degrees, one in science, one in computing," Hugo boasted.

"Yes," agreed Laurie, "I was watching you working on the computer – a twelve-year-old boy could have done better."

"I didn't say I had those degrees," said Hugo. "I got into the police force because my father had a high position in the government!"

Hans interrupted them rudely, waving his brandy glass in the air. "I can go one better than that. I got into the police because I knew the wife of a very important government minister, intimately, if you get my meaning."

"I don't shag old women!" exclaimed Hugo.

"You don't know what you're missing; all that experience and expertise. That's the best part," Hans said.

"There are some things in life you don't want to experience, like cholera, bubonic plague and very old women," Hugo asserted.

Interrupting their bragging, Erik shouted, "The evening is progressing but we're still sober. Another round of drinks, waiter, and you lot, give up your showing off and be nice to one another or I'll call my mum and she'll beat you over the head with her rolling pin!"

"Do you mean to say," said Laurie, "that your mother still has a rolling pin?"

"Of course," said Erik, "otherwise how would she keep my father under control? Are your parents both alive?"

Laurie groaned. "Yes, they are, and always asking me why I don't find a nice German girl and settle down. They want grandchildren."

"You mean you haven't told them about the little bastards you've fathered and who you spend all your money on?" asked Erik jokingly.

"As it happens," said Laurie seriously, "I'm trying to build up my own football team to win medals and cups for me."

Gradually, as the evening went on, their speech became a little slurred and Laurie and Hugo's Dutch took a severe beating trying to understand the quick conversation of Erik and Hans. In the end, Erik nearly slid off his chair and they decided it was time to go back to their respective residences and call it a night.

Laurie was announcing that he was going to order two taxis, when Hans said, "I have something really important I have to say," and he stood up carefully, balancing himself against the table. "I just wish my mother had called me Hugo instead of Hans!" He sat down and shook Hugo's hand.

Seeing as he was the only one who appeared to have been left with any brains, Laurie called the waiter over and asked him to bring the bill and ring for two taxis. He looked at the column of figures on the bill, trying to work out the total amount. Finally, he looked up at the waiter and said, clearly enunciating each word very carefully, "Is this the bill for the food and drinks we've consumed or have we purchased this restaurant?" This struck him as being very funny and he started to laugh. Unfortunately for him, he hadn't realised he'd said it in German and the waiter had no idea what he had said. Laurie reached into his pocket and found his credit card, which he gave to the waiter. "This'll take some explaining to the Commander," he said – still in German – and started to laugh again.

When the taxis arrived, Hans and Hugo supported Erik, who was murmuring to himself with a broad smile on his face. Laurie told Hans to make sure he got home and to make him some strong coffee before he left to go to his own home.

"I've seen him much worse than this and he still turns up for work on time in the morning," said Hans. "Now we're in the fresh air, I feel almost sober!"

"Good," said Laurie. "I'll check on him tomorrow." He turned to Hugo and said, "Let's get back to the hotel. You must get a good night's sleep if you're flying off to see your wife and kids tomorrow."

At the hotel, it seemed to Laurie as if he barely had time to get into bed before Hugo was knocking on his door to take him to the office. Nothing warned him of the terrible chain of events that was about to be set in motion.

Chapter 31

They were all a little late to work and it was after nine o'clock, after the third mug of coffee, before they could concentrate fully on the case. Of the four of them, Erik had the thickest head and he glared at Laurie when he asked, solicitously, how he was feeling.

"There's no need to shout at me. Not that you really care, but if you did, I feel fine, okay?"

"Well, if you feel 'fine'," said Laurie, "you'll be able to concentrate on our discussion. If you feel lousy and have a thick head, you should have stayed at home and slept it off."

With dignity, Erik said, "I feel it's my duty to be here, to stop you three doing anything idiotic! I'll just go and get some really black, black coffee and I'll be raring to go. Come on, Hans; leave these two slave-drivers to their deliberations."

When they had gone in search of more coffee, Hugo said, "What can we do next?"

"You're catching the three o'clock flight, so we can't really accomplish much this morning. I don't fancy going down the list of addresses to find out who lives in the last four houses," said Laurie. "Let's just talk about the case in general and see if we've overlooked anything obvious. They must have had a house already waiting for them when they set off. They were a long way from Amsterdam and yet they managed to find a house to rent immediately. When they arrived at the house, they had to move all their luggage – we think there would have been large amounts of bulky items, because there was nothing left in the other house – out of a removal van. Can you imagine a big removal van arriving at a house in a select area with possibly eight or ten Asian men unloading their boxes and packages, probably in a great hurry? It would arouse a great deal of interest if anybody were to see it, and that's the last thing they'd want, particularly when you remember that three of them had their pictures published in the newspapers."

Hugo pondered on the problem before saying, "However they did it, they certainly managed to do it efficiently, but the photographs weren't published in Holland, so once they were over the border, they might think themselves safe."

Erik and Hans returned with their coffee, but there was little more they could add to the discussion. Hugo gave his hotel room key card to Erik at lunchtime and went on his way to catch the flight for Frankfurt.

The two inspectors met in the hotel bar after they had finished work, and Erik promised to take Laurie sightseeing around Amsterdam in the morning. In the meantime, they both decided on an early night.

After breakfast the following morning, they set off for the city centre and looked around some of the usual tourist attractions until Laurie said, "Enough is enough. All this walking's about wearing out my shoe leather. Let's have something to eat before the next marathon."

They found a self-service café, and when they had eaten large amounts of excellent goulash, Laurie asked if the palace they had seen was where the Dutch royal family actually lived.

"Yes, they actually live there," said Erik with a grin. "We don't make such a fuss over our royals like they do in Britain."

"What about all the sex shops and cinemas right in the middle of family shopping areas? How do you stop children and young people seeing it all?"

"The adverts are only a small part of the shop front and people are used to it. This afternoon I'll take you to see the sex museum." Erik roared with laughter at the expression on Laurie's face. "Haven't you heard? Amsterdam is famous for its sex industry. You straight-laced Germans; you should see the look on your face. Come on; I can see I'll have to educate you. All the cinemas, by the way, are usually in cellars with no windows, so no one can see anything from street level."

Laurie felt he had to explain. "In Germany, all that sort of thing is usually confined to one specific area of a city, not usually the in places where ordinary people go for entertainment or to do their shopping. Anyone seeking sexual pastimes has to go to these areas!"

"I'm looking forward to seeing your face after we've been round the sex museum," chuckled Erik, "but first, let's take a boat trip along some of the canals and I'll tell you about the little boy who saved Holland from flooding by putting his hand in the dyke wall."

Laurie was unimpressed. "We have a lot of mythical heroes too."

As they walked along the side of the canal in the pleasant afternoon sunshine, Laurie suddenly thought how marvellous it would be if Liza were walking alongside him, laughing and chatting. Suddenly he wanted to see her; so strongly did he feel the need to see her, talk to her, to just be with her. he looked realy sad.

Erik suddenly realised that Laurie was not answering his questions and nudged him slightly. "What's occupying your thoughts all of a sudden? I've asked you three questions in the last three minutes and you're a mile away."

"Sorry. I was remembering the teacher who taught Hugo and me Dutch. I can't get her out of my mind. At any time when my mind isn't taken up trying to solve this case, I find myself thinking about her. Not that she gave me any encouragement and I think, from something she said, that she has a boyfriend, although they don't live together."

"Today you're with me and I want to make sure you enjoy this weekend and not go around looking sombre with thoughts about some female. Come on; let yourself go a bit. Stop thinking about something that never was and concentrate on enjoying yourself here. In my company. I'll be insulted if you look miserable while you're with me!"

They went to the sex museum and spent over an hour looking at the various exhibits. When they came out, Erik looked at Laurie. "Okay, tell me what you thought of it."

"It's quite disgusting, all of it."

"You're not one of those prudes, are you?"

"I think I must be. When it comes to sex, I'm very broad-minded, but for me, sex is between a man and a woman, and in that sense I'm happy to be innovative and explore, giving pleasure to both. But what I saw in there has very little to do with seeking pleasure. Most of it was indulging in deviant acts for men to take some pleasure in degrading their partners, male or female!"

"Oh dear, you do take a high moral ground," Erik mocked.

"Tell me, did you get any kind of feeling, apart from revulsion, from most of those exhibits? Was there any suggestion of love in any of them?"

"It's not supposed to be about love; it's about lust and what sort of practices a human being will indulge in to satisfy his lust. Let's forget this and start planning where to go for our evening meal. You tell me what your favourite kind of food is and I'll take you to a restaurant which specialises in cooking it." Erik waited expectantly with his head on one side, a bit like a small terrier, and Laurie had to laugh.

"I'm not really into spicy or exotic foods," he confessed. "What I really like is tender, juicy steak, fried potatoes, maybe some vegetables and gravy, followed by a dessert and coffee. Nothing very spectacular."

"Sounds like you're a man with very similar tastes to mine," said Erik, "and I know just the place to go!"

They entered the restaurant and the waiter showed them to a table. "Are you two gentlemen dining alone?" he asked.

"Unless you have two lovely ladies to accompany us," said Erik.

"Yes, sir. Would you like an aperitif while you're studying the menu?"

"What do you suggest?"

"Fran Limon is quite popular, sir."

"What does that consist of?"

"Vodka, gin and tequila in equal parts topped up with lemon and ice."

"And how much is this fantastic cocktail?"

"I believe it's fifteen euros, sir," replied the waiter, without batting an eyelid.

"Thank you. I'll have a gin and tonic and so will my friend, and you can save your exotic drinks for your more adventurous customers. Okay with you, Laurie?"

"Yes, that's fine with me. Now, let's look at the menu."

While they were studying the menu, out of the corner of his eye, Laurie saw the waiter ushering in two women and asking them where they would like to sit. They finally decided to sit at one which happened to be the next but one to theirs. Not wanting to be too obvious, he glanced discreetly in their direction and then looked away, having taken in the fact that one was older than the other, probably in her late thirties, while the younger one appeared to be around twenty. They looked very similar and both were attractive with good figures; perhaps they were sisters. A thought struck him: if not sisters, perhaps they were lesbians. He glanced their way again and caught the older woman looking at him. He tried a smile but there was no response.

When the waiter had taken their order, he returned with two drinks for the women and announced with a flourish, "Two Fran Limon for you, Mesdames," and placed them on their table.

Erik said in a penetrating voice, "It'd be nice to have enough money to order fancy drinks. We poor office workers have to save up before we can afford to go out for a meal and a drink now and then!"

Laurie leaned over to Erik and said quietly, "You're wasting your time; those two are probably lesbians." Erik gave him an enquiring look. "A few moments ago I gave the older one a smile and there was no response at all."

Erik laughed. "Well, they must be lesbians if they didn't respond to a tall, handsome, virile young man like you when you gave them a come-on smile. Oh dear, have I hurt your feelings?"

Laurie was somewhat annoyed by Erik's laughter. "I was only trying to save you some embarrassment."

A moment later, the waiter appeared at their table with two Fran Limon and said, "With the compliments of the two ladies over there."

Both men were stunned into silence. They turned to the adjacent table, raised their glasses and said politely, "Salut." The women nodded in acknowledgement and all four sipped their drinks in unison. "Me Erik, him Laurie," said Erik.

They laughed and the older woman said, "Me Christina and her Greta."

"Me and him single," said Erik.

"Me divorced, she's still single," Christina replied.

"Me and him very pleased to meet you two ladies. How about if we all sit at the same table and then we can stop speaking in pidgin language?"

The women looked at each other and nodded. Erik summoned the waiter to move all four of them to a larger table.

Once they were seated and had been served with their meals, Erik asked if the women were friends, but Christina said they were sisters who only managed to go out together every two or three weeks, even though they shared a large apartment, but they liked to get together and check how each other's lives were progressing.

He asked them what their plans were for the rest of the evening. Christina looked at Greta and said, "What was that song that was so popular recently? 'Smooth operator'. We'll have to see. We only planned to have a quiet meal. What about you?"

"Well, it's my friend Laurie's first weekend in our lovely city and I was going to show him some of our dens of depravity, but I since found out that he's a bit of a prude, so I don't know whether it's worth it!"

"Does your friend speak Dutch or does he not speak at all?" asked Greta.

"Oh, he speaks very good Dutch, but he classed you two ladies as lesbians and the fact that you're not has thrown him off balance. Normally he's quite chatty."

There was a moment's silence until a bewildered Greta said in amazement, "What on earth made him think we were lesbians?"

"Apparently, he gave Christina one of his most seductive smiles and was ignored. As he thinks he's totally irresistible to women, he decided that only a lesbian would have spurned him like that."

Greta looked annoyed and Laurie knew he had to apologise quickly. "I'm very, very sorry I said that. I'd never have put it so crudely as my so-called friend has done." He glared at Erik who was laughing.

"He can speak after all," said Greta.

"What can I do to make it up to you?"

"That's the trouble with society today. A friend of mine took his seventeen-year-old son out for a meal and people were giving them funny looks as though they were two homosexuals, an older man with a younger man. So because one of us is older and one younger, you assumed we were lesbians?"

Laurie groaned. "I'm never going to live that down, am I? I apologise most profusely."

"Okay, you're forgiven," said Greta sternly.

"Can I kiss you now?" smiled Laurie.

"I'm not that forgiving!" she said.

The rest of the evening went by quickly. The restaurant filled up with customers and the waiter hovered nearby with their bills. He had decided not to assume anything and, to avoid causing any difficulty, had one bill for the ladies and one for the men.

Erik asked the sisters what they were going to do for the rest of the evening. Christina told him that they had ordered a taxi to pick them up at eleven o'clock.

"We've enjoyed your company so much this evening; we must see you safely home," he said.

The women looked at each other and Greta said, "I think you're being cheeky now. What makes you think we'll let you take us home? There probably won't be enough room in the taxi to take four of us anyway."

Laurie looked very serious and said, "Then I'll run all the way behind it."

The waiter, very happy with the generous tips from both couples, announced that their taxi had arrived. Somehow, they all managed to squash in. It took twenty minutes to get to the large apartment block where Christina and Greta lived. There was a big lounge with a neat kitchen at the side of it, three bedrooms and two bathrooms, and was very comfortably furnished throughout. Laurie thought how much larger it was than his own place, but he supposed two women sharing an apartment needed more space than just one man.

Greta offered them a drink from the small bar unit in a corner of the lounge. They laughed at Erik's ridiculous jokes and Laurie's attempts at Dutch impersonations until Greta came up to Laurie and whispered, "Now's the time to kiss me, to show I really forgive you."

The following morning, he awoke with a fairly thick head to find himself in bed with Greta. She was still asleep with her back to him, her upper half uncovered. He thought what a perfect shape she had, with her blonde hair covering the nape of her neck with little curls. As she stirred, he kissed her neck, her shoulders, working all the way down her back with soft gentle kisses. He hadn't kissed a woman like this for a long time; it was usually a sexual encounter with no affection or tenderness.

She woke and turned to him saying shyly, "I'm so glad to find you here."

They made love again, and this time he was absolutely sober. He was to remember that encounter for many years to come.

Chapter 32

On Sunday, Laurie and Erik spent a quiet day at the hotel, watching sport and vintage films, until Erik went back his own apartment. Laurie didn't ask how it had been with Christina or whether they should make arrangements to meet them again. Perhaps it was better to leave it like that; they would see.

Monday morning found them all back at work, and nobody went into any details about how their time had been spent at the weekend in case it spoiled the idyllic memories.

Laurie decided to ring the same property-renting agency he had contacted before, in case there was any further information which had been overlooked. A woman answered the phone.

"This is Police Inspector Mueller. I wish to speak to the man I spoke to previously."

"I'm sorry, sir, but the gentleman you spoke to before disappeared shortly after you spoke to him and has been missing ever since. We reported him as a missing person to the police but we've heard nothing."

"He's not been in touch with anyone; his friends or work colleagues?"

"No," she replied firmly, "we've not seen him."

Laurie put the phone down and looked round at the others. "This sounds like one for you, Erik. The agency clerk has been missing ever since I rang him last week and there's not a sign of him anywhere. I've a feeling this is tied up somehow to our case."

"Why's that?"

"Because I got all the information from him about renting properties with minimum contact with customers and I think that's how our group from Germany rented their property. Could you get in touch with your HQ and find out what's happening, if there have been any results from their investigations? I think the terrorists are protecting their safe house by making sure no one can reveal any information about them."

Erik picked up his phone to get in touch with an old friend who would be sure to let him know any inside information. "He owes me a favour," he said.

Meanwhile, Laurie and Hugo went to check another property that the agency clerk had told them about. After driving past the house, they parked where no one could observe them, except possibly from the end bedroom window. They waited there for most of the morning, but there was virtually no movement along the length of the road. Eventually, Hugo, longing to stretch his legs, said, "I'll see if I can find a neighbour who might be able to tell us something."

As he walked away, Laurie continued to observe the house, which seemed deserted. Suddenly, he thought he saw a flicker of movement at one of the windows on the second floor, just as though someone had accidentally touched the curtain with a pair of binoculars. He got out of the car and leaned against it casually, looking around as if he were waiting for someone, and allowed his eyes to glance towards the house. He couldn't make up his mind whether he was imagining the slight movement of the curtain or whether his eyes had accurately noticed the twitch of the fabric.

When Hugo returned, he told his boss that the only neighbours he found lived three doors away and thought the house was empty – they had never seen anyone moving in.

They were both hungry, so drove until they found a small bistro, where they ordered some pasta and a salad.

"Had a heavy weekend, sir?"

"You know Erik by now; he has a hearty appetite, eats like a horse and does his best to encourage others to do the same, so I'm trying to clear my system of my weekend excesses." He was not sure what they should do next. "Daylight surveillance seems to be a waste of time."

"I agree with you, sir," said Hugo. "What do you think their plans are now?"

"They can't have been sent here just to hide in a safe house; they must be planning other operations."

"I don't know about that, sir. Perhaps they're establishing some sort of 'terrorist embassy', but if that were the case, Interpol has information about three of them. There would be no point in keeping them in EU countries where they could be recognised at any time. But it might be worth hiding them if they're experts in a particular field of operations, say bomb making."

Frustrated by their lack of progress, Laurie said, "I guess we'd better get back to the office and see if the others have had any success in finding the agency clerk."

Erik told them his item of information as soon as they walked into the room. "My friend at Police HQ has come up with the info you wanted. The man was reported missing last Friday, but as you know, they always wait twenty-four hours before any action is taken. They checked all the usual places, casualties in road accidents, admissions to hospital etc., but nothing turned up. Then this morning, they found the body of a man floating in the canal and they are at this moment doing a post mortem. My friend will let me know what the results are."

"You've got to take me there," insisted Laurie.

"Why, have you seen him?"

"Well, no, but—"

Erik was equally as insistent. "So there's not much point in going there until he's been officially identified, is there?"

"We'll go to the agency," said Laurie. "I'm sure it's the missing clerk and we'll try and get a photo of him before we go to the morgue."

At the agency, Laurie explained that he thought the police had found the missing man but that they needed a photograph of him to make sure.

She went into the back room and brought back a small photograph frame showing a rather indistinct picture of a man and woman, possibly taken some time in the summer. "This is Johann Gruebber, the clerk, and his wife," she said. "Perhaps I ought to get in touch with her, but I'm not sure how, because I know she went to see some relatives in South Africa recently and intended to spend six months there. Oh dear, what do you think I should do?"

Laurie reassured her that there had been no official identification as yet and it could all be a mistake. The police would trace his wife in South Africa if necessary, but in the meantime, all she should do was inform her employer that the police were looking into things and would let her know. He would let her have the photo back when they had finished with it.

He rang Erik and asked him for directions to the morgue, telling him about the photograph. He and Hugo found the building without too much difficulty and asked to see the body recovered from the canal that morning.

"Hang on a minute," said the receptionist. "I'll get someone to take you down there. Can't have you wandering round on your own, can we?"

An attendant in overalls and rubber gloves appeared. "You want to see the one we fished out of the water this morning? Come this way!" He showed them into the cold room where the bodies were kept in drawers. He consulted a list on the wall and pulled out a drawer and folded back the sheet to reveal the body of a young man. Even though he had been in the water for a number of hours, it was obviously the same person as in the photograph.

Laurie showed the morgue attendant the photograph. "His name's Johann Gruebber and he worked at a housing rental agency until last Thursday."

"He'll have to be formally identified by a close relative," said the attendant.

"Yes, I know that, but you should get in touch with the police working on the missing person's case. Apparently he has a wife, but she may not be in this country at the moment. I'll leave this photo with you and give you the phone number and address of the agency, because I'm dealing with an entirely different case; it was completely accidental that I happened to know who he was."

The attendant took the photo and closed the drawer noisily.

Back in the car, Laurie tried to put the pieces in order. "We know now that he was killed to keep him quiet, whether or not he had any important information he could have divulged."

"So where does that leave us?" asked Hugo.

"I think it confirms that the house was rented by our group of terrorists through this agency and Johann was the man who set it all up. He ended up paying for it with his life."

"Do you think he knew who they were?"

"Maybe he didn't know anything about the people, but he knew the address of the house they moved into, and after our enquiries, even though we didn't say we were policemen, he might have checked the phone number I gave him and found out it was a police station. He wouldn't find it difficult to work out that they had something to hide and that the police were looking for them."

"Unfortunately, sir, this doesn't get us any closer to their whereabouts."

"This could be their first mistake here; it could open up a trail of evidence that we'll be able to pick up. They were very foolish to kill someone; that immediately intensified our suspicions. We'll wait for the results of the post mortem; it may provide us with more information."

Erik was waiting to hear the results of their visit to the morgue.

"The body was that of Johann Gruebber, the man from the rental agency," Laurie confirmed, "but we'll have to wait for the PM results before we know how he died."

"I thought he was pulled out of the canal," said Erik.

"Yes, but it doesn't mean he drowned; what I want to know is what caused his death. Was he held under the water until he drowned? After all, you can kill someone and throw them in the water to destroy some evidence or you can drown the man in a bathtub, throw the body in the canal and hope when the body's found it's classed as a suicide."

When they got a copy of the post mortem findings a few days later, Erik read out the salient points. Gruebber had been tortured: both his legs had been broken by having a heavy weight dropped on them and the soles of his feet had been beaten with a stick, an old Eastern form of punishment, but the actual cause of death had been drowning. However, the water samples taken from his lungs did not match the samples of canal water and the examining surgeon assumed that the victim had been murdered.

They sat in silence when Erik came to the end of the report and Laurie swore silently under his breath for several minutes. When he spoke aloud he said bitterly, "What sort of uncivilised savage could do that to another man? He didn't know anything and he couldn't tell them anything; their cruelty was all for nothing. And we're still no further forward in tracking them down, no further leads we can follow up, nothing."

"The one fragile lead we have is the address he gave you. We have to confirm that," said Erik.

"How are we going to do that?" asked Laurie.

Erik looked at them with grim determination on his face. "By walking up to the door and knocking until someone answers; then we'll know for sure."

"Hey, wait a moment; let's think this through," said Laurie. "What if some dear little old lady answers the door and says she's lived there for fifty years?"

"In that case, we'll apologise profusely and withdraw in good order down the drive, but somehow I don't think that will happen. We'll go fully armed, ready to shoot if there's any trouble, so I hope your small arms training is up to date!"

With some misgivings, Laurie went with Erik to draw firearms and ammunition from the weapons store and watched as Erik carelessly scribbled his signature on the official form and cheerfully selected two sniper rifles and two handguns, with appropriate ammunition, and four flak jackets.

Back in the office they planned their raid, making sure each of them knew the part he had to play.

"We shoot only if our lives are in danger," said Erik. "Laurie and I will go up to the door while Hans and Hugo cover us with rifles from the car. We're single and unattached, but these two are married with kids! We knock on the door and then it depends on what they do as to how we handle the situation. Everybody clear? Okay, let's get to it."

Laurie wasn't sure how the authorities would see this raid; if it were successful there would be nothing but praise, but if it all went belly up, they might get thrown out of the police force.

Erik drove and parked the car in plain sight at the end of the drive. He warned Hans and Hugo to watch their backs very carefully and to be ready to bring in reinforcements if necessary.

Their nerves were stretched to breaking point as they walked up the drive and knocked on the large front door. They saw a bell push and there was a jangling sound when they pressed it, but nothing happened. They rang again, but still nothing happened. The house was quiet and no lights were on, but somehow they felt an evil presence.

There was a sudden wailing noise and two police cars came roaring down the road and screeched to a halt behind their car. Several armed men jumped out and surrounded it, shouting, "Come out of the car and lie on the floor, now!" The two sergeants didn't know what was happening and just sat there, unsure what they should do.

Hans was the first to recover his wits. "Do just as they say," he told Hugo. "This is the Dutch Police Armed Response Unit, and they might shoot first and ask questions afterwards if we don't jump to it. Let's put our guns down very gently and put our hands up to show we aren't going to be any trouble."

"This is very humiliating," said Hugo.

"Yes, but if we don't do that, they might shoot us. Put your weapon down and we can get out of the car without starting a riot!"

They lowered their guns to the floor, struggled out of the car with their hands up and were told to lay flat on the pavement with their hands behind their backs.

"Any funny moves and you could be dead!" someone shouted.

When they were both lying flat out, they were handcuffed and told to lie still.

"Okay, you've had your fun," said Hans. "You can take the cuffs off. We're police sergeants. Our identity cards are in our inside pockets. I'm Sergeant Hans Vogel and he's Sergeant Hugo Kalman of the German Police. He and his superior officer are liaising with us on a very important case. Ask my boss over there at the house and he'll confirm what I say."

Erik and Laurie hurried over to where they were lying on the ground. Furious, Erik asked, "What's going on? Why have you handcuffed our men?"

"Let's see your badges," said the senior officer in charge of the detachment. "I want identification that you two are police officers before I let those two get up."

Erik fished inside his jacket and flourished his identification at the officer before asking what Armed Response was doing there. Once they had proved themselves to be genuine police officers, Erik asked how they came to be there.

"At HQ they received a phone call that some old people at this address were very frightened because some armed men had surrounded their house and were trying to knock the door down. HQ told us to respond to the call with two cars and here we are. It appears to have been a hoax call. I can only apologise," he said stiffly.

Erik was furious but realised that he had to put them in the picture. "These clever bastards are, we think, terrorists, and we suspect that this is one of their safe houses. We want to find out who lives here, but there was no response. They must have rung the police and told them a pack of lies and that's how you became involved."

"Perhaps there's no one in, sir," suggested Hans.

"If there's no one in, then who rang the police?" asked Erik impatiently.

"What do we do now?" asked Laurie, trying to calm the situation before aggression built up and tempers were lost.

Erik looked at the Armed Response officer and said quietly, "Look, I can't give you the whole story but there are some unusual things occurring with this case. Unfortunately, we don't have a warrant to search the property so we were just trying to establish who lives there. This more or less confirms our theories, but there's not much we can do without that warrant. Even if we gained admittance and could produce some evidence, it would not be admissible in court, as any two-bit lawyer would say that it was obtained illegally. The only thing we can do is to apply for a warrant to search the premises. They have refused to respond to our knocking on the door so we just have to go back to the office. Unfortunately, we can't leave anyone here on surveillance, as they now know we're onto them and it would be too dangerous for anyone to remain. These are desperate, vicious men who are cornered like rats and none of us know what they'll do to escape."

The four policemen returned to their office, knowing they had probably blown their chance of catching the torturers and murderers of poor Johann, who happened to work in the wrong place at the wrong time.

The process for applying for a warrant to search the house began. Erik went into his desk drawer and extracted a large folder, which he threw across the room to Laurie. "There you are," he said. "In Holland, that's what you need before you can apply to a judge for a warrant, and before you start reading it, I'll tell you now: we have nothing like enough evidence to produce a good case. It's very difficult here to get a search warrant because of a suspect's human rights, plus the fact that the owner can sue the police for a large sum in damages if we get it wrong. That payout comes from the police budget. So you can see what we're up against from the start."

"So what happens if we shoot them when they're outside," asked Hugo.

"Then the family sues the police!"

Chapter 33

In the isolated house on the outskirts of the city of Islamabad, three men knelt on a luxurious carpet in an attitude of prayer. When they had finished, the man in the centre looking straight ahead said "There's very bad news from Holland. The police are getting extremely close to finding our warriors," he said.

"Yes," said the man on his right. "I think from what our informants say, we have two weeks at the most before the police will act. Do we have a team ready to replace them?"

"We do have men ready to take their places, but we cannot go on replacing those who are betrayed," said the man on the left. "Training and placing our men in other countries is very expensive and takes time. Our sponsors will soon be asking what we've achieved by spending their generous donations. Finding the right men is not easy – we have plenty of volunteers but we need men with the right skills, and that is a very different matter."

"I agree," said the man in the middle. "We must keep four men where they are and move the others to Britain, because we could always use more skilled personnel. The four men who remain in Holland will be those three whose faces have appeared in the media and the one who's experienced in constructing bombs. We'll teach the people in Holland not to interfere with someone who does not interfere with them. We'll target their police, especially the two inspectors and two sergeants who are getting close on our trail."

The other men nodded and their meeting broke up as each man shouted, "Allah be praised; may he help us with our endeavours!"

Chapter 34

Little progress had been made that week and both Laurie and Hugo were battling with their frustrations. It seemed that the terrorists were winning every round. There was no chance of getting a search warrant and there seemed to be no other way to get at the terrorist cell; they had gone to ground. Now and then, they would drive out to the house and spend an hour sitting in the car watching it, but nothing ever happened. It was as though the house were empty.

On Friday, all four policemen attended the funeral of the murdered agency clerk, placing a large arrangement of flowers on his coffin; they felt it was the least they could do. On Friday afternoon, Hugo caught the three o'clock plane for his weekend at home and Erik moved into his room at the hotel. He and Laurie spent Saturday afternoon in the city and in the evening they called at their ladies' flat, but no one replied to their knock.

"Let's go to that restaurant again," suggested Erik, "and have a meal there."

"Good idea," agreed Laurie. "Even if they aren't there, I liked the food."

When they arrived at the restaurant, the same waiter as before said to them, "The two ladies are waiting; shall I take you gentlemen to their table?"

"Indeed, please do," said Erik. Christina and Greta were looking lovely. "Thank God for that," Erik whispered to Laurie. "I thought I'd have to drag you round the red light district again."

When they got to the table, Greta said, "We were just beginning to think you were the sort of men who took advantage of poor innocent girls and once you'd had your wicked way with us, you'd disappear."

Erik looked pained and said, "We actually called at your flat, riding on white horses and carrying bouquets of beautiful flowers and chocolates, but no one answered the door, so we took the horses and the flowers back!"

"Well, you could at least have left the chocolates and flowers outside our door," said Christina.

As happened when they had first met each other, they chatted, telling each other outrageous jokes and enjoying each other's company. Laurie felt almost like a boy on his first date, remembering kissing Greta and hoping to hold her close to him again.

The weekend went by in a flash and all too quickly it was Monday morning again. When Erik tried to start his car to drive to work, the engine gave a couple of muffled grunts and died on him. He thought that was a bit odd, because the battery had been perfectly all right when he'd last driven the car; it wouldn't go flat overnight. He put his hand on the ignition key to make another attempt when a faint memory, something at the back of his mind, maybe a TV programme he had seen, came to him and he froze with horror. The programme had been about a car which had been wired to explode when the ignition key was turned. Trembling with tension, he carefully opened the car door and eased himself out – no quick movements, no sharp bangs, nothing to trigger any explosion – and phoned the Bomb Squad. It took them fifteen interminable minutes to arrive.

"What kept you?" Erik said irritably to their team leader.

He just shrugged and said, "Traffic." Obviously a man of few words.

Erik thought he recognised him. "It's Alberto, isn't it?"

Alberto nodded and said, "What makes you think the car is rigged to explode?"

"When I put the key in the ignition, the engine stalled as though the battery had gone flat, but it was okay yesterday. I suddenly remembered a film I'd seen about a car being wired up to explode when the ignition was switched on and, I can tell you, I got out of that car pretty damn quick."

Alberto crouched down and very carefully looked under the car. When he stood up he told Erik that he was one very lucky man. It was a miracle it hadn't exploded the first time he used the ignition key. It was a large device, which would have completely destroyed the car and anyone inside and would have blown out all the windows of the buildings nearby.

Erik realised that he had been holding his breath and he released it in a long sigh, trying not to shudder. His immediate reaction was a mixture of joy that his life had not gone up in smoke and fear because he realised how much danger he was in. This would probably not be the last time he would have to use his sixth sense to save himself.

The Bomb Squad cordoned off the area and defused the explosive charge under the car, and Alberto promised to let Erik have the report asap after Forensics had done their work.

"I don't think they'll find much," he told Erik. "It looks like a real pro job. See you around!"

When he eventually appeared in the office, Laurie looked up at him in surprise. "You suffering from the after effects of the weekend?" he queried. "Or have you seen a ghost? You look very pale."

Erik glared at the men sitting at their desks and said, rather dramatically, "So would you if you'd come within inches of meeting St Peter at the pearly gates!"

"What happened?" asked Hans, who could see that his boss had suffered some sort of trauma.

Erik calmed down and gave a short, succinct explanation as to why he was late arriving. There was a moment of shocked silence. Eventually, Laurie said, "This is very bad news. This means that the four of us are marked men because we're getting too close. We have to do something to protect ourselves. What about you, Hans?"

Hans thought carefully before saying, "I don't think they've ever seen me sitting in the car outside their house, so I don't think I'm in much danger."

"Okay, you can still live at your home address, but take every precaution you can to protect yourself; check and double-check everything in your surroundings to make sure nothing is booby-trapped. Erik, I think you should come and live at the hotel with Hugo and me. The security is very good there and we can get them to step it up a few notches. At least we now know what we're dealing with."

Erik agreed with him and decided to collect what he needed for a short stay at the hotel straight away. "We can't go on like this for long," he said. "We have to solve this problem for good."

"That goes without saying," said Laurie. "After this incident, do you think they'll grant a search warrant for the house?"

"No, I shouldn't think so; the bomb could have come from anywhere; a terrorist cell in Belgium say, or even a jealous lover! No matter how frustrating it is, we have to wait for some more definite evidence before that'll come about."

"You mean until one of us is blown up and the bomber hands himself in at the reception desk," said Laurie cynically.

The following day, the train driver of the eight o'clock express Amsterdam to Paris train reported a strange object on the line, just outside the city. It did not affect the train and he did not stop. The police found a man's jacket covering something at the side of the track, so the line was temporarily closed while they examined it. It was a large parcel, which turned out to be a photocell bomb. It would have worked with a similar mechanism as a speed camera, but instead of a flashing light, the current would have been used to trigger an explosion. Whether the train had not been going fast enough, having only just left the station, or there had been some other fault, mercifully, the device had not exploded.

This incident escalated the country's security to its highest possible level and there was an immediate emergency meeting of the heads of all departments responsible for countrywide security, including the police and the secret service. A question was asked of all of them: what could be done to stop this kind of attack on the train services?

"The answer to that is nothing," the Head of Home Security said bluntly. "Do you realise how many kilometres of train tracks there are? It's physically impossible to cover all that ground all the time."

"What about our Secret Service?" the chairman asked. "Is there any way they can trace anyone suspected of planting bombs?"

"We're bugging the telephone lines of anyone suspected, but with the advent of mobile phones, this can easily be overcome; they simply move to a different place and make calls with perhaps a pre-arranged code. It becomes more and more difficult to pin them down. Still, we're working on some American equipment which has shown some very promising results, but I'm afraid that's for the future; nothing that can help us very much at the moment."

"What about you?" The chairman of the meeting looked directly at the Chief of Police. "The last time your people got it right we had no trouble for some time. Is there anything you can contribute which would be of help in this situation?"

The Chief of Police shook his head slightly and said, "We're doing our best, but the Human Rights Act is tying our hands to a great extent. We have to make absolutely sure that the evidence is one hundred per cent before we can even think about taking action, otherwise the so-called victims can sue us for thousands of euros in compensation. I wouldn't be at all surprised if some of that money, in the past, has not found its way back to terrorist cells. Also, the compensation money comes out of our police budget, which leaves even less money for policing."

The meeting broke up with no real decisions being made.

A few days later, Laurie and Hugo went to have another look at the house. They were super keen on security and checked their surroundings, their cars and their mail both at the office and the hotel, but they thought that they would be quite safe if they just sat in the car, observing the area to see if the occupants stirred or made any moves. It was another boring morning which produced nothing except an argument as to which football team would win in their next match.

They were driving back to the office, just turning into the main road, when a motorbike appeared in the rear-view mirror. As usual, Hugo was driving.

"Let this maniac get past us," said Laurie.

Hugo grinned. "Shall I stop him, sir, and book him for not obeying the speed limit?"

"If he overtakes, we'll wait and see what he does."

But the motorbike did not overtake; it just kept dawdling behind them.

"He must know we're police," suggested Laurie.

"If he knows we're police, we're in no danger," said Hugo, "but as we're in civilian clothes in an unmarked police car, how could he know?"

"He could have driven out of the garage after we left the area. Are you armed, Sergeant?"

"No, sir, are you?"

"No. I think he's waiting for an opportunity to strike, perhaps when we get to a quieter area." He pulled out his phone to call Erik for help as the motorbike drew level with them. The rider was balancing a gun, pointed at the car, on his right arm. Hugo yanked the steering wheel to the left and steered the car straight at him just as the gun went off. The high-velocity bullet shattered Hugo's window but missed its target and lodged in the roof of the car. Desperately trying to keep his balance, the rider took aim again.

"Ram his back wheel!" shouted Laurie. Before Hugo could get into position to ram the bike without crashing the car, the rider zigzagged out of the way and accelerated through the oncoming traffic, and was soon out of sight.

Hugo brought the car to a standstill and slumped onto the steering wheel with a loud exhalation. "I think we'd better wait here for a few minutes until backup arrives," he managed to say. "You never know; he might be waiting round the corner to take another shot at us."

Laurie rang Erik and explained the situation and asked for an armed escort to take them back to the office.

"From now on, none of us go out unarmed," said Erik, who was pleased to see them in one piece. "I don't suppose you noticed the motorbike's registration number, did you?"

"Actually," said Laurie sarcastically, "we were too busy trying to avoid being killed. In any case, I can't imagine they'd leave the correct registration number on it. The bike could have been stolen. It's probably been dumped and torched by now. The question is what do we do now?"

"They appear to have been very clever; as neither of you saw him leave the house, it won't help us get a search warrant. The only thing it has confirmed is that they're definitely out to kill us. I'm fed up with this situation. We're going to have to take some action. I'd be quite happy to devise a plan to have them all killed!"

"How could we do that?" asked Laurie cautiously.

"Give them a taste of their own medicine and blow the building up. We could put a story around that they were making and arming a bomb when it went off accidentally."

There was a moment of silence while they took this in.

"That's an outrageous suggestion, boss," Hans said eventually. "It would take a lot of planning and organising and the fewer people who knew about it the better."

"If there were an investigation, which there would be, it would reveal that they really were making a bomb," Erik explained.

"Yes, but you know how skilled Forensics are nowadays. Wouldn't they think there was something fishy going on if they found the explosion took place outside the house, for instance?"

"If you set off a bomb big enough and include canisters of gas or petrol, it would start such a huge fire that if the blast doesn't kill them, the fire will."

"That theory is fine," chipped in Laurie, "but there are two problems with it. First of all, a powerful explosion might kill or injure a number of innocent people, and secondly, they'll just infiltrate another bunch of murderous bastards into the country to exact revenge. So rather than removing the threat to our lives, the dangers will be increased tenfold."

"Why are you always so damn right?" said Erik.

"Look at it this way," said Laurie. "It's fairly easy to arrange a killing but it's having to deal with the consequences that would cause problems – a great many problems – and I don't want to end up in prison as a result."

"What about getting a professional hit man to do it?" mused Erik.

Scornfully, Laurie said, "You are joking; we don't have enough money between us to do that. A really good professional killer, which it would have to be, would cost you a million or two euros, and if he were caught and tortured like the agency clerk, then what?"

"So you're saying there's nothing we can do but sit here waiting like lambs to be slaughtered?"

"We can do some good police work to ensure we get them in the end," suggested Laurie.

"Pardon me while I have a good laugh," said Erik, "before I'm blown up or shot! I swear I'll come back and haunt them to death."

Chapter 35

A security company that supervised one of the airport car parks sent Erik an email stating that a car had been left in a restricted area. None of their personnel remembered it being left there and no surveillance cameras overlooked the area.

Erik rang the security office supervisor to ask him about it.

"Yes, Inspector, we found the vehicle this morning, parked forty metres from the airport perimeter in a no-parking zone. I expect you'd like to check the car before it's moved."

"Leave it with us," Erik told him. "We'll send somebody round straightaway."

"Thank you very much, Inspector."

"In the current climate I suppose we'd better get the Bomb Squad to check it over before any poor sod moves it."

Erik rang the Bomb Squad office to apprise them of the situation. "Be with you in ten minutes," said the voice on the other end of the phone.

Erik turned to his colleagues. "Well, I don't know about you lot," he said, "but I'm going to take a look at our comrades investigating what's probably a completely harmless abandoned car, left there by some drunk after a night out."

They drove to the airport perimeter fence, where they could see the car, and sat waiting for the Bomb Disposal Unit to arrive. The car was an old red Toyota Carina, and when Erik rang the Vehicle Registration Office to check the number plates, he was told that there was no such number, which meant that the plates were false.

"How did the car get into this area?" asked Hugo. "Did they cut the perimeter fence?"

"I hope not," said Erik. "There's a first-class security system here; if anything gets to within a metre of the fence, an alarm is triggered, both near the perimeter and in the office, which shows exactly where the problem is occurring."

"The security response would be very quick and they'd be armed, so how did that car get here?" queried Laurie.

Erik shrugged his shoulders. "Obviously, at this point we don't know, but we'll have to leave that till later because here comes the Bomb Squad."

Four men got out of the van, including Alberto. "Inspector, we meet again!" he said jovially.

"Thought I'd keep you busy," said Erik "This car is illegally parked and has false number plates, so as we don't want anybody to get blown up if they try to move it, we immediately thought of you."

Alberto moved everybody fifty metres away from the car and ordered his men to don their protective clothing. With a mirror stick in his hand, he approached the car and carefully squatted down beside it so he could slide it underneath. He whistled. "It's a beauty," he told them when he got back. "They don't make 'em small, do they?"

"Not worth bringing you out here if it wasn't seriously big," joked Erik. "What's the best way to deal with it?"

"It's similar to the one we fixed for you the other day," said Alberto, "so I think I'll tackle it the same way."

"Let one of your team do that," said Erik. "You don't have to do it all yourself."

"No, I know that, but this team is fairly new and they don't have the experience yet."

"And they'll never get the experience if you always do everything yourself," argued Erik.

Alberto asked politely if everyone could take cover behind their vehicles, picked up his toolkit and walked back towards the red Toyota. He wriggled very carefully under the car. There was silence while he worked. It only took him about five minutes, but it seemed like an eternity to the onlookers. At last he emerged with a large bundle, which he handed to a member of his team. They would inspect it further later.

"That stopped it making a nasty big hole in the concrete and the fence," he joked. "I'll just go and check the inside of the car."

As he pulled open the front nearside door, an explosion blew him twenty metres from the car, where he lay unnaturally still. Nobody moved for a few seconds, deafened and shocked by the noise. Hugo started to run towards Alberto, but Laurie shouted to him to come back; there could be other delayed booby traps waiting to go off. But Hugo was already standing over the body, his feeling of helplessness showing on his face. The paramedics were there in minutes, but looked towards Laurie and with a slight shake of the head, indicated that there was no hope. It was little consolation to be told that the force of the explosion had probably killed him outright and that he wouldn't have suffered.

Laurie looked around at his men and saw that Erik hadn't moved; he looked frozen with shock, and the other two were not much better.

"The doctor's on his way," said the medic. "Looks like he'll have to treat some of these blokes for shock." He kept talking while they moved Alberto's body into the ambulance, but Laurie didn't hear a word; the seriousness of the threat they were all under had come home to him with a vicious blow. What if it had been Hugo, married with children, or Hans or Erik or himself? He shuddered and tried to listen to what the paramedic said. "The doctor will examine the body and declare him dead, and then there'll be a post mortem. You'll get the official report when it's been completed. Meanwhile, it looks as if some of your men need attention."

Laurie remembered what Alberto had said about his team not having had much experience and hurried over to see how they were coping. "The doctor will be over in a minute," he said, realising how completely inadequate that remark was. He returned to Erik, who was still not moving or speaking. As soon as the doctor arrived, Laurie called him over. He looked closely into Erik's eyes, checked his pulse and asked if he could hear him. There was no response.

"This man is suffering from severe shock and must go to hospital for a complete check-up. I can't do it here in these circumstances," the doctor said.

He decided that the rest of Alberto's team were okay, apart from their white faces, but insisted they make their statements to the police as soon as possible, as doing so would release some of the tension and allow them to get back to as near normal as they could ever be. "What about you?" he said shrewdly to Laurie. "Was the victim a close friend of yours? Tell me what happened here; I assume it was some kind of terrorist activity."

Laurie spoke slowly, marshalling his thoughts, and explained what had happened.

Erik was persuaded to get into another ambulance so that he could be taken to hospital for the check-up he urgently needed, and Laurie asked Hans to get the Bomb Squad to ensure that the car was safe to be moved for the inevitable forensic examination. They checked the remains of the vehicle and pronounced it safe.

Hans turned to Laurie and said hesitantly, "As my boss is not here, sir, I think you're in charge of the investigation as to how the car came to be left here, so would you like to examine the wreckage in case we can pick up on anything?"

"Yes, I think we should all look at the remains of the vehicle. We might see something that triggers off an idea. Three heads are better than one." He tried to sound optimistic. "Don't let the Bomb Squad move it for the time being. We can start tomorrow morning; we've all had a bad shock today and I must go and see how Erik's getting on. If I know him, as soon as he recovers slightly he'll sign himself out and perhaps go home and get drunk. I think I'd like to join him in that, but someone has to keep sober." His mild joke fell on deaf ears.

Laurie and Hugo went back to the hotel, promising to meet at dinnertime. Laurie lay on his bed, thinking of the day's tragedy. He rang the hospital to see if he could speak to Erik but was told he'd been given a mild sedative and encouraged to rest. He told the doctor that he would enquire how things were going in the morning; perhaps he could pick him up tomorrow. He had seen some unpleasant incidents during his career with the police, but this had come so close to home that it was going to take a long time before he could come to terms with the horrible outcome. It was never easy to accept a man's death, especially when he had only been doing his duty.

Chapter 36

By the morning, Laurie had recovered his composure to a great extent and he rang the hospital from his desk. Erik was suffering from severe shock and as there was no one to keep an eye on him if he were discharged, they were keeping him in for a few days for 'observation'.

"We'd better get some flowers and a bunch of grapes," said Laurie, hoping to lighten the atmosphere. "What sort of magazines does he like? Those from the top shelf at the bookstore? Oh, I'd forgotten; we're in Holland and sex magazines are displayed all over the counter!"

The two sergeants looked at each other and decided to humour their older colleague by laughing at his attempts to lighten the situation.

"We have to find out how they managed to get that Toyota into one of the most secure airports in Europe," said Hans.

"Well, it's obviously not as secure as we thought it was, so let's try and pin down some facts," said Laurie. "First, they got it through the gate. How many entrances are there?"

"Two," said Hans. "One for passengers and one for goods vehicles."

"Right, that's where we start. I'll ring the security office and speak to whoever's in charge." When the phone was answered, he said, "I'm Inspector Albert Mueller and I'm temporarily in charge of the investigation into the bomb incident that happened yesterday. What's your name, by the way? I like to know who I'm talking to."

"Tomas Henkel, Inspector. May I say that we're very sorry for the family of the man who was killed and wondered about the health of the other policeman who was taken to hospital, I believe. How may I help you?"

"I'd like to inspect the entrance for goods vehicles. Do you have CCTV camera cover for the last twenty-four hours? If so, I'd like my men to study the coverage for the hours before the vehicle was noted and we were informed."

"Yes, Inspector, we have that footage."

"What about the guard who was on duty at the time?"

"He's off-duty at the moment, Inspector, but we can ring him at home."

Laurie told Hugo to stay in the office in case any of the top brass wanted information about the present position of the investigation. He took Hans with him because he was familiar with the airport and its layout.

After a short conversation about the current situation, Laurie spoke to Henkel and explained his theory about how the Toyota could not have been driven into the airport and dumped. "No sane person would drive a car with two explosive charges attached to it, and an Asian driver would have to obtain security clearance at the entrance. They just couldn't take that chance of being stopped and searched. The second reason is that the driver would still have to get out of the airport and he couldn't just stroll out because it would have seemed suspicious to the guards on duty. That's why I think it was smuggled into the airport through the goods entrance inside a delivery lorry or a very large van, and was then left in the no-parking area during the hours of darkness."

"It would have to be at a fairly reasonable time – no deliveries are made between midnight and 5 a.m., said Henkel.

"Right, so we need to concentrate on the video say from 8 p.m. until midnight."

"Right you are," said Henkel. "I'll get my IT guy to go through it and pick out any large vehicles which could have been used. May I offer you some coffee while you're waiting?"

It was the best part of half an hour before they were taken through to the laboratory and shown the results of the search. Only five large lorries had passed through the entrance and three of them were fuel tankers, which ruled them out. Of the other two vehicles, one was delivering beer and one had the name of a large frozen-food chain on its side and presumably contained groceries of some sort. Laurie was bitterly disappointed; it looked as if his theory had crashed. But he could not accept that there was any other way that the vehicle could have been taken to the forbidden parking area. The cameras were foolproof: even if a cable had been severed, an alarm would have sounded and security guards would immediately be on the scene. All recording was done in the lab, twenty-four hours a day, three hundred and sixty-five days a year. There was no way they could have missed anything.

"Somehow or other, a red Toyota was smuggled in here, booby-trapped and left to kill one of our men. We'd better find out how they did it before something similar happens again," said Laurie. "Thanks for your help."

On the way back to the office, he and Hans were silently engrossed in their own thoughts. Hugo looked up as they came through the door and asked if they had found anything out.

"Yes," said Laurie. "I've been mulling over the film footage we saw and I'm almost certain it came in the back of the lorry marked with the name of a frozen-food firm. It was big enough to hold a car, and all you'd need is two ramps to get it on and off."

"What about the security guards?" queried Hugo.

"I think we need to check on two men," said Laurie. "The security guard on duty between 8 p.m. and midnight and the driver of the frozen-food delivery van."

"Why the delivery driver?" asked Hans, puzzled.

"They could only have got away with this if it was a regular driver who the guard knew. If it was a usual delivery and the guard knew the driver, there would be no reason for him to suspect anything. I must contact him without delay."

They obtained the home telephone number of the off-duty security guard and Laurie questioned him closely, asking if he remembered if he had checked the frozen-food lorry through the goods vehicle entrance between 8 p.m. and midnight two nights ago.

"I remember all the lorries that came through at that time in the evening. There weren't very many. Most of them come in during working hours. These drivers only work late if it's worth their while in overtime. Just a few of them are regular and always come after eight."

He was starting to ramble on so Laurie brought him back to the subject. "I'm only interested in the food lorry. Was it the usual driver?"

"Yes, it was the regular driver. I know him quite well. I checked his docket and it was all in order. I didn't open the doors because if the food's frozen, the drivers don't like it; they complain that it affects the temperature and then they get into trouble if it's not first-class quality. Did I do something wrong?"

"Well, it would have been better if you had checked his lorry, but it's too late now. You've probably had a lucky escape. If there were terrorists in the back of the lorry, they would probably have silenced you in some way." Laurie heard a sudden intake of breath, and it was a few moments before the guard managed to speak again. He understood exactly what Laurie was telling him; he had his life but another man was dead because he had not insisted on opening two doors. "Thank you," said Laurie quietly. "I can trust you not to mention this to anyone else while I check out this information, can't I? It could mean another death if you don't keep your mouth shut."

"Yes, yes," gabbled the security guard, "I won't say a word."

"What about the driver?" asked Hans. "Was he in on their plan, do you think?"

"He couldn't have unloaded the car and positioned it on his own, so he was probably persuaded into helping them, possibly by threatening him or his family in some way. We'll have to be armed when we go to his home address."

Hugo phoned the frozen-food company and, after being passed from person to person, eventually discovered the driver's name, address and telephone number. Laurie dialled the number and waited several minutes before a man answered. "I'm Inspector Mueller—"

Before he could go on, the phone was put down abruptly. "He must be scared out of his wits. We have to get to his house as soon as possible. Hans, you drive; you know this city better than any of us."

The drive took twenty minutes and then they had to find the right apartment, number three on the first floor. The two sergeants asked Laurie the best way to approach the situation. He had been mulling this over and over in his mind all the way there and said, "Hide your guns and leave the shotgun in the car boot. Hugo, you stay in the car and if anyone comes running out, stop them but don't shoot if at all possible. You come with me, Hans, and we'll try to talk to the driver, if he's free. If not, we'll have to play it by ear." He knocked on the door and shouted, "Police! Open up!" There was no reply. He shouted again "This is the police. Open the door or we'll have to break it down."

The door opened slowly and a pale and frightened face peered round it. Laurie showed his badge and the door was grudgingly opened a little further. Politely, Laurie said, "If we may come in, I think it would be more private for you." He was aware that his Dutch was not quite sufficient to interrogate this obviously frightened man, so he used a conciliatory tone and said soothingly, "We have only a few simple questions for you. We won't take up much of your time. Do you have a wife and children here?" The driver turned paler. Laurie said to Hans, "Would you make a note of our conversation, please, Sergeant. I wish to have a record of what this man says." That should frighten him into telling me what I want to know, he thought. "You're the driver who made a delivery in a frozen-food container lorry to the airport two nights ago?" The man nodded his head. "I want you to listen to me carefully," said Laurie. "A good man was killed by an explosion the following day and we suspect it was caused by something delivered by that vehicle." The man glanced away and said nothing. "If this was due to something connected with that delivery, you'll be an accessory to his murder. You must tell us everything that happened that night."

The man made a sound between a cry and a gasp and wailed, "Please, what about my family, what about my child? I can't stand this any longer."

Laurie glanced triumphantly at Hans and said soothingly, "We can protect you all, but only if you tell us everything you know about what happened that night."

The words came tumbling out so fast that Hans could not keep up with his attempts to write it all down, and he listened in gathering fury to the situation the driver was explaining.

There had been the three of them in the apartment – his wife, himself and his fourteen-year-old daughter – when at about eight o'clock he had answered a knock on the door and three armed men pushed their way in. They were told to sit down and keep quiet and one of them told him what they must do if they wanted to stay alive. They threatened to kill his wife and daughter if he didn't do exactly as he was told. Two of them went with him to the lorry park to collect his vehicle and then he was driven somewhere else. He was not sure where because they put a hood over his head. He heard the doors at the back being opened and something that seemed very heavy and cumbersome loaded. They then drove him to the main road on the way to the airport, took off the hood and told him to drive as if he were making a normal delivery. They hid at the back of the cab and one of them warned him that if he put so much as a finger out of place, it would be the last thing he did, and his wife and daughter would also pay with their lives. He then made some disgusting suggestions about what they would do to his teenage daughter before they killed her.

The driver had been almost paralysed with fright when he remembered that he'd need a delivery note to be allowed through. After more threats from his kidnappers he remembered that he had a blank pad of delivery notes in his cab; they were occasionally needed if a load had to be split up and taken to two different destinations. The leader watched him while with trembling fingers he made up a list of goods and forged a very creditable copy of his boss's signature. They told him that once through the gate, he was to pull up before he got to his usual delivery point and wait. They then told him that there was a huge bomb in the back of his lorry.

There had been no difficulty in gaining entrance to the airport and the two men told him where to drive and park. They made him help them open the doors and use the ramps to unload a car, which he thought was red but it was a bit difficult to tell in the sodium lights around the perimeter fence. The car was rolled into position in a no-parking area. Then they made the driver take them out of the airport, as if he had just made a delivery, and allowed him to drive nearer to his home. They knocked on his door and assured their compatriot that everything had been completed satisfactorily, but before they allowed the driver inside, they told him that if he called the police, they would be back to kill them all. They had a car parked out of sight around the corner, so he didn't have a chance to see what it was.

"Can you describe what they looked like, what they were wearing?" asked Laurie.

"They all looked Asian, young, wearing black bomber jackets with hoods, trainers, dark jeans, in fact everything was black; they all looked alike."

"The man who stayed behind with your wife and daughter, did he say anything, anything at all to them? Did he boast about what they were going to do, insult them or try to explain their motives or ideologies? Did he eat or drink anything?"

The driver shook his head and said pleadingly, "We'd help you if we could but my wife's a nervous wreck; she can't sleep for fear they'll come back or get my daughter if she goes to school or out shopping with her mates or something. I'll do my best to try and think of something, but at the moment all we can think of is if the next knock on the door will be the last thing we hear."

"You've helped us already and I'm sure if anything comes back to you, you'll let us know," Laurie said soothingly. "In the meantime, I want to make sure you're quite safe so we'll move you into the airport hotel, where I am staying with my sergeant. That way you'll have nothing to worry about."

The driver looked very happy at first, but than a thought occurred to him. "What about my job and my daughter's education?"

"As for your job, I'll arrange for you to take a long sick leave, due to the trauma you've suffered, and I'll discreetly inform your company that you'll be available for work in due course, but at the moment you're a vital witness in a very dangerous and complicated case we're working on; that should keep them quiet. And I'm sure your wife will appreciate an all-expenses-paid holiday in a luxurious hotel for as long as it takes. I'd also like you all to have a chat with a doctor, who'll be able to help you get over this upsetting incident, and if you need any medication, I'm sure he'll prescribe something mild for you. As for your daughter's education, she can carry on going to school, because I'll assign a police officer to escort her, stay there and then bring her back to the hotel. He'll be fully armed and instructed to shoot if necessary. Now, go and pack a few necessities you might need – clothes, toiletries, etc. – and we'll take you to the hotel without delay."

Chapter 37

At the airport hotel reception desk, Laurie used all his charm and authority to arrange accommodation for the family, explaining that they would be staying for about two weeks, but perhaps longer, depending on circumstances. They were to have anything the hotel could supply and any bills were to be forwarded to the Police Accounts Division. The receptionist was quite impressed and called the porter to take the guests to their suite.

Laurie inspected the two rooms, each complete with a lounge and bathroom, to make sure everything was suitable, and told the family to settle in and to try and relax; one of his men would be outside to make sure they were not bothered by anyone. He also told them that someone would visit them the following day, not too early, to ask them a few more questions, and the doctor may also call. Their daughter would have to have a short holiday from school while he arranged her escort.

As Laurie and Hans left the hotel, Laurie heaved a sigh of relief that that was over. "Let's go back to the office and get that driver's story typed out, then the three of us can kick around some ideas about the next steps to take," he said to Hans.

When Hugo had heard the driver's story, he said, "You were absolutely right, sir. I thought your idea was a bit far-fetched, but it was spot on. Those poor people. At least none of them were hurt physically, but it might affect them psychologically, don't you think so, Hans?" Hans nodded his agreement. "Has it helped in any way?" Hugo asked Laurie.

"Not really," said Laurie. "Although his description of events is very accurate, is it definite enough to help us get a search warrant for the house?"

"That I don't know," said Vogel, "and without that we're back to square one."

"Tomorrow's Friday," said Laurie, "and I hope that Erik will be back." But when he rang the hospital, they told him that they were not discharging him before the weekend.

Laurie rang the driver's company to ascertain if they knew where their lorry was, but they didn't know what had happened to it. He then gave the driver's boss an abbreviated account of what had happened and told him that he and his family had been taken into safe custody until the terrorists had been caught. Laurie finished by saying, "We're hoping that the whole situation will be resolved shortly." He could almost feel the driver's boss shrugging his shoulders over the phone and anticipated his reply.

"So we lost a van and a driver, and while I have every sympathy for the driver and his family…" Liar, thought Laurie. "…being caught up in something he had no control over, it doesn't help us to run our business."

No sympathy there, thought Laurie. In his iciest voice he said coldly, "You can put in a claim to your insurance company for the lorry and lost working hours; the police will support it. As for the driver, consider him to be on holiday – paid holiday."

"Sure, sure. Anything you say, Inspector. I'll have the claim forms sent to you right away so that you can authenticate the statements and, er, thanks for letting us know about this." As an afterthought, he added that he hoped the driver and his family would make a quick recovery from their ordeal.

Laurie made a face as he put down the phone. "He's all heart, that one. Hopes they make a quick recovery but can't wait to send us the insurance claim forms so that we can back him up and he can get some money out of the situation! As I said, all heart."

The rest of the day was spent checking over what was being done to further the case. They rang Forensics to see if the airport site had been cleared and was told that the car was in their laboratory, but so far had yielded very little information and they were still completing their investigations. A report would be with them as soon as possible.

Hans disappeared late afternoon to visit his boss, so Laurie told Hugo he would see him in the hotel bar about 6.30 p.m.

As they sat in the bar sipping their first drink of the evening, Hugo said abruptly, "This particular assignment is very frustrating; we take one step forward and seem to take two steps back. All that time in Germany and now here, and we're still chasing the same three men with very little to show for it except a number of dead bodies."

"I'm beginning to feel we might have been better to hire a professional hit man, strictly off the record of course. They don't have the same constraints that we do."

"Could we do that?" asked Hugo, wondering if his boss were serious. Laurie just smiled.

The following evening, Laurie was eating dinner in the hotel restaurant. He had checked on the driver and his family and found them to be settling in well, and had spoken to the armed guard patrolling outside their suite, just to make sure nothing unusual had happened, but all was in order. He was wondering how he was going to occupy himself at the weekend without Erik. He decided he didn't want to just sit in his room watching television, so he gravitated towards the bar, wondering if there might be some interesting company he could talk to about anything than the present case. He worked his way through a large beer and a considerable amount of salted peanuts; the barman, recognising him as an almost permanent resident of the hotel, kept filling up the nut and crisp containers assiduously.

Out of the corner of his eye, Laurie became aware of two women sitting at a table near the entrance, and as he got up to get himself another beer, the barman put a drink on his table. "Compliments of the two ladies over there," he said.

Laurie turned to the table and raised his glass in salute, swiftly assessing the two women, who looked like they might be mother and daughter; there was a faint resemblance between them. The older one was, at a guess, in her mid-forties and the younger one maybe in her early twenties. She was very slim with light brown hair and was wearing a tight red trouser suit with a low-cut, frilly white blouse.

Everything looked expensive. The overall picture – seven out of ten was his mark! The older woman had a fuller figure, the same light brown hair, which looked as if she had just come from a fashionable hairdressing establishment, and a very attractive face. Laurie thought that of the two, she looked better, because her daughter was too skinny for his taste, and he awarded her, mentally, nine marks out of ten. The bar was now getting quite noisy and he couldn't very well shout to them over all the other conversations, but almost before he could take another sip of beer, the younger woman was standing near him saying, "If the prophet won't come to the mountain, the mountain has to come to the prophet." She smiled down at him. Nice teeth, thought Laurie. "Why don't you came and sit with us? It's too loud to have a conversation from one end of the bar to the other."

He moved over to their table with his beer, and the older woman introduced herself as Margo and her daughter as Katia.

"Laurie," he said, smiling and holding out his hand. "Laurie Mueller. But I have an admission to make: I'm a police inspector by occupation." Margo looked puzzled and asked if there were anything wrong with being a policeman. "You'd be surprised how many people shun the police. I was once enjoying an evening out with a lady and we were getting on very well. I happened to mention what I did for a living and before I knew it, she stood up and walked out on me. Could have been guilty conscience. But I can see you two ladies have nothing to worry your heads about!"

"You were better off without her," said Margo.

"Well, now that you've told us you're a policeman, what are you policing?" asked Katia.

"Well, at this point I'm sitting next to two lovely ladies and guarding them from the attentions of any men who might try to steal them from me. I know what men are like, being one myself, and I know they're only after one thing – no, maybe two things or perhaps three things!" said Laurie facetiously.

Margo raised an eyebrow and, entering into the silliness of the conversation, said, "You wouldn't advise us to go with them?"

"No, they're underhanded and cunning; they'll tell you one thing and mean another."

"And you're not like that; you don't want one or two or three things?" continued Margo.

"Oh yes I do," said Laurie, keeping a straight face, "but I'm straight, I'm honourable, I just say are we going to bed or not?"

"And this is better?" said Margo. "Do you get many positive replies to that question?"

Laurie pretended to think and said innocently, "I'm trying this out for the first time, and so far, I've had no reaction."

"What do you think, Katia?" asked Margo.

"I don't think it'll catch on," she said.

"No, neither do I. It's not going to appeal to many women," agreed Margo.

"Ouch," said Laurie. "What else can I say? It's going to be a lonely night for me tonight. Of course, you realise I was only speaking hypothetically. I'd never use that sort of approach to any woman, particularly to such beautiful, refined ladies like yourselves!"

"Ah, look, Katia; he's retreating now, going back on what he said."

"Yes, the usual back-tracking, denying he said anything of the sort. Typical man."

Laurie pulled himself up straight and said in a hurt way, "I was only trying to describe how most of these lusty men would go about things!"

"Shall we let him off, Katia?" said Margo archly.

"I suppose so; it's sad to see a man in this situation, trying to talk his way out of a tricky situation and only digging himself deeper into a hole."

"Phew," said Laurie. "You ladies are being very kind and forgiving tonight. Perhaps it'll continue for the rest of the evening. What are you doing in this palatial establishment tonight?"

"We've just flown in from Rome and Katia has brought me here to meet her fiancé."

"Oh, I see. Do you both live in Rome?"

"Yes. Katia is finishing a post-graduate course and I work in the Dutch Embassy there."

"What are you doing here, all on your own and lonely?" asked Katia lightly.

Laurie considered rapidly how much he should tell them and decided to keep it to the very minimum. No point in complicating things. "I'm only on my own because my colleagues are away this weekend, but fortunately or unfortunately, they'll be back on Monday, so then there'll be four of us."

Katia stood up and gathered her purse and wrap, saying, "I'll leave you two to enjoy yourselves. I'm going to have an early night; busy weekend starting tomorrow."

When she had gone, Laurie asked, "Is there a Mr Margo?"

Margo looked straight at him and said evenly, "No, not tonight."

Laurie felt he had to clarify this and said with a smile, "You mean there is someone, at certain times, when you want to arrange it?"

She thought for a moment and said slowly, "Ever since my divorce, I've not wanted to get too involved with any particular man, so I think very carefully before I – how shall I put it – make an appointment in my diary."

Laurie laughed. "You mean like going to the dentist or the hairdresser? Never having been married I don't know much about these things, but I suppose the ending of any long-term relationship is painful. Once bitten, twice shy, as the saying goes."

"What about you?" asked Margo.

"In my case, I lack commitment," Laurie said lightly, "plus being a policeman puts women off; they don't want to put up with the unsociable hours, the possible danger of death or disablement. I think they tend to go for the civil servant or office manager type, someone who'll bring home a regular salary and work regular hours."

They continued to make light-hearted, flirtatious conversation and Laurie realised that he was getting slightly inebriated. He thought that if he didn't go for it he wouldn't be capable of anything later on. "Do you think something is building up between us or are we just going to continue our conversation and then say goodnight?" he asked Margo.

"I was waiting for you to say something," she replied. "I'm not the sort of woman who makes the first move, not like some of our sex; I wait to be asked."

Laurie smiled. "May I ask you to share my lonely bed tonight?"

"Do you know, I think I'd like that." She smiled at him.

"Shall we make a run for it or shall we saunter out like an old married couple, arm in arm?"

"You might leave me some dignity," she said. "I'm not running anywhere; we'll stroll casually to the lift as if we're married – but perhaps not to each other!"

They tipped the barman lavishly and went up in the lift to Laurie's room. Once inside, with the door locked, they came together, kissing as if the end of the world was coming and they must experience every feeling they could before that happened. They undressed each other and fell on the bed, luxuriating in the way their bodies blended into one another.

"Has it been a long time since you last made love?" asked Laurie.

"Ssh, or you'll spoil the best moments."

Afterwards, they lay together, Margo's arms clasped around Laurie, and she gave him the answer to his question. "Yes, you're the first man I've been with since my divorce five years ago."

They fell asleep and when Laurie woke, Margo had gone.

He showered, dressed and went down to breakfast, looking around the dining room carefully, but the two women were not there. As he drank his coffee he thought how odd life was when two strangers could meet like that, purely by chance, and enjoy making love, then each go their own way. The only thing he knew about her was her first name. The rest of the weekend was going to be decidedly dull.

He was trying to decide whether to go out or watch an old film or sport on television when what felt very much like a gun jabbed him in the spine. A voice behind him said very menacingly, "Are you going to eat all that food? Because if you do, I'll have to shoot you!"

"Erik! Where did you come from? How are you? Sit down. Tell me how you come to be here. They were going to keep you in till

Monday. Boy, am I glad to see you. How did you escape?" Laurie said, all in one breath.

"I take it you're glad to see me," said Erik. "I discovered the way to get out of a straightjacket and I wasn't going to stay in that damn hospital being observed like some weird phenomenon."

Laurie was glad to see his colleague apparently fully recovered and back on form. "And I thought you'd be loving it, laying in bed being stroked and pampered by all those gorgeous nurses," he said.

"What, those old battleaxes? You have to be dying before someone comes to attend to your needs and the best-looking nurses refused point blank to get into bed with me."

"I'm not surprised about that," said Laurie. "It's supposed to be a hospital, not a house of ill repute. But if we have any luck, your 'special needs' will be taken care of tonight."

"Never mind that, bring me up to date with the case."

Laurie told him everything that had happened since he had been taken into hospital.

"It seems as if we're getting somewhere now," said Erik, "but I think we might be in more danger as we get nearer to finding them. What's the next step?"

"We'll discuss it on Monday, but let's not spoil the weekend," said Laurie. "But one thing I will tell you now: I'm going to resolve this once and for all in the next few days."

"You took the words right out of my mouth," agreed Erik. "Even if I have to plant a huge bomb under the bastards personally, it'll come to an end and I can pay them back for killing a good man right in front of my eyes. No waiting for a good reason for a search warrant while they intimidate families and kill our men."

"I agree with you wholeheartedly, but we have to do this in the correct police way."

"We'll do it that way if it works," said Erik, "but if it doesn't, I'll do it any way I can, and that's a promise."

"Calm down and have something to eat. How did you get on in hospital? We were all concerned about you."

"Actually, I don't remember much after the explosion. The noise and the shock of seeing poor old Alberto's mutilated body just lying there made my mind a blank. After a few seconds I couldn't take it in. One minute we were chatting and the next… he was…" He hesitated before he could carry on. "Well, luckily everyone rallied round. The paramedic gave me something which nearly sent me to sleep, and when I came to I didn't know where I was. It turned out to be nine o'clock the next day. Then the memories started to come flooding back and I kept on seeing Alberto's body; I couldn't get it out of my mind. So they gave me some pills and I seemed to spend the rest of my time dozing."

After a moment of silence, they both started to talk at once.

"Let's not talk about it any more," said Laurie. "Think about meeting the girls tonight; think of a good place to have a meal and a few drinks. You're the expert."

"I think we'd better carry weapons when we go out," Erik said, almost to himself.

"Are you joking? Do you really think we'll need them to subdue two ladies?"

Erik looked at him seriously. "I've a feeling they've been given orders to kill us."

At the armoury, they withdrew an automatic pistol each and some ammunition, and then they went to pick up Erik's car.

"This is the car they tried to blow up, isn't it?" said Laurie in an odd tone of voice.

"Yes, why?"

"So it's well known to the terrorists. Perhaps we should have taken my car. Keep on these busy roads."

"They're all pretty busy at this time of night," said Erik. "Why?"

"We appear to have a motorcycle following us."

Erik looked in the rear-view mirror and swore under his breath. "How long has he been there?"

"For the last three or four minutes."

"We'd better not pick up the ladies yet. If there's going to be any trouble we can't expose them to any danger. What I'll do is lead him away from where we're going and see if he really is following us. Since we're armed and there are just the two of us, I'll turn left at the next junction and see what this guy does."

Two junctions later he turned left again, heading for a quiet stretch of road. The motorcycle was still following them but holding back behind some cars.

"I take it you're looking for a lonely spot along this road," said Laurie.

"There's a disused garage somewhere just along here, to the right, and I'm going to pull in there and stop. Then we'll see what our motorcyclist does."

"What are we going to do? Shoot it out?"

"We can't drive round all night waiting for him to do something; and besides, I'm beginning to feel hungry and in need of a little female companionship, so I'm pulling in here at this old petrol station forecourt and waiting to see what he does. Have your gun ready!"

"Did you see him go past?" asked Laurie.

"No, damn it, I was concentrating on the turn off and stopping without bumping into anything." Before he could look round, a bullet flew past his head through the open window and smashed into a corner of the windscreen. They both ducked, but Erik managed to start the engine again and they drove clumsily around the disused petrol pumps, trying not to expose their heads as targets.

"Where is he?" hissed Laurie.

"I don't know for sure, but the bastard seems to be a good shot. I should think he's in that ditch at the side of the road."

"There are two of us. I'll go round the back of the building; you stay here. When I get into position, I'll fire one shot as a signal. Then we'll have him from both ends and we can open fire." Laurie's Dutch was getting rather ragged in the heat of the moment. He eased himself out of the passenger seat and keeping as low as he could, worked his way to the back of the derelict building, banging his shins on some protruding rubble on the way. As soon as he was in position, he fired the prearranged shot. Erik opened fire in the general direction of where he thought the motorcyclist was hidden, and at the same time, Laurie shot at a shadowy figure in the ditch and shouted to him to come out and throw down his gun.

"You're surrounded by armed police! Come out or we'll be forced to shoot!" Erik yelled.

For a few moments there was complete silence. Then came the roar of a motorcycle engine. The rider shot past their car and onto the road, disappearing in the direction of the city before they could get back in their car and start the engine.

Erik was fuming with rage. "We lost our only chance of getting him. There were two of us, fully armed, and we let him slip through our fingers."

"I think he chickened out. It was a damn good idea of yours to come armed, Erik."

"Well, now it's going to be a matter of their honour being challenged. They cannot countenance failure in any way. They'll want us very badly now, but I don't think there'll be any more planned for tonight. He'll go back and make a report and then they'll plan some more."

"In the meantime, let's make a note to have our office swept for bugs," said Laurie. "They might have somehow managed to plant one. Now I come to consider it, I bet there are bugs in our cars."

"I guess that puts an end to our going out with the ladies tonight," said Erik sadly. "That motorcyclist might still be hanging around the area, so even if he doesn't attack us again, he could follow us and find out where they live. That would put them in danger. Terrorists would have no scruples about using them to blackmail us or even kidnapping and torturing them."

"We can't involve them in any way that would endanger their lives," said Laurie.

"You can be so annoying when you get that high and mighty tone in your voice," said Erik furiously. "Why do you always have to be right? I've just been through a terrible ordeal and was hoping for some sexual healing and now I have nothing to look forward to tonight, or any night for that matter."

"Do you have their phone number?" asked Laurie reasonably. "Perhaps if we ring them they might come to the hotel?"

"Do you have their phone number?" demanded Erik. "No, well neither do I. I'd look a right fool ringing up directory enquiries asking for Christina and Greta's phone number who live in No. 3 of that big apartment building, somewhere in the suburbs, wouldn't I?"

"Calm down, Erik. I happened to meet someone last night, a lovely, sexy, divorced lady, and—"

Erik changed gear with a grinding clutch. "And I'm supposed to feel happy for you, am I?"

"Sorry, sorry. Wrong thing to say. What can I do to cheer you up?"

"Nothing. I think we both need some shooting practice."

"It was dark," said Laurie defensively. "I couldn't see anything so I aimed at where I thought he was!"

"It was dark for him too, but he didn't miss my head by much! We've been lucky this time but we'd better not to rely on luck; it has a nasty habit of running out just when you need it most."

They returned to the hotel and after a quick shower and change of clothes met in the bar. Gradually the tension began to ease as the alcohol took effect and they started to think about going in for a meal.

"I'm not really hungry at the moment," said Erik. "Perhaps later."

"Don't drink too much before you eat," Laurie said jokingly, "or it'll make you impotent."

"Why would I want to be sexually potent when we haven't the prospect of getting laid tonight? Come on, let's go and eat."

CHAPTER 38

BACK AT WORK ON MONDAY, Erik took his car to the police garage to check for electronic bugs. The mechanic found two, one in the boot of the car, hidden under the carpet lining, and the other behind the rear drive.

"They must have known exactly where we were at any given moment," he told Laurie. "We wouldn't have stood a cat in hell's chance if they'd been trailing us. The terrorists must have some fairly sophisticated tracking mechanisms, which means they're well established; they must have been in Amsterdam for a considerable time." He called a meeting with his three colleagues.

"I'm going to plan how to destroy these maggots once and for all," he announced. "They're making my life, sorry, our lives, as difficult as it gets and I'm not taking it any more. Now they can't locate the position of my car, I'll be able to plan a surprise attack!"

"What are you planning to do?" Hugo asked eagerly.

"I'm going to give them some of their own medicine."

"Like what?"

"There are several ways to do it; one is to gas them all – carbon monoxide gas is the best because it's not easily detected: it has no smell, you can't see it and it overcomes the victim very quickly, depending on age and weight. If we could get enough of it into the house it would look like a gas leak."

"It would be very difficult to ensure that the gas overcomes them all," Hugo said cautiously. "If any of them survive, the revenge would be brutal."

"Okay," said Erik impatiently, "it'll have to be a large bomb that'll blow the whole place to pieces. I can't see anyone surviving that."

"I hate to put a damper on your bloodthirsty plans," Laurie said, "but the whole thing is completely illegal. If even the slightest hint of a leak got out about it, it would cause an international incident of megaton capacity. Besides, to destroy the whole building you'd have to crash a lorry load of explosives through the wall into the house and hope the explosion caused a fire to make sure of complete destruction. I've seen demolition gangs at work, placing explosives where they'll bring the building crashing down, and believe me, it's not an easy job. It takes a long time for an expert to place the charges in exactly the right place so that the whole building becomes unstable and collapses without causing any damage to it's surroundings."

"Well, thank you very much. All you lot have done is tell me what won't work! Why don't you tell me what will work, because I'm determined to do something very soon." Erik sat back in his chair, knocking over an empty coffee cup in the process.

"Look," said Laurie, trying to placate him, "we have to do it the right way, the police way. We're not terrorists and if we start acting like them, we'll be as bad as they are. We'll lose the support of all the organisations at present backing us, the police, the Bomb Squad, public opinion, you name it they're going to say we're thugs and not to be trusted. I'm as sure as you are that they're planning some atrocity; all the signs point that way. It could be tonight or tomorrow, we just don't know, but I can't imagine them going out anywhere much before eleven o'clock at night. They won't want to be noticed, so the fewer people about the better. The four of us, two in each car and very well armed with say a pump-action shotgun, sniper's rifles with night-vision scopes, stun grenades and handguns, could stake out their house and wait for them to make a move. What do the rest of you think?"

Hans spoke for the first time. "Our local armoury will never issue us with all that firepower."

With increasing enthusiasm, Erik looked around at the other three men. "We won't go to our local armoury. We'll go to the sergeant at the central armoury. As long as we sign the form, he'll be off the hook and there'll be no comeback on him afterwards if there's a cock-up. Laurie, my friend, you've hit the proverbial nail on the head, as usual. We can draw the arms and start on watch tonight. Do we all agree?"

They did.

Chapter 39

They had no difficulty withdrawing the weapons they wanted from the sergeant at the central armoury, who said sarcastically, "Remember, no blood or body parts on any of the weapons when you return them; it's very difficult to get them clean!"

At ten o'clock both cars arrived quietly on the scene. They had agreed before leaving that they should park each side of the gates, so that when the terrorists came out of the drive, their vehicle could be blocked.

"If they appear through the gates, we switch our lights fully on to dazzle and surprise them," Erik had told them. "If they make any attempt to ram either of our cars, shoot to kill, driver first. We mustn't hold back, otherwise we'll be the ones to die. We all know they'll not have the slightest compunction or hesitation about killing us; they're trained assassins."

Monday night produced nothing and they left the scene at 5 a.m. as it became light. Tuesday night was the same, and although they had slept during the day, their body clocks, being unused to the change in routine, left them feeling weary and out of sorts.

On Wednesday, they were all eating their evening meal at the hotel. Laurie was thinking about something that had been bothering him. Finally, he said to Erik, "I think there's a flaw in our plan and we've got to sort it out, otherwise we could lose our chance of getting them. We have to wait until their vehicles – if there's more than one – are completely outside the drive gates and on the public highway. If we hit them while part of their vehicle is still in the grounds of the house, technically we're trespassing. Unless we wait until they've turned left or right, they could reverse back into their compound. Then, because we have no authority to enter their property, if we attack them, we'll be totally in the wrong. You remember what happened last time. If that happens again, in complete darkness, the Armed Response Unit will shoot first, and as there's no way of identifying ourselves, it'll mean a shoot-out between two sets of armed policemen."

"Yes," agreed Erik. "I wonder what the papers and media would make of it when it all came to light? I can see the headlines now: Police shoot-out between officers on the same force, etc., etc. They'd have a field day, especially if there are any casualties!"

"I'm not joking," said Laurie. "So here's what we should do. We have to wait until they've turned into the road, as I said before, dazzle them with our headlights at full beam, and one of our cars has to get behind them to prevent them reversing before they've fully realised what's going on. It'll be a matter of split-second timing, because the other car has then to get in front of them so they can't drive off. We have to block them back and front in those few seconds while they're confused and disorientated. Then we can shout that we're armed police and they must get out of the car and put down any firearms they have. Not that I've much hope of them doing that. They'll probably try to ram us. But remember, as soon as you pull up, have your door open and your weapons ready and slip out quickly, keeping low, because that's when I think the shooting will start."

"You want us to take all our weapons with us?" asked Hans.

"Whichever you prefer to use, as long as you get out of the car pronto."

They all looked at each other, feeling slightly anxious, and tried to smile as they considered what they were going to do.

"Hopefully, the speed of our action and the dazzling headlamps will give us a few vital seconds of advantage, and considering everything, we may just carry it off," said Laurie. "You know they'll shoot to kill. They're highly trained and motivated by their beliefs, which have been drilled into them from infancy. They'll do anything to achieve their goals, so remember: there's none of this nonsense about giving them a fair chance and asking them to surrender, because to put it plainly, either they die or we die. End of sermon, I've finished."

Hugo cleared his throat. "It'd be very useful to know which direction they were going to turn when they get to the end of the drive. I don't suppose they'll be flashing their indicators!" he said.

"Erik, you know that part of the city," said Laurie. "Which way do you think they'll be heading?"

"I need to study a large-scale map closely, but I'd guess right, the driver would be heading into the city, left he'd be heading for the quieter, more residential area."

After their meal they returned to the office to study the wall map, trying to second-guess which way their assailants would turn.

"Okay," said Erik, "which team is going to take the left-hand position and which the right? They're both equally dangerous, so Hans and I will take the right, which leaves you and Hugo at the left. If you're ready, gentlemen, it's time to go."

They drove swiftly to take up their positions, trying to ignore their fast-beating hearts and the heightened awareness of what might come before the end of the night. They switched off their headlights and settled down to wait.

"What do we do if nothing happens tonight?" Hugo whispered to Laurie.

"We carry on tomorrow."

"What about Friday?"

"Friday, you go home as usual."

"But what about you, sir?"

"That'll probably depend on Erik, but I suppose we'll carry on until there's a result. Thanks for thinking about me, anyway."

Another night went by and nothing happened.

At the weekend, with both Hugo and Hans visiting their families, Laurie and Erik sat in the hotel bar trying to come to some decision about their next step.

"There's really no decision to make. Either we stay here in the hotel or go on night watch outside our terrorists' hiding place," Erik said lightly. "Personally, I'd rather go and resolve this situation once and for all. How about you?"

"In that case," said Laurie, "we'd better stay off the alcohol."

"That's a shame," joked Erik, "when I was just looking forward to imbibing large amounts of vodka and falling off my bar stool. Nevertheless, sacrifices must be made." Serious again, he continued, "I have this gut feeling that something definite will happen tonight."

They ate their meal and idled the time away until they needed to collect their cars and set out for their destination, each suddenly glad that they had no one with them, no one else to feel responsible for. They parked quietly at either side of the drive and settled into their usual routine, trying to keep themselves awake, almost convinced that nothing was going to happen.

Both were half asleep when they heard the low sound of a car engine being started. Laurie felt a surge of adrenalin and was suddenly wide-awake. He could see the dull reflection of dipped headlights behind the wall. The engine was turning over quietly, almost purring, and he knew that it would start moving at any moment.

Erik was equally wide-awake. The next thing he saw was the nose of a 4x4 vehicle appearing through the open gates. The driver hesitated, swiftly looking to see if the way was clear. Erik ducked down behind the dashboard for a split second to avoid being seen and heard the engine revving. Looking up, he could see that they were going to turn left, but for some reason the driver hesitated, as if waiting for something, and he knew that as soon as the driver did turn left, he would accelerate quickly, so he had to get into the right position to either follow him or overtake and block his progress. There didn't seem to be any response from Laurie, and Erik, grinding his teeth with fury, thought, if that bastard's fallen asleep, I'll kill him myself.

In the other car, Laurie was fuming, thinking what's the idiot waiting for – an invitation? Block the driver's retreat for God's sake!

Erik decided to start his car and switched his headlights on at full beam. He drove at the 4x4 too fast, ramming into its rear. Pulling on his handbrake, with his heart pumping like crazy, he flung open his door and slid out onto the road, holding his pump-action shotgun close to his chest, trying to escape the murderous firepower coming from the terrorists' vehicle. He saw Laurie's car slewed across the road, thankfully blocking the forward escape route, and Laurie was trying to shelter from the heavy gunfire which was slowly annihilating his car.

Erik took what cover he could and started to aim for the rear of the 4x4, nearly taking the back panel off, such was the firepower of his gun. He dodged back behind his car, but not before he saw the passengers desperately trying to focus on his position. Someone managed to escape from the car and was running, keeping low and weaving from side to side in an effort to avoid bullets, making for the comparative safety of the house.

Erik yelled to Laurie, "Shoot him! If he reaches the house we'll never get him!"

Laurie dropped onto one knee, took careful aim at the moving figure and shot twice, bringing the man down before he could reach comparative safety. A split second later came the flash of a bullet from the 4x4, and to his horror, Erik saw Laurie crash down as if pole-axed.

Coldly and systematically, Erik kept up a fusillade of shots at the terrorists' vehicle until he ran out of ammunition, then fumbled inside his car and brought out another gun he'd stashed under the seat. He carried on firing until in a sudden and unnerving silence, all firing from the ruined vehicle ceased. The silence was deafening. Erik shook his head to try and clear his thoughts and carefully walked towards the 4x4. There were three bodies in the car, all dead – he made quite sure of that – so he turned to where he'd seen Laurie go down after taking a bullet in his back. He blinked rapidly, a confused line of thinking going round in his head. Amazed, he saw Laurie stagger to his feet and struggle to get to the man he had shot, intent on making sure his bullet had finished the job as he had intended. Erik felt light-headed and sauntered over to his friend in the unnerving silence.

"You all right?" he asked laconically. "Need any help? Could have sworn you were hit; saw a flash from the 4x4 and thought you might be swinging the lead, trying to get a few days' extra leave if you were wounded."

Laurie grinned. "Which 4x4 are you talking about? You mean that heap of wreckage at the end of the drive?"

As an overwhelming feeling of relief came over them that now, hopefully, they had completed what they had set out to do, they shook hands solemnly, grinning like idiots at each other. Laurie winced slightly and Erik asked him where he'd been hit, getting out his phone to call in the paramedics and all the other departments who would have to be notified about this confrontation. Rather shamefacedly, Laurie explained that he'd not been hit; when he had aimed at the terrorist, in the excitement of the moment he'd forgotten the powerful recoil from his gun and as a result, the jerk to his shoulder had nearly dislocated it, at least it felt like that. When Erik had enthusiastically shaken his hand, his arm had throbbed.

"But for heaven's sake, don't tell anyone I'm injured or I'll be laughed off the police force and never live it down," he pleaded.

Erik couldn't stop laughing and when he had finished his calls, told Laurie that he would expect a great many favours from him in the future if he was not to regale the rest of the department with the funniest story of the decade.

"Let's get our story straight before anybody turns up," Erik said, serious once more. "How does this sound: we were following a tip-off from an informer about a couple of terrorists we had our eyes on and they led us to this house. We staked out the place for three nights and nothing happened, but tonight, this 4x4 came speeding down the drive, so we jumped out of our cars and shouted at them to stop, telling them that we were police officers conducting an investigation, but they only slowed down a little. That's when the shooting started. We were forced to take cover and return fire, if only to protect ourselves."

"And what about our cars blocking their vehicle front and rear?" asked Laurie.

"We did that before the shooting started, when we shouted to them to stop."

"Okay, go on," said Laurie.

Erik continued, giving full rein to his inventive streak. "You only have to look at the state of the two police cars to appreciate the very real danger we were in. We thought that the suspected terrorists were not going to give either of us a chance to stay alive to, er, tell the tale. One of them made a break for it, trying to get back into the house, and my brave colleague chased after him while I covered his back by continually firing at the car. I saw the flash of a shot going in your direction, saw you go down and thought you'd been killed, so I kept firing until there was no response. How does that sound? Any flaws, loopholes? Do you think the powers that be will believe our version of events?"

"We've got to hope that they do, otherwise things could get tricky for us. God, I could do with a stiff drink right at this moment. Any convenient bars nearby?"

They leant against the wall, wondering if the shooting had woken any of the other residents in the street, but if it had, no lights were on and no one appeared. It was another thirty minutes before the cavalry arrived in the form of the Bomb Squad, Forensics and two policemen with yards of white tape to seal off the surrounding area.

A man from Forensics looked inside the 4x4 and turned to Erik with an amazed expression on his face. "Have you two done all this?"

Erik launched into a brief explanation of the circumstances, broadly keeping to the lines he and Laurie had agreed upon. "I thought they'd shot and killed Inspector Mueller, so I kept on firing at them to prevent them killing me and getting away," he said defensively.

"The inside of this vehicle looks like a battle zone, not that I can't appreciate that you did what you had to do in that situation. But you do realise, don't you, that this has destroyed a lot of important forensic evidence?" said the man plaintively.

As a reaction to their recent gamble with death, Erik could barely contain his impatience with this attitude, but Laurie murmured a calming word in his ear, emphasising just how precarious their situation was if the facts came out.

Between gritted teeth, Erik managed to say, "Oh, I don't think you'll be short of forensic evidence for your investigation; there's plenty to keep you all occupied for weeks and you haven't even started on the house. Wait till the Bomb Squad have been through it and discovered any booby traps, and you can forage to your heart's content! Is it all right if my fellow hero and myself go for a well-deserved drink before we both fall down with exhaustion?"

The man looked doubtful. He was not officially in charge of the incident, but he knew enough about procedure to know that these two should not leave the area until they had been fully checked out by the paramedics, who would make a discreet assessment of their state of mind. After all, if they were insane, gun-toting mass murderers, it wouldn't look very good on his CV if he let them disappear into the nearest bar without having been checked over! He looked around for anybody senior to him so he could offload his problem. Laurie, seeing the difficult situation he was in, said to Erik, "Let's go up to the house and see if the Bomb Squad have found anything interesting. I'd like to know if there's some evidence of what they've been up to in the past few weeks while we've been tailing them. That drink'll have to wait until we've had a look round, or before we know it they'll be breathalysing us and saying we imagined it all!" He steered Erik off in the direction of the house, and the forensics man watched them stroll up the drive before turning to the much more interesting examination of the badly damaged vehicle.

They were soon questioning the leader of the Bomb Squad team, who had been hastily promoted after Alberto's death; they all had some memories of the last time they met after the airport bomb. Erik spotted a police inspector, newly arrived on the scene, who greeted them with: "Looks as though there was a battle royal here. What have you been getting yourself involved in now?"

Erik introduced Inspector Grunwald to Laurie and replied with great dignity, "What makes you think this is my handiwork? My colleague here was the one who did all the shooting; I was just here trying to keep him out of trouble, him being a German foreigner!"

Laurie shrugged his shoulders and said, "Unfortunately, it was necessary. There were only the two of us without any backup and there were four terrorists shooting at us. Odds of fifty to one, so if we hadn't returned their fire, we wouldn't be here talking to you."

"I'm not criticising you," Grunwald said, "just sorry it had to happen on my shift. You wouldn't believe the paperwork I'll have to do to cover all aspects of this." He waved his hand vaguely, taking in the ruined vehicles, the gardens and the house. "And I'll have to interview you both as well when the paramedics have checked you out!"

"May I ask a bit of a favour from you?" said Erik. "We've been on night duty for the past week and we're dead beat. Can we leave things in your capable hands so that we can get back to our beds for a couple of hours' shut-eye? Then our brains can function in the morning. I should think all hell will break loose then and we'll be called on to account for every bullet fired!"

Grunwald looked around, quickly assessing the immediate situation, and mentally ticked off the progress made so far. "Bomb Squad clearing the house of any explosive devices, Forensics checking every minute speck of evidence; there's no fire so the fire service won't be needed, and in any case, nothing must be disturbed until they give the all-clear, which, in my experience, will be about six months ahead! Hopefully we can keep the press and media at a distance, so you two had better be anonymous in the meantime until the Chief's decided how he wants to play this situation. When we get the okay, the bodies can be removed to the mortuary for post mortem. The only thing I need to ask you is to check your weapons back into the armoury. They'll have to be examined to trace which bullets were fired from which gun, you know the drill; and a very detailed report will be necessary, given the difficult circumstances in this incident." He gave them a quick, sideways glance and said in a low tone, "I hope you both know what you've got yourselves into. This has all the makings of an international diplomatic incident, so make very sure you get your version of events straight. Watch your backs, because it would be a shame to have any glitches occurring in your careers at this stage of the game, and as you well know, if a scapegoat is needed, one of you will be sacrificed on the altar of diplomacy!"

"Tut, tut," said Erik, returning his look. "As if such things could happen in this day and age. Come on, Laurie, let's get back to civilisation and check in our weapons at the armoury. After that we might well be able to get a drink or three."

"We'll need a lift to get back to HQ," Laurie said. "Both our cars will probably be write-offs, and besides, they'll no doubt be needed for evidence."

A vehicle and driver were eventually found to take them to the armoury, where they handed over the weapons they had checked out.

"What about all that spare ammo I let you have?" queried the sergeant in charge with a questioning look and a lifted eyebrow. "Never tell me you used it all!"

"It was a very tense situation," said Erik defensively. "There was a lot of shooting, and if I were you, I would be very careful to store each gun separately in a labelled container, duly signed and witnessed, as I think there's going to be a great deal of interest shown in them. Come to think of it, Laurie, I'm not sure we should have removed them from the scene. Perhaps we ought to hang on to them, because if they were to disappear mysteriously…" He turned to the sergeant. "You're my witness and I want a signed statement from you, here and now, that Inspector Mueller and I have handed back to you the exact weapons we checked out earlier this week. I don't want there to be any confusion about this, now or at any future time."

The sergeant looked at his tense, white face and, grumbling, took out a pen and some writing paper and wrote out the statement Erik had demanded. He gave him the paper and took exaggerated care to put each weapon into a separate bag and clearly labelled them. "Does that satisfy you, Mon General?" he said sarcastically.

"Yeah, great," said Erik, stuffing the sheet of paper into his jacket pocket and feeling vaguely satisfied with his cautious action. "Right, driver," he said, "drop us somewhere in the city within easy reach of women and booze and you've done your duty for tonight!" Once they were in the car, he said to Laurie, "You didn't want to go back to the hotel, did you?"

Laurie shook his head. "No, we need some time to unwind after all that's happened tonight. Lead me to wherever the drinks are cheap and the women are pricey, or do I mean it the other way round?" He started to laugh at his poor joke and Erik sighed.

"You must be in need of both to try and crack a joke like that at this time of the night, or I should say morning," he said.

They ended up in a place Erik knew and ordered a large glass of beer each. Relaxing in the comfortable chairs, they started to come to terms with what had happened to them that evening.

"I was worried when I saw you fall," Erik said abruptly.

"You were worried; how do you think I felt with bullets whistling past my head?" said Laurie. "I fell down and played dead and hoped they'd stop firing."

"I made sure of that," said Erik smugly. "I kept on firing until there was no returning fire. When they stopped firing I went and made quite sure they were all dead."

"You do realise that we've killed four people tonight, don't you?" said Laurie.

"Of course I do, but I ceased to regard them as human beings when I considered the inhuman, sadistic torture they performed on blameless people who simply happened to be in their way. The little man from the estate agency; he never deserved what they did to him, poor bugger, and how many other people have they killed in their short, busy careers, setting the world to rights, according to them? No, the only regret I have is that we couldn't have done it sooner."

"How does that make you feel about Asian and Muslim people?"

"If these four were Muslims they bore no relation to the ones you meet every day! The Muslims you know are the ones who live on the same street as you or the same block of apartments and are aiming for the best they can achieve for themselves and their children; they're hard working, honest and polite and they just want to get on with their lives. The terrorist organisation attracts the worst kind of thugs and sadists, no matter how they try to disguise it as religion, and they kill those who don't agree with their view of civilisation. If they ever had consciences, these absolve them from feeling any guilt. Right, that's enough about tonight's events. We'll have to go over it time and time again in the near future, so let's think about something else. Are there any good-looking women in here waiting to be seduced?"

"You randy sod," said Laurie. "You're going to see Christina in less than twenty-four hours."

"Yes, but that's tomorrow and they say that fear makes you want to have sex – something to do with the need to reproduce before your life ends, or so I've been told. How about trying two working girls?"

"No thanks. I've never been with one and I'm not going to start now. But you go ahead, if that's what you want."

"What, and leave you all on your own, sitting here, getting drunk without me?"

"I have my mum's permission to wear long trousers and go out on my own," said Laurie, laughing.

"So if I leave you alone, you'll be all right?"

"You go, my friend. You probably saved my life tonight, so I'll just sit here and wait for you with my beer to keep me company. But don't forget to come back here, or if it's going to be an all-night thing, phone me, cos I don't want to end up sleeping here. I have a very comfortable bed back at the hotel and I'm really going to enjoy getting into a hot shower and sleeping for a week."

"Don't worry; I'll be back before you know it!"

"Bragging again. Mind you don't bring anything back with you; you know, something you could pass on to Christina."

"Of course not," said Erik scornfully, already half drunk. "That's reserved for the tourists, but I know better. See you later."

Laurie sat comfortably relaxed in his chair, sipping his beer and feeling happy, because for once they were getting somewhere with their investigations. He looked round the room, studying the faces of the other people. As his glance slowly encompassed the room, he realised that there were a number of attractive women present and suddenly realised what he must look like, straight from a gun battle, crawling over the grass to escape the bullets, possibly covered with soil and mud. Not being a vain man, he hadn't checked himself before they came out. Leaving his beer on the table, he found the toilets and grimaced at himself in the mirror. He'd seen better-looking tramps. He did his best with soap and water, brushing the mud from his jacket and trousers and combing his hair into some semblance of order. He went back to his beer, feeling a little happier, and noticed two younger women, one of whom was indicating a 'thumbs-up' to him. It must mean that there had been an improvement in his appearance. He signalled his thanks to them and was rewarded by a smile and a little wave of the hand, beckoning him in their direction.

Erik returned to the bar a couple of hours later and glanced around to the place where he had left Laurie sitting. Two couples now occupied the seats, and he wondered where Laurie was. He spotted him eventually, sitting with two attractive young women.

"I see you were expecting me," he said as he picked up the beer Laurie had just got for himself.

Laurie introduced him guardedly, not being quite sure of his reaction, but Erik dragged up another chair and plunged into conversation with the two girls.

When the girls decided it was time to go home, Erik and Laurie saw them safely into a taxi and then flagged one down for themselves. Half an hour later they were both fast asleep in their hotel rooms.

Chapter 40

What seemed just moments later, but was in fact 8.30 in the morning, the phone began to ring monotonously and continually, waking Laurie from the depths of slumber. Groggily, he picked up the receiver and was told by Erik's Chief that he was wanted at a meeting at ten o'clock and to make sure that Erik was with him, as so far they had been unable to wake him.

Laurie tried to ignore a partial hangover and aching muscles while he got ready and then went to find Erik. He was not in his room and the cleaning staff looked blank when he asked them where the occupant was. He was very glad when he went into the restaurant to find him cheerfully eating his breakfast and consuming large quantities of strong black coffee.

"For heaven's sake sit down," he said to Laurie. "If you feel as bad as you look, you should have come with me last night and enjoyed a little relaxation!"

Laurie wondered how he was able to appear so cheerful after the night they had experienced, but that was Erik. He told him about the meeting they were commanded to attend at Headquarters with his Chief, and Erik groaned. "Now it starts, the inquest and post mortem and why we did what we did; and I bet you they won't give us any medals. Be prepared for a very tough attitude – they don't like junior inspectors taking it into their heads to carry out assignments they haven't been instructed, in triplicate, to do. Hold onto your sense of humour but don't show it!"

They were shown into the Chief's office, where he and a chief inspector were waiting for them, to be greeted with the words: "I'd like to know what the hell you two were up to last night."

Erik took a swift sideways look at Laurie and said politely, "I'm not quite sure what you mean, sir."

"What I mean is that the two of you have killed four young men and destroyed a Toyota 4x4 vehicle, caused two police vehicles to become complete write-offs and used enough bullets to provide spent cartridges to fill two buckets. You seem to have started World War Three all on your own."

Erik spoke carefully and clearly. "Well, sir, it would appear that we've destroyed a terrorist cell which had been causing mayhem throughout our country and Germany, to say nothing of possible plans to cause havoc in Great Britain. We exposed their safe house and we have, I think, prevented them from causing any more damage in the immediate future. Further than that, I wouldn't like to say, but it might be considered fully justified for the mere loss of a few bullets and two slightly damaged police cars, the only reason for my using one being that this same cell tried to blow me up in mine. They also shot at me in another attempt to kill me, and Inspector Mueller can tell you of the murders they committed in his neck of the woods. With all due respect, sir, I think our devotion to duty in trailing and annihilating these men, at great risk to ourselves, amounts to…" He trailed to a halt, unable to think of the right word.

"Cocky lot, aren't they?" said the Chief to the Chief Inspector. Turning to the two men, he said, "Tell us how it happened."

"Well, sir, our investigations gave a strong indication that the house we were watching contained a bomb-making workshop and four, or possibly more, assassins just waiting for an opportunity to strike. As you know, sir, they've already tried to blow up the police station and we have reason to think they tortured and murdered a clerk who worked in the estate agency who rented them the house. His body was found and the post mortem showed that he'd been made to suffer; I won't go into the gory details. Yesterday, we decided to continue our surveillance, although we had done this for the four previous nights with no result, not even a light going on at the front of the house. We had no concrete evidence to apply for a search warrant so, as before, we parked in the street outside the drive to the house, starting at ten o'clock in the evening. Because there were only two of us – our sergeants are on weekend leave – we made sure we were well armed with pump-action shotguns and hunting rifles with night-vision scopes and used two police cars so that in the event they left the property and failed to stop when requested, we could block their route both front and rear. The grounds of the house are surrounded by two-metre-high walls, and the only way in or out is through a metal gate.

"At about midnight, they emerged onto the road through this metal gate and turned onto the road, a public highway. We blocked their way and shouted that we were armed police officers and wanted to ask them some questions about an incident which had taken place recently. That's when they started firing. We had to take evasive action by getting out of our vehicles and returning fire and it was then that the Toyota 4x4 was damaged. They carried on firing at our cars, which led to quite a lot of damage, and then one of the suspected terrorists tried to head back to the house. Inspector Mueller pursued and shot him. I thought he'd been hit by their random fire, so I was left with only one option: to keep firing until they surrendered, which as you know, sir, eventually led to them all being killed. If Inspector Mueller hadn't pursued the escaping man and therefore drawn their attention to himself, it would have been three to one against me and the firepower would have overwhelmed me. As it happened…" He threw a quick glance at Laurie. "Inspector Mueller had thrown himself onto the ground to escape their bullets and fortunately only suffered bruises to his arm and shoulder."

"Why didn't you call for backup?" the Chief asked abruptly.

Laurie decided that it was time he opened his mouth and answered the question. "Sir, all this happened in just a few minutes. We were crouched against our vehicles and with all the noise going on, we had to concentrate on protecting ourselves; there was simply no time to radio for help."

The Chief tapped his fingers on the top of his desk before saying, almost grudgingly, "There's no doubt you've both acted very bravely in incredibly difficult circumstances, but there's also no doubt that there's a lot more to this than you're telling me. However, we'll let this go for the moment. We're still waiting for confirmation that all four men were terrorists. Have we any way to verify this?" Erik told him about the weapons left at the scene, the forensic evidence which would be found in the house and Inspector Mueller's video film of three of them arriving at Frankfurt Airport as they went through passport control. "Are they good quality videos, clearly showing these men?" asked the Chief.

Laurie nodded. "Very clear, sir."

"Why were they not arrested then?"

"Well, sir, they came in several days apart, one at a time. Their passports were in perfect order and they were well-dressed, polite young men with absolutely nothing suspicious about them. It wasn't until one of the airport employees started to rethink the situation, after there'd been a terrorist incident, that he was struck by the similarity of the type of young men – it was just a gut reaction, sir. Then the coincidences were noticed."

"Yes, I understand that," said the Chief. "And with the new human rights rulings we have to be very careful not to tread on anyone's toes, so to speak. Chief Inspector, do you have any questions you'd like to ask at this point?"

"No, sir, I think they've covered the main points. I would just like to add that in the circumstances, they've done well. If the four men do not prove to be terrorists, they're obviously top level villains with that amount of firepower in their possession and were probably about to commit some crime."

The Chief of Police shook hands with Laurie and Erik and told them to go and enjoy what remained of their weekend.

Outside the office, they both heaved a sigh of relief.

"That was skilfully done," said Laurie admiringly. "How did you manage to avoid all the subjects which would've been difficult to deal with, but make it sound as if you were explaining everything in minute detail and not missing out anything important?"

"Okay, okay," shrugged Erik, "but we did some good work too!"

"You mean I did most of it," Laurie said, making a face.

"Did you now." Erik sounded somewhat irritated.

"I'll let you win this time," said Laurie.

"Let's face it," said Erik, "one way or another we got away with it all for the one and a half hours we spent being interrogated in that office. If it hadn't been for my skill in telling the story, we'd have been in that office till the Chief of Police and the Chief Inspector had fallen asleep, which would have been some time tonight!"

"Remind me to mint a special medal for the number one storyteller supreme," laughed Laurie, "and I know where I'll put it when it's presented to you."

"Thanks for your appreciation. It's nice to be well thought of. Now, let's go back to the hotel for a well-deserved lunch. You can pay because you made sure I spent all my money last night, or do I mean this morning? It's all becoming a bit confusing, what with lack of sleep and telling inspired versions or events."

"Why the hotel?" queried Laurie. "I thought you were feeling trapped and isolated having to spend all your spare time in a luxury hotel with nearly every facility you could think of, except one, at the press of a button – so you said to me the other day."

"Well, look at it like this: you can charge everything to expenses but our country isn't as rich as yours and our police budget is very tight, so any hotel payments are charged to the central police expenses account but meals are claimed on a separate system. There, have I explained it clearly to you?"

Erik was enjoying himself hugely, laughing at the baffled look on Laurie's face, who in the end said, "I give up; let's go eat!"

Chapter 41

Monday morning arrived only too soon, and when Laurie and Erik got to the office they gave their sergeants a brief outline of what had happened. Their reactions were mixed: they regretted missing the action but were thankful that they had avoided the danger. They both secretly wondered what they would have done had they been present.

"Do you mean to say you shot four men who were trying to escape from that house we were watching?" said Hugo, unable to believe it.

"You'd better believe it. And for that moment of doubt about your senior officers, you'll now come to the morgue and view the bodies," said Laurie.

They took prints from the videos from Frankfurt Airport to use for identification. The men's features could clearly be recognised.

"At least now we can inform the families of the two dead police officers in Germany, the wife of the estate agency clerk and Alberto's wife and children that the men who killed them have been brought to justice and are themselves now dead. As if that's really any consolation," Laurie said sadly.

Erik said quietly, "This finishes our part of the investigation for the time being, but I don't suppose it's the end of the problem. Have you two seen enough bodies for today?"

Hugo and Hans nodded.

Back in the office they tried to settle into a routine by catching up with the paperwork, typing their report for the Chief Inspector and waiting for the preliminary findings of Forensics. After three days of unexciting routine, they received news from Forensics that they had found definite traces of at least nine people staying in the house. This meant that five of them were still at large; they must have left before they had started the surveillance.

"At least they'll not be able to use that house again," said Hugo.

"I'm not so sure about that," said Erik. "When the police investigations are finished, the house must be handed back to the owner. If the rent's been paid for say a year in advance, the terrorists might slip in some new faces. At the end of the day, there's no legal reason why they shouldn't occupy a property they've paid the rent for."

"I don't think they'd dare do that; it's too much of a risk for them. But when the police have finished there, who knows?" Laurie said. "We won't be able to enter the house again without a search warrant, and we all know how difficult it is to obtain one of them!"

A gloomy silence descended on the group.

"For the moment, there's not a lot we can do except keep our ears open," said Erik. "And let's all cheer up; this isn't the end of the world."

Chapter 42

The following Saturday, a red Ford car pulled up at the airport entrance gate, driven by a young Asian man with a passenger. He politely asked where he could park his vehicle, as he and his friend were returning on Wednesday afternoon from Geneva. The attendant replied that when they got inside the airport perimeter, they would be shown where the short-stay car park was situated, but in the meantime, would he just get out of the car and open the boot.

"But we're going to Geneva on the two-thirty flight and we'll be back by Wednesday," said the young man. "I've only got a couple of holdalls in there and we'll check those in as usual."

"Yes, sir, but I'd still like you to open your boot for me," said the attendant implacably.

"Do you check the boot of all the cars which come through here or is it just because I'm Asian?" the young man asked.

"Please open the boot of your car, sir."

"You're picking on us because we're Asian. This is a violation of our human rights and we're going to complain to the highest authority about your attitude!"

"I don't want to have to repeat this again, sir, but please step out of your car and open the boot."

An armed policeman moved forward to back up the airport official as the driver said shrilly, "What will you do if I just drive straight through the gates?"

Calmly, the policeman said, "We're all fully armed and I strongly advise you to do as you've been asked. You're not going to drive into the airport until both your car and yourselves have been fully searched."

It was a battle of wills and no one was going to be the first to stand down.

As the policeman advanced towards the car, with his weapon pointing at the driver, the engine started and the car reversed at top speed with a shrieking of tyres, did a three-point turn and headed off at top speed towards the city.

The policeman was on his radio immediately. "Suspect red Ford car." He gave details of the registration number. "Carrying two young males, Asian in appearance, heading away from the airport towards the city. The suspects could be armed and dangerous. Use extreme caution to apprehend, as the car could be carrying explosives." He repeated his message, which was relayed to all Armed Response Units, who were told to intercept and arrest the suspects.

The red car turned left and headed west, then turned to head east, as if they were not sure of their direction. Eventually, they turned onto the A9, then the A2, heading south. A police helicopter was launched and concentrated on the city area. A message went out to all police cars within thirty miles of Amsterdam to look out for the red vehicle and to report any sightings to Police HQ. The vehicle was approaching Utrecht, still on the A2.

The first sighting of the car was beyond Utrecht, but the police car was going in the opposite direction. The driver reported the sighting, but by the time he could turn around, the red car was out of sight. The police helicopter was diverted onto the A2, but by now it was well behind the fast moving vehicle, so police in Eindhoven were alerted and asked to intercept it on the A2, but the car turned onto the A15, heading west, and then onto the A27, heading for Breda. There was a sighting just before it got to the outskirts of Breda. This time the police car was facing in the right direction and hotly pursued it with lights flashing and sirens blaring. Another police car containing members of the Armed Response Unit joined the pursuit as the red Ford turned off the main highway and onto a deserted country road. It seemed to increase speed, the driver, no doubt, hoping that the lack of traffic would enable him to out-distance his pursuers, unaware that the helicopter had spotted them from the air and was now closing in. The first police car was gaining when a bullet shattered their windscreen, completely obscuring their vision and causing them to pull off the road. The following Armed Response car accelerated past them, gradually overtaking the red car's erratically driven course; the driver, although an expert, was not as experienced as the Armed Response driver and the Ford was not built to travel at these excessive speeds.

The two men realised that their situation was desperate and the passenger turned and began to fire high-velocity bullets at the chasing police car. One of the Armed Response team was forced to lean out of the car and try to shoot out the tyres. Whether it was a tyre, a wheel or perhaps the boot, there was a massive explosion and the red car completely disintegrated, vanishing into deadly shards of shrapnel, which rained down on the police, who were desperately trying to avoid the wreckage. There was a huge pall of smoke and pieces of the burning car fell onto the road. It was a long moment before the police officers could make sure they were all uninjured, although their car would probably end up on the scrap heap. They radioed in, requesting the fire and ambulance services, and on shaky legs got out of their car and leaned against it, out of the way of the smoke and heat. There didn't seem much point in checking to see if anyone was alive in that inferno: the odds were thousands against.

The driver said to his team-mate, "What the hell were you shooting at?"

"I was aiming at the right-hand tyre, more or less."

"Well, it looks as though you hit the petrol tank."

"Don't think so; just hitting the tank makes petrol spill all over the road and the bullet usually goes straight through."

"Hey, I just remembered," said the driver. "Didn't they say that the car was stopped by the guard at the airport gate? These two bastards must have planned to leave it in the car park and fly off somewhere with explosives timed to go off after they'd left. The short-stay car park is so near the airport buildings, it would have caused major damage, destruction and probably numerous fatalities. What did we ever do to them?"

"I know what I'd like to do to them, if they weren't already in hell."

CHAPTER 43

It was the following day before Erik, Laurie, Hans and Hugo heard about the chase and the explosion.

"Maybe they were hoping the four of us would be there when it went off," Laurie said thoughtfully. "The bomb disposal team reckon it was four times as powerful as the last one, going by the size of the crater left in the road!"

"What happened to the people in the car?" asked Hugo.

"There wasn't much left after what happened, maybe not even enough for identification purposes," explained Laurie.

"We're not safe now, any more than last time, are we?" said Erik.

"It's not quite the same; the car had Belgian number plates so it could have been a special unit sent from there, but I was under the impression that we had police looking out for Asian men, especially young men travelling on their own, at border crossings," queried Laurie.

"I'm going to find out what's gone wrong here," said Erik, picking up the phone. After about an hour, he put the phone down. "According to my colleagues, every border crossing is manned by police with instructions to stop and search any car carrying men of Asian appearance, but nothing was reported. So we have to assume that no car of that description attempted to cross into Holland yesterday. Of course, it could have crossed several days ago, in which case where were they hiding? It was also the only way they could smuggle large amounts of explosives into the country."

"We know one way they could do it: in a large removal van or something similar," said Laurie. "But it would still have to be unloaded inside a large shed or warehouse and then an expert would have to make it into a bomb. If anyone had seen them unloading, it would've looked really odd, and they wouldn't want anybody seeing them and asking questions."

"That's very true," agreed Erik. "It seems a very difficult way to go about it, but they've done it before."

"Yes, but before they actually took the car right into the airport, and they had an accomplice, albeit an unwilling one. How could they get a van, load it in Belgium and drive it over the border, find a place to unload it uninterrupted and then send it back to Belgium? It's not on," said Laurie.

"I suppose they might have paid someone enough money and told them some cock and bull story to get them to do it. After all, it seems as if they don't stop commercial vehicles at the border, so the driver would have no problems crossing back, particularly with an empty van," said Erik.

"But what would such a person think if these two insisted on travelling in the back of the vehicle? How would it look?" Laurie asked.

Erik mulled over the idea. "They wouldn't sit in the cab with the driver and the vehicle would just go past the policeman at the crossing without any difficulty with two men in the back."

"You could be right; that's one way of getting away with it," said Laurie.

They sat in silence, mulling over this latest idea, until Erik looked round and asked if anyone had anything to contribute.

Hugo spoke up. "I think there are a lot of ifs and buts about the van theory. Wouldn't it be a lot easier for them to get a young Asian woman with a small baby to travel with them in a car? She doesn't have to even know them; she could just be told that they'd give her so much money if she travelled with them to Amsterdam. Once in the city, they could buy her a rail ticket to get her home again. Three men, a woman and a baby would arouse no suspicion at all and would have no difficulty crossing the border, particularly if one of them posed as her husband."

"You're right, Sergeant," agreed Erik. "That would certainly divert any suspicion away from them. So what happens next?"

"We follow up on this theory," said Laurie, "and start checking railway stations, asking if someone bought a mother and baby a single ticket to a town in Belgium and if so, were they of Asian appearance. One thing that strikes me is that Asian women very rarely travel anywhere alone, but the only way to find out is to ask. I suppose the time would be roughly between ten and twelve o'clock in the morning."

"Could I just ask why we're doing all this?" said a rather puzzled Hans.

"Because we want to know if they came here from Belgium or if they're local," Laurie explained. "If they're local it means there's another terrorist cell still present in Amsterdam, and that would mean that for all our recent efforts we're no better off and are still in danger. If they were sent from Belgium or anywhere else for that matter, we're now clear of suspected terrorists, at least in Amsterdam."

"Okay, I see where you're heading," said Hans cheerfully. "Let's get going."

At the railway station, they split into four and started asking traders who worked on the station if they had seen a young Asian couple with a baby buying a ticket during the previous morning.

The woman serving behind the counter at the news stand told Laurie that she had seen a couple very similar to that, and something had struck her as a bit odd because the woman, not much more than a girl really, had what looked like twenty-euro notes in her hand, but not just one, a thick wad of them. "Anyway," she went on, "she was holding the baby and trying to stuff this wad of money into a little shopping bag, and her husband never even gave her a hand or offered to hold the baby while she was struggling like that. Some men have no idea how difficult it is to manage a wriggling baby. And then he went off and left her to get her own ticket. I ask you."

"Yes, I'm sure," said Laurie politely, "but would this have been say ten to twelve o'clock yesterday morning?"

Well into her stride about the iniquities of young husbands leaving struggling mothers with small babies, she carried on. "I thought he could at least have waited until she put the money away, because there are people who prey on passengers round here and wouldn't think twice before knocking her down and running off with a large amount like that. Anyway, in the end she managed it and, poor thing, I don't think she could read the signs, because it took her some time before she managed to get to the right ticket window. I think she got a bit lost, but eventually she must have found the right one and I didn't see after that. She only had to come and ask me and I would've helped," she said triumphantly.

Finally escaping, Laurie went to the ticket window indicated by his chatty informant and showed the ticket officer his warrant card. "I'm a police inspector making enquiries about an incident. Were you working here yesterday between ten and twelve o'clock?"

"Yes, I was on duty yesterday. What's it about?"

So far so good, thought Laurie. "Do you remember a young Asian woman with a baby, buying a ticket?"

"There were a lot of people buying tickets yesterday. I don't know if I recall that one."

"This woman had a small baby in her arms and might have been holding some twenty-euro notes in her hand; she might have appeared confused or a bit lost."

"Wait a minute; I do remember such a person, yes, that's it. She was a bit unsure where exactly she wanted to go. At first she kept on saying 'Belgium' and I tried to explain it to her. In the end, I started to read out a few destinations to her, 'cause the queue was starting to build up and people was beginning to get impatient, and when I came to Bruxelles, she just nodded with a smile, so I sold her a ticket and that was the last I saw of her; she just disappeared into the station. That's all I can tell you, officer."

Laurie was exultant. "You've been a great help. Thanks a lot." He went in search of the rest of the team to tell them the news.

Erik was amazed at the speed with which they'd gleaned the information. "Let's get back to the office and discuss this," he said. "Where are we now exactly?" he asked back at the police station.

"I think we just confirmed that there are now no terrorist cells or safe houses in Amsterdam, and I'd think the same goes for the whole of the country, although we can't rule it out completely," said Laurie.

"That makes a great deal of sense," said Erik. "I can't imagine them sending a team all the way from Belgium and risking a stop and search at a border crossing if they still had anybody left on the spot."

"So what's going to happen to our little group?" asked Hans.

Laurie sighed, not knowing whether to be pleased or disappointed. "Hugo and I go back to our jobs in Frankfurt."

"Was there anyone doing your job while you were away?" asked Erik.

"Probably, but we were sent on this assignment by the Chief Constable, so it'll be back to the same sort of thing, I assume."

"So you have faith in your Chief do you?" queried Hans.

"I'll ring Police HQ in the morning and find out what the Chief has in mind for us, but tonight we celebrate! If we do it in the hotel, we can put it all on the bill. What about you, Hans; can you make it for tonight?"

"You just try and stop me."

"Good; that means the whole team can celebrate and the German police will pay the bill, seeing as your country is so poor. What time shall we meet?"

"Straight after work. I've got some reports to finish," said Erik.

"I don't suppose Hugo and I'll need to come to the office in the morning, so this will be a farewell party."

"What will happen if the higher ranks say they want us to continue the investigation into Belgium?" asked Erik.

"There's nothing to carry on for; the two men I was following have died, the link is broken and, as far as I know, the terror cell in Belgium isn't active. If it's not active, there's nothing to pursue. You know the old saying – if it's not broke, don't try to mend it."

"Are you saying that we don't pursue terrorist groups unless they're actually blowing things up and killing people?" asked Hans.

"Look, there are a lot of evil people all around the world, in every country on this planet, but you know the law: everyone is innocent until proven guilty, so that's the way we have to play it," said Laurie.

"I'll miss you two," said Erik. "We've been through quite a lot together these past few months. I can't say it hasn't been exciting and we worked well together."

The following morning, Laurie phoned the Chief at Frankfurt Police HQ to tell him of the outcome of their assignment and suggested that he and his sergeant returned without delay. There was just the tiniest hesitation in the Chief's voice as he said heartily, "Well, it's great to hear that everything turned out so well and I look forward to seeing you in person. But in the meantime, you both deserve a couple of weeks' leave. I'm sure you have some owed to you, so take some time off and I'll see you next month."

Trying not to sound accusing, Laurie asked, "You haven't given my job to someone else, have you, sir?"

"Another officer had to fill your post temporarily, while you were absent on this special assignment, but I assure you," said the Chief, trying to sound sincere, "it was only a stop-gap solution and a short period of time is needed for the officers to, er, complete their paperwork before they can hand the job back to you."

Laurie thought that he would call the Chief's bluff. "Oh good, sir. In that case we can start taking over the day after tomorrow, because we're flying back tonight." He knew he had to act swiftly to outmanoeuvre the foxy Chief, because if he took two weeks' leave, by the time he got back his job would have disappeared. He thought dispassionately that perhaps they had expected him to get killed.

That afternoon, Laurie and Hugo said a last goodbye to Erik and Hans, packed their few belongings and flew back to Frankfurt.

"It's going to be odd speaking German all the time after we became so fluent in Dutch," mused Laurie, "although you were back here every weekend, so it won't seem so different for you."

Chapter 44

On the outskirts of Islamabad, the three men held a meeting at their usual venue. The man in the centre of the trio said, "We've received a message from our benefactor. We are to stop our policy of revenge against the police immediately; there have been too many lives lost, lives that were valuable to the overall strategy and lost to very little advantage. There will be no more of that kind of activity. All effort must be concentrated on the main objective with no diversions from our main task. With the help of Allah, the main operation will take place soon and its success will provide more than just revenge for all the previous setbacks. Its scale will send our enemies into a state of shock for months, perhaps even years, to come."

The man on the right said, "The main product is not yet complete—"

"But I've been assured that it will be ready and delivered soon," interrupted the third man.

Once again, the man in the centre spoke. "What about the men?"

"Recruitment of men of that quality and dedication is not easy, but we're maintaining our training schedules and continually searching for warriors with high ideals who yearn to accomplish our aims. Apart from that, I don't think I've anything more to add."

The man in the centre turned first left and then right, querying whether either of them wanted to speak again, but both shook their heads. "Then let Allah be praised." The meeting was over.

Chapter 45

The operation in Britain was not making any noticeable progress. The investigation into the murder of the prostitute near Peterborough did not appear to be getting anywhere; the media had dropped the story for other more current news and the police were on the point of putting it on the back burner, in view of the lack of further information, and were about to be moved to more urgent cases.

The murder of the prostitute in Manchester was still being pursued with vigour, with a weekly review of the evidence by the Chief Constable. At the review, the Chief listened carefully to the update of information given by Chief Inspector Derek Young. When he came to a halt, he said, "So there's not been any recent progress, I take it?"

"It's not for the lack of effort, sir, believe me, but we can't manufacture evidence where there is none," said Derek reluctantly. "As we know, whoever did this is extremely adept at leaving behind nothing to connect him with the murder and there's no apparent motive."

"So you maintain that your theory about this being a person who's showing us just how clever he is and what he's capable of doing still holds firm?"

"To me, it's the only motive that makes sense. It's like he's saying see how brutal I can be, what I can do to you if you don't co-operate with me."

"What about the terrorists demanding the release of some of their members from jail?"

"As far as I know, we've not imprisoned any person if importance to the terrorists; all the ones in this country are amateurs, just disposable volunteers, and they would never be of any use to Al Qaida after they were released anyway."

"So what are we left with? Is there anything we can pursue?"

Derek counted the items off on his fingers. "There are the tyre tracks, so we know the make of tyre, which is the commonest type. If only we knew where they were fitted and to what sort of car, then we'd be a lot further forward, sir, but even then, we're grasping at straws, because it could take a long time to trace the car, assuming the driver hasn't renewed his tyres in the meantime!"

"Well, you've depressed me enough for one day," said the Chief Constable. "Carry on working with your team, but I'll have to reconsider the investigation if nothing positive comes to light soon."

Outside his office, Derek found himself considering all the facts again, going over and over them like a dog with an unchewable bone. He wondered if the same car was used for both murders.

He phoned Peterborough police and asked for CID, eventually being put through to their extension. "This is Chief Inspector Derek Young of Manchester CID," he announced. "Can you check something for me very quickly? It's important."

"Yes, sir, I'll do my best," said a cheerful voice.

"I must have a copy of the tyre impressions left at the scene of the prostitute's murder. Can you fax one to me?"

"Can you leave it with me, sir? You'll appreciate that this information isn't kept in this office. I've made a note of your number and I'll do this as soon as I can."

"You do understand, don't you, that this is very important?"

"Yes, sir, I'm onto it straightaway."

Derek had to be satisfied with that.

Maidstone police were a little less co-operative, but after stressing the importance of his request, he was assured that the information would be faxed to him as soon as possible. Putting the phone down, Derek sighed and hoped it was worth his efforts.

By the end of the following day he had received both faxes. He compared them with the tyre marks left at the scene of the Manchester murder. They looked identical to him. But it would have to be confirmed by the forensic lab, although he felt it in his bones. He tried not to put two and two together before his idea was confirmed but was sure that the same car had been used in all three murders. He felt excitement, because this indicated that some individual was involved in all three murders, perhaps someone with a deranged mind and hate of women. Or perhaps it was some kind of Mafia plot to extort a huge sum of money from the government, with gang members willing to go to any lengths to get it. At this point, Derek could not see how all this helped the investigation, but at last he had a possible reason for the murders.

The next day, he presented his new information to the team, attaching the three faxes to the whiteboard, and asked if it rang any bells or set off some theories. Total silence.

"Okay, I want some fresh ideas from you all as to what use we can put this new information. What help is it to us that the same car was used in at least three murders at three widely differing sites, and what, if anything, connects the whole lot together? At my meeting with the Chief this week, he told me he wants this investigation to go on, so we have to have something, anything, to keep going. I'm relying on you to come up with some ideas. That said, you can get back to work!"

Derek called over his sergeant, George Green. "How do you think this investigation is going so far?" he asked.

George thought for a moment and then said in his usual measured way, "I think we've gone as far as we can, sir. All these men would be better employed on other police work."

"For heaven's sake, don't say that to anyone else or it'll get straight back to the Chief. He says he needs this investigation to go on and he's sure that sooner or later we'll crack the case; all it needs is one hint of a clue and we can do it, I know we can. There's just some fact eluding us, probably staring us in the face, and we can't see it. Also, the Home Secretary is under a great deal of pressure to get results and wouldn't be happy to see things peter out, so he makes the Chief his excuse for the lack of arrests. I think it's all getting a bit too political."

George shrugged. "Well, I've told you my honest opinion, guv, and to my mind we've done as much as humanly possible. But you know the top brass; if they say they want us to carry on, then carry on we must."

"I think we need to refocus on this investigation," said Derek. "At the moment we're just following routine procedures, as we've done in all previous murder cases, because before it worked and led to an arrest. But in this case, we're not dealing with the usual type of murderer. He appears to be a serial killer, for a reason which we have yet to establish. Perhaps he's insane, perhaps he has a psychotic personality, but why would he travel from Maidstone to Peterborough to Manchester? What we have to do is check all hotels…" He ignored George's loud groan. "…around these areas, one, for a list of people staying there on or about the date of the murder, and two, did they take the registration numbers of cars parked in their hotel car park?" He looked at George apologetically and continued. "We're only interested in a period of two or three days before the bodies were found. If we can come up with a name to go with the registration number, we've cracked it – I think, don't you?"

"Sir, you must be well aware that we'll need an army of policemen to find all the hotels, check through records and collate the information, and if even one person is missed, the whole scheme goes belly-up. Where are you going to find a dedicated team of coppers willing to slog through hotel records when you have to be eagle-eyed to spot even a tiny link in a chain? I'm not saying my lads can't do it, but it's a very slim chance they'll find anything." He looked at his boss's expression and added, "I might as well hold my breath, mightn't I, because that's what you want us to do. I suppose this is a positive move and that's what we can tell the Chief. Shall I call them back into the office and let you explain what their next few months' work is going to consist of?"

"First we have to form the teams and decide where they'll be located. Perhaps we can get some help from Maidstone and Peterborough forces, if we put it to them diplomatically."

When they had complete the layout, Derek left his sergeant to do the paperwork and went to look at the site, examining the area where the car had been parked in relation to exactly where the body was found. The forensic report was embedded in his memory and he tried to imagine himself in the place of the murderer. There had been no blood under the body, so it had been concluded that she had been dead when dumped there. It had been a dark night, no moon and overcast. He would have used only dipped headlights and must have known the area, perhaps having selected it during daylight hours, so it was not chosen at random. The question was how do you find a place like this? It wouldn't be on any map, so it presupposed local knowledge. Or had they managed to recruit somebody local who knew of a derelict building site, perhaps someone living rough around the area? One man would be more than capable of carrying the body from the car to where it was found – she weighed less than eight and a half stone – and her throat was slashed elsewhere. So where had he come from? Perhaps within half a mile. He obeyed all the speed limits, made sure he didn't attract attention to his car or himself, turned onto this derelict building site using only his sidelights, checked that no one was in the area and removed the body from the boot. Perhaps there were two of them, one to keep watch; even better if the other one was a woman, because you could make out like you were lovers and had had an argument.

There was no point in spending any more time there, so Derek got in his car and started to drive slowly round the area, spending nearly an hour checking the various approaches to the site. Then he went into the nearest café and bought a mug of tea and a chocolate bar. Sitting near the steamy window, he came to the conclusion that the houses, in small terraces, were mainly occupied by Asians. He had nothing against Asian people. In general he found that crime was a lot lower in the areas where they had settled than in areas that were predominantly white, and they tended to be very family orientated. But the fact was that so far, all the terrorists they had arrested were Asian. As the younger ones grew up they were fertile ground for recruiting into organisations like Al Qaida, and it had been shown that terrorists were capable of killing innocent people. So it might not be East European mafia after all. Something like fifty-two people in the London bombing had been killed completely at random; they had no connection to any causes or political goals or any religious affiliations; they had been people who just wanted to get on with their lives. Can anything be more cruel than that? Some kind of terrorist plot might be on the cards for all he knew.

A woman's voice startled him. "Is there anything wrong with that tea? You've not drunk any of it and you're staring into space like you were lost!"

Derek hastily picked up his mug of tea, which was now cold, and started to drink it, trying not to grimace at the unpalatable taste.

"Give it here," she said. "I'll get you a fresh one."

"No, no, thank you, I like my tea cold. Please don't bother. But thanks for asking."

"I put my customers first and if there's anything wrong with anything, you only have to say."

He finished his chocolate bar with the last of his cold tea and went back to the office, thinking that the Asian woman who ran the café had been polite and interested enough to ask him about his drink – how many white café owners would have done that!

He rang the Chief's office to ask for a meeting at ten o'clock the next day and asked Sergeant Green if any of the team had made progress in tracing the car or driver they were looking for.

"Give us a chance to get going, sir," he responded. "You must think we're greased lightning. We've only had a few hours so far and it's like looking for a needle in a haystack!"

The next morning, Derek faced the Chief, who asked him if he were bringing him good news.

"Well, I'd like to say that," said Derek cautiously, "but not exactly. However, it is very important." He told him of the plan he had put into operation to check hotels and car registration numbers, trying to match them up. "But that wasn't the main reason I asked for this meeting," he went on. "I feel most strongly, sir, that these murders have been carried out by a terrorist group and that the next incident is going to be the biggest yet. I think they're planning to involve large numbers of their people and use a lot of their money and that these murders have just been a decoy, getting police forces all over the country chasing their tails while they go on preparing for the main operation without any distractions."

The Chief of Police looked thoughtful. "While all things are possible, so far you've not produced a shred of evidence to support this theory. I accept that at this point the only thing we can do is theorise, and it does fit in with what's happened. But we've got to rely on facts and evidence, and so far you haven't got any," he said bluntly. "In any case, what would you have me do? I can pass the information on to the Home Office and let them take over, because they have the resources to track the culprits down countrywide, but we can only deal with events in our area. If I go with this story to the Home Office, they'll think that I've spent too much time in this job and it's time for me to 'broaden my horizons', in other words retire or take a posting to the Outer Hebrides! They already have many people employed undercover, watching out for terrorist intentions. If we point anything out that doesn't fit in with their ideas, we'll be told very politely to mind our own business. They'll say it's all under consideration, they're dealing with it or a paper is being written about just that subject. They don't really like anyone giving them information because they like to think they're ahead of the police and may think that we're telling them how to do their jobs. But I'd like to stay with this idea and be kept informed of any progress. In the meantime, don't go upsetting our Muslim community.

"Thank you, sir," said Derek politely, "but it's not my intention to upset any community, whatever their faith. I'm only going after the criminals, be they Jews, Catholics, Hindi, Irish, white, coloured, Red Indian or Muslim. It's whether or not they're guilty that concerns me."

"Very well, Chief Inspector; I take full note of your intentions. Let me be the first to know of any promising results, and good luck."

Back at the office, one of Derek's men looked up from his notebook and said, "Sir, I've found one car registered at a hotel in both Maidstone and Peterborough during the dates we're concerned with."

"What's the name and address in the hotel register?"

"I've just checked them and they're false. And the man paid in cash, sir."

"Does anyone remember him? Have they got a description of any sort?"

"I've asked each hotel receptionist that, but they both say it was some time ago and they see so many people, so they can't remember him."

"But nowadays it's so unusual to pay in cash. I didn't know it was still accepted." Derek came to a decision. "I'm going to drive over to Peterborough to check this out. What's the name, address and phone number of the hotel and what's the registration number of the car?"

"Here you are, sir; it's all here." He handed Derek a piece of paper. "Shall we keep on checking?"

"Yes, you're doing a great job. Now if only someone can pick up that car registered to someone at a hotel in Manchester, we've got it made."

He drove to Peterborough and found the hotel after a little difficulty; it was in a side street, a little away from the city centre. The receptionist eventually appeared after Derek banged repeatedly on an ancient bell. "Can I help you, sir?" she asked, not looking particularly interested.

Derek put on his official demeanour and showed her his warrant card. "Can I see the manager, please," he asked coldly.

"Is it a complaint, sir?"

"No, I'd just like to ask him some questions about a person who stayed at the hotel." He consulted the information his constable had given him, quoting the dates he was interested in.

She disappeared into another room and returned after a few minutes with a man who looked to be in his fifties. "Come into my office," he said. The 'office' was a cluttered room housing two filing cabinets, a desk piled high with assorted papers, an old-fashioned, bulky computer and a grubby telephone. "What can I do for you, Chief Inspector?" he said, smiling. Always be polite to policemen, he thought. It didn't do to have them poking their noses into your business if you didn't appear helpful.

"You had a man staying here on these dates. He's given a false name and address and we're trying to trace him with regard to our enquiries about a prostitute who was murdered then. He quoted his car registration number on the card he filled in when he registered here and we'd also like to trace that."

The manager appeared to be thinking back to the dates in question, but he answered, "I'm sorry, Chief Inspector, but I can't really help you with this. I don't think I saw this man you're looking for, but I'll ask my staff if anyone remembers him. What does he look like?"

"That's the point," said Derek, who was becoming irritated. "That's what we want, a description of him. He paid you in cash. Does that ring a bell? What would happen to the money once he'd paid? Where would you keep it?"

"It would be put in the safe until I was ready to take it to the bank, and of course it would've been recorded on the computer for our accounts."

"Would whoever accepted the money to settle the bill have noticed what the man looked like? He or she must have glanced up at him while they were writing out the receipt."

The manager was doubtful. "I'll get my receptionist in here and see if she remembers anything. Apart from her, with it being a small hotel, we don't have many staff – a couple of domestics and my wife who does the cooking – but you can question them all," he said generously. "I'm sure they'll help you if they can. Oh, I was forgetting the part-timers. Most of 'em won't be here at this time of day." Derek realised he should have brought some members of his team to track down those not at work, but after questioning the receptionist with no result, he left, telling them to contact him should they remember the slightest detail.

During the drive back to Manchester, Derek racked his brains for a solution and an idea came to him. All's fair in love and war, he thought. What about trying to bluff the man and make him think the police were a lot nearer to arresting him than they were?

Back in his office, he phoned a reporter he knew and asked him if he wanted a 'statement' from the police, an unofficial official story. The reporter could hardly believe his ears.

"You're my favourite chief inspector," he said. "What have you got to tell me? I can't promise anything, but if it's good, it should make quite a stir."

"I want you to print the piece as 'according to my police source, I have been informed' etc.," Derek said.

"Go ahead," said the reporter. "I'm all ears."

"Police are on the trail of a murderer, who, to our knowledge, has now killed three women, one in Maidstone in Kent, one in Peterborough in Cambridgeshire and one in Manchester. We know that the same car was used to carry the bodies to the places where they were dumped in all three cases, and the police are very close to arresting the owner of that car."

"Thanks, Derek. Can I quote you as my source?" said the reporter with his tongue in his cheek.

"As written in a well-known TV drama, I couldn't possibly comment. Don't mention my name or it'll be the last tip you ever get from me."

Derek waited in vain for a reaction to the article. After a few days, he went to the local bar for a beer, and seeing the local Manchester paper, he spotted the headline saying that a burned-out car had been found in the canal. He picked up the paper and read the whole article. He made a note of the recovery company who had pulled the vehicle out of the canal and next morning told his sergeant that he was going to check on it.

He arranged for the car to be taken to the police forensic laboratory, but before that happened he wanted to take a look at it. The mechanic took him outside to see the wreck.

"What make is it?" Derek asked.

"It's a Toyota Carina," the mechanic at the recovery depot told him. "Don't really know how old it is, but it must be at least ten years old."

"What about the tyres? What state are they in?"

"Well, there's some tread left on them but mostly they've just melted away. Whoever did this didn't intend there to be anything left at all. Is it connected with some crime, Inspector?"

"Might just be the car we've been looking for. Have to get it examined first. Thanks. If you need any papers signing before releasing it into police custody, I'll do it for you in the office." He watched as the burned-out car was hoisted aboard the low-loader and followed it back to the lab. He so hoped that a detailed inspection of the vehicle would reveal a great deal of information.

He knew the laboratory inspector, but had not seen him for some time. The inspector studied the unprepossessing heap of junk and said, "I take it you want me to perform my usual miracle with whatever that used to be and give you a detailed report including the make, year, colour, mileage, tyre pressure, radio frequency, where it's been for the past year – have I got that right? – all by tomorrow morning?"

"Sarcasm," said Derek, "will get you nowhere. Do a good job on this and I'll recommend you for promotion to Lord High Admiral, or I might even buy you a pint of ale! No, seriously. You've heard about these three murders which we think are somehow connected by the bloke using the same car each time. Well, this could be the car, so anything you find when you examine it might give us the lead we're searching for. Could you particularly examine the tyres, because we have three sets of identical tyre prints, each found near where the bodies were dumped. That could prove it's the vehicle we're looking for. I'll ring my sergeant now and tell him to email the prints over to you."

The burned-out car was raised on a ramp and the careful and thorough inspection began. The wheels were removed and the tyres, the treads of which had mostly melted in the fierce heat, were compared with the prints. On one small section, a match could be made. Photographs were taken for a more detailed comparison, which would take a lot more work by the Manchester laboratory – a mould of the tyre marks would be made to finally confirm that these were the same tyres.

Derek felt deep satisfaction, because now they were getting somewhere; this might just lead to an outcome, perhaps even the killer.

"It worked, then," said George, referring to the report in the paper.

"So it seems. They couldn't take a chance on the story not being true, so they took a gamble that by destroying the car they would destroy all the evidence to connect the driver to the murders."

"So you think that these murders were committed by a person or persons who live in this area and therefore wouldn't have stayed at a hotel? That narrows the search down. When we get the report from Forensics, who knows what information we'll get."

"What I'm afraid of is that no matter what evidence we gather, no matter what case we can bring against the man or men that perpetrated these crimes, if cornered they'd prefer shoot it out and die rather than surrender, and who can tell what other casualties there might be."

"That's frightening," agreed George. "It's like a suicide bomber who'd blow himself up rather than give in, regardless of the consequences."

The forensic report was much as Derek had expected. The fire had destroyed any evidence in the torched interior but the remains of the tyre treads supported his theory that the same car had been used in all three murders. But there was nothing to trace the car back to its previous owners, which had probably been many in view of the car's age and condition.

He now had only George working with him and a young detective constable, twenty-three-year-old Tony Bruce, who had a reputation as a bit of a computer genius. As there were only three of them working together, Derek told them to forget rank and use Christian names; it made for better communication. He set Tony to work entering every known fact about the three cases into their office computer, which was also linked to the main police database. He asked George to be in charge of the office and then set off for Manchester Airport to make some enquiries in the passport control department.

He was greeted with a cautious, "What can we do for you, Chief Inspector? Not looking for one of us, are you?" Derek explained that he was investigating the murder of a local woman, a prostitute. "Oh yes, I've read about that in the papers. Shocking, isn't it, when this kind of thing keeps happening." The passport official was going to launch into a tirade about the state of the world today and what he would do to the politicians who were making such a mess of everything, but Derek interrupted smoothly.

"Yes, I couldn't agree with you more, but I want to know if any of your people recall a case where problems were caused at the checking-in desk by someone entering the country. I'm only interested in Asian people."

There was silence while the official collected his startled thoughts and he gave Derek what could only be described as a funny look. "I'm not quite sure what you mean by that, sir. Is this some kind of a crackdown on illegal immigrants or have the police got something against Asians? Because if so, I'll have to refer you to—"

"No, no," said Derek, realising he'd started off on the wrong foot. "I'm just checking if anyone had a dodgy passport or stood out for some reason, anything your people would have picked up on, because I know how good they are at their jobs. It could be extremely important if the murderer entered Britain via Manchester Airport."

"You appreciate, don't you, Inspector, that we have a large number of Asian people coming and going through the airport. It'd be like looking for a needle in a haystack to pick out one person on one day sometime in the past year or so. Could you narrow it down at all?"

"The majority of passengers would be classified as routine. I'm only looking for anything concerning a man, probably early to mid-twenties, well-dressed in European clothes, very little luggage, perhaps coming from one of the EU countries, where your people were put under some kind of pressure, anything like that."

"You'll have to give me some time to question all my operatives. There are a number of people not on duty at the moment."

"You don't keep any kind of incident log of things which you need to put on record, people who were stopped for further investigation?" asked Derek.

"Cases like that are passed on to another authority and the individual is held in a secure unit, so it's out of our hands. Our job here is, as you say, routine. We either let them through because their paperwork is in order, or the airport police take over."

"Do you have police officers on duty here?" Derek asked.

"Yes, Chief Inspector. I'll take you to their office."

The officer on duty was a woman. Having identified himself, Derek asked her who was in overall charge of the small force deployed at the airport.

"That'll be Inspector Graham Pollock, sir, but he's not on duty today."

Derek gave her his hundred-watt smile and said, "You might be able to help me, Sergeant. I'm looking into several incidents which may be connected with the murder of a prostitute. The kind of thing I'm looking for is any passport checks where Asian men have been involved, where there might have been an attempt to enter the country illegally and the officer on the passport desk became suspicious, for whatever reason, and reported it to you. Would you keep a record of that kind of thing?"

"I remember that murder," she said. "How far would you like me to go back?"

"About the last six months."

She clicked her tongue and said, "It may take half an hour or more to get the details for you. Why don't you go to the café and have a coffee."

"That would be great."

Derek strolled round the airport terminal buildings, familiarising himself with the layout. Three quarters of an hour later he was back in the policewoman's office. She passed him a folder.

"There are nine entries in the last six months; five men were deported to their country of origin after an investigation into their cases, and in four cases, all men, they were released and allowed to enter the country."

"Was there any follow-up after these four cases?"

"No, sir. As they'd already been investigated, all the papers were simply filed, as you can see from the folder. Would you mind if I asked you a question, sir?"

Derek looked up from the folder in surprise. "No, of course not. What do you want to know?"

"Are you married or divorced?"

"Why? What makes you ask that?"

"It's just that I've seen the look you have before, totally absorbed in your job, which usually means a neglected wife or partner."

Derek looked at her and smiled. "You speaking from experience?" he enquired.

"Well, sir, we're both in the police force and have similar job demands, so yes, I suppose you could say I speak from experience."

Derek looked at her as a person for the first time and made a quick assessment of her in his mind. No make-up, or perhaps a very subtle touch here and there, and the uniform did nothing really positive for her shape. He found himself wondering what she looked like in a tight dress! But she had a very attractive face and was perhaps in her late twenties. "Are you married, Sergeant?" he asked.

"No. I've recently broken up with my long-term partner after five years. He couldn't cope with my irregular hours and the friendships I had with other officers. He has a nine-to-five job and doesn't understand that you have to be on good terms with the team you work with, and he wasn't prepared to meet my friends, so we just agreed to call it a day."

"Why don't you let me buy you some lunch and we can discuss the shortcomings of the police force in more detail," Derek offered.

As she picked up her coat, he asked her what her name was.

"Call me Helen," she said. "I'm Helen to my friends and Sergeant D. Baker to anyone else who might be asking. What shall I call you? Or should I just stick to 'sir'?"

"You can call me whatever you like, Helen, but my friends call me Derek. Everyone else, depending on rank of course, calls me 'sir' or 'oi, you over there!" They both laughed.

They started to get to know each other over their meal. Chatting up a bird, so to speak, was a bit of a novelty for Derek after what seemed a long time without female company.

"Do you go out much in the evenings?" he asked.

"Not very often, and when I do, it's usually with other officers. I seem to have lost touch with the friends I had before I joined the police force. What about you, Derek?"

"Pretty much the same, really. I go out occasionally for a couple of pints with the lads, but by the time I've finished work, got back home, made myself a meal, watched a bit of TV, the evening's gone. Aren't we a couple of sad cases!" he said lightly.

"I take it you've lost interest in women?" she said with a smile.

"I wouldn't say that, but my wife left me for another man. She said I was a poor husband and in the divorce proceedings she claimed I totally neglected her, putting my job first. As we had no children, she didn't ask for much, so I kept the house we were buying. I made her a one-off, final monetary settlement and that was that. I haven't seen her for, oh, it must be months now. She went to live in her bloke's big house and so the place I've got suits me fine."

"You've been very lucky. I've heard some dreadful stories about couples fighting over who should pay for what, and people I know with kids, well, they ought to be ashamed of themselves. But in the end I think it's better if they split up, provided they don't start bad-mouthing each other."

"I suppose I was fortunate. It's not that I didn't want kids, but by the time we got round to going in for a family, she decided she wanted to be with someone else. What did you do? Did you have to sell your house?"

"No, we only had a flat, which we were buying together, and I still live in it. He moved out and I've taken over the mortgage. On my salary, I could do with a paying lodger!" she joked.

They ate their lunch in companionable silence and when the bill was placed discreetly on Derek's side of the table, she offered to share the cost with him. Derek was rather nonplussed. He had never known a woman to offer to pay her share and he refused. "Of course not. I asked you out to lunch so now I settle the bill!"

As they were walking back to her office, she quizzed him. "Do you intend to continue not thinking about women in the foreseeable future?"

Derek looked down at her and said in his most patronising voice, "Actually, I was thinking of asking you to come out for a meal on Saturday evening, but if you're going to be cheeky about it, I'll have to think again."

"Oh no, you don't get away as easily as that," she laughed.

"Okay, I'll pick you up at about seven o'clock, but you'd better tell me your address or I'm going to have a great deal of difficulty finding you!"

"That sounds great." She quickly scribbled her address on a scrap of paper. As they got nearer to her office, her thoughts returned to the case that Derek was working on. "You never said exactly what you were looking for, but if it's a case of tracing illegal entries into the UK, Heathrow is the best place to look."

"The people I'm looking for are already in this country," he answered.

"From our experience, they usually arrive at Heathrow and then catch a train to their final destination. They had a lot of trouble in Frankfurt and Amsterdam with terrorists who had forged passports, and Interpol gave every major airport a warning. But you know how these things are: a couple of weeks later and other stuff comes up and it gets forgotten, or at least overlooked."

"This is just the kind of information I'm looking for," said Derek, delighted by this young officer's intelligence. "Tell me any more you can."

"Do you mean terrorist acts like bombings and shootings?"

"Do you have any first-hand knowledge of that, or is it just rumour?"

"It's not rumour," she said, "but we haven't any actual details, apart from the fact that this kind of thing is going on. Occasionally there might be a headline in a foreign-language newspaper. But you could always find out by phoning their police department. I'm sure they'll give you all the gen."

Derek made a face and said ruefully, "I don't speak either language; only did Latin at school and I don't think that would be much use."

"Look, there's sure to be someone on the switchboard who speaks English at both locations. You could phone first to explain and then arrange to fly out there and talk to the detectives who are working on the cases. Anyway, do you think there are some terrorists in this area that came in illegally? There's been no trouble here has there?"

"I'm afraid there are people who would like to kill and maim the population round here. Our only problem is finding them before they carry out their atrocities. Thanks for your help, Sergeant. See you on Saturday."

Chapter 46

When he got back to his office, Derek asked his new recruit to put through a call to Amsterdam Airport, the police section, for him.

"Is there such a section there?" asked Tony.

"So far as I know, there's a police officer at every major airport in Europe."

Tony got through and asked very clearly, "Can anyone speak English? This is the Manchester Police Force. Chief Inspector Derek Young wishes to speak to the police officer on duty at the airport." He put his hand over the mouthpiece and said to Derek, "They've gone to find someone who speaks good English, sir, someone called Alex Mengis. Here he is." He handed the phone over to Derek.

Derek cleared his throat, feeling suddenly awkward, not quite knowing what to say, when suddenly the words came to him. He started by telling Mengis who he was and the nature of his enquiry, but was interrupted by him saying that he was only the translator. The man who dealt with security at the airport was Inspector Erik van Eyck. "He's sitting next to me and I'm translating what you're saying."

"Something has come up at Manchester Airport which I can't discuss over the phone. I'd like to talk to him personally. Perhaps I could fly over with my own translator sometime soon. Would that be in order?"

There was some hurried conversation at the other end of the line before Mr Mengis said, "If you could manage to fly out first thing on

Monday, Inspector van Eyck will be free all day to discuss anything that you wish. Is that convenient for you?"

Derek accepted and rang off, wondering where he was going to find someone fluent in both English and Dutch before Monday.

When consulted, Tony said that he knew of some Dutch students at the university, who were obviously bilingual, so perhaps he could find one of them to take on the role of translator. "But what about security?" he queried. "Would they be considered a security risk in view of what you want to discuss?"

"Just find me someone who can translate and can fly to Amsterdam late Sunday night, returning on Monday, and book us two seats, will you?" Derek knew he had to consider what Tony had said, but that could wait until later. Tony got in touch with the university and found someone suitable to act as translator. But because of the red tape involved to get them security clearance, he was unable to travel with Derek and had to take a later flight.

Chapter 47

On Saturday evening, Derek arrived at Helen's apartment. Before she came to the door he was ready to say something silly like, "Your carriage awaits you, my lady," but the words froze on his lips when he saw her. She was wearing a tight-fitting clingy black dress that barely reached her knees. The top of her dress revealed a glimpse of her slender neck and exposed her flawless back. Her shining shoulder-length brown hair framed her face. As he took in her appearance, he noticed the very high-heeled black shoes, which brought her eyes to the same level with his own.

Seeing his slightly dazed expression, she laughed. "Were you going to say something?" she asked.

"Yes, but I think I'm at the wrong apartment. The gorgeous girl in front of me must be waiting for a tall, handsome prince, or at least a millionaire, not a humble chief inspector like me."

"But this humble police sergeant wants to go out with you, seeing as you're the only one who has knocked at my door tonight, so let's go, shall we?"

"I hope you like Italian food," said Derek, "because I've booked a table at La Traviata. I should've asked you first, shouldn't I?"

"I do like Italian food and I love Italian wine," she reassured him.

In the ten minutes it took them to get to the restaurant, they discussed their favourite dishes and what they might order. A waiter led them to a corner table where they could watch the comings and goings of the rest of the customers and Derek ordered a bottle of Chianti.

"I don't really know an awful lot about wine, do you?" he asked.

"Not really. Somehow I've never had the money to splash out on bottles of wine," Helen responded frankly.

"Well, if we don't like Chianti – do you like gin and tonic?"

"Yes, or rum and coke."

They studied the menu and decided that they didn't want a starter but might indulge in a dessert if they weren't too full of pasta. Then conversation came to a halt, and both of them tried desperately to think of something to talk about.

When the waiter went away with their order, Derek said, "I feel a bit like a teenager on his first important date; on his best behaviour and wondering what he can do to impress his new girl."

Helen laughed. "You won't feel all that lucky when you get the bill. Anyway, tell me a bit about you, what makes you tick."

"There's not really all that much to know. I was an only child of a middle-class family. I went to grammar school then university, took a job in the civil service and then transferred to the police force."

"How old are you?"

"Thirty-one. What about you?"

"I'm twenty-eight, with a working-class background. My dad is a carpenter. He has a small business, and my mum works as a counter clerk for an insurance company. I did go to grammar school because I passed my eleven-plus exam. I got three A levels but I decided not to go to university. Instead I worked in a solicitor's office but gave that up, as it was boring. I thought I'd have more excitement in the police force so I joined up!"

"Do you like your job now?"

"It's like every job; sometimes you like it, sometimes not. How did you meet your wife? Was it at university?"

"Yes, I met her in my second year and we had an on-and-off relationship for years. Eventually it seemed to blossom and we decided to get married. By that time I was a young police sergeant, very much driven by the need to get on. Looking back, getting married was not a good move at that time. It made me feel very insecure and I drove myself even harder, trying to succeed. In the end it cost me my marriage."

The waiter arrived with the wine and poured out two glasses with a flourish. When he had gone, Helen said sympathetically, "It was a good job you didn't have any children."

"It would have been heartbreaking for me if we had. Somehow when you have kids you always think your marriage is going to be like your parents' was, last forever, and when it doesn't you feel so let down, but nobody was hurt but the two of us. If I'm honest, we never really talked about having kids. What about you, Helen, did you want children?"

Helen hesitated for a moment and then shrugged her shoulders slightly. "I was undecided about it, but he most definitely didn't want any. Perhaps in his mind he could never see our relationship lasting. It's probably the only thing I can thank him for! Come on, let's forget about our ex-partners and enjoy our meal."

As the evening wore on, they found themselves enjoying each other's company more and more. After a couple of gin and tonics, Derek asked Helen if they were going to see each other again.

"I hope so," Helen said lightly. "I've invested three hours of my time on you; five hours if you include getting ready."

Derek was serious for a minute and tried to put his feelings into words. "I like you very much already, so if we do continue to see each other, I don't want to be let down."

"You get quite intense about things, don't you," observed Helen. "There are no guarantees in this life or in relationships; you just have to take life as it comes."

"So you're saying we should keep this low key."

"Sometimes very intense relationships fail because they are so intense."

Derek didn't reply; it wasn't what he wanted to hear. He thought that at last he had found someone he could fall for in a big way, but he realised that he was expecting too much on their first date. "I'm sorry," he said at last. "I'm not very good at this dating game; a bit out of practice."

"Okay," she said, "we'll consider it just a friendly meal, a bit of a night out for two mates."

She changed the subject and told him that she had a brother in the navy, that her parents were still working and that they still lived in the house where she was born. She asked about his family.

"As I told you, I'm the only one. My mother took one look at me and said, 'God, if this is the best I can do then it's no more for me'."

"Oh, pull the other one. You're a handsome man and must be very talented to make Chief Inspector at such a young age."

"She wasn't to know that at the time. It's getting late. I'll call a taxi to take you home."

"Why? Aren't you coming with me?"

"Sure, I'll take you home and then the driver can take me back."

"Aren't you coming in for a drink or something?"

"No, I'm flying to Amsterdam first thing tomorrow and I still have some preparatory work to get through," he said without thinking.

Disappointment showed clearly on Helen's face. "Did I put my foot in it somewhere along the line?" she asked abruptly.

Derek realised that he'd been a little short with her and tried to smooth things over. "No, no, honestly, not at all. You were quite right; it's my fault, rushing things at you like that. Here we are, out for a first date and me talking about relationships in the first five minutes. I must have frightened you to death. Forget what I said and let's just take things as they come."

"You're sure you're not coming in?" Helen asked when the taxi pulled up outside her apartment building.

"Thanks, but I have to go. Goodnight."

Not even a goodnight kiss, thought Helen as she put her key in the door.

Chapter 48

The plane landed at Amsterdam and Derek went straight to his hotel. He took a brief look round, unpacked his overnight bag, had a shower and went downstairs into the bar. It was quite busy, and after he had managed to get a large glass of lager, he found a comfortable chair at a vacant table and sat down. A moment later, a rather scantily clad woman came up to him and said something in Dutch. Not understanding what she said he just nodded. To his surprise, she sat down next to him and started to talk to him. It suddenly dawned on him that she was a prostitute, so he tried to tell he that he wasn't interested. She didn't understand, or pretended not to, and Derek was starting to get a little irritated. While he was struggling to get the message across, a young man, casually dressed, walked into the bar, obviously looking for someone. He asked the barman a question, and he pointed towards Derek. He walked over and asked politely in English, "Are you Chief Inspector Derek Young?"

"Yes, I am."

"I'd like to introduce myself. My name is Gert and my surname is so long, English people find it very difficult to pronounce, so just call me Gert, if you wish."

Derek stood up and they shook hands, very formally. "Nice to meet you, Gert. You must be the student from Manchester University who's going to translate for me when I meet the Dutch police. Well, your first job is to tell this 'lady' to take her business elsewhere."

Gert spoke to the woman in Dutch and she flounced off in a huff.

"What did you say to her?" asked Derek.

"I just told her you're not interested and asked her to go before I called security and had her escorted out of the hotel."

"I thought the Dutch were quite liberal about prostitution?"

"Well, we are, but they're not allowed to pester people who aren't interested."

"Thanks for that; she just wouldn't go away!"

"That's because you're English and don't know anything about how Dutch law applies to prostitution. There have been cases in the past where prostitutes have accused someone like you of abusing them, telling them they would take them to court. Afraid of any publicity, men pay out to keep them quiet, to make them go away. Have you eaten yet?"

"No, I was just having a drink before going for a meal."

"Were you thinking of eating in the hotel?"

"Yes, it's all included in my expenses and I don't know anywhere else."

Gert told Derek that he knew of a small restaurant nearby where the food was much better than that served in the hotel and suggested visiting it before going on a tour of Amsterdam's night life.

"I know this'll sound pretty mundane to you, but food is something I eat as fuel to keep me going, and as long as it's decently cooked, I'm not all that bothered. As for the nightlife…" He laughed. "I think I've seen most of it before. You live in Manchester and you know we have a similar sort of thing there – red light district, sleazy clubs, porno cinemas – only it's probably not quite so international. I've got at least one important meeting tomorrow and I want to get the most information I can from it. But this doesn't apply to you; you're not a policeman and can do what you wish."

"Okay. It would be a shame to miss a night out when I'm only home for one day. I'll see you at breakfast in the morning."

They met at breakfast, Gert showing absolutely no signs of a hangover after his evening's foray into Amsterdam. They walked to the office used by the police at the airport. A man stood up when they were shown in and introduced himself as Inspector Erik van Eyck.

"I'm here to translate for you," explained Gert.

The two inspectors shook hands and Erik offered them coffee, which he was never without. Derek smiled but said he would wait until later, as he had just eaten, and guessed when Erik laughed that he said something about not being able to work without coffee. Derek had prepared himself well, because he knew that having a conversation through a third person was going to be a slow process, so he restricted himself to specific questions.

"When was the first time you became aware of having terrorists working in Amsterdam?"

"Several months ago when a man was stopped by passport control."

"What sort of security system do you use for checking passports?"

"All non-EU passport holders are inspected as they pass a desk. Also, they're filmed twenty-four hours a day, every day. No non-EU passport holders can pass through the airport without being filmed."

"How many terrorists have been located in Amsterdam?"

"Known to us, about twenty and they've all been accounted for," said Erik with pride, obvious in any language.

"Did you ever find out what they were doing in your city? By that I mean did they carry out any bombing attacks or killings of your people?"

"No, in fact we never knew they were here until we stopped one at the airport."

"What do you think was their objective?"

"We know now that they were wanting to move on. We think they were heading for England. In fact, one of our inspectors, who was sadly killed by terrorists, sent a warning to your Secret Service and Interpol, including a photocopy of the suspect's passport, and we deported him back to Islamabad, but the copy was in case he tried to enter from a different country."

This was the information that Derek wanted and he felt he now understood the situation a lot better. He thanked Erik for all this information and, refusing the offer of lunch, said he was going back on the earliest flight to add these facts to those he already possessed. He asked Gert to request a report from the Amsterdam police if any more incidents took place and assured Erik that he was ready to welcome him to Manchester if he ever wanted to come. Gert decided to take up their offer of lunch so that he could stay a little longer in his own country and take a later flight back.

On the short flight back to Manchester, Derek started to systematically place the information he'd been given in time and date order. One or two facts became fairly obvious. The terrorists had been using Amsterdam Airport as a kind of transit destination, together with, who knew how many, other continental airports to get their operatives into the EU, poised to enter Great Britain by train, ferry or short flights to various UK airports. Their passports would be good enough to get them through all but the most stringent checks.

On arrival at Manchester, he stopped to see the passport checking process in operation at the desk for non-EU passport holders and nearly got arrested for loitering. The system was similar to that in Amsterdam, with CCTV in constant use.

Back in his office, he checked his messages and was pleased to see that there was one from Helen asking him to phone after 7 p.m. There was also a message from the Chief Constable saying that he wanted to see him asap. Derek rang and made arrangements to see him the following day at eleven o'clock, wondering what the hurry was.

George and Tony were interested to hear what information he had been given by the Dutch police. Derek gave them a précis of what he had been told by Inspector van Eyck. "There's a very good security system at all passport checking desks with twenty-four-hour CCTV footage. The recorded information is stored so they can look at people they allowed through whenever they want," he explained. "Because of this, a watchful young man came up with a few suspects. Our problem is that a number of terrorists entered Holland and then disappeared, and Inspector van Eyck feels sure that they ended up in England, getting here by a variety of means: ferries, train or short distance flights, going through the Channel Islands or perhaps Ireland.

"Let's face it; we're not dealing with a bunch of bungling amateurs. These are fit, young, highly trained men, well versed in every aspect of killing and bombing. They're determined and, if necessary, will die for their cause. These men are extremely dangerous and will kill instantly, on sight, but what they're planning to do, as yet we have no idea, but we must find out. It's probably something spectacular, with the maximum number of dead and injured, so it's up to us to put a stop to them or suffer huge consequences if we fail."

"Who the hell is going to stop them?" asked George indignantly. "There are only the three of us; how much can we do?"

Although he was not feeling calm, Derek said calmly, "We have the resources of the whole of Britain behind us; it's just a question of mobilising them and directing them at the right targets. I have a meeting arranged with the Chief Constable tomorrow morning and I hope to start the ball rolling then. Have there been any incidents countrywide which could be linked to our investigations?"

"It's a bit difficult," said Tony "because there are always incidents somewhere, but can we prove they're linked in some way?"

"The sort of incidents we should be looking for would be the abduction of females, murders or bombing attempts which remain unsolved. Can you get onto that, Tony?"

"What I'll do is trawl the Internet and other police networks to see what I can find, then I can co-ordinate likely cases into a file. What I can't understand is why they would be committing these sorts of crimes. I mean, three murders of prostitutes – exactly what does that achieve?"

Derek explained his theory that it takes policemen away from routine policing, chasing around trying to solve cases while the terrorists are given less attention and can go on with their preparations. "To look at it coldly, it gives their members some practical experience, and you know what they say: practice makes perfect."

Chapter 49

Back at Derek's house, there was a message from Helen on the answerphone asking him to phone her after seven. He made himself a meal, all the while watching the hands move slowly round the clock face. He took a quick shower and unpacked his overnight bag. It was amazing to think about what had happened during the last forty-eight hours. He should feel tired after travelling, but he was on tenterhooks, wondering what Helen was going to say. He told himself to stop being so ridiculous and behaving like a moonstruck teenager. Perhaps she was going to tell him that he'd left something in her flat.

"You idiot," he told himself, aware that he was talking to himself out loud.

At seven o'clock he forced himself to wait another ten minutes before phoning her. The phone rang and rang but there was no reply. So that's it, he thought; she's probably gone out and forgotten all about me phoning her. He considered going to the pub and getting drunk, but decided to give it one more try. She answered after the first ring.

He intended to sound cool, but instead blurted out, "Helen, I'm so pleased to hear your voice."

"Derek, I wasn't sure you were going to ring."

"I was dying to ring you to apologise for my boorish behaviour the other night."

"Why don't you come over; that is if you can remember where I live."

He was knocking on her apartment door ten minutes later.

She was dressed in black jeans and a low-necked black sweater, which showed off her full figure and revealed a glimpse of her lacy bra. It was all he could do not to grab her in his arms.

"Come in," she said. "I won't bite you."

They walked into the main room, where there was a television showing some news programme, a comfortable settee and a coffee table with a laptop PC open on it.

"I rang about seven but there was no reply, so thought you might have gone out," said Derek.

"No, actually I was in the bath, and by the time I got to the phone it had stopped ringing, which is always what happens, isn't it?"

"Well anyway, as I said, I wanted to apologise for the way I spoke the other night."

"I wasn't much better. It only occurred to me later when I was thinking about what you said, that after your wife walked out on you, you were looking for some kind of reassurance that it wasn't going to happen again. I thought you might be a possessive person, always asking where I was and who I was with and always suspecting the worst. I wanted to say that I would like a much calmer and relaxed relationship; that is if we carried on seeing each other. My ex-partner was jealous and in the end he left. I'm not a flirt and I'd see any relationship as a long one. The last one went on for several years and I really thought we had a future. Then he left. I don't know whether to be glad or sorry!"

Derek took her hand. "I can assure you I'm not the possessive type. I let my wife get away with murder, figuratively speaking. I always trusted her completely and she left me. Now let's stop talking about this. I think you look lovely tonight."

Helen flushed a little and said, "Why thank you kindly, sir. Can I get you a drink? I've got some cans of lager in the fridge."

"Not at the moment," he murmured, and gently started to kiss her mouth. For a moment she hesitated and then put her arms around his neck. They revelled in the heat of their bodies; mouths open, exploring each other's lips. He could feel her firm breasts against him, and the passion they had been holding back threw aside any barriers they had put up between themselves. Somehow they were feverishly undressing each other, eager to make love, rolling on the carpet naked, enjoying the sheer animal passion and she moaned with ecstasy. They fell asleep where they lay, exhausted but satisfied, both thinking that next time they would make it last longer in the comfort of a double bed.

Derek woke first, not sure where he was. They still had their arms around one another. Helen stirred as he pulled his arm out from beneath her. He started to kiss her and nuzzle her neck until she woke up with a start.

"Sorry to disturb you," he grinned, "but my left arm went to sleep."

She yawned and stood up, completely unaware she was naked until, suddenly realising she wasn't wearing a stitch of clothing, she rushed off to the bathroom, shouting as she went, "Don't you dare disappear before I come back!"

"No chance," he replied and pulled some of his own things on. She emerged wearing a bathrobe and sat down next to him.

"Are you hungry?" she asked. "I am."

"Well, I did eat earlier on, but if you're having something, I'll join you."

She went into the tiny kitchen, humming a tune. There was the sound of rattling pans and cupboard doors opening and shutting, and after a few minutes she set a ham omelette in front of Derek. He found he was suddenly ravenous.

When they had finished eating, she swept everything into the dishwasher and they cuddled up on the settee.

"I know I shouldn't ask," Derek said, "but did I live up to your expectations?"

"You mean sexually?" she said honestly. "One, I have to tell you I have had very few men in my life, so that doesn't make me any kind of a judge, and two, you were brilliant!"

"It's been a long time between drinks, if you know what I mean."

"It's been a long time for me too. I enjoy sex as much as any young woman, but you can't make it the be all and end all of your existence. Now, what shall we do tomorrow night?"

"I'll call for you and we can go out for something to eat; about seven o'clock?"

"I'll be ready by then. Come as early as you can."

They spent the rest of the evening curled up together on the settee.

Chapter 50

Derek was kept waiting in the Chief Constable's office and was beginning to feel very impatient at his time being wasted. When the Chief appeared, he apologised; something had come up which he had to deal with.

"What did you learn in Amsterdam?" he asked.

"It confirmed my worst fears."

"Explain what you mean by that." The Chief was looking very worried.

"Inspector van Eyck told me that by the time their airport check caught one terrorist trying to enter Holland, an unknown number had slipped into the country and had apparently moved on, probably to the UK. He thinks they're planning something big, although, of course, he hasn't got any proof of this, nor does he know what form it'll take. But the trouble in this game, if you can call it that, is that we only seem to find out the full extent of the atrocities they commit after the event, when it's too late to do anything about it."

"What do you suggest should be our next move? What can we do to prevent it?"

Derek looked him squarely in the face and said, "We have to pull out all the stops. We have to mobilise all our forces – MI5, MI6, Special Branch and every police authority countrywide – and we need to find out what their plan is and stop them before they can carry it out."

"How do you suggest we do that?"

"As you know, sir, I don't have the authority to mobilise the whole country. That will have to come from the Home Office. But I suggest you get in touch with them now, immediately, and stress the urgency of the situation. Did you know that the inspector at Amsterdam Airport who deported a suspected terrorist back to Islamabad had informed Interpol and Scotland Yard, sending them photocopies of his passport and identifying footage from the surveillance cameras?"

"If the suspected terrorist had been sent back to Islamabad, no further action was needed, was it?"

"The following week he was killed by a bomb attached to his car. I think the man he deported was a very important key person in the terrorists' plans and the inspector was killed in revenge. They'd have probably tried to get him into Britain again through another route, but once his face and details were on record he was of no use to them."

"Okay, I've heard enough. You've convinced me of the urgency of the matter. I'll get in touch with the Home Office immediately and see if it's possible to see the Home Secretary."

There was some delay while the Chief tried to get through, and Derek had to tell himself to be patient, although every minute that passed seemed to take hours off his life. Why are they never there when they're wanted?

Eventually, an appointment was arranged and he heard the Chief grunt his assent. "Eleven o'clock Thursday be all right with you?" he asked Derek, looking at him over the top of his spectacles. "I'll need you to come with me to emphasise the urgency of the thing. They take their own sweet time about things, don't they? Home Secretary's out somewhere declaring the opening of a new office building or some such rubbish, but I managed to get over the importance of what you had to say and they say he'll be there, even if they have to strap him into a chair." The Chief seemed to find this amusing, but his smile was short-lived. "Anything else while you're here?"

"Yes. I think we can put the murder of the prostitute to one side for the moment. It's my opinion that all three women were murdered as a diversion, to occupy police resources, and although the same car was used, I don't think we'll ever find the killer. It was done cold-bloodedly, professionally, at random, possibly as an exercise in planning, with no apparent motive. We'd be better off concentrating on discovering what the terrorists plan to do and making sure we stop them."

"Okay, Chief Inspector, as the team investigating that murder was told to return to their former duties, you'd better get them all back and organise your strategy to deal with this situation. I'm putting you in to head the operation, then on Thursday, when we see the Home Secretary..." He stopped to consider whether it would be best to travel by car or train.

"The quickest way is to fly, sir. But if we want to be there on time, perhaps we should go down the night before by train. Getting from an airport into the city depends so much on the traffic you meet; delays are almost inevitable."

Back in his office, Derek told George and Tony what was happening and to get on the phone to the members of his original team. "I'm going down to London tomorrow night to see the Home Secretary with the Chief Constable, and I'd like everyone here to be fully briefed by Friday if possible. When I get back we'll have to work like hell. Plenty of overtime for everyone. We're going to stop their little game if we have to die in the event!"

Derek arrived at Euston the next day and took a taxi to the Clarendon Hotel. He hadn't seen the Chief on the train, but he expected to see him at the hotel. However, that was not to be and after a late meal and a drink in the bar, he went to bed. Before he went to sleep, he went over in his mind the eye-opening, sensuous behaviour of Helen the night before. He tried to concentrate on what he was going to tell the Home Secretary in the morning, but it was not much use; his mind kept straying.

In the morning, the Chief came into the restaurant for breakfast and proceeded to demolish bacon, eggs, sausages, mushrooms, four slices of toast with butter and marmalade and a large pot of coffee. He looked rather shame-faced and said hastily, "I only indulge like this when I'm at a hotel. Normally, I hardly eat anything at breakfast. My wife's very keen on this low-fat diet thing, so I make do with yoghurt and cereal."

At the Home Office, the Chief said that he would see the Home Secretary first to explain the situation and would then call Derek in to contribute his ideas to the meeting.

Derek waited impatiently in the anteroom, fiddling with the papers he'd put together hastily in case anyone wanted a few facts and figures. A few minutes later, he was called into the office.

"Are you trying to frighten us?" the Home Secretary said bluntly.

"No," said Derek, equally bluntly. "If you mean do I have any proof of what they're planning, I can only tell you that I'm trying to avoid some nasty event. The people who are planning this aren't likely to give out any details. If anyone came to us with information, they would be killed without any hesitation."

There was silence for a moment. "What can we do?" asked the Home Secretary eventually.

Derek cleared his throat and said, "We could get every police officer throughout England and Wales to report anything, even the smallest detail, that could be related in any way to a terrorist act. I can draw up a specific list of events to look for, because we don't want to be inundated with crank calls telling us someone's loitering near a government building. We would enter these details onto a computer and analyse the findings. I have an IT specialist working for me who's a bit of a whizz-kid at that sort of thing. He could highlight coincidences and bring together random items of information which would help us in our search. The main thing is it must all come to a central point, otherwise it'll get lost in the ether. In Holland they have terrorist response units located in various parts of the country with well-trained and fully armed men who can respond in a very short time."

"Holland is a small country in relation to the UK," the Home Secretary said thoughtfully.

"Yes, sir, but transport could be arranged to get the teams into position, say using helicopters and fast 4x4 vehicles."

"We do have SAS units."

"Yes, sir, but they could not be dedicated to this task and we don't know how quickly they could respond. That's why I was going to suggest specially trained units of Royal Marines, experienced in using all weapons and who know basic information about atomic devices."

"Why?" asked the Home Secretary in a raised voice.

"There's been talk about exploding a dirty atomic device for some time – this could be the time."

"God, now you're really frightening me," the Home Secretary said, bringing out an immaculate white handkerchief from his breast pocket and mopping his forehead.

"There's nothing wrong in being prepared. Before the London Underground bombings, no one thought it could happen, but it did. Hoping it may never happen doesn't prevent it from happening, and we have to take the worst-case scenario into our calculations."

The Home Secretary turned to the Chief Constable, saying with a wry smile, "He's very convincing, isn't he? He should have been a politician." He came to a decision and looked hard at Derek. "Look, we could talk about this all day, but unfortunately I have other people to see. But I'll tell you what I'll do." He counted the items off on his fingers. "One, you send me a report – keep it short mind – of incidents countrywide which might be connected. Two, you want to be the central point collating all information; as from now, you are. And three, rapid terrorist response units using Royal Marine resources – well, I can't promise anything here, because that would come under the Ministry of Defence and I'd have to consult my colleague there. If the situation deteriorates and you have a specific location in mind, we could certainly let you have a platoon of Royal Marines. But to deploy special units on spec, as it were, is just not possible, because most of our special units are serving in Iraq and many other parts of the world, including Afghanistan. The Ministry would not sanction such a move back here and I wouldn't even ask. I'll leave it up to you on those points already agreed. Thank you for your time. You will, of course, keep me in the picture at all times. I'll be extremely interested in the outcome of your investigations."

Outside the Home Office building, as they walked towards the taxi rank, the Chief said to Derek, "You're learning to be the politician, aren't you?"

"Yes, sir!"

During the journey back to Manchester, the Chief asked him what his immediate plans were.

"I'll draw up a list of events I want reports on, and I want written confirmation from the Home Office that I'm the designated UK Terrorist Investigations Co-ordinator. Then I'll use the information sent in to catch them before they can act."

"That's a tall order!" said the Chief.

"I'm aware of that, sir, but we'll have to try."

Back in his office, Derek put all his powers of concentration into the job at hand. "George, I want you to find out for me where all the mail goes when it's received by Scotland Yard before it's redistributed to the various departments. Specifically, I'm looking for mail received from the Dutch police."

"I'll get onto it right away, sir."

"Tony, a job for you. Can you look up on the Internet and any other source that you know of for terrorist incidents and try to assess if they're the kind of thing that should have been spotted or would indicate possible future terrorist activity. For instance, if it had been established that the perpetrators of these activities were all young Asian men living at the same address, or people buying large amounts of home chemicals, like nail polish or similar products, or if new arrivals had moved into a house and there's a lot of activity, coming and going at all hours of the day and night. I know it's a tall order, but I'm banking on your keen eye and analytical mind to pick up something that you think is completely out of the ordinary. Heaven knows, nowadays people lead the most peculiar lives and nothing might be unusual to them, but make a start. Who knows where it will lead. Once we have a list, the three of us can discuss it and the items we choose can be sent to all UK police forces so that every policeman can look out for and report to us anything similar happening in their area."

Derek managed to get through his workload by 6 p.m. and left Tony still staring at his computer screen and talking to himself. He murmured goodnight as Derek went out of the door, eager to see Helen.

"Have you eaten?" he asked her.

"No, I was waiting for you."

"Shall we go out?"

"Whatever you want to do," she said.

"What I want to do has nothing to do with eating!"

"If I didn't feel exactly the same, I could accuse you of being a sex maniac. Let's order in a Chinese or pizza."

Derek reached for his mobile and ordered two pizzas. After they had eaten their fill, they made love, slowly at first and then urgently, as if it were the last time they were going to see each other.

Afterwards, Helen asked Derek what the outcome had been of his meeting with the Home Secretary. She was concerned when he told her, her face showing her anxiety. "You will be careful, won't you?" she said. "Chasing terrorists is a very dangerous business and you never know if they have someone getting information from a contact in the police. If they find out who you are, and it wouldn't take them long to do that, there's a chance they'll target you, and if they think you're a danger to them, they'll kill you without hesitation. I've heard what they did in Holland."

"How did you get to hear about that?" he asked, a little surprised.

"Don't forget, I work at the airport police office. We heard that the investigations started at Amsterdam Airport."

"So, what did you hear?"

"I heard that the police inspector deported a suspicious traveller who was probably a terrorist trying to get into Holland on a forged passport. Soon afterwards he was killed in a car bomb explosion and his successor nearly met with a similar fate. Apparently, his car engine was turning over as if it had a flat battery, so he got the bomb disposal boys, who found a huge bomb under it."

"That was Erik van Eyck. I was talking to him the other day when I flew over to Amsterdam."

"I don't know his name; I just heard he was very lucky to escape without being blown to smithereens." Helen shuddered.

They lay in silence, holding each other closely. "I wasn't aware of that; he never mentioned it. He's a very brave man," Derek observed.

Chapter 51

The next day all hell broke loose when a fourteen-year-old girl was abducted on her way home from school. She was later found with horrific sexual injuries and her throat had been cut. Alice Groves had been an only child; both her parents collapsed when told of their daughter's murder and had to be sedated. They were so shocked that a nurse had to be sent to care for them.

Alice had been abducted in the Middleton area of Manchester, an area not normally associated with a crime of this sort, and the newspapers were full of the story. TV reporters and cameramen were in the area, trying to get some footage of the house where Alice had lived or interviews with the devastated parents.

The Chief wanted to see Derek immediately. Before he had a chance to open his mouth, the Chief said irately, "Well, has this something to do with your investigations?"

"Of course not, sir. I haven't even started to organise things since I got back from London with you."

"So what do you think this is all about? Is it a continuation of the same tactics, to get the police running round in circles, disrupting the force from crime prevention and above all, tracing the terrorists, as you suggested?"

"I haven't been able to get the full details yet, sir, but as you rightly say, it would appear to be exactly that, and I expect we'll find it's been done very professionally, similar to the other three murders. But unfortunately, we're not likely to make any arrests in the near future."

"You're not suggesting we just ignore it are you?" shouted the Chief.

"Of course not, sir. We have to assemble a murder enquiry team and appoint a good man to lead it, but please, don't take any of my men away from the task at hand, because the only way we're going to stop these murders is by apprehending the terrorists."

The Chief sat in silence, rapidly assessing Derek's remarks. "If you ever decide to become a politician, I'll vote for you," he said ruefully. "Okay, carry on for the moment, until we see how things develop, but I'm warning you; there have to be results or it's my head on the block, never mind yours!"

Derek heaved a silent sigh of relief. Back in his office, he asked Tony how he was progressing with the list he'd asked him to compile.

"I've come up with a list of ten items, but until we go through it I don't know how comprehensive you'll think it is."

"Okay, the three of us can discuss it in a moment. What about you, George? Have you managed to get that information for me?"

"All the mail delivered to Scotland Yard goes to their post room, as you would expect. There it's sorted and redistributed to various offices, but if it's addressed to a certain person, i.e. the Chief Commissioner or a divisional commander, it's hand delivered straight away, after being carefully checked for explosives or anything of a similar sort. So any envelope or package from overseas would be considered urgent and treated in the same way. I've got the phone number here of the Mail Enquiries Department if you want to ring them."

Derek rang the number and asked the name of the person who answered.

"I'm sorry, sir," said the voice smoothly, "but we're not allowed to give our names for security reasons."

"Right, Mr No-name, if you can help me I'd be very grateful. Some time ago, I'm not sure of the exact date, at Amsterdam Airport, a young Asian man was denied entry because his passport was out of order and he was sent back to the country he came from. The policeman on duty had the presence of mind to photocopy all his passport documents and, for some reason, was convinced that the man had been heading for Britain. Thinking that he might be connected with the terrorist movement, he sent the copies of the documents, with an explanatory letter, to Scotland Yard. I need that package, urgently. Can you help me?"

"Who would this be addressed to?" asked the disembodied voice.

"This I don't know. Since he sent this package to Scotland Yard the inspector has been blown up and killed in a car explosion. All we know is that he sent those important details to someone in Scotland Yard. Let's assume he didn't know a name or title or which department to send it to, so he would have put on it something like 'For the urgent attention of the Commander of Scotland Yard', or the Head or the Chief or something like that. Where would you send it? Which office? Something like that would have been sent via some sort of registered mail."

"When the mail is sorted, if an item cannot be assigned right away it's put to one side to be attended to later when the first rush is over. We still have some items put to one side looking for a home, so to speak. Do you want me to go and have a look at them and ring you back, sir?"

"Yes, right away, if you could. It should be fairly easy to spot: it'll have Amsterdam Airport markings on it, and I shouldn't think you get much mail from there, do you?"

"Right you are, sir. Give me your extension number and I'll get onto it." Twenty minutes later the phone rang. "Sorry, sir," said the now familiar voice. "I put the bit of paper with your extension number on my desk and someone dumped a pile of paper on top. That's what took me so long." Derek had the feeling that the caller had also been checking up on him to make quite sure he was who he said he was. "Anyway, I've found what could be your parcel, sir; well, it's more of a thick envelope really. It has Amsterdam markings on it but it's addressed to the Head of Scotland Yard Security Department, and as we don't have any such person, someone's put it on one side to deal with later and it's got a bit overlooked. What do you want me to do with it, sir?

"Open it and fax me the contents, then package it up again and send it to me pdq, and please try not to mislay it. By the way, thanks a lot; you may have managed to avert a catastrophe!" Turning to George and Tony he said, "This could be the breakthrough we've been waiting for. At last we'll have the face of a terrorist, assuming he's entered the country. Let's hope he was one of the key men and so they somehow had to try again to get him into the UK. Tony, book me on the first flight to Heathrow in the morning."

On arrival at Heathrow, he headed for the passport control office. "I'd like to speak to your Head of Passport Control," he told the officer who answered the door.

The officer hesitated and it was clear that he had been instructed to vet carefully anybody who turned up asking to meet his senior officer. Derek realised that he should have telephoned earlier to establish his credentials and was forced to kick his heels outside the office until his warrant card had been authenticated. He was finally shown into another room where he was introduced to Chief Inspector Don Harris. Derek complimented him on his security, quoting the difficulty he had had getting past his other staff.

Harris laughed. "This is a big airport and I'm kept pretty busy, so I have to make sure that what I do no one else can handle. I assume your trip here is very urgent."

"I've been appointed by the Home Secretary to co-ordinate all actions against terrorist activities for the whole country."

"What about the Secret Service, MI5, MI6, Special Branch?"

"This doesn't affect any of them; they continue to carry on with whatever they're doing. This is a separate enquiry. I'm looking at a specific threat by, as far as we know, a special terrorist group. These people have been carefully selected, trained and funded by Muslim fanatics. They've been smuggled into the UK by various routes. So far they've carried out three murders and an abduction and murder of a schoolgirl, and they're probably responsible for a hoax bomb scare at a football stadium. We haven't been able to connect them with anything else as yet, but we think they're testing police reaction to these events to see what we do when faced with a problem."

"I'm not quite sure I follow your reasoning. In what way do committing these crimes help them?"

"If you form a team to investigate a murder, say, you pick the best officers available who work full time on just one crime. If we look at the original three murders, you have separate teams from Kent, Cambridgeshire and Manchester all engaged in murder enquiries, which have now become high-profile cases. Then we have the abduction and very brutal murder of a schoolgirl and all hell breaks loose. The Home Secretary is jumping up and down – figuratively speaking – and my Chief is crying in his beer!"

"Right, I get your meaning. So what is it I can do for you?"

"I have here a photograph of a terrorist suspect, originally from Islamabad, trying to get into Holland at Amsterdam Airport. Entry was refused and he was deported. The officer whose decision it was to refuse him entry was convinced he was heading for the UK – some gut instinct, I think – so he photocopied his passport and documents and sent them with a covering note to Scotland Yard Head of Security. Because there's actually no one with that title, it was put to one side in the post room before deciding to which person it should be delivered. Unfortunately, it went into the wrong tray and it wasn't until I heard about it and realised the possibilities of actually having a picture of a suspect that a vigilant worker quickly discovered it and copied it to me. The officer who sent the details paid for his action with his life; he was blown up and killed in a car bomb explosion very shortly afterwards. It's essential that this man's found. The photo is a good one, very clear, and we've had it enlarged. Could you circulate it, discreetly, amongst your passport control staff? Maybe one of your officers will have their memory jogged and remember him going through. His passport and any other papers he carried with him would have been perfect and there would have been no reason to stop him, but he could have been a bit nervous, knowing that if he were sent back again they'd probably kill him."

"What kind of people are they?" murmured Don. "Leave it to me. I'll circulate this photo immediately. With any luck, one of my staff will remember him. I'll get back to you as soon as we have any results."

Back in the office, George asked him how things had gone.

"Well, I managed to convince Chief Inspector Harris how important it is to find this man and he promised full co-operation. He was going to circulate the photo and question his staff to see if they remembered anything."

"By the way," George said, "the Chief wants you to ring him asap."

Derek phoned him there and then.

"What were you doing in London?" asked the Chief.

"I went to London to check with the passport control office at Heathrow if anyone had passed through who looked like the man in the photograph I had sent up from Scotland Yard."

"Why did you think he was a terrorist?"

"Because a copy of his passport was sent to Scotland Yard from Amsterdam Airport with a warning note," said Derek patiently.

"Why wasn't he arrested in Amsterdam?"

"Look, sir, it would take too long to explain at the moment and I have to get on with some current enquiries. You'll be getting my usual report quite soon; I'll give you all the details then."

Derek was just about to put the phone down when the Chief said, "I still want to talk to you about the call I had from the Home Secretary. You can forget what was said in his office until we catch the killer of the schoolgirl. You said yourself that it's linked to the terrorist enquiry, so I want you to go and talk to the team."

"Who's in charge?" asked Derek.

"Inspector Hank Knowles, I've been informed."

Derek was just about to say, "Hank Knowles?" but stopped himself, because he knew that if he said anything he would be put on the case. Knowles was probably the right man for the job. He thought it would be a waste of his time in any case. When he put the phone down he added to himself, "Don't hold your breath!"

George was looking at him, grinning. "How do you manage to get away with it, the way you speak to the Chief?" he asked.

Derek ignored him. "We don't have to worry about the list," he said to his two colleagues. "The Home Secretary wants us to concentrate on finding the killer of the schoolgirl."

"It's all over the nationals and on TV," said George.

"It'll be the same people who murdered the three prostitutes, so I doubt they'll have left any clues. But in this case, they might have made a mistake by murdering a young, innocent schoolgirl. It'll make people think more carefully if they've seen anything which might point to the killer. The general public are apt to resent that sort of thing and consider the dangers to their own daughters or young relatives. I'll talk to Inspector Knowles tomorrow and see if he's getting any co-operation from the general public."

"What's our next step?" asked Tony.

"Have you finished that list?" asked Derek.

"Asking that is like asking how long a piece of string is," said Tony. "How long do you want it to be?"

"Terrorism goes back centuries," said Derek, "but we're talking about recent events; we're talking about a group of people who've set themselves a task, and in this case the task is to kill and maim as many people as possible and get away with it. To them, the more people they kill the better. If we put ourselves in their shoes, we might just get an idea of how to catch them – before they can put their plan into operation. So how would you go about killing the maximum number of people?"

"Okay," said Tony, "ruling out natural disasters like earthquakes, it would have to be something like an atomic explosion."

"You would have to drop an atomic bomb, and somehow I don't think the terrorists have enough sophisticated equipment to pull that one off. What we have to do is go over every practical, and in some cases impractical, ideas. Then tomorrow we can have a brainstorming session and toss a few theories around. It's amazing what you can come up with. But right now I'm bushed and in need of a shower and a good meal!"

CHAPTER 52

At his flat, Derek had a shower, and while he was preparing to go to Helen's flat, he switched on his TV, which was showing the early evening news programme. The main item was the murder of the schoolgirl and they were showing a live interview with Inspector Knowles. He gave the usual replies to the reporter's questions: it was early days; looked like it was going to be a long one; the girl had been moved from the murder site and dumped where she'd been found, perhaps during the night; no witnesses; the body was completely naked and the post mortem was being carried out. Other reporters shouted indistinct questions: "Any suspects?"

"No, not at the moment."

"Any indications as to who the killer might be?"

"At the moment we're still sifting the information we're getting."

"How long before you can make an arrest?"

"As I said before, early days." And so on.

The news then switched to the Home Office, whose spokesman said that they were giving all their support to Manchester CID and would send someone from Scotland Yard if it became necessary. The parents were still too distressed to be interviewed and the police officer in charge hoped that their privacy would be respected.

Derek switched channels, watching various sports results, before ringing Helen. "Hello, it's me."

"Are you coming round now?"

"Only if you're ready and waiting for me."

She laughed. "I might be, but you'll have to hurry or I might lose interest."

When he got to her flat, she opened the door to his knock almost as if she had been waiting behind it. She was wearing a short black skirt and a filmy white blouse which clung closely to her breasts. He stood admiring her.

"Are you coming in or shall we hold a conversation in the hall?" she asked with a raised eyebrow and a cheeky grin.

He went in and closed the door behind himself, leaning lightly back against the panels. "Come here. I want to kiss you, amongst other things."

As they kissed, gently at first, she drew back from him, looking into his face. "Are you feeling tired," she enquired challengingly.

"What makes you think that? It seems a shame to tear off your clothes and ravish you when you look so delicious."

"Have you eaten? I haven't because I was waiting for you."

"Do you want to go to a restaurant?"

Helen thought for a moment. "If we go out to a restaurant, there won't be much time for ourselves when we get back." She carefully avoided saying 'back home', because it seemed too fraught with meaning. "If it were a Friday or Saturday when we could laze in bed the following morning, it would be okay, but—"

"I don't want you to start cooking every time I come here," Derek interrupted.

"So as I was saying, let's order a takeaway," finished Helen.

"Isn't there a MacDonald's near here?" asked Derek. "Why don't we just get something from there? I love their chips. You could have a salad, if you wanted."

When they returned, Helen told Derek to wait in the lounge and went into the tiny bathroom to undress. She came out wearing her bathrobe.

"I'm having difficulties. I can't manage the hooks on the back of my bra. Can you help me?" Turning her back to him, she slipped the robe down her arms and waited for him to unhook her bra. Derek stroked her shoulders and unhooked the little fasteners, freeing her breasts, and turned her towards him, marvelling at the full firmness of her body. Somehow they were in the bedroom, he undressing as he moved against her, kissing, struggling, almost fighting in their urge to satisfy each other. He kissed her neck, the delightful triangle of curls covering her neck. They both moaned with satisfaction as they climaxed together. They fell asleep almost immediately.

Derek was the first to wake and found that they were curled up on the bed, Helen with her back against him. He began to kiss her, little kisses on her neck, and she shivered with delight, slowly turning to face him. He rested on his elbow and frowned down at her. "I think I've fallen in love with you and I'm not sure what to do about it. Seriously, looking back I don't think I've ever been in love before. I didn't love my wife and that's probably why she left me."

"Women are much more aware of these things than men. What are you going to do about it?" asked Helen prosaically.

"I'm going to impress you and court you and make love to you until you fall in love with me, and if that fails, I'm going to pull rank and order you to became my personal slave policewoman until you agree to make love to me every day for the rest of my life!" he said.

"There's no need to get all excited," she laughed. "I think I've fallen for you too. We don't want to rush into anything do we?"

"We've got plenty of time to enjoy life. After all, it's only the first time we've been to bed together, isn't it!"

"I hope you're coming round tomorrow night. I can't wait for this to happen again," said Helen.

"Unless I tell you I can't make it, you can assume I'll be coming," said Derek, giving her a lingering kiss as he reluctantly left to go home.

Chapter 53

The following day, the discussion about how to put themselves in the place of the terrorists started as soon as they were all present in the office.

"How could we kill the maximum number of people?" The question was posed by Derek. "We've overruled atomic bombs and large explosive devices, so what does that leave us with? There's been speculation for some time about when terrorist groups will get their hands on some of the larger devices used by the armed forces. It's said that if you have enough money you can buy anything, and we know that some rich supporters back various terrorist groups. This is possibly what they're waiting for. In the meantime, they're keeping the police forces all around the country busy with murder cases, and other crimes for all we know."

"Even if we assume that this is true," said Tony, "it doesn't help us to catch them."

"Not at this point," agreed Derek, "but if we know what their objective is, we may be able to pinpoint their target. If we know what and how, we're more likely to find where. With these three questions answered we can stop them."

"These are all speculations," George said, "but in reality we have nothing, not at the moment."

"I know, but let's speculate further on this possible atomic device. Even with something like that there's a limit to how many people it could kill. Now, there has been some talk about a so-called dirty bomb, which could cause more deaths in the future."

George pulled a face. "There's not much point in carrying on with that line of reasoning unless it brings us closer to catching them."

"What we have to do is prepare for the worst, and if it doesn't happen, we're happy. However, if we're prepared, we can minimise the damage."

"Only if we know where it's likely to happen," said Tony. "What can we actually do?"

Derek looked around and asked what they knew about atomic devices. "I have a more or less basic knowledge. What about you, Tony?"

"I understand the basic principles, but that's all."

"I think that applies to us all," said Derek. "So what we do now is learn as much as we can about nuclear power stations and explosives; this could be important. And George, you and I have to learn how to use the media to our advantage in case we want to put out a story which could influence the terrorists in some way. For example, we could send a photo of a suspected terrorist to an agency which supplies stories to all the media with a few lines of copy, something like here's a picture of a suspected terrorist that the police are hunting; get in touch if you have any information, or words to that effect. We could then check who's rung and check the information given."

"Why go to all this trouble?" asked George.

"One police inspector has already been blown up by a car bomb in Amsterdam. Another escaped the same fate by his presence of mind, getting out of his car before trying to start the engine a second time. The Bomb Squad found a huge bomb underneath his car."

"What do you mean about starting the engine for a second time?" asked George.

"Apparently, when they wire a car bomb into the engine starter circuit, turning the key gives the impression of a flat battery, as the engine turns over very slowly. If you're lucky, and don't keep trying to start the engine, and get out of the car and run away very fast, you might be lucky and survive."

"That's something worth knowing," said Tony ruefully.

"What happened to him, the inspector who survived?" asked George.

"Nothing; he was fine."

"Is he still serving in the police force?" asked Tony.

"Yeah, I met him when I went over to Amsterdam."

"He must be a very brave man."

"Okay, George, I'll leave it to you to find out the best way to manipulate press releases to our advantage. I'm going to see Inspector Knowles to find out how their investigation is going. I'll see you both later."

He found Knowles' incident room, which was set up in the police station nearest to where the girl's body was found, and asked to see Inspector Knowles.

"He's not here at the moment, sir," said the sergeant after inspecting Derek's warrant card very closely, "but if you'd like to wait in the room he's using as his office."

Derek followed a young policewoman through the organised chaos which was standing in as an incident room, noting that most of the officers were in civilian clothes, not police uniform. Everybody had their heads down, some looking at their computer screens and some talking on the phone, but everyone seemed very busy.

It was not long before Inspector Knowles appeared. Derek knew Knowles slightly, so he said, "Hank, I was wondering how things were going in this case."

Hank looked at him a little suspiciously. "Has the Chief sent you to take over?"

"Absolutely not. I've got far too much on my plate at the moment to take anything as big as this on board."

Hank looked relieved. Satisfied that Derek was only there to discuss the case, he squeezed into the tiny space behind the makeshift desk and shouted to someone to bring two coffees for him and his guest. "What do you want to know?"

Derek explained that he was still investigating the murder of the prostitute and he wondered if anything had come up which might link the two murders.

"I'll tell you what I know so far and you can judge for yourself. I've got a preliminary post mortem report – you can have a copy of that if you wish. Basically, the girl was tortured, sexually assaulted with some kind of metal object and beaten but was still alive before her throat was cut." He cleared his throat in distaste. "Why all that inhumane torture?"

"In my opinion, it was done specifically to cause outrage, so that more police would be used in the investigation to try to catch the killer. I think it's laying a false trail to divert attention away from something, some atrocity being planned."

Hank shook his head, disgusted with the fact that a girl might have been murdered most sickeningly to divert attention from – what? "What's being planned?" he asked. "Have you any idea, any hint or suspicion?"

"We're working through a list of possibilities," Derek lied, "but at the moment we're trying to narrow things down to possible events. Has your team come up with any information?"

"I have to say that at the moment nothing really useful has come up, but we're working very hard, using every possible line of enquiry, and information is coming in all the time. We're collating it and a report will go through to the Chief as soon as … er … well … as soon as something comes up," Hank finished lamely.

Derek persevered by asking if any vehicle tracks had been found.

"No. It's been unusually dry for the Manchester area just lately and we concluded that she was tossed from a vehicle parked at the roadside, probably by two people, and that was done so that they would not leave any kind of track. She was completely naked and had been thoroughly washed by persons wearing gloves. The whole operation was so cold-blooded and clinical, they left no clues at all."

"What about the actual kidnap, the abduction?"

"She was at school; everything was completely normal and then she was snatched in broad daylight."

"How could that happen with no witnesses?"

"This is the most crucial part of the investigation, and we're pursuing this enquiry most vigorously. If anyone even glimpsed her being taken, it could be the one breakthrough we need."

For a moment, both men sat in silence, each considering his own thoughts on the matter.

"Have you talked to her parents yet?" asked Derek.

"They're still very distressed, so not yet."

"Which school did she go to?"

"Middleton Comprehensive."

"Well, thanks for your time, Hank. I wish you luck!"

After a quick sandwich, Derek drove to Middleton Comprehensive School and parked in the staff car park. As he went in through the main entrance he was stopped by someone he took to be a teacher, who asked him who he was and what he was doing there. Derek produced his warrant card and asked directions to the form teacher who taught the murdered girl.

"I think you need to talk to Mr Ramsay, Jack Ramsay, but he's taking a class just at the moment. Is it urgent?"

"I have to talk to him about the murder," explained Derek.

"Good heavens; he's not under any kind of suspicion, is he?"

"No, of course not, unless you know something we don't," said Derek a trifle sarcastically.

"Well, I can take over his class for him if it's really urgent," said the teacher.

"I would really appreciate it if you could tell Mr Ramsay that I'd like a word. It is quite urgent." He stressed the word 'urgent'. How much more urgent was solving a murder case, he wondered.

"Come this way then, and I'll get Mr Ramsay."

They walked down the nearly silent corridor and Derek wondered how noisy it would be when six or seven hundred pupils came out of their classrooms. The teacher asked him to wait outside Room 8 and came out moments later with another man, whom he introduced as Jack Ramsay. Derek asked Ramsay if there was somewhere private where he could ask him some questions. "Just to assist with police enquiries, you know. There might be something you can tell us which would be helpful."

They went into an empty classroom and sat down, feeling rather foolish, at adjacent desks. Derek studied Ramsay closely and noted that he was probably in his early forties, nearly bald and a little overweight for his height. Almost without thinking, he pulled in his stomach and wondered if he should start working out in the police gym. "I'm making enquiries about Alice Groves' murder and it would help our investigation if we knew a little more about her. In fact anything you can tell us would be appreciated," he said. "First of all, what sort of a girl was she?"

Mr Ramsay considered carefully before he replied. "She was quiet, sensible, very nice, not a beauty but always clean and polite, and although not an Einstein, she came in the upper twenty per cent in most of her classes."

"Thank you; that's a very comprehensive description."

Before he could say anything else, Ramsay said, "She'd never accept a lift from a strange man, you know!"

"Are you quite sure about that?" queried Derek. "Not even if he was driving an expensive car, stopped to ask her for directions or something, and was young and good-looking? She was fourteen plus, just the right age to be interested in boys."

"It's possible, but as far as I know, her mother met her at the school gates every day, possibly drove her home, I don't know. It might be possible to interview some of her school friends, but they would have to have their parent or guardian present, and I don't think they'd be very open with you. Kids nowadays clam up when you start to ask them questions, particularly in a case like this. If there was anything in Alice's life they didn't want you to know about, there's no way they would tell you."

"Not even if it meant catching her murderer?"

"Well, of course, if you put it that way, perhaps a casual question or two might be in order, provided I'm in the room all the time. There's a break in lessons coming up in a few minutes and one or two pupils who appeared to be quite friendly with Alice will be having a free period. I think I can arrange to ask them quietly to co-operate with you. You will be careful won't you, how you talk to them, because they've been very upset by this. I can't have them complaining to their parents or the head that you've said anything out of place."

"I can assure you, Mr Ramsay, that anything I say to these children is only designed to elicit information which could help us to discover who did this and perhaps prevent him from doing it to some other poor innocent girl."

Mr Ramsay disappeared and returned minutes later with a tall, blonde-haired girl. He ushered her into the room and introduced her as Gillian Hughes. He said that he had explained the circumstances to her and that she was willing to give as much help as she could. He went over to the window and Derek started to talk to Gillian.

"Hello, Gillian," he said gently. "I'd like to ask you some very straightforward questions and perhaps your information may help us to arrest someone." Gillian's face went white and she nodded silently. "Were you and Alice close friends?"

"Yes," she muttered nervously, "at school, and we lived fairly close to each other as well."

"Did you come to school together and go home by the same route?"

"Not always; more on the way home than coming to school."

"When you went home together, how did you travel?"

"We would take a bus along Accrington Road, get off at Dorset Drive and walk the rest of the way."

"Always the same way?"

"Not always; sometimes if it was a nice day we'd walk all the way home."

"What happened the day she went missing?"

"I wasn't at school that day because I had a very bad cold and my mum made me stay at home."

"Have you talked to any other of Alice's friends about how she meant to travel home that day?"

"As far as I know, she was going to catch the bus."

"Did anyone actually see her getting on the bus?"

Tears were welling up in Gillian's eyes as she thought about her friend. She gulped and said, "As far as I know, no one said they did."

Very quietly and gently, Derek said, "You've been absolutely brilliant so far. I just have one more question to ask. Could you say from knowledge of your friend, would she accept a lift in a vehicle from a young man?"

With a complete change of attitude, the schoolgirl giggled and said, "If he was young, good-looking and had a flash car and talked nicely to her, course she would!"

"Haven't you girls been told about the danger of accepting lifts from strangers?"

Gillian tossed her head. "Don't do this, don't do that. Adults are always telling you what to do. You never learn to look after yourself that way. We wouldn't do anything silly, but where's the laugh in behaving like a nun and walking home like a good little girl every day after school?"

Derek looked at her severely, suddenly out of patience with the teenager's attitude. "Sadly, Alice may have paid the ultimate price, assuming she did accept a lift."

"She may have been taken by force," said Gillian.

"In which case you're right, but I hope this event will stop you from ever accepting a lift with a stranger." Gillian shrugged her shoulders and pouted. "Well, thank you very much for your time and your honest contribution, Gillian. Mr Ramsay, would you take Gillian back to her class and, as a last favour, ask the whole class if anyone saw Alice get on the bus that afternoon. This is very important."

"Yes, of course."

Derek reflected that so far, nothing had come of his visit to the school, which was confirmed when Mr Ramsay came back, shaking his head and saying that none of the pupils had actually seen Alice board the bus.

On his way back to the office, Derek theorised that if only he could find out what Alice had done when she came out of school that afternoon, whether she had decided to walk home or catch the bus, it would clear up the point as to whether she could have been picked up by someone. In any case, hadn't Mr Ramsay said something about Alice's mother meeting her after school each day? There was some discrepancy here, but he must be very careful not to tread on Hank's toes by seeming to interfere in his case and putting questions to anybody whom he thought might be involved. He mulled over what Gillian had said earlier, about them both liking big, shiny cars, and realised it was a possibility that they had seen one or more of these vehicles, which might have been observing them, even stalking them. It was a very lucky cold that had kept Gillian at home that day, or she may have been the one that was enticed into a big 4x4 with blacked-out windows.

He wondered if there were any CCTV cameras on that stretch of the road, but there appeared to be only one speed camera, which would not pick up anyone obeying the speed limit, as he was sure the kidnappers would have worked out beforehand if they had planned it as carefully as he thought they had.

Back at the office, he asked Tony to check if there were any cameras on Accrington Road.

"Do you mean cameras observing traffic situations or cameras for speeding cars?"

"Both; anything you can pick up in that area."

"How did things go?" asked George.

Derek sighed ruefully. "I did just what I said I wouldn't do, and got involved in another inspector's murder case. I can only hope Hank Knowles doesn't take offence, and if anything should come of my enquiries he can have all the credit. According to all the people I've spoken to so far, Alice Groves didn't get on her usual bus to go home from school, and her best friend said that she might have been tempted to accept a lift if the driver was young and good-looking and the car was big and flashy, say a 4x4."

"Why a 4x4?" asked George.

"I think from something her friend said it's because they're big and impressive looking. You sit higher up off the road, kind of looking down on other car drivers and your schoolmates, and it makes them feel more powerful. Come to think of it, older women like them too!"

Tony interrupted to tell Derek the results on the check he had made about cameras in the Accrington Road area. "There are only two recording cameras on the whole of that road; one near the beginning and one about a mile further on."

"This could be very important. Can you check how they relate to the position of Middleton Comprehensive, but before you do that, Tony, you're a tall, good-looking young man, so you've got a girlfriend, right?"

"Why? Do you want her to arrange a date for you, boss?" Tony quipped.

"No thanks. I've quite enough to handle in that department. I was going to ask you what sort of cars she likes."

"Big and expensive!" said Tony.

"No, I didn't mean your girlfriend," said Derek, getting his own back, "I meant what sort of car does she like?"

"The answer's the same in both cases," laughed Tony.

Derek tried again. "What sort of car do you drive?"

"Me? I have a fairly old Vauxhall Astra. It goes like a bat out of hell," he answered enthusiastically. Derek looked sceptical. "It does, honestly. I do my own servicing and repairs and nothing can overtake me on an open road. Not that I break the speed limit," he added virtuously. "I'm a law-abiding police officer! Anyway, I've got through to Traffic and you can see the results on my screen. There are the cameras and there's the school."

"Print it out for me." A few minutes later, Derek could see that the first camera was right at the beginning of the road, a long way from the school. No joy there. The second camera was a long way past the school, but he asked George to get any recordings on file from the day of Alice's abduction, between three and four o'clock being the most important time, and to ask Tony to direct him to the correct department. "You're a family man, aren't you, George?"

"Yes, I've got two girls, one twelve and one fourteen." He quickly whipped out his wallet and showed Derek a snap of the whole family.

"Well, you can understand the feelings of her parents, can't you? If there are any difficulties, get Tony to back you up. I'm sure he has the gift of the gab and will point you in the right direction."

George leaned towards Derek and muttered darkly, "I should watch that one, if I were you. I think he's taken a fancy to you."

"It won't do him any good," rejoined Derek. "I'm already spoken for. I'll give you a written requisition for the copy films; there should be no difficulty."

That night, after making love, Derek looked at Helen, who was curled up fast asleep against him, and wondered if he should wake her. He was worried and wanted to talk to her, so he started to blow gently in her ear. She stirred and moved her hand over her ear but did not wake. He gently kissed her and gradually she became aware of him and smiled sleepily.

"What is it? Do you have to go so soon?"

"No, it's not that. I wanted to know what sort of things you did before you met me."

Helen smothered a laugh, realising that he was quite serious and that something was worrying him. She sat up, and said, equally seriously, "I told you that I was in a relationship and we were living together. We did the usual things that couples do. Do you want to hear examples?"

"No, I just wondered how long it is since you broke up."

"It must be ten or eleven months. Why?"

He persevered, knowing he was beginning to sound ridiculous. "What sort of things did you do during that time?"

"For the past month I've been with you."

"I meant before that."

"You mean after my ex had moved out and before I met you? You want to know how many other men I had in that time and am I a promiscuous floozy."

"No, of course not," Derek said, aware he was treading on very thin ice. "I just meant I'm very much in love with you and I'm enjoying our life very much, but I worry that you might become bored with this routine."

"What routine?"

"Me coming over here, eating, making love, staying in, just enjoying each other's company."

"Oh, so that's what you are getting at. You think I'll get bored, fed up and just up and go."

"Yes, that's exactly what I mean," said Derek. "That's what happened in my marriage, although my dedication to my job was to blame to a certain extent…" He trailed off and finished quietly, "I couldn't bear it if it were to turn out like that again."

Helen knew that this was the turning point in their new relationship. "Look at me, Derek. We have to settle this once and for all. I don't know your ex-wife so I can't comment on her. All I can tell you is I've had three dates in the ten months before I met you and I only went out with one of them twice. I didn't have sex with any of them, and if you want me to repeat that on a stack of Bibles, I can only say you're not the man I thought you were. I'm just not promiscuous, if that's what you thought."

Derek wished he had never opened his mouth, knowing how clumsily he had handled the situation. "No, that's not what I meant at all. What I was so ineptly trying to tell you was that if you want to go out with the girls or do something different, then tell me and we can either do it together or you can spend time with your friends. I don't think I could bear to lose you now."

He turned away from her and Helen hugged him, trying to put all her feelings into what she said. "I'm not the person to suffer being unhappy without saying so and if I think we're getting out of touch with one another, you can bet I'm going to let you know. I'm not going to let you go without a fight," she said playfully and gave him a soft punch on his chin.

Chapter 54

Next morning, Derek arrived at work early, before the other two got in. George would have gone to pick up the copies of the tapes and Tony came in looking somewhat hung over.

"Sorry, guv," he said, "it was my fiancée's birthday yesterday and the celebrations went on for too long."

"What's her name," asked Derek, realising how little he knew about Tony.

"It's Louise, actually."

"Nice name. Reminds me of that song 'Every little breeze seems to whisper Louise'."

"Do you mind," laughed Tony. "She absolutely hates that song."

"What happens, just as a matter of interest, if I wanted some slightly illegal phone tapping done," asked Derek.

Tony typed something on his computer keyboard and said, "Says here that from April, all communication work including phones, radios, Internet etc. will be done by a contractor called G. G. Barker Communications and it gives all their details here. Shall I print you out a copy?" Derek took the sheet of paper, folded it and put it in his inside pocket. "What is it you want doing?" asked Tony.

"I know what I want done, but whether they can actually do it is another matter."

Tony realised that his boss wasn't going to tell him, so he just wished him good luck and went to find a cup of coffee and an aspirin.

Derek went in search of Barker Communications and finally found it. Looking around, he thought what a dump it was. From the outside it looked like an old garage. He knocked on the door and waited. The door was finally opened by a youngish man of medium height and looking as if he had not had a square meal in days. He was wearing faded blue overalls, which were somewhat threadbare in places, and glasses, the nosepiece of which had been mended with a piece of grubby plaster. "Yes?" he asked.

"I'd like to speak to the manager," said Derek politely.

"Yes," he replied.

Puzzled, Derek looked closely at the young man, wondering if he had caught him on a bad day. "No, I want to speak to whoever is in charge here," he explained, knowing he sounded very pompous.

"That's me; owner, manager and complete work force."

It's incredible, thought Derek. This scruffy kid has the whole of the Manchester Police Force contract for any kind of communication work. They must be crazy, depending on someone like this.

"Are you with the police or are you here to look at the premises? If you want the usual guided tour, I've got five minutes to spare."

"Sorry," said Derek, trying to take in the situation. He showed him his warrant card and asked if he could come inside.

The place was even worse inside than the shabby outside. Seeing his look, the 'manager' said, "Don't worry about what it looks like. So far, your police force has been more than satisfied by the work we've done for them."

"You said 'we'; who exactly is 'we'?"

"Normally there's me and the lad over there."

Derek noticed someone sitting at a bench with some complicated electronic gear, which he appeared to be stripping down.

"Yes, there's me and him; his name is Julian Clay. He's a brilliant electronics engineer."

In total disbelief, Derek said, "He doesn't look as if he's old enough to work!"

"What do you mean? He's a married man with two children."

"How old is he?"

"He's twenty."

"What, twenty years old, with two children?"

"Yes, why not? My name's Michael Barker, by the way."

"What happened to G. G. Barker?"

"George Graham Barker was my father and he gave me the money to start up in business."

"So it should really be Barker & Son?"

"It will be when I pay him the money back! Now, what can I do for you, Chief Inspector?" He emphasised the word 'Chief'.

Derek went into a long explanation, and when he had finished, he said, "Can you do it?"

"Can we do it?" Michael said scornfully. "We can both do it in our sleep. You want us to install a communication box, well away from your office, which must be able to receive and record phone calls on a certain number, so you can ring from your office phone, be directly connected to that number and listen to the recorded calls. Have I got it right so far?"

"Perfect."

"You also want the phone box to be used as a normal outgoing call service but fix it so you can ring from your office but nobody can trace the call back to you. In other words, you'd be anonymous and untraceable."

"Perfect," said Derek again.

"Correct me if I'm wrong, but don't you need permission for that from someone higher up?" asked Michael.

"No, because we're not monitoring anyone else's calls. The incoming calls will be for us anyway, and going in the other direction, when we make calls we don't want anyone to be able to trace who called!"

"Sounds a bit dodgy to me," said Michael. "You could be a stalker, harassing some poor young lady or something like that!"

"Michael, we're the police," said Derek. "I'm doing this because I want to catch the murderers of a schoolgirl who was abducted, tortured and raped. A stalker is a lone person; we're talking about a team of police officers trying to take every advantage of modern technology to help us solve an apparently unsolvable crime. By the way, when you install the box, make sure you leave no indication of who you are and be very careful that there's nothing to be traced back to you. These people shoot first and then discuss it afterwards; they'll go to any lengths to protect themselves."

"If you're trying to frighten me then you've succeeded," said Michael.

"Do this job and say nothing to anyone," emphasised Derek. "I assume you've already signed the Official Secrets Act when you started to work for the police, so you won't discuss this job outside your place of work or with anyone else. This is very important. It's amazing how quickly rumours start and the press get hold of things and try to work up a story. Not that I have anything against reporters, but I want to catch these killers. If anything should go wrong, it might lead to other tragedies, and I'm working very hard to prevent that."

"First things first," said Michael. "What shall I do with the bill?"

A reluctant smile came over Derek's face. "First things first, indeed. Right, you are a young businessman, for want of a better word, send the bill to this address in a plain brown envelope and I can guarantee it'll be settled immediately. You're going to do the job?"

"Course we are, Chief. We'll get onto it straight away. I'll let you know when the system is up and running."

"Thank you, Michael. Hope to speak to you soon."

Derek returned to the office to find that George had brought back the video copies and was setting up the equipment so they could study them.

"What exactly are we looking for?" asked Tony.

"We're not likely to see any of the schoolchildren – one camera was too far before the school and the other was about a mile past it – but Gillian said they both liked black shiny 4x4 cars, like Shoguns, Jeeps or Toyota Cruisers, possibly even BMWs. We're looking for cars driving sedately along the road, obeying the speed limit, but maybe slowing down when they go past a lone female."

Each camera had provided one hour of film to watch. They settled down to the boring job, trying not to lose their concentration. Twenty minutes passed. Suddenly, George made Tony and Derek jump by growling, "Yes, yes. It's gone past. Rewind it or whatever." Suddenly alert, all three men focused on the screen as they slowly rewound the tape. "It was just how you described it," said George. "A flashy Jeep. Get the registration number, quick." He beamed at them in satisfaction.

Derek made a note of the number. "Now continue in case there are any more vehicles that fit the description."

All tiredness and boredom gone, the three men gazed at the screen until Derek said with huge satisfaction, "There's another." It was a black BMW, a streamlined model with tinted windows, impossible to see inside, driving in just the way Derek had described. He made a note of the number and they watched the recorded film to the end. "What have we got?" he said. "I know there were other 4x4s, but they were fairly old and had different paint jobs."

"What do we do now?" asked Tony.

"We watch the second film and see if we can match up the vehicles further along the road, after they've passed the school." But nothing further happened except that the black BMW appeared and drove along the stretch of road covered by the camera. The Jeep had not been recorded, so perhaps it had turned off somewhere.

They checked with Vehicle Registration and were told that the Jeep was owned by a Mr Gregory Joseph Smythe, who had a Manchester address, but apparently the BMW did not exist; it was being driven with false number plates. Derek felt a surge of triumph as he said, "We can start looking for that car straightaway, because it's on the road illegally! First, I'll get in touch with the Chief's office with a request to trace this vehicle as soon as possible; then I want every policeman in Manchester and all surrounding areas to be alerted to look out for it. But on no account must they try to stop it or apprehend the driver in any way. If no one reports seeing it in the next forty-eight hours, we'll go to the media and get the public involved."

"They're liable to get shot at if anyone tries to challenge them," said George.

"Yes, I'm perfectly well aware of that," snapped Derek. "Hopefully, our own special call box will be up and running very shortly."

"It looks like it was the terrorists driving the car," said George. "It fits in with our supposition as to what took place. The poor girl couldn't have seen the danger. After all, she'd just come out of school, it was broad daylight on a fairly busy main road and there might well have been other people about. Once inside the vehicle, nobody could have seen what happened to her through those heavily tinted windows. Unfortunately, her nightmare had begun, poor kid."

"Poor parents. At least her suffering is over, but theirs has only just begun."

"Where would the next camera be sited? Further along that road?" pondered George.

"That's a job you can start on now, checking for cameras in the neighbourhood," said Derek. "We may have to commandeer more people onto our team to check all the footage on or after 3.30 p.m. on that day for say the following half hour. That should do it. Then we can get an idea of where they were heading. Everything's starting to move in the right direction! What are you doing, Tony?"

He was rewinding and playing the film over and over again. "I'm slowing it down and trying to establish if anything can be seen inside the car. If you get a real expert to play about with the images, sometimes they can narrow it down to quite a good picture. I'm not an expert in that field so I can't do that, but I know a man who can."

"If we need to do that, I'll ask you who your friend is," said Derek, "but we've got a picture of the vehicle which was most likely used in the abduction, we know it's got false number plates and whoever's using it is unaware that we're onto them. I'm pretty certain that if we can trace the vehicle, there's bound to be some forensic evidence of Alice's presence in it. We can be sure the users will resist arrest, and this will prove to us that they're terrorists involved in a suspected plot. It all sounds rather dramatic, but we can set the ball rolling at last."

"What if the vehicle's stolen and they're just car thieves?" asked Tony.

"Well, that's going to depend on any evidence we find in the car, but even if they're not the fanatics we've been looking for, they're still murderers and gangsters and we'll be doing the public a service by eliminating them from society."

Forty-eight hours passed, a nail-biting time for Derek's team, during which they checked every tiny detail of the information they had. Short of driving around the city, personally searching for the BMW, there was not much else they could do but wait. The phone call recording device was tested and was ready to take any calls. Michael even provided Derek with a small device that when attached to his receiver, altered the sound of his voice so that he could not be identified unless special equipment was used.

After waiting for any information to be passed on by police patrols, Derek knew that the time had come to get the media involved. He took several copies of the rather blurred picture of the BMW and went to a news agency with which he had collaborated before.

Ernest Beckenshaw was a tall, thin man who looked about sixty and walked with a slight stoop. "It's not often a Chief Inspector of Manchester CID turns out to visit us," he said with a twinkle, "unless it's something very urgent or very important, or you want some help."

Derek smiled. "You got me banged to rights, guvnor. I confess to everything." Ernest knew when he was being kidded and lit a cigarette. Derek surveyed the ashtray, which was overflowing with butt ends, and said mildly, "Correct me if I'm wrong, but isn't it illegal to smoke in the workplace, to say nothing of just about everywhere else?"

"Course it is," said Beckenshaw, "but it's my office, my lungs. I make the rules here. You goin' to arrest me?"

"Naw, it's not worth it. You'd never survive the cooking in the nick, and you can be more useful to me alive than dead. Besides, 'Elf and Safety' will be after you before long."

"I thought you might say that," said Ernest. "Fire away; what do you want me to incriminate myself in?"

"Nothing," said Derek, pretending indignation. "I'd like you to look at some photographs I have here, taken from a CCTV camera, of a black, shiny new BMW car with heavily tinted windows – that is a very important fact – and I want it published in the media. It's very urgent that we locate this vehicle, because it has false number plates and we suspect it was used to kidnap a young girl."

"What about using conventional police procedure?"

"We've tried that, but so far it's come to nothing. Apparently, it's not been seen anywhere and we must trace it, which is where you come in." He told him what the copy should say to go with the photo and finished by saying, "If you can get that out pronto, it would be much appreciated."

"News is a bit scarce just now, so I expect we could fit this in somewhere on, say, page three."

"I want it on the front, taking up at least half the page," said Derek "And I can tell you this, without revealing the reason; a lot of peoples' lives might be saved and perhaps a national catastrophe averted."

"Well, if that's how you put it," Ernest said, with tongue in cheek, thinking that Derek was exaggerating, "I'll pull out all the stops and get onto it right away." He pretended to tug his forelock.

Outside the smoke-filled room, Derek breathed deeply several times to clear his lungs and then headed back to his own office. He put Tony onto checking if any BMWs had been booked for speeding or parking infringements, but after carefully studying the records, nothing turned up. The next morning, most of the dailies carried the picture of the BMW and the police request for information and the all-important telephone number, and on the midday news bulletins, every channel ran an item on the police appeal, quoting the special number to ring for anyone who thought they had any information or could give any help.

It was late afternoon before they heard a 'bleep, bleep' sound, indicating that someone was ringing the special number. "I strongly advise you to drop the investigation into that vehicle," the caller said. "This is nothing to do with you. This is a warning and you'll not get another."

"Now what?" asked George.

"Now nothing," said Derek, looking up from his desk. "They can't trace the number or get to us in any way. I'll inform the Chief now and make an appointment to see him tomorrow, to keep him informed."

The following morning, the Chief asked Derek what was so urgent. Derek played a recording of the message they had received and emphasised that they should reinforce their warnings to all personnel involved in the search for the car, particularly Hank Knowles and his team.

"I think they know we're getting closer and there's a little bit of panic setting in. My one thought is that they'll take the car out somewhere and torch it, destroying any evidence, even at the risk of being seen when they do it."

The Chief balanced on the edge of his desk and appeared deep in thought. "I'll issue a general warning to all personnel, but it'll have to be low key; we can't have everyone panicking. You talk to Hank Knowles and put whatever urgency you think into your discussion, and keep me informed."

Twenty minutes later he faced Hank, who had a scowl on his face. "I have a bone to pick with you, Chief Inspector. You should have spoken to me about this vehicle before you went public!"

"That's exactly what I'm here about now," said Derek, hoping to smooth Hank's offended feelings. "Originally, we picked up on this vehicle because it has false number plates. At the time, it was not connected with your case in any way. It's an expensive car and it seemed odd that it had false plates, so we tried to trace it and find out whether it was stolen or whether it had been sold with forged documents to some unsuspecting punter. Then we got this message telling us to lay off." He played the tape for Hank.

"And you think we should take this seriously?" he said.

"You're out there on the patch and all your team should take it very seriously," Derek emphasised. "We think these people have a lot of support in this country as a whole and I'm sure they can identify you all. They know you're investigating the death of Alice Groves and they're desperate that you should not get too close to any of their operatives."

"What do you expect me to do; stop everything?"

"No, of course not," Derek said impatiently, "but you have to take this into account, be extra aware and understand that someone might try and harm a member of your team. If I could, I'd put an armed response unit on guard outside this station, but the Chief says to play it cool and not to blow everything out of proportion!"

Hank gave a laugh. "Tell me the old, old story: don't make a mountain out of a molehill, when what they really mean is they don't have the money to pay for extra security."

"Oh, another thing, Hank. Make absolutely sure that no cars are left unattended outside this station; one of their favourite pastimes is putting bombs underneath cars, and if ever there's the slightest doubt, make sure vehicles are checked underneath. Better safe than sorry."

The next morning, Hank rang Derek to tell him that Alice Groves' parents had been found dead, apparently having taken overdoses of sleeping tablets washed down with alcohol. They had discharged themselves from hospital the previous day and the nurse discovered their door was unlocked when she went for a routine visit. She had found them apparently asleep in each other's arms. This meant that the perpetrators were now responsible for three deaths.

The next morning, news of the suicide was in every national and local paper with headlines such as 'Tragedy of the Groves family: daughter killed, parents commit suicide'.

The Chief was on the phone as soon as Derek walked into the office, asking him if he had seen the headlines. He had some news for him. "The Home Secretary's been asking when we're going to catch the killer and what could I tell him. I said we were doing our best, but the outcome of that was they're sending a commander from Scotland Yard to 'assist us'."

"Whatever you do, don't tell him about my team or anything about what we're doing. The last thing we need is some wise guy telling us how to run things."

"Okay, but where exactly are you and your team?"

"We're awaiting reports of sightings of the BMW."

"So, no further forward really."

"Chief, you know it's painfully slow, but I'm sure something's going to break any time now."

Chapter 55

At six o'clock the next morning, a police officer working in Hank's team went outside for a smoke and noticed a white van parked in a prohibited area. He finished his cigarette and went inside to tell the desk sergeant to send someone to put a clamp on the vehicle or have it towed to the compound. The desk sergeant pointed to a large notice on the wall. "See what it says there," he said. "Any vehicle parked during the night is to be reported to Inspector Knowles *immediately*."

It was a long time before the phone was finally answered and the desk sergeant, realising that he was waking Knowles from a deep and satisfying sleep, said diplomatically, "Sorry to disturb you, sir, but someone's left a white van parked outside the station and—"

Before he could finish his sentence, Hank yelled, "Get onto the Bomb Squad immediately and make sure no one goes anywhere near it. Get everyone out of the building by the rear entrance and keep away from that vehicle, do you understand?"

"Yes, sir. I'll get onto that right away." Lot of fuss about nothing, thought the desk sergeant. But always carry out your orders and then you're in the clear. He rang the Bomb Squad and then gave the instructions to empty the building as if it were a fire alarm, ushering some very grumpy police officers out into the early morning fresh air.

Hank's wife kissed him and watched as he went out to his car and almost laughed as he got down on his hands and knees to examine underneath it. Holding his breath, he opened the driver's door and slowly slid in his car key, turning it gingerly, but the engine roared into life. He gave a sigh of relief and set off.

His arrival at the station coincided with that of the Bomb Squad, and the leader waved him to the designated parking area.

"You in charge?" asked Hank.

"Yeah, I'm Lieutenant Gerry Parker. You're Hank Knowles? I expect you've told your men to be careful and I just want to emphasise this. It ain't going to be no picnic and I've got a bad feeling about this sucker. What makes you think there might be explosives in this van?"

"I can't swear to it, of course," said Hank, "but not only do I think there are explosives in the van but it's probably booby-trapped as well. We're working on a very difficult case and just as we thought we were getting somewhere, we get a threatening message telling us to keep our noses out. Then, out of the blue, this turns up. It's not a coincidence."

"Well, thanks for the info," said Gerry. "Could you get to the back of the building with your team and we'll get cracking."

They got out Robbie the robot and guided it in the direction of the van. Everyone waited in complete silence. A mobile phone started to ring using a popular song as its ring tone and went on ringing and ringing. Everyone dived for cover behind the nearest wall and waited, hearts pounding. Then silence reigned once more.

"Whose was that bloody phone?" snarled Hank. "I'll have his guts when I can get to him."

"I thought that might have been the signal to trigger the explosion," Lieutenant Parker said coolly. "If so, poor Robbie. We've lost more robots than you've had hot dinners, and they come very expensive, all that metalwork. Carry on, guys."

The rear windows were covered inside with some black material, so they directed the robot to the driver's window and the camera showed the two front seats. Nothing remarkable there.

"I'm going to put a small charge on the rear doors and blow them open. Everybody in the vicinity has been moved back behind the barriers, haven't they?"

"Yes, Lieutenant."

Parker took a small device from his own vehicle, attached a coil of wire to it, walked over to the van and placed the magnetised box very carefully next to the door handle. Once back behind the temporary crash barrier his team had erected at the side of their vehicle, he shouted, "Heads down!" There was a small explosion, which left the doors hanging off their hinges.

The robot now trundled forward, peered into the back of the vehicle and showed them the interior.

Gerry whistled. "Well, blow me," he said. "They've put enough explosives in there to blow up Colditz Castle." There were four gas containers, a demijohn with some liquid in it, and bags of what looked like fertiliser. "It's going to be a tricky job," Gerry went on, "but if we can disarm it, we can take the vehicle back to base. Who knows what information we can get from it. It must have been that mobile phone ringing that should have set it off, so it would appear there's something wrong with the circuit. It must still be in there somewhere and we'll have to find it to make sure it doesn't trigger a booby trap or any other little surprise."

He brought out a device which appeared to have a camera and light on one end and a long aluminium pipe at the other. He pushed a switch and the light went on at the camera end. Walking carefully over to the back doors of the van, he examined the interior by carefully moving the camera and finally found the mobile phone. "I can see the phone," he said and returned holding it gingerly in his left hand. "Don't know why it didn't set things off, but we'll have to investigate when we get back. In the meantime, the driver and/or passenger doors will almost certainly be rigged to go off with a bang, so that's what we'll do – only from a safe distance," he said cheerfully.

The small charges were fixed to both doors and triggered when everybody was at a safe distance and after checking and rechecking that the area was safe.

"Okay, folks, show's over. Time for a strong drink or failing that, a nice cup of tea!"

Hank ushered his staff back inside, making sure everyone was present and correct and had suffered no ill effects from the tense period they had just experienced. He rang Derek and told him what had happened. "The Lieutenant deserves a medal for what he's done. I wouldn't have his job for all the tea in china," he said thankfully.

"From what you say, he was brilliant," said Derek "but if it hadn't been for a dodgy circuit or a flat battery or something, the number of casualties could have been horrific."

"If it hadn't been for my sergeant craving a smoke or the desk sergeant insisting that he should ring me…" Hank shuddered.

"I don't think it's safe for you to continue working at that police station; it's possible they could try something else," Derek announced. "I think we'll have to move you to another location."

"I've just been thinking about that," said Hank, "but there's not much point in moving us. I have the feeling that they would find out. I'll put a rush job out and get some cameras installed today, with a screen next to the duty sergeant's desk so he can see what's going on all round the building. And we'll have to take more precautions, up our security level. No one's going to frighten us off the job – I am frightened, but now we're getting somewhere, we'll carry on to the bitter end."

Derek laughed. "Good on you, mate. Let me know if you have any difficulties getting the cameras put in. I'll ring the Chief and tell him about our little incident this morning. Keep me updated with any results, won't you. If anything, this should ram home to the disbelievers how determined the terrorists are to destroy anyone or anything getting in their way. Speak to you later."

Later that day, Chief Inspector Don Harris phoned with some information for Derek. "Sorry to have taken such a long time to get back to you, but I can now confirm what you probably suspected all along. The young Asian man whose passport you copied is somewhere in the UK. A young female passport control inspector remembered him. Something triggered her memory and she described him to me perfectly: young, good-looking, smartly dressed, dark suit and tie. He'd tried to chat her up while she was examining his passport, which was in order."

"Thank her very much and praise her for her excellent memory. We could do with more like her," said Derek. "It was his second attempt to gain entry to the UK, so his bosses would have made quite sure his passport and any other paperwork he needed were flawless. He would have practised his charm offensive to try and hide his nerves. Judging by the sketchy information we have, he must have an important role in whatever they're planning to do, because let's face it, they'd never go to all this trouble to get a simple foot soldier into Britain."

"So where does that leave us now?" queried Don. "Are you leading the investigation into terrorism in the whole of the UK?"

"Yes, the Home Secretary appointed me as Information Co-ordinator. Our information line is security protected so no one can find out who's actually behind it. It's vital that our officers have complete anonymity. The Bomb Squad have just defused a huge bomb which was left in an old white van outside the police station where Inspector Knowles and his team of detectives are working."

"My God, who would have done that?"

"Well, considering that his team are investigating the abduction and vicious murder of a schoolgirl, which, by the way, we're sure was done as a sort of sideline to their real target, we're certain it was done by terrorists."

"I find all this very difficult to believe," said Don.

Derek tried to contain his impatience. "Well, unless you're prepared to constantly look for bombs under your car, outside your house, outside your office, don't get involved. I'd have thought living near London you would be having warnings and bomb alerts every time some half-witted passenger leaves a suitcase unattended on a station platform. All I ask from you is to get that photo published locally with an accompanying story, warning the public not to tackle him because he's armed and dangerous, etc., and publish our telephone number. We'll do enough worrying for you, so there's no need for you to get involved. Thanks for finding the photo! Cheerio." He turned to Tony. "Are you logging all this information into the computer?"

"Sure am."

"Well, add this: an Asian man, pictured on the copy of a passport sent to Scotland Yard by a police officer in Amsterdam and later passed to us, has been allowed to enter the UK through Heathrow and is now somewhere in this country. Chief Inspector Harris is going to issue a press release to the daily newspapers with our number."

Tony turned to his computer, brought up the correct file and typed in the information.

"Have we had any more messages on our phone line?" Derek asked George. George checked, but there was only the one threatening message, not even the usual calls from people who were sure he had stolen their washing or kidnapped their cat!

The Chief rang and told Derek that the funeral of Mr and Mrs Groves had been arranged and that a police contingent would be going to show respect. Derek commented that he didn't think that anyone should be in uniform, as the higher-ranking officers, who were rarely seen in public, could be targeted. The Chief accepted what he was saying, even though that rather cancelled out their show of solidarity and sympathy with the bereaved, who might think that the police didn't care enough to attend. "Service at eleven o'clock at St Luke's Church and then interment at Lawnswood Cemetery, next to Alice."

It was a very sombre occasion. There were only about twenty people there, including neighbours and an older brother of Mr Groves with his wife. Most of the married police officers had asked their wives to attend the service with them to maintain a sense of normality.

After the service and interment, Mr Groves' brother told the Chief that they were all welcome to join the family at The Anchor for a drink, but he declined. "I've got to have all my men back at work sober, but thank you for the offer."

Derek, George and Tony returned to the office to find a message from Inspector Harris. It said: 'Watch out in tomorrow's papers.'

Chapter 56

Derek planned to take Helen out to a newly opened restaurant that night, and when she answered the door, he liked what he saw. Her red dress fitted closely and she had completed the look with black high-heeled shoes and fishnet stockings. He began to wonder if it was such a good idea to go out. He looked longingly at the comfortable sofa, and when she asked him what he was thinking, he said, "You don't want to know. It looks as if I'll have to put up with every man who sees you waiting to get me out of the way so he can ogle you and make me jealous."

"Oh dear, I thought you might like this outfit. Never mind, I've got a pair of navy blue overalls in the kitchen. I could put those on with a pair of my police boots and a crash helmet. Would that suit you?" responded Helen innocently.

Derek grinned. "Any more of that cheek and impudence from you, madam, and you'll find yourself in the cells on bread and water instead of the gourmet meal I was planning! I guess I'll just have to fight off the opposition."

"What's this about a gourmet meal?"

"I've booked a table at La Taverna. Is that okay?"

"Anywhere that serves food and drink is okay with me," said Helen. "Come on, let's get moving. I'm starving."

They were studying the menu when a man's voice said loudly, "Hello, Helen. Long time since I saw you, isn't it?"

Derek looked up to see a young couple standing by the next table while a waiter hovered around, pulling out a chair for the woman. The man was wearing a dinner jacket and his partner a long evening gown, which was very flattering to her rather plump figure and obviously very expensive. The young man was possibly six foot tall and in the dim light of the restaurant appeared athletic and handsome.

"Can I introduce you to my fiancée Barbara?" the man went on. "Helen – Barbara, Barbara – Helen. And who's this?"

Helen turned to Derek and said tonelessly, "Derek, meet Inspector Colin Jackson. Colin, this is my fiancé Chief Inspector Derek Young." She placed a slight emphasis on 'fiancé and 'Chief'. "Colin works at the same police station as I do, but I don't work for him."

"Looks like I'm outranked," Colin said pointedly. You've done quite well for yourself then. Funny, I thought I was in charge of the whole station."

"The station yes, but me no."

Colin put his hand out to Derek so that they could shake hands.

When Derek withdrew his hand he felt an impulse to wipe it clean on a napkin. "I didn't really come out tonight to compare ranks and to discuss police matters," he said. "I brought Helen here so we could relax, have a good meal and a few drinks and enjoy ourselves."

Colin laughed rather noisily, as if he had already had a number of drinks, and said, "No good asking you to join us then is it? You two obviously want to be alone." But inevitably, as they were seated at adjoining tables, conversation started between the two couples and Derek forced himself to become sociable.

Helen squeezed his hand under the tablecloth.

"I don't want to spoil anyone's evening," said Barbara, "so let's give the waiter our order for drinks and then we can see what's on the menu."

Derek asked her what her job was while Colin shouted to the waiter for attention.

"Actually, I'm a civil servant and I work as a tax inspector," she replied. "Pretty routine stuff, you know."

"Hmm. I must come and get you to check my tax return," Derek joked.

"Do you want a private visit?"

"I didn't realise that tax inspectors did home visits."

Giggling, she said, "In your case, Derek, I could make an exception."

"Well, that seems like a fair offer," Derek said, wondering why he had started this conversation.

Colin raised his glass and announced, "I don't mind swapping partners."

"But I do," said Helen icily.

"So what shall we do now?" asked Colin, looking around the restaurant.

Glancing at Barbara, Derek asked, "Does he always go on like this?"

"You mean does he always go on and on? Yes, he does tend to. I think he's afraid that if he stops talking someone will see through him for what he is!"

"Hey, what do you mean?" asked Colin indignantly.

Barbara tickled his chin and said in a cooing voice, "I mean you lack confidence, my darling, and that makes you nervous."

"I didn't know you were a psychiatrist as well as a tax inspector," said Colin sarcastically.

"Ah, that's where you're wrong," said Barbara. "To become a tax inspector you have to be a psychiatrist, so you're getting two professional people for the price of one. Aren't you lucky?"

Derek knew that these two were the last people Helen wanted to share their intimate dinner with, but it would be very rude to just walk out. Apart from that, the waiter was approaching their table with the meal they had ordered. The only thing Derek could do was to try to steer the conversation away from themselves and attempt to bring some humour to their remarks. He changed the subject to holidays, thinking that was a safe topic to discuss, but it proved unfortunate.

"Don't talk to me about holidays," said Barbara indignantly. "He goes to some Spanish resort with his so-called mates, boozes all night, then lays on the beach trying to recover, and then they pick up some girls and take them back to their hotel rooms. Some of the videos he's taken would pop your eyes out." Barbara was getting well into her subject of Colin's peccadilloes.

Colin replied indignantly, raising his voice slightly to cover her remarks, "I wouldn't have to do that if you were a bit more cooperative; all that 'when we're married we'll do all those things you want me to do' is a load of crap. You're a cold fish and if you won't give me what I want now, what will you be like with a ring on your finger?"

Derek tried not to look at Helen and wished they could crawl under the table, leaving the other two to bicker and squabble all they wanted.

"You're too old to go on these laddish holidays," Barbara was saying.

"I'm not that old and I want some fun. It's more exciting than taking you to a dinner dance," Colin retorted.

"I've told you..."

And so the evening dragged on. Finally, after they had finished their food, Helen turned to Derek and asked him to take her home, using a headache as an excuse. He paid the bill and they left the engaged couple to their full-scale row, fuelled by several rounds of drinks. Luckily, they hardly noticed when Derek and Helen made their escape.

When they got back to Helen's flat, she looked at him with a quizzical glance. "And you wanted to go out more! They ruined our evening!"

"I didn't want to be rude to them. After all, he is your boss."

"I have nothing to do with him. The other women think he's a pest. He goes round acting like he's Mr Wonderful, chatting up all the females. He once pinched a secretary's bottom. She threatened him by saying she was going to report the incident to his boss and the Chief, and he apologised, promised not to do it again and bought her a big box of chocolates. After that, she got a transfer. Now listen. I want a word with you! You've ruined my evening but you're not going to ruin my night as well. I'm just going into the bathroom and when I come out, I want you in that bed, ready to make up for it!"

"Yes, ma'am."

Chapter 57

On Saturday morning, Derek bought two newspapers. Both carried the photo of the terrorist suspect and underneath was printed: 'The police are looking for this man, who is suspected of terrorist acts. If you see him, do not attempt to approach him, as he may be armed and will shoot on sight. Phone this number to pass on any information you have'.

Derek went back to Helen's flat. She was still in the shower. She stepped out smelling delicious, and as she walked past him into the kitchen.

"Have you had any breakfast?"

"Who would want to eat when such a gorgeous woman is standing in front of them?"

"Oh, never mind that. What's in the papers?"

"They've published our request for information and the photo."

She looked at the headline in the *Daily Express* and asked whether the man was a terrorist.

"You can bet he is," said Derek. "He's one of their key men."

"So what happens now?"

"What we're hoping for is dozens of eagle-eyed citizens who've spotted him and can't wait to ring our number to inform us. Then we'll flush him out of wherever he's gone to ground and the case will be solved, I'll get a medal and the Queen will thank me personally. I wish."

Helen looked worried. "You're playing a very dangerous game. You've nearly had an entire police station blown up and you know the odds are that next time you may not be that lucky."

"We know that, but we have to do something; we can't just sit around and wait for them to blow up innocent people just because they happen to feel like it. We have to make every effort to prevent them doing something bad. We're the police and we're here to stop crime and protect our people; that's what we're being paid for."

Helen put her arms around Derek's neck and gave him a long kiss. "Don't you dare let anything happen to you, understand?"

"Okay, and what's going to be my reward?"

On Monday morning, Derek was first to arrive at work. The phone was buzzing like an angry bee. Skipping the first message, he listened to the second. It was another threat: "You are stupid people and you will die." Not very original, he thought. When George and Tony appeared, he replayed both threats to them.

"That's not much help to us, is it?" said Tony.

"Well, in a way it might be," said Derek. "If we look at the things we know for certain, perhaps we might be able to frighten them into making a mistake. So for starters, we have a photo of one of the terrorists and one of the BMW and there are a couple of things we've not done yet. The car must've come from somewhere – that's your job, Tony. Find out whether it was stolen, bought from some garage or a private sale. There can't be too many of that very expensive model in the whole of the country. If you have to, contact the manufacturers and importers and find out how many new vehicles were sold or rented in the UK over the last year. That should keep you quiet for an afternoon!"

Tony made a face, but said, "I'm on it, boss," and turned to his trusty computer screen.

"Now, George, we have to make some assumptions. We know this vehicle passed both cameras and then there were no more sightings and nothing showed on the speed camera. I'm beginning to wonder if that means they didn't go much further. In other words, they turned off Accrington Road shortly after passing the second camera to their safe house. This is a big if. What sort of property would they use as a safe house? It would have to fill all their requirements including a good-sized garage so the car could be kept out of sight. But thinking about it, they must have more than one vehicle, so a large garage would be essential. Privacy is also very important. We know they'll kill anyone who gets close to them, even at the risk of giving away their location. They'll always have somewhere to fall back on, so somewhere after the second camera, within say a two-mile radius, they'll have bought, or possibly rented, a property which has all these advantages. If it's being rented, it might be on a short lease, say three to six months at a time."

"How would they pay? Cheques are easily traced," George chipped in.

"I don't think anyone cares about that as long as the rent gets paid and the cheques don't bounce. Pay your money on time and no one is going to bother you."

"Okay," said George. "Shall I start checking with estate agents?"

"Hang on a minute," Derek said. "Let's think about that. We have to be very careful how we go about this, because we don't want to risk the lives of innocent people. We have to approach it as though we wanted to rent a house of a similar specification so that we can get as much information as possible. All it takes is for one gossipy clerk in an estate agent's office to start mentioning any details to a mate, just in idle conversation, and the terrorists might be alerted. We also can't let them think the police are involved in any way. So let's all walk on eggshells, as it were. If you make contact with an estate agent, always give them our special contact number. Tell them to leave a message because we're never sure when we're going to be there, and never quote our office number."

George had never worked on a case where so much secrecy was necessary and he asked if such caution was always going to be required.

"Better be cautious and alive than a blabbermouth and dead. I'll leave it with you and you can start right away." Derek studied the Ordnance Survey Map. "At least you'll have a good idea of promising sounding houses in the area we've decided on."

At lunch, Tony approached Derek with an invitation. "Louise and I would like you and your lady to come for a meal this Friday evening."

Derek tried to conceal his surprise and said that they would be delighted to come. Keeping a straight face, he asked if George and his wife were also invited. Tony looked somewhat embarrassed and answered that George and his wife were a bit old for them and as they still had children at home, they might have had to extend the invitation to them and their flat was not that big! Derek grinned at Tony's obvious embarrassment and said innocently, "But won't Helen and I be a bit old for you?"

"Oh no, Louise thinks we should start to have more mature company now. She thinks most of our present friends are a bit adolescent and immature," Tony explained.

Derek stopped teasing him and assured him that they would be delighted to come and that he wouldn't mention the subject in front of George.

The rest of the week passed more or less uneventfully. Tony was still trying to trace the BMW and George was having very little luck with the estate agents. Something's got to turn up next week, thought Derek. For all they knew, time may be running out.

When he went to pick Helen up on Friday evening, all thoughts of work vanished as she answered the door with a smile and the question, "Will I do?"

Derek took in the short black skirt and high-heeled shoes, the close-fitting, lacy white blouse with a discreetly plunging neckline and gave a whistle. "You look absolutely scrumptious; enough to turn any man's head. But I won't have to be jealous tonight. Tony's madly in love with Louise so I have nothing to worry about," he said gallantly.

"Oh damn! I was hoping to steal him for myself," said Helen with a smile. "What's Tony like? I know he's in the force but I've never come across him."

"Young, tall, good-looking, plays rugby for some club, cricket in the summer, a very sporty type."

"Sounds like a real catch for some designing female," teased Helen.

Derek chose to ignore this last remark. "You can do the navigating, seeing as I haven't got satnav. Here's the bit of paper Tony gave me. See if you can find out which way to go."

"I don't know if I can accept such a responsibility," said Helen. "You won't shout at me if I get lost, will you?"

Derek pretended to growl and said, "Get on with it, woman! You're in the police force, for heaven's sake. Don't tell me you can't find your way around your home patch!"

Eventually, they found Tony and Louise's flat on one of the newly built estates that were springing up all round the outskirts of Manchester. It was a mixture of detached houses, town houses and low-rise blocks of flats. They found the right number and Tony came to the door immediately, closely followed by Louise. He introduced her as his fiancée and Derek introduced Helen as his fiancée. Introductions over, Tony and Louise showed Derek and Helen over their home. There was a small fitted kitchen, a lounge with dining area, two large bedrooms, one with the obligatory en suite shower room, and a separate bathroom. Derek and Helen complimented them on their decorating taste and comfortable furniture and said how nice the surrounding estate seemed. Louise and Helen then disappeared into the kitchen for some 'girl-talk'.

Tony offered Derek a choice of drinks and they settled down to discuss sport while the girls put the finishing touches to the meal.

The food was simple: pasta with a delicious cheese sauce, side dishes of broccoli, roasted tomatoes, garlic bread and a large dish of salad leaves, all washed down with copious amounts of Italian wine. A homemade raspberry trifle and cheese and biscuits followed for anyone who still had room. By the end of the meal they were all on good terms with each other. Louise and Helen discovered a mutual interest in ancient history. Louise wanted to know what Tony was like to work with.

"Why?" said Derek innocently. "Is he supposed to work when he's with us?"

"That's what he says he does," said Louise.

"Does he work hard at home?" asked Derek.

"He works very hard at home," she said seriously.

"I thought he must do. After all the rest and sleep he gets in the office, he has to make up for it somewhere."

"Don't listen to him," Helen said. "That's just his perverse sense of humour!"

Derek asked how long Tony and Louise had known each other and it turned out they had met at university.

"He was standing outside the library looking all lost and forlorn, so I went up to him and asked him whether he'd lost his mummy, because I felt so sympathetic towards him."

Tony told her that she was a cheeky madam and claimed that she used to come and admire his body when he was training in the gym. Helen looked at Louise and asked her if Tony looked nice in shorts.

"He looked very nice in shorts and had lovely legs, even nicer than me."

"Nicer than *mine*," corrected Tony, smirking.

"That's just one of his annoying little habits; correcting me when he thinks I'm wrong. You can go off people, you know!"

"Well, for a teacher of the English language, you could do better," said Tony smugly.

"You two should definitely get married," said Derek when they had all stopped laughing. "Actually, you have all the symptoms of being married already!"

"Did you say you were married?" asked Louise.

"No," answered Helen, "I've not broken him in yet."

"I've been married once already," said Derek.

"So what was it like?" asked Tony.

"She can't have thought very much of it because she left me for another man."

"That must have felt bad."

"Do you mean for me or the other man?"

"Did you not get on?" asked Louise.

"At first things were great, but then the work started to take over my life and that came between us. Anyway, let's not talk about my marriage. Tell us all about your university life." Derek was drinking very sparingly, as he was driving back, but his hosts were well into their third bottle of wine.

Helen looked at Tony critically and said, "You don't look like a rugby player to me. They're usually over six foot tall, built like brick walls and have cauliflower ears!"

"Ah," explained Tony, beaming at her, "but I play on the wing – you know, like the proverbial bird on the wing – and I fly up and down at the edge of the pitch, being caught and manhandled very rarely, so that accounts for my wonderful physique and superb legs!"

Louise put her empty glass down by the side of her chair. "If we're going to start comparing legs, I'm going to change into something more suitable!" And she disappeared into one of the bedrooms.

Derek was wondering if the time had come when they should be making their farewells. Louise was a very attractive lady, slim with curves in all the right places, and it was no wonder that Tony was attracted to her. When she reappeared wearing a short red mini-dress, she was certainly showing a very long and shapely pair of legs. She had pulled her hair into a ponytail and looked for all the world like an American high school cheerleader or drum majorette in some pageant.

Derek stared, quite blatantly, Helen thought, at what was on display. Quite by accident, Louise, when fastening up the zip of her dress, had caught it in her black lacy bra and she was displaying an eyeful of her soft breasts, which were nearly falling out of her tight underwear.

Helen gave Derek a sharp nudge in the ribs and hissed, "Stop staring like that! You look as if you'd been pole-axed!"

"Very nice," he said weakly. "I'm sure your legs are far superior to Tony's, given that he's a rugby player and you're…" He ran out of anything to say.

"Don't encourage her," said Tony. "Next thing we know, she'll be taking the rest of her things off and doing a pole dance!"

"No, I wouldn't! How can you say that about me? You know I wouldn't." Louise looked as if she were about to burst into tears, then gave a little giggle and flung her arms round Tony, hugging him and nuzzling his neck.

Tony gave a desperate glance towards Derek, who rose to his feet, pulling Helen with him, and said smoothly, "Thanks for a lovely meal, Louise. We'll have to arrange for you both to come to us sometime soon. Must get going now. It's long past Helen's bedtime and we have a lot to do tomorrow!"

Louise gave them a lovely smile and sat down rather suddenly as Tony went off to get the coats. Tony hoped that Derek's opinion of him hadn't have been affected and Louise was beginning to realise what the wine had done to her inhibitions!

"Are you sure you're okay to drive?" asked Helen.

"Course I am," responded Derek. "I had one can of lager and made my glass of wine last all evening, so I shouldn't get picked up for dodgy driving." He decided not to mention any of the evening's events, but Helen wanted to know what he thought about Louise's quick-change act. Before long they were laughing, but Helen's laugh died when she glanced in the wing mirror.

"I don't want to worry you, love," she said quietly, "but it looks like a car is following us."

"Perhaps he's just going in the same direction as us," Derek suggested.

"Well, maybe, but I don't think so. He's sticking too close behind us."

The car behind accelerated and came close to the rear of their car, flashing its lights. Derek put his foot down and pulled away, but the other vehicle was soon close behind them again.

"What shall we do?" said Helen shakily. "Do you think it's something to do with the case you're working on?"

He didn't want to frighten Helen, but this had gone through his mind as well. "This is a good fast car and I've just had it serviced. I'm going to try and lose him in the back streets. I know my way around here fairly well; it shouldn't be too difficult."

"There are at least three of them in the car."

"Hold onto your handbag. Here we go!"

Along the narrow streets of terraced houses he drove, concentrating every effort on getting away from the pursuing car. But despite his skill, the following driver had just as much skill and expertise as he had and was not afraid to cut corners in an effort to ambush them in the quiet streets. The two cars were racing through the narrow, narrow streets with engines roaring and brakes squealing. God knows what the people living in the terrace houses were thinking of it all. Neither car giving any space to the other, nor getting anywhere either.

It gradually dawned on Derek what would happen to Helen if he were forced to stop or crashed into another vehicle and they were injured. They just wanted him dead, but Helen's death might not be an easy one. In a cold sweat of fright, he turned back towards the main road, intent on finding the nearest police station and wondering why he hadn't thought of that before. With squealing brakes and skidding tyres, he avoided a car reversing out into the road, swerved round it and came to a large roundabout, where he was held up waiting for a break in the traffic. I'll drive round the roundabout, he thought and then put my foot down and try and come up behind them. But unbelievably, the other car passed them with the window wound down. Derek cringed, waiting for the bullets to come. Instead, three white youths yelled obscenities at them. "That'll teach you old farts to try and race us! Hope we frightened the life out of you!" one of them shouted, and they roared off.

Derek looked at Helen's white face, and despite the fact that a large queue of traffic was building up behind them with irate drivers poking their heads out of windows, he pulled her against his shoulder and let her sob out her fear and tension.

"Will you marry me?" Derek asked. "Sorry I can't go in for the bended knee and diamond engagement ring scene."

Helen sobbed even harder, thumping his chest in retribution for his silly proposal. "It would serve you right," she choked, "if I took you at your word and made you go with me to the registry office in the morning and get a licence. I'll make you pay for this night's fiasco."

Derek affected a pained expression and said mournfully, "Do you mind; I can't get married in a registry office. I'm a good Catholic boy and that might be a sin!"

"Words fail me," said Helen. "Don't you think we'd better get moving before we're murdered by any one of the drivers behind us?"

They drove to Helen's flat in silence. After making sure that all the windows and doors were securely locked, Helen asked Derek to stay the night. He poured himself a drink and told her that of course he would, if that was what she wanted. "It's just that those young yobbos unnerved me and it would be nice to wake up in the morning feeling safe, with you here," she explained.

They both slept late and when Derek woke, he slid out of bed carefully, so as not to wake Helen, and went to a local shop to buy a toothbrush and razor, trusting that she would have everything else he needed.

When he got back she greeted him with, "I thought you'd gone without saying goodbye."

"I'd never do that. I just went to get a razor and a toothbrush so I can make myself look presentable. If you ask me to stay the night again, I'll be prepared. Are you coming back to bed or staying up?"

"That depends on you. But if you come back to bed, I'll show you that my legs are better than Tony's."

"All the way up?"

"Yes, all the way to my chin!"

"Then I'm coming to bed."

Afterwards they fell asleep again. Hunger woke them about midday.

"Come on," said Derek, "I'll buy you a huge meal. There's one of those superstores that serve all-day breakfasts and other meals nearby. You drive."

He tossed his ignition keys to her, which she caught deftly. Putting her head on one side, she said, "Your car? Aren't you afraid I might scratch the paintwork or clash the gears or something?"

"Of course not. You're quite a good driver – for a woman." He sped down the stairs before she could catch him.

They spent the rest of the weekend relaxing and making love, completely absorbed in one another.

Chapter 58

When Derek arrived at his office on Monday morning, he was surprised to find Tony already there.

"I wanted to catch you before George came in, to apologise for Friday night," he said.

"Why, what happened on Friday night?"

"You know; the way Louise behaved."

"Look, Tony, I didn't see anything wrong with her behaviour, as you put it. She was just having a bit of fun. I've seen more surprising things going on at the police Christmas party. Louise has a nice shapely figure and she was just showing it off a bit."

"I thought you two might have been offended by it."

"Well, you're quite wrong there. In fact it was a very pleasant evening and thank you for inviting us. Any joy with the BMW yet?"

Tony heaved a quiet sigh of relief and turned to the information that he'd discovered about black BMWs with tinted windows. "Bit of a dead end, really. Only six were sold by dealers in the UK, and they've all been accounted for; all sold to white people. I've checked them out. They all carry the correct number plates which check with customs records, so they haven't been smuggled in, but there's the possibility one could have been bought abroad and then brought to the UK and had the number plates changed to fool customs, so that anyone checking with the authorities would be told there was nothing on record.

"Okay, Tony, that's your next line of enquiry. If that comes to a dead end, we'll have to think again, unless you can think of any other way they could have obtained that sort of a vehicle in this country."

George came bustling in and Derek asked him if there were any results from his enquiries with the estate agents.

"Most agents rent properties for varying lengths of time, but on the whole, they're flats, terraced houses, maybe the odd semi-detached, very rarely large detached houses of the sort we're looking for."

"It's uncanny," Derek said. "Every trail we open up comes to nothing; it's as though a veil has been thrown over it. We have four murders and that parcel incident at the football ground and in each case they leave nothing to lead back to them. Come on, guys, can you think of anything, anything at all, we can do to follow up these cases?"

"Hang on a minute," said Tony. "We haven't listened to the answerphone since we came in. Estate agents are usually busy over the weekend; there just might be something recorded that'll be of help." They listened. "Heard that one; heard that one. Wait, this one's new! Came in at 11.20 on Saturday."

The message said that the agents had two properties of the kind they were interested in, one available for immediate occupancy, which could be inspected at any time, and another that would be available in two weeks' time, as the tenants were vacating it at the end of their lease.

This is it, thought Derek. I can feel it in my bones. "This sounds like the one," he said. "We'd better get a move on. It looks like we have less than two weeks to get them before they blow up their target. If only we knew what it was! I'm going to call at this agency and make enquiries; then I'll drive casually past the house and see how things are placed. I'll get back to you later. In the meantime, if the Chief should ring wanting to know how things are going, be a bit cagey about where I am and say I'll contact him as soon as I come in!"

"Hey, wait a minute," said George. "I thought you told us on no account should we get in touch personally with any of these agents in case word got out that the police were taking an interest."

"We only have a very limited time now and we have to take the risk!"

Derek got into his car and consulted his map. The area was one he didn't know well and was further away from Accrington Road than he had calculated; in fact, it was well outside the two-mile radius he thought might contain the safe house.

He found the office with no difficulty and pretended to be looking at the various properties for sale hung all round the walls. When asked if he needed assistance, he said that he had had a phone call about a property he was thinking of renting, and could he have some details, because he happened to be in the area at the moment. He was given a sheaf of papers showing a rather murky picture of each house and a description of the various rooms and facilities they offered. He made one or two comments about the area the houses were situated in and was told that their firm was well known for offering only the highest quality rented homes. "Oh, just one thing," he added. "Could you tell me how you'd want to be paid?"

"Well, sir, we'd want three months' rent in advance before you get the keys to the property and then every month by way of a cheque, cash, direct debit or banker's draft, whichever is most convenient for you. Any missed payments would, of course, be regarded as one month's notice to quit."

He thanked them and, as a shot in the dark, asked how the present tenants paid. He couldn't believe his luck when the agent told him that it was by banker's draft. The lessee had worked in a bank, but he had already left; but the other tenants had also paid by banker's draft from the Bank of Dubai.

Derek was almost choking with excitement, but he tried to contain his feelings and said casually, "They must have been an interesting family to meet."

He was assured that no one would dream of calling on them once they had moved into the property, as security and privacy were their bywords. As long as the rent was paid and the neighbours didn't complain about noise or anything else, there was absolutely no need to intrude.

Derek made his way back to his car, hardly daring to breathe, and hoped he hadn't been too indiscreet by asking questions about the tenants. He drove to the house, which was now vacant, and saw immediately that this property would also have been ideal. According to the details he had read in the agent's blurb, it had all the facilities to ensure the comfort of several persons. He wondered if he had the nerve to drive past the other address, only a mile away from Accrington Road. He read the details of the second property: 'Would suit a large family; large kitchen, dining room to seat twelve, large sitting room, TV/computer/study room leading off a spacious hall, and upstairs four big bedrooms, all en suite, two smaller bedrooms, two bathrooms, and outside, a double garage with utility area, enough space to park four cars on the driveway and well-stocked gardens with a lawn at the front.'

After driving past once, Derek parked his car well away and slowly sauntered past the house, wishing he had a dog or something so he had an excuse for walking so slowly. He tried not to obviously stare and took in the fact that the drive curved away from the entrance and that there were trees obscuring the view of the house.

"I'm almost sure I've found it," he told George and Tony back at the office. "I'll fill you in with the details after I've had a word with the Chief."

After some delay, the Chief's secretary told him that the Chief was out, opening a new old people's home or something similar, and she wasn't expecting him back for some time. Indeed, he might well go on to his next engagement without coming back to the office.

"Could you contact him urgently?"

"I'll do my best, but I'll have to tell him what it concerns. What's so urgent that you have to speak to him immediately?"

Derek wasn't sure how much to tell her, so he tried to make it sound as important as possible without giving any details away. He turned to his expectant colleagues, who were waiting for him to give them the details of what he had discovered, and he didn't disappoint them. "Out of the two properties, only one is of interest to us. The empty one is obviously not harbouring any terrorists but the other has all the characteristics of a safe house." He showed them the agent's details. "We have to put it under twenty-four-hour surveillance; that was what I was going to ask the Chief about. He'll probably say it's too costly, particularly when I haven't a scrap of concrete evidence to place the terrorists in that location. Bit of a catch-22 situation here: until we get the evidence we can't have the surveillance, but unless we have the surveillance we won't be able to get the evidence. Crazy! Whatever we do, we mustn't spook them into disappearing or we've lost it."

It was late afternoon before the Chief rang. "What's so urgent you couldn't tell my secretary about? She's quite hurt you wouldn't trust her!" he said jovially, feeling the effects of a generous lunch.

Derek took a deep breath. "Thing is, Chief, I think we've found the safe house where the terrorists are living, but we need twenty-four-hour surveillance to make absolutely sure." He paused.

"That's all, is it?" said the Chief sarcastically. "Just the one building, say six observers, twenty-four hours a day? Do you realise how much that would cost? On my over-stretched budget? When you haven't the slightest scrap of evidence to put to me and you don't even know what's involved? I can't do it, Derek. You'll have to try to get Home Office approval. Put the case to them to justify the very large expense involved. I can't give my approval until they've been put in the picture."

Derek tried to contain his impatience, knowing it would gain him nothing if he irritated the Chief too much, so he said calmly, "I don't want to stretch the budget too much and I don't want one of their little black vans parked outside in the road pretending to be a gas pipe repair crew or something; that would immediately make them suspicious. However, I've been informed by the estate agent that they're getting out in two weeks, which means we have less than twelve days to find out what they're up to and prevent a possible disaster. Now we've got this hint of where they are, I have to follow it up. What I suggest, completely off the record of course, is that some sort of machinery is set up to track all vehicles leaving and entering the grounds of the house and my team and I will do the rest."

"So you and your merry men will undertake all the surveillance necessary and let me have a report in due course?"

"This work has to be done as soon as possible; we have to get started without delay."

The Chief consented.

First thing in the morning, two men came into the office and introduced themselves as Allan and Gerry from the surveillance unit. They were there to install the equipment Chief Inspector Young had requested.

Derek was pleased at the speed of the operation, and after some consultation between the two surveillance men and some fancy wiring work, they announced that they had finished and were off for a coffee. Before they went they showed them how it worked.

"Last night we installed the equipment you asked for at the address you gave us. Now we've attached a circuit to complete the work in this office. It's similar to a TV satellite dish. On your desk is a receiver, which is attached to your PC screen."

Tony was taking all this in, fascinated by the electronic wizardry involved. He memorised the instructions they were being given, as he had a canny feeling that the other two might be a bit confused.

"When a vehicle enters of leaves that address, the movement triggers a device which transmits to your dish outside this building and starts recording into your little black box for as long as the vehicle is moving. When you want to view the information recorded, you just point your mouse at the icon I've put on your screen and press the left hand button. You'll get type of vehicle, colour and registration number."

"How do I know if anything's been recorded?" asked Derek.

"You just have to play it and see! Here's my phone number. If you have any difficulties or it doesn't work for some reason, give me a bell and I'll come round. But we are a bit busy at the moment!"

As soon as they had left the office, Tony tried it out. The system worked perfectly, although, of course, nothing had yet been recorded.

The following morning when they switched on their computers and clicked on the icon to view the previous night's recording, they were rewarded by the sight of a black Mercedes leaving at 19.20 and returning at 22.15; it had a Belgian registration number.

"Quickest way to check the details is to get on to the Belgian police. What we need is who owns it and their address or any other details on record. Can you do that, Tony?" asked Derek.

"Onto it right away, boss."

While Tony was checking, Derek listened to the 'magic box' to check if there had been any more messages, but there were none.

The Belgian police had promised Tony that they would ring back. He emphasised the urgency and sat impatiently awaiting their reply.

The Chief rang to ask whether the special equipment had been installed and Derek thanked him for arranging things so promptly. "Very much appreciated, Chief," he said. "We've already had results: a Mercedes with Belgian number plates. We're getting the Belgians to check on the owner and get back to us."

"You do realise that I had to go down on my bended knees to get that gadgetry installed so quickly. I owe several people several large favours, so I hope it's justified, otherwise you'll find yourself directing traffic in the middle of a football crowd who've just lost the cup!"

"I'm certain it won't come to that."

"Any results on that photo you had published in the papers?" the Chief asked.

"Nothing so far, but it strikes me as a bit odd. Whereas before they reacted straight away by murdering the girl, this time there appears to be no reaction at all. It makes me suspicious."

"Well, we don't want bombs exploding and people getting killed, do we?"

"The thing that worries me is the message telling us we're stupid and would die like all stupid people, but nothing has happened since, which makes me think that the main event is very near so they won't risk another incident. They don't want to be distracted from what they see as their main task. They might think that when this comes off there'll be so much destruction and so many casualties that we'll be punished enough for daring to try and stop them."

"Chief Inspector Young," said the Chief before he rang off, "I don't know why I bother to talk to you; after every conversation we have I always end up very depressed!"

"Are you quite sure about what you just said, about the terrorists preparing for their final event?" queried George. "Or were you trying to get the Chief pissed off?"

"Course not. I really think something's going to happen very soon and I'm racking my brains to think of what it could be."

"Shouldn't we be doing something about it?" asked George.

"Like what? We don't know what, we don't know where and we don't know when; we've done everything we could possibly do, followed up every tiny lead, looked at every record and we can only hope that we've narrowed it down to the address we're watching at the moment. More than that, it's impossible."

"Any good calling in MI5, MI6 or Special Branch to see if they can help us?"

Before Derek could give any comment, the phone rang; it was the Belgian police with the information they had requested about the Mercedes.

"The car was bought by a businessman from Dubai called Assad Ben Saayed, and he still owns it. His bank pays all the bills for it and he has no criminal record in Belgium nor Interpol."

Derek told the others what had been said. "This is another dead end; leads us nowhere."

"What's eating you, boss?" asked Tony. "There's obviously more to this than you've told us, and unless you explain a bit more, we can't really be of any great help."

Derek thought for a moment and made a decision. "What I'm going to tell you is my deduction from the events we know about so far, but it's only my theory, nothing substantial, nothing definite. If you can imagine some very high up terrorist plotter coming up with an outrageous plan more spectacular than Nine-Eleven and far, far worse that the London bombings, they would obviously need a great deal of organisation and large amounts of money. The organisation would not be much of a problem; they have plenty of young men, perhaps university graduates, skilled in chemistry, physics, engineering etc., and can take their pick. In the background, never seen or contacted, are the skilled organisers, and everybody is a dedicated follower of Allah. They've got it into their minds that the West has a 'down' on people of the Muslim faith. They believe that we're totally immune to the suffering and dying of Muslim people and the proof of that is in Iraq and Afghanistan. So they form this group and approach very rich known sympathisers and put their devastating plan to them and ask for funding. A number of rich men volunteer, although some need a bit of persuasion, and proceed to form what's known as a bank. Then the whole thing is up and running."

Tony and George took all this in and opened their mouths to comment, but Derek said, "Don't say anything just yet; there's a bit more to add. To my way of thinking, they'd need at least forty people in the country where this objective is going to be achieved. Their first choice would obviously be the United States, but since Nine-Eleven, security has been tightened up so much it would be almost impossible to get that number of young Asian people into the country at roughly the same time. I'm of the opinion that it would've been impossible to recruit local Americans, train them to their high standards and have them all in the right place at the crucial time. Their second choice would have been the United Kingdom, because there are so many ways you can get people here through other EU countries, since border security is a bit of a joke! Since Blair became PM, Britain has become the fifty-first state of America and we're worth far more in supporting their government's policies than any one of their fifty other states! I now think that some months ago they started moving the people they wanted to locations in the UK via France, Belgium, Holland and even some African countries like South Africa. As always happens, the best-made plans can go wrong and the first balls-up was in Amsterdam Airport. It seems, from what I can gather, that one of their leaders was stopped and sent back to his country of origin. However, some bright-thinking official had the brains to send photocopies of his passport to Scotland Yard, the photograph we published recently. That Amsterdam official would appear to have paid for doing his duty by being killed a short time later, and the terrorist got in at the second attempt via Heathrow. They also had trouble at Frankfurt Airport and I've been told they lost a lot of their men in Holland, nine at one safe house and four at another. Sadly, a lot of policemen were killed in the process and the men they lost will almost certainly have been replaced."

"Where does that leave us then?" asked Tony.

"I'm convinced that their spectacular event is going to be soon, possibly within the next few days. The two houses we got details of were very similar and would be ideal as safe houses: quiet areas, no nosy neighbours, large enough to accommodate nine or ten people, a big garage to keep their vehicles out of sight, which is what you would have to do if you carried false number plates."

"They'd be very expensive to buy," commented George.

"They just send one of their operatives into the area to do a recce, find a suitable property and then arrange to rent it for say a year or however many months they think they're going to need it; everything sorted! As you know, one of the houses is already vacant and the other will be free in two weeks. What does that tell you? Hopefully, we can keep them under surveillance and will be able to track them when they leave. I only hope they have some kind of large van to load all their equipment into. That should give us the opportunity to see what's going on."

Tony was looking at the estate agent's illustration of the house. "I don't think you'll be able to see very much because of those trees near the house," he pointed out.

"Damn," said Derek. "You're right, Tony, but hopefully we'll be able to tell by the increased traffic."

"If all your assumptions are correct," said Tony, "we're relying too much on hope. What we need is something a bit more positive. Even if we do spot vehicles moving in and out of the driveway, how are we going to follow them without them spotting us?"

"All good points, but at the moment I can't give you any answers. If we knew for certain there was a terrorist cell planning an attack we could get the Armed Response Unit, SAS Units, Marine Commandos, Old Uncle Tom Cobbley and all lined up and we could wipe them out. But as I told you, we don't have that information, and we can't lay siege to private property without a warrant to search the premises. We're not even allowed to enter the grounds without a warrant. And no judge is going to issue a warrant on my suspicions!"

"If we can't break the law," suggested George, "perhaps we can bend it a bit. Couldn't we arrange a break-in, make it look like a robbery and get evidence that way?"

"George, I'm ashamed of you," said Derek, shaking his head in mock outrage. "You must know that any evidence obtained by those means would be illegal and couldn't be used in court. Also, we know that this group is only a small part of a much larger number, so to eliminate them without finding who else is involved defeats the object of cutting out and destroying root and branch of the plot. What we want is to follow them and hope they lead us to the chief plotters and indicate where the crime is to take place. But most important of all, we must stop them carrying this out."

"So the only action we can take is really no action at all – we have to sit and wait," sighed Tony.

"Sadly, that's the way the law works. You can only arrest a person while they're committing a crime or after they've committed it, but not before."

"What exactly do you think they're planning to do?" asked George.

"I can only guess, but the most scary events have been perpetrated by man himself. Events like Nine-Eleven, Chernobyl, the genocide in Rwanda and Colombia and other places, the London bombings, explosions in Madrid when more than three hundred people died, the bombing of a nightclub in Bali when it's thought nearly one hundred were killed. I could go on and on. I think it's some kind of bombing campaign and I suppose the obvious targets would be football stadiums. Some stadiums have regular attendances of forty thousand plus."

"What about explosions on passenger planes? They hold around three hundred?"

"No, I don't think so; you'd have to explode a lot of passenger planes to equal a casualty number from a football stadium. I think they've done the dummy run already."

"Would one bomb kill many people in a stadium?" queried George.

"On a match day, the police won't let you park your car within miles of the ground, and if you were thinking of exploding a bomb against the outside wall, you wouldn't be able to do that undetected, so I think it has to be several football grounds for it to be really effective," said Derek decisively.

"So far, we've got nowhere," said Tony. "What about Chernobyl? Although there are many different estimates as to how many died, the resultant fallout is still killing people. Some of our nuclear power stations aren't out in the wilds of the Ukraine. There's that one in Kent less than sixty miles from London and then there's Harwell, that big one on the Suffolk coast, and what about Windscale in Cumbria? I seem to remember reading that farmers in Cumbria weren't allowed to sell their sheep after they'd been contaminated by fallout from Chernobyl, and that was hundreds of miles away, so think what it would mean if there were to be any fallout from UK plants."

"We're just going round and round in circles and achieving nothing," said Derek. "I still think the best thing we can do is try to follow these people when they move and try to second-guess what they intend to do. Any messages?"

"No," said George, "just the ones we've already heard."

"I'm going to give Inspector Knowles a buzz and asked how they're progressing," said Derek.

Hank had nothing new to add except statements from a couple of people who remembered seeing a black BMW drawn up at the kerb; they remembered that the driver was talking to someone about ten to four on the same afternoon that Alice disappeared. Unfortunately, they had been on the other side of the road, so they couldn't see who the driver was talking to. But it had seemed a little odd that when the BMW pulled away from the kerb, no one was left standing there.

"Why on earth didn't they report it after the advertisement and photograph appeared in the papers?"

"They said that a lot of mothers collect their children from school and drive 4x4s; it could have been a mum offering a lift to a school friend of their own child when they saw them walking home on their own."

"It's probably too late now, anyway," said Derek. "They would have changed its appearance and had it thoroughly cleaned to get rid of any evidence that could place Alice inside."

"That's my conclusion as well," said Hank, "and I said as much to the Chief. My team would be better employed somewhere else."

"What did he say?"

"He said to keep things going a bit longer; another crisis might emerge soon which would be a priority case and we'd then have to downsize the team, although we'd keep the case on the books as we always do in case a breakthrough occurred. You know the old saying: we never close."

"Whatever happened to the Commander who came up from Scotland Yard to make sure you were doing everything correctly?" Derek asked.

Hank laughed. "He told us he'd never been so far north before!"

"Goodness me, that must've been a shock to his system. Did you tell him that the atmosphere is a lot lighter here and we have to use oxygen masks to survive?"

"He had the nerve to say it was a lot cleaner than he expected!"

"They don't expect that north of Watford. So what happened to him?"

"When he appeared and saw all the lights and security cameras all round our building he asked me why so many, so I told him about the attempted bombing and the size of the explosive charges used to make the bomb. He went a little bit green, spent the next two days checking what we were doing and at the end of the second day told me we were doing everything right and to just keep at it! There wasn't much else he could do to help us and he had some very important work back at Scotland Yard. He left that evening for London. If you ask me, I think he was a bit scared to work at this police station in case another bomb was planted outside."

Derek chuckled and made a comment about 'soft southerners'. "I'll keep in touch in case I come across any information which might help you."

Derek was soon on his way home to shower and change before he went over to Helen's flat. She answered the door wearing her bathrobe.

"I thought we'd eat in tonight," she said. "Do you like my outfit?" She slipped the robe off her shoulders. She was wearing a miniskirt, which barely covered the tops of her black stockings, and a frilly white blouse tied round her midriff, showing her taut waistline. The blouse did nothing to hide a black lace bra, which pushed her generous breasts up, and the outfit was completed with a black velvet choker and high-heeled stiletto shoes.

"Why bother eating?" suggested Derek. "Who wants food at a time like this?"

Helen avoided his arms and said demurely, "This is a surprise evening. We eat first and then there's a surprise for you."

"You certainly know how to torture a guy, don't you? Okay, but if you see steam coming out of my ears, you might have to call an ambulance."

"Nonsense," said Helen briskly. "If I see steam coming out I'll simply throw a bucket of water over you."

Derek pretended to groan.

They were soon sitting at the dining table, sipping white wine and eating pasta followed by strawberries and homemade ice cream.

"Cheese and biscuits?" queried Helen.

"Yes, and how about some more of that wine. Have you got another bottle hidden somewhere?" Derek helped himself to a generous glass, making sure that Helen's glass was equally full. "What did you put in the pasta to make it so appetising?"

"Oh, just a little sachet of 'Revitalise' to make sure we had an enjoyable evening!"

"Sounds like it should have gone in the bath water, but it's certainly done the trick with me. I feel eighteen again."

"Well, that would make me fourteen and not old enough for sex, so you could be arrested for what you're about to do to me!"

"And who's going to arrest me? Some rookie policeman trying to clap me in handcuffs? I don't think so. Now come here and let me take that miniskirt off you to make you feel more comfortable."

"What about the washing-up? I never have sex before I've left the kitchen clean and tidy!"

"Sod the washing up, woman. Do you want me to come over there and chastise you?"

"Ooh, yes please!" Helen tried to run into the kitchen, but Derek grabbed her and kissed her, fumbling for the fastening of her skirt.

The wine was doing its work and they were both intoxicated with each other; it would have been the same with or without the alcohol.

"What are you doing to me? You shouldn't be kissing me down there; my mummy told me that's a secret place where babies come from."

"Well, that's okay then; I won't kiss your mummy!"

The bed received them gratefully and then the 'Revitalise' really started to work.

Derek woke and heard Helen in the bathroom, so he lay there until she returned.

"You having a bath?" she asked. "There's plenty of hot water."

"I had a bath last year," he said loftily, "and I don't need another just yet. Come here, woman, that 'Revitalise' hasn't finished working yet."

"I'm just going to get some wine and then I want to talk to you about something." She disappeared into the kitchen and Derek stood up, pretending he was Tarzan, beating his naked chest and yelling like Tarzan in the jungle. Helen rushed back in with the bottle and glasses. "For heaven's sake, shut up, or you'll have the neighbours battering the door down, thinking I'm being murdered," she laughed. "Put some clothes on before your dangly bits fall off."

Derek put on his pants and jeans and asked if that was sufficient. Helen made a face at him and said that she couldn't have naked men all over the place, baying like sex-starved moose. "Come over here and sit down. Tell me all about yourself."

"You already know everything there is to know about me."

"No, I mean when you were a kid. Were you a big baby? When did you start to walk? What can you remember about your early life? Things like that."

"I was walking as soon as they cut the umbilical cord and told my mother I was free at last."

"You're an only child, aren't you? Didn't your parents want any more children?"

"As far as I can remember, my parents spent most of their time building up their business and I was a bit of a nuisance to them. They sent me to the best schools and I was a bit of a swot and not too popular with the average Joe. Don't get me wrong; they were good parents, just not the type to hug and praise you. I think for this reason, I've grown up to be a very independent but responsible sort of person."

"Poor you," said Helen. "But you must have had girls falling all over you, a tall, handsome, rich guy like you!"

"I've been brought up very strictly as a Catholic and always stuck by my principles," he said with tongue in cheek.

For a moment she said nothing. "You mean you were taught to think that sex was sinful. You must be pretty unusual, though, if you never had sexy dreams or wanted to watch girls in the bath or shower or undress in front of you?"

A little too airily, he said, "I just said 'get thee behind me, Satan', and thought pure thoughts."

"You're having me on, aren't you? I'm beginning to tell when you're taking the mickey," Helen said indignantly.

"Cross my heart and hope to die," Derek said innocently. "As if I'd ever to try and pull the wool over your eyes, Sergeant Baker."

Helen was determined to find out whether or not he was serious about his teenage years and persisted. "Didn't you ever want to see what girls looked like?"

"You mean being invited to go behind the bike shed for a close examination? I did once have an invitation from Betty 'Drop my Drawers' Hillington, but I had to refuse and sent Trigger instead."

"Who or what on earth was 'Trigger'?"

"We called him Trigger because he was quick on the draw, and if you ask what that means, I'll draw you a picture!"

"No thank you. I'm not all that interested!" Helen moved onto another subject. "Did you sit A levels at your posh school?"

"Yes, I told you I was a bit of a swot. I got two As and two Bs; English, Maths, Latin and Law."

"Why Latin?"

"I was going to university to study law and that helped me to impress the other lawyers and, later on, judges. I could also insult them without them realising. Later on, I started working in a solicitor's office, but I didn't seem to be getting anywhere. I had an acquaintance who had joined the police force and he told me about the work. It sounded interesting, so with my legal training, they welcomed me, and here I am. That's quite enough about me," he finished firmly.

"Okay, here's my potted life story. Working-class parents, lived in a semi, passed my eleven-plus, as it was called in those days, and went to a grammar school, but not the same one as you, obviously. I went into the sixth form and came out with three A levels in English, History and Geography, went to City University and got a degree in English and Geography, which for some reason is known as a 'bad' degree. After that I worked first in one office, then another, but I didn't really like it. So I joined the police force. Now, do you want me to tell you about my sex life?"

"If you want to."

"Well, you're in luck, because there's not really all that much to tell." Derek started to kiss her neck. "Whoa; down, boy. There's a lot we still have to talk about before we get to the kissing stage again. Well, here goes. We've known each other for some time now, haven't we?" Derek nodded. "How about we try to live together?"

"Funny you should mention that. I've been thinking that for some time but I didn't want to rush you."

"Let's try it!" said Helen. "When are you going to move in here?"

Derek paused and said thoughtfully, "The one thing my ex-wife did for me was to leave me with the house. I had to pay her a large lump sum, mind, and extend my mortgage ten years to be able to afford the repayments. But it's fairly new, and at the risk of sounding like an estate agent, it has the following mod cons: entrance hall with separate WC, lounge, dining room and kitchen to the rear, garage with paved drive, four bedrooms, two en suite, separate bathroom with WC, well-stocked rear garden, a corner position and a pleasant outlook. How does that sound to you? Tell you what we could do: you pack a few things tomorrow; we can do some shopping on the way there and you can take a look around. That way we can spend the weekend there and you can see what it feels like from your point of view."

Helen thought for a moment. "You think I should move in with you? I suppose it might work. It is much larger than my place, so it seems logical."

"We can try it as many times as you like until you feel happy to live there. And if you really hate it, we can think about selling and buying somewhere else. How does that sound to you? Can we now go back to bed?" A scrap of black lace on the floor caught Derek's eye as she wriggled her hips slightly under her bathrobe.

"You're not attacking my knickers again!" she said as she moved towards the bed.

Next morning, Helen packed a few clothes into a holdall, gathered her make-up and other essentials together and they set off for Derek's house, stopping at the supermarket for food and wine. Helen was a little apprehensive, having never seen Derek's house before. But it was nothing out of the ordinary; quite pleasant but nothing outstanding.

Derek opened the front door and said, "Remind me to get another set of keys cut for you. Now for the official tour!"

Helen found the place curiously bland; it was completely without any feminine touches. But thankfully, there was nothing there to remind her of his ex-wife. Everywhere was comfortably if a bit sparsely furnished. When Helen went upstairs to dump her bags while Derek put the shopping away, she knew that she could be very comfortable there. She peeped into the smallest bedroom and saw that Derek used it as a study; there was a small TV and bookshelves, and a computer was set up in the corner. The other two medium-sized bedrooms were completely featureless and already she was beginning to furnish them mentally to her own taste.

Derek called up the stairs, "Want a coffee now you've finished peering in all the cupboards and opening all the drawers?"

Helen pretended to be insulted. "Nothing of the sort. I was just putting my things away. I assume the master bedroom is yours?"

"No, actually it's ours. My ex-wife took all the household stuff with her – pillows, duvets, sheets and everything like that – so it's all fairly new. Even with my limited brainpower, I know that no woman wants to use stuff that another woman's used. By the way, I bought a new bed, in case you were wondering!"

"You've thought of everything, haven't you? Who's a clever so and so? I'll have to bring you down a peg or two before you get even more big-headed." But she was thinking how considerate he was to think of things that might upset her and try and put them right.

The weekend was something to remember. They just lazed about, cooked a little, made love, enjoyed each other's body in bed, under the shower and curled up on the sofa watching a film. All too soon it was Monday morning.

Chapter 59

Derek arrived at the office to find the other two already there. He had to shake his head and concentrate on the task they were confronted with and firmly put all thoughts of the weekend out of his head.

"We've got a message on our magic box," said George. He dialled the number and listened to the threatening voice: "Your days are numbered; your death will not come swiftly but will be painful and slow. We're expert in extending life, even when you long to die."

Derek rang his contact at the news agency.

"What can I do for you, Chief Inspector Young?" said the sixty-cigs-a-day man.

"Can you do me a favour? We're getting threatening messages over our answering service. If I give you a recording of the message, can you ask for it to be played on TV, say during the news, and ask if anyone recognises the voice and the person behind it? You can have that as an exclusive."

"That sounds like a good deal to me. Consider it done."

"How's the stop-smoking resolution going?"

"It's not going at all," said the editor.

"Come on; save the planet, and yourself, of course."

"What's the bloody planet got to do with it?"

"Cigarette smoke has poisonous gases in it; it pollutes the planet, your body, clothes, office, destroys your lungs and rots your teeth!"

"Goodbye, Chief Inspector." The editor hung up.

"I can only assume he didn't like what I was saying," laughed Derek.

"What was that?" asked Tony.

"I was just telling him in a most friendly and concerned manner about the evils of smoking, and he had the nerve to hang up on me! Dear, dear; what is the world coming to?" said Derek mournfully. "By the way, something funny happened when I was driving Helen home from a restaurant a couple of weeks ago one Friday night. We were followed very closely by a car, and no matter how I drove, it stuck to us like glue. I was beginning to suspect the worst when it pulled level with us and the window opened. I thought it was going to be a terrorist thug shooting at us, but it turned out to be a car full of jeering teenage yobbos, yelling and shouting that we shouldn't try to insult them by trying to race them. I can't explain why they suddenly happened to pick on us, but I don't think there was anything too sinister about it."

"Did you get their number? What sort of car was it? Why didn't you report it to the police?" said Tony. They all looked at one another and each gave a shout of laughter and repeated in unison, "But we are the police!"

The news agency rang later and the editor told him the name of the man who had made the threatening calls. "His name is Sam Drinkwater, an out of work actor I happen to know. As far as I know, he wouldn't hurt a fly."

"Where can I find him?" asked Derek.

"I'll give you his number if you promise to hear him out. This is completely out of character; he's a quiet kind of chap."

"All I want to do is ask him a few questions. If he's the quiet man you say he is, there's nothing to bother him."

"I'll give you his phone number, but I don't know his address."

Turning to Tony, Derek said, "If I give you this number, can you trace the address?"

"Should be easy. Is he ex-directory?"

"You could say that."

With the address Tony had written down for him, Derek drove slowly along Liverpool Road looking for No. 29. Usually, blocks of flats have names, but this one didn't. It turned out to be a low-rise block containing six apartments. He drove past and parked out of sight, then walked slowly back to the entrance. The door was securely locked, so he looked at the names next to the illuminated bells and found, to his surprise, that Drinkwater lived at No. 2. He pressed the bell and when someone answered, mumbled, "Parcel delivery for Mr Drinkwater," into the intercom. A buzzer sounded and the door opened wheezily. He knocked on the man's door and as soon as the catch was loosened, he pushed inside to face a pale, skinny man, maybe five feet nine inches tall and aged about forty. He showed him his warrant card.

"You said it was a parcel delivery," the man said accusingly. "Pushing in here under false pretences. You might not even be a policeman." He was clearly nervous.

Derek said unpleasantly, "I can assure you that I am a policeman, a Chief Inspector, actually, and I think you've been a naughty boy, haven't you?"

"What are you saying I've done?" the man asked plaintively.

Derek immediately recognised the voice. "I think you've been making threatening telephone calls, Mr Drinkwater, which, as you must know, is a criminal offence."

Drinkwater sat down abruptly, a look of misery on his pale face. He was almost in tears. "I'm very sorry, Inspector. I've been out of work now for a long time. Just can't seem to land a job anywhere. So when I was offered three hundred and fifty pounds for each recording, well, I couldn't resist it. The rent for my flat is overdue and I'm living on beans on toast, so I thought there's no real harm in it, is there? Just a little phone call. He said it was a joke on a friend, that's all. I suppose I should've known there's no such thing as easy money."

Derek almost felt sorry for him, but said sternly, "If you co-operate with the police now, we might be able to drop any criminal charges."

Pathetically grateful, Drinkwater said, "Anything you say, Inspector."

"How did it begin?"

"I got a phone call from a man, who asked me if I wanted to earn three hundred and fifty pounds for a small voice-over job. Of course, I was delighted and thought my luck was changing. I'm an actor, you know; you might have seen me on *Coronation Street*. I was in a number of episodes, just a bit-part, but they were going to extend the part for me—"

"Yes, yes, I understand. Just stick to the point."

"Yes, well of course I accepted and said I'd be delighted. He said he'd coach me on what to say and how to say it, you know, taking full advantage of my dramatic training, and he said he'd come in the next day and pay me cash at the same time. So the next day he popped into my flat and…"

Derek could feel his optimism rising; at last, an eyewitness, somebody who had actually seen a terrorist or someone closely connected to them. "Could you describe this person?" he asked.

"Well, you know, I'm used to observing people – it comes in very useful when you're playing a part. I'd say he was young, possibly a student – you know what they're like, playing jokes on each other – casually dressed, jeans and trainers but stylish – quite expensive I would've thought – average height, say five foot nine or thereabouts, and spoke with a local accent."

"Yes, but what did he look like?" asked Derek urgently.

"Oh, you know; dark hair, brown eyes, second-generation Asian, probably born round the corner. There's quite a few Asians in Manchester you know. If you heard him on the phone, you'd never think he was Asian – very confident, knew just what he wanted done and how. He had one of those hand-held recording devices. I don't know the proper name for them."

Thank God there's something you don't know, thought Derek, but he let him carry on centre stage, in his element.

"He had an A4 sheet of paper with what he wanted me to say written down on it. Then we had a little rehearsal, a sort of trial run so I could get used to the machine. When he was satisfied, he erased it and we did the whole thing in one take. He said my voice was very dramatic and just what he wanted. He paid me the money in cash and took everything away he'd brought with him. That's the last I saw of him."

"If I bring round a police sketch artist, would you be able to describe him well enough?"

Drinkwater sat back in his chair, thinking something over. "Would you pay me for making a sketch of the young man?" he said at last.

"Why, can you draw?"

The actor bristled with indignation. "As a matter of fact, I can both draw and paint. I'm very artistic, you see, and it was a toss-up whether I became an actor or trained professionally to become an artist. In the end, I decided to go on the stage."

"If you're sure you can make an accurate likeness, by all means go ahead. An independent person will appraise the drawing and you'll be paid according to his evaluation, okay? Can you do that right away?"

Drinkwater hunted around for the largest piece of paper he could find and a pencil with a point on it, closed his eyes to picture his caller and then, with a few sure strokes, he began.

Derek sat quietly, glancing around the shabby flat, feeling pity for the 'resting' actor, making no movement in case it broke the concentration of the artist.

When the sketch was finished it was an excellent likeness, but of whom? It showed a young Asian man, perhaps of Pakistani or Indian ancestry, black mid-length hair, with a clear complexion but nothing outstanding about the face. It could be anyone you might see in the high street of many a northern town. On the back of the paper were the only personal details known: brown eyes, wore jeans, trainers, might be a student.

"Thank you very much," said Derek. "And now I have to tell you that you've managed to get involved with some very nasty people. I'm not exaggerating when I tell you they'll kill or torture you if they have the slightest suspicion you've co-operated with the police or anyone they think might be a danger to them. Do you understand what I'm saying?" The actor nodded slowly, beginning to look worried. "If you stick to the instructions I'm going to give you, you'll be all right."

"I'll do whatever you say. Who are these people anyway? A mafia sort of gang or something?"

"I can't tell you that at the moment, but you should carry on normally, doing whatever you do each day, keeping to your usual routine in case anybody's watching you. If he contacts you again, you must ring the special number I'm going to give you; put it somewhere it won't immediately be found, in a drawer or hidden in a book—"

"But he doesn't ring, he just comes," Drinkwater interrupted urgently.

"What happens if you're out? Does he call again? Does he come straight into the building and knock on your door?"

"No, he rings the outside bell first to see if I'm in. At least that's what he's done before."

"That's good. You've got a little time before you have to answer the door. How do you know it's him?"

"My flat's on the front so I can see who's ringing the bell. Besides, I don't get many callers; you're the first person I've spoken to for ages."

"That makes it fairly simple. What sort of a car does he drive?"

"I've never seen him get out of a car; if he's got one, he doesn't park it anywhere I can see it."

"That's a pity, but never mind. This is what I'd like you to do: ring the number I'm going to give you and just say, 'The parcel has arrived', and then put the phone down. That's all you need to do, understand? Don't rush it; make sure the person at the other end can hear you and after that, just act normally. I'm sure an actor of your experience will have no difficulty in playing the role. Now you won't hear from us until we've cleared up the case, but remember what I said: these people will do anything to prevent anyone identifying them, so be very careful. Any questions?"

"Yes, Inspector. Will I get paid in cash for the drawing and for the information I've given you?"

Chapter 60

DEREK MUNCHED A SANDWICH WHILE he was entertaining his two colleagues with an interesting version of his meeting with Sam Drinkwater, actor. They roared with laughter when he told them about his loss of rank, being demoted to inspector, and the actor's skill at sketching and asking for money. They both agreed that the sketch was very fair and that the man would be easily identified if only they could spot him among the crowds in Manchester's streets.

"We've got to be on the alert for his phone call and hopefully, while the actor takes on his greatest acting role, we can be round there."

"Why don't we publish the sketch?" asked George.

"Only if you want Drinkwater killed straight away," said Derek dryly. "They'll know where it came from and they'll eliminate him to make quite sure he doesn't reveal any more information."

"So if we're not allowed to touch this guy, why did we bother to do anything anyway?"

"I know it's frustrating, but perhaps we could provoke them into issuing another threat."

"Like what?" asked Tony.

"We could insert a short article in the paper; nothing special but something along the lines that we're closing in on a major terrorist organisation and arrests are imminent. We could pad it out to make it sound really plausible and see if this has any effect on the situation."

Derek had a long conversation with the news agency editor. When he put the phone down, he told his colleagues, "He says it's the last time he's going to allow total bullshit to be put out on the media!"

"Why?" asked Tony. "Most of it's true, particularly that bit about the terrorists, although the bit about us closing in on them might be considered exaggerated."

"Well, they'll have to allow for some poetic licence," said George.

"I'd better ring the Chief and bring him up to date with the present situation," said Derek.

The following day, the information 'from a reliable police source' appeared in most of the dailies and on television news reports. Derek rang the Chief to ask him if he had seen their little bit of news and had to listen to him calling it 'fantasy-land' and an exaggeration of the circumstances, which placed him in a very vulnerable position if nothing positive happened. He was clearly not happy and when Derek said firmly that he wanted an Armed Response Unit available to respond immediately if called upon, he said sarcastically, in his usual manner, "Only one? Why not have three units, the Bomb Squad and a tank at your disposal if you really want to clinch the arrest!"

"Sir, it's only like a kite-flying exercise, trying to provoke a response with the hope that they start to panic and make mistakes."

"It seems to me," said the Chief, "the best result would be if they just walked in here and gave themselves up. However, there's not the ghost of a chance of that happening. How long do we have to wait?"

Derek did his best to smooth things over, stating his case for using the unit whose special skills were needed to arrest the suspect when he was committing an offence, knowing he was walking a very fine line between possible promotion and demotion.

Before putting the phone down, the Chief reluctantly offered two armed policemen and an unmarked car, and Derek had to be content with that.

True to his word, an hour later the two men were shown into Derek's office. They were no one he knew personally, but beggars can't be choosers. He put them in the picture. "We've set a trap for a terrorist suspect who may or may not be armed, but his supporters will be fully armed and very dangerous. It's a bit of a waiting game, to see if he turns up, but if he does, we only have a maximum of twenty minutes to get there and arrest him before he disappears into thin air. I don't know how you want to play this, but the suspect is going to be at Flat 2 at No. 29 Liverpool Road. If he doesn't appear in three days, we'll just have to abandon the idea."

"I know Liverpool Road, sir," said one of the men. "Where do you want us to be on standby?"

"That depends on the length of the shifts you're working."

"That's pretty much up to you, sir, as this is a special op. If we were on standby at our own station, we could work from ten in the morning to six at night. We'd be minutes away from Liverpool Road and our response time would be very quick whenever you alert us. Here's my mobile number and the number of the station sergeant, who's only a shout away from us. Just ring either number and say 'Car five on standby'. We'll start straight away after a quick recce round the district to see how the land lies."

"Right," said Derek, "let's go over this so we know what we're doing. I, or Tony or George here, will ring this number and say 'Car five on standby'. You two go to No. 29 Liverpool Road and wait till this chap comes out of the building and heads for his car, which, by the way, will probably be parked some distance away. The timing is a bit tricky but try and arrest him when he gets into his car, handcuff him and read him his rights, no matter what protestations he makes. Caution him, tell him the charges will be read to him at the station and then ring me. If possible, prevent him getting in touch with anyone: friend, solicitor, whoever. Play it by the book and reassure him that he'll be allowed to phone, but not until after I get there."

"What if someone else comes out of the building, someone who's not involved in the case at all?"

Derek showed them the sketch of the suspect. "This is the one you're going to arrest. I'm told it's a very good likeness, so there should be no mix-up."

"Hmm; looks like he might be a student."

"He may well be a student, but he's the suspect and I want him. He could be the key to the case I'm working on. The man who lives in Flat 2 is co-operating with us; he's on our side. But as far as you're concerned, you know nothing about him and he's not concerned with this arrest."

Nothing happened the following day. Derek thought his nerves could stretch no further. He stayed in the office until nine o'clock in the evening, catching up with his neglected paperwork.

Drinkwater phoned the next day and left the agreed message. Derek was galvanised into action instantly and contacted the armed police officers to tell them that their quarry had arrived.

With nothing he could do to help, he paced up and down his office, praying that the officers would be able to arrest the suspect without any difficulty. He imagined the suspect sprinting away, evading capture, shooting passers-by and disappearing into a labyrinth of narrow streets, in fact anything that could go wrong. When the phone shrilled he was almost reluctant to put it to his ear.

A voice with a broad Lancashire accent announced, "I'm Station Sergeant Jack Wright. Am I speaking to Chief Inspector Young?"

"Yes, this is Chief Inspector Young. What is it?"

"Well, sir, two police officers have arrested a gentleman who refuses to give his name and they say I should contact you because you're conversant with the facts. Is that so?"

Derek collected his thoughts. "Quite right, Sergeant. I'm coming down straight away to interview this gentleman in relation to a serious case I'm working on. I'd be greatly obliged if you could hold him in custody until I get there. I'll be with you in ten minutes. In the meantime, please make sure he's held incommunicado, for reasons I'll explain when I see you."

"Very well, sir."

When Derek arrived at the police station, he looked through the inspection window of the cell and was amazed at the accuracy of Drinkwater's sketch. The youth lying casually on the bench at the back of the cell looked exactly like the picture drawn by the actor.

Derek knew Sergeant Wright from his younger days in the police force and swiftly explained to him that he needed a secure interview room where he would not be disturbed and that the suspect was to be charged with threatening a police officer.

"Well, sir, he's at last condescended to give us his name and address, which I'm having checked discreetly to make sure it's correct."

"Great. Now if you could usher him into the interview room and station an officer inside with me and one outside the door, we can get things going."

Derek sat in the interview room facing the young man. He switched on the tape recorder and related all the relevant facts, finishing by asking the police constable if the suspect had had his rights read to him after his arrest. "Do you understand?" he asked the suspect.

The young man answered in a well-educated voice. "I understand but I do not seem to have 'rights', as you put it."

"We're going to talk about the offences you're being charged with, but I'd like you to confirm your name, address and occupation. You say your name is Joseph Anatoby and you live in student accommodation on the university campus, Block B, Room 292. Is that correct?"

"Yes," sneered the young man.

"You're from Dubai and you're here on a student's visa to attend courses at the university with a view to gaining an engineering degree, yes?"

"Yes."

Derek leaned back and studied him for a moment. "I'd strongly advise you to change your attitude. The charges you're facing will almost certainly lead to you being deported, which I can arrange immediately should you fail to co-operate fully." The young man was silent, his expression difficult to read. "If you don't answer my questions I'll have you put back in a cell where you'll stay until you're ready to comply."

There was silence and then a grudging, "Okay."

"The charges are that on several occasions you procured the services of a third party to record threatening messages which were later left at the Manchester Metropolitan Police Department with the aim of persuading the police to drop their enquiries and investigations into terrorist activities within the Metropolitan area of that city. These charges are covered by the Terrorist Detention Act. Do you understand?"

"I understand them but I've not been involved in any such activities."

"We'll now proceed to discuss the evidence we have, which is three recordings of threats which you asked another person to make and paid three hundred and fifty pounds for on each occasion. We have the recordings and we have some ten and twenty pound notes which you used to pay that person and which, when examined, will show your fingerprints. This afternoon you were arrested as you left No. 29 Liverpool Road; the person who resides in Flat 2 will confirms this. We also have your hand-written note containing the wording of the message to be recorded and your recording machine. This was recovered from your car after the policemen arrested you."

"All this has been planted in my car by your corrupt police!"

"Oh, come on, Joseph; you're an intelligent young man. Why would the police arrest you unless you were there and the evidence was found in your possession? We've got better things to do than fabricate evidence against some idealistic student. Tell me, what were you doing there? It's nowhere near the university. Slumming, were you? Not exactly your sort of area, is it? And it's not exactly on the tourist visitor's map!" Joseph said nothing. "Of course, if you admit to all this, we can move the process forward, but if you keep on denying you were there and the evidence has been trumped up against you, well, under the Terrorist Act we can hold you in prison while we investigate the matter further for twenty-eight days. It is twenty-eight days, isn't it, officer?" Derek looked towards the police officer for denial or confirmation.

"I'll have to check on that, sir," he responded dispassionately. "Wasn't there some alteration about length of time a couple of weeks ago?"

"You're probably right," said Derek cheerfully. "It could be even longer now!"

"What happens if I admit the charges?" asked Joseph unwillingly.

"Well, in that case, you'd have to attend court for sentencing, and depending on how busy the courts are, you might be given bail, so you could be out on bail before you know it."

"I need a lawyer to get some advice."

"Certainly. You can call your own solicitor or you can have the one on duty, appointed by the courts, but you'll remain here while you're making up your mind. Put him back in the cell, officer." On his way out, Derek spoke to Sergeant Wright. "Make sure his treatment is strictly by the book; we can't have anything going wrong with the case. He wants to consult his own solicitor, but if that's not possible, get the duty solicitor to advise him. I'm going to speak to the Chief, but I'll be back shortly."

The Chief's secretary looked up at him over her spectacles. "Well?" she said uncompromisingly.

"You're the most beautiful person I've seen all day!" said Derek.

She thawed noticeably, but said, "Knowing the sort of company you keep, that's hardly a compliment!"

Derek pretended to clutch his heart and said, "You've cut me to the quick; my heart is breaking."

"What sort of remark is that? Don't try and bullshit me with your charm. What is it you want?"

"If things were different, I'd want a lot from you, but in the meantime, I must see the Chief."

"Don't tell me; it's urgent, as usual." She pressed the intercom. "There's a lost soul out here waiting to see you, Chief."

The Chief looked up as Derek walked into his office. "What have you been doing now that can't be undone? Did those two officers I sent you turn up on time?"

"Yes, they did, and together we've achieved a great deal."

"Why do I find that so difficult to believe?"

"That's because you're a cynic, sir, whereas I'm an optimist. I need just a bit more help."

The Chief's face started to go red. "More assistance? You're employing half my force already!"

"No, sir, not really; I've only got two armed policeman and their unmarked car," Derek said soothingly.

"What do you want now?" asked the Chief suspiciously.

"I have a suspect in custody, thanks to my informant. This man we're holding is a direct link to the terrorists, and once he contacts a lawyer, the hours of my informant's life are numbered. If I don't protect him, the terrorists will kill him."

"You seem very confident about that."

"A terrorist's key weapon is, as the name implies, terror, and if anyone betrays them, they exact revenge immediately to show that if others step out of line they'll suffer the same fate. This is why they stick together so closely and there tends to be very few informants; they all know the consequences."

"I am fairly conversant with the methods used. Who's your informant?"

"It's an actor they used to record some threatening messages so that they didn't use their own voices, which might have been recognised."

"Just tell me what you want; you've given me a headache already."

"It's simple. They know exactly where he lives and they'll probably send someone to kill him."

"What do you intend to do?"

"I'll move this man out as soon as I leave your office, but this is an excellent opportunity to lay a trap for them and capture one or two more of them in the act, so to speak. We need to conceal an experienced armed unit around the block of flats, before eight o'clock tonight, and wait for the killer or killers to come. It could be an all-night job, but it's very important that they are cought Not only would we be eliminating some more terrorists but we'd be protecting innocent people as well. It could also mess up their plans for whatever atrocity they have planned."

"You've convinced me. Leave it to me and I'll have a word in the right ears, but you'll have to put your case to the inspector or whoever's in charge of planning this operation to set this whole thing up. Make a note of this number; give me half an hour to speak to the people in charge at the top and then ring it. I don't know any names; secretive lot they are. Now leave before you come up with another hare-brained scheme to decimate the Manchester Police Force. And by the way, leave my secretary alone; no more insults or she's threatened to shoot you!"

Derek rang car five and told them what he wanted them to do. "Go back to Flat 2, No. 29 Liverpool Road as unobtrusively as you can and tell Mr Drinkwater that his life is in danger. Persuade him to leave as quietly as possible and tell him to pretend to go to the supermarket or the betting shop or something. He must take no luggage and be very casual. When he's moved well away from his flat, pick him up and take him to a friend or relative's place, outside Manchester if possible, and keep an eye on him; make sure he doesn't panic. Tell him to close his bedroom curtains, leave his television on and perhaps a lamp lit to make it look as though he's still in residence. You know the drill. Let me know if there's nowhere he can go and if so, take him to your operational building and arrange a bed in the section house for him while we think of something else. Come back to me and let me know when all this has been done."

Derek waited half an hour and then rang the number the Chief had given him. "This is Chief Inspector Young. May I speak to the person in charge of your unit?"

"There's only Inspector Ford here at the moment," was the reply.

"Can I speak to him, then? It's rather urgent," said Derek impatiently.

After a long wait, a voice said, "Inspector Brian Ford. What can I do you for?"

Derek ignored the witticism and asked if the Chief had been in touch with him.

"Yes, sir. How many men would you be wanting?"

"I don't think there'd be more than two operatives on this job, one to break into the flat and kill and perhaps one to keep watch, three at the very outside. They'll either try to abduct the victim or, most likely, kill him on the spot. Since he has very little information to impart, they'll probably kill him immediately."

"Very well, sir. I suggest sending four of my men, giving them no chance to kill any of ours and get away. That suit you, Chief Inspector Young?"

Derek had the feeling that he was taking the mickey. "Yes, that sounds okay. The address is Flat 2, No. 29 Liverpool Road. The building's on the main road so your men will have to take positions at the side of the building – there's designated parking at the rear. And please, Inspector Ford, I'll be eternally grateful if you can get them alive; no fancy shooting. They probably hold the key to a crucial situation the whole country wants to avoid. Anyway, best of luck to you all. One more thing: when you arrest them, make sure they're put in very secure cells, and no rough stuff. And make sure none of them try to commit hara-kiri or anything like that. As I said, I want them alive and kicking!"

"Anything to oblige, sir. Two or three suspects, alive and kicking, will be awaiting your visit!"

On impulse, after a quick glance at his watch, he decided to join Inspector Ford and his men. He would go home, have a brief nap, change his clothes for something suitable for a night watch, have a quick meal and drive to Liverpool Road later in the evening in good time to observe the operation.

His mobile rang. It was the driver of car five to say that they had delivered Drinkwater to a friend of his in Leeds where he would be quite safe.

"Thanks for ringing. You've done a great job. Fax a copy of the address to my office and I think your part in this is over. Some time soon I hope to tell you what you've achieved." Now for the next event, he thought.

After a quick snack and a drink, he was on his way to meet the four men who would be his companions for the evening. He drove his car into a side street, just off Liverpool Road, and started to walk casually towards the flats. He was just approaching the road entrance when he was seized from behind and put into a painful arm lock. His first thought was, God, they're good; I never even saw them. Then he realised he had been mistaken for a terrorist. He tried to tell them who he was, but someone was stuffing a wad of material into his mouth to stop him shouting out.

He was roughly searched and his warrant card pulled out of his inner pocket. A voice hissed, "Sorry, sir. What are you doing here? Nobody told us you were coming."

Derek tried to regain a little dignity and pulled the gag out of his mouth, rubbing his arm where it had been twisted behind his back. "Look, I'm sorry," he whispered to the man who had manhandled him. "I wanted to know what happens and I thought you might need an extra pair of hands."

"If anybody's seen you approaching, you might have given us away. For heaven's sake, sir, go back to your car and leave us to handle things."

Derek felt he had to explain to him the importance of what was going to happen. "We've been after them for a long time and we know that in the last three months they've infiltrated this country in ones and twos, entering through France, Germany, Belgium or Ireland using false passports. These are not homegrown insurgents; they're the best, highly trained and totally dedicated fanatics. We're desperate to discover their plans and put a stop to whatever they want to do, and we have to know when and where it's going to happen. If we can get just one of them to talk, boast or give a hint of what's coming, we stand a good chance of saving lives."

"Very well, sir. I'm Sergeant Tim Wallis and I can assure you we'll do our very best to apprehend these men."

"Be very careful. They'll kill without the slightest hesitation. They know there's no death penalty in this country and terrorists get long sentences in jail, so to them it doesn't matter how many they kill. They're religious fanatics, and taking the life of a non-believer or dying in the attempt means they'll go straight to heaven."

"Thanks for the warning. We'd better get completely out of sight and stop talking."

Time passed very slowly. Ten o'clock came, then eleven o'clock and still nothing happened. What little traffic there was had died down and the occasional pedestrian walked past without noticing them in the shadows at the side of the building. Derek tried to stave off cramp and boredom by quietly rubbing his legs and arms.

Suddenly, a single headlamp was seen up the road. It belonged to a motorcycle carrying two passengers, their faces covered by their crash helmets. It slowly passed the building and Derek froze against the wall, hoping his face was not visible as a white blur. The motorcycle turned around and came slowly back down the road, as if searching for an address. The pillion passenger was carrying a large flat box, which looked like a pizza.

They came to a halt, the engine stopped and the lights were switched off. The pillion passenger eased himself off the bike, still carrying his flat box, and started to move towards the entrance of the flats. Suddenly, men were converging on the two riders, four of them armed.

The Sergeant shouted, "Armed police! Lay down on the ground with your arms stretched out! You're surrounded and we'll shoot unless you do exactly as you're told!"

For a moment, the two riders froze, but then the one carrying the pizza box dropped it and leapt back on the rear seat of the bike and the other gunned the engine into life and tried to accelerate away, but the machine overbalanced and the pillion passenger fell to the ground. The rider roared away.

"Shoot him before he gets away!" shouted Derek, but it was too late. The bike disappeared into the distance before anyone could take a shot.

The officers grabbed the pillion passenger and wrestled him to the ground, handcuffing him securely.

"Take him straight to the interrogation cell at the station," Derek said, trying to make it sound as intimidating as he could. "I don't think another attempt will be made to kill the occupant of Flat 2; when the motorcyclist gets back to their HQ they'll know the building's being guarded. What a pity we didn't have a vehicle ready to chase after him. We might even have found out where they're living. They'll now be really worried that we have one of their operatives in custody, and I'm sure he'll have some very interesting information to give us. Remember what I said: don't allow him any freedom at all, keep at least two officers with him all the time even if he wants to take a slash, and give him a complete body search to make sure he has no concealed weapons. Watch him like a hawk."

Once he'd seen that the pillion rider was safely in the police car, he turned to Sergeant Wallis and said, "I hope I didn't muck things up for you, but you did a great job. I'll be interrogating him in the morning. It won't do him any harm to cool his heels for a while and start to think about the difficulties he's in. Goodnight, or is it good morning? I've lost track of time a bit!"

He went home, but lay awake for most of what was left of the night, planning his interrogation of the suspect. Suddenly the phone shrilled, making him realise he had nodded off at last. It was George with a message for him.

"Sergeant Wallis has asked me to get in touch with you, sir," he said stiffly. "It appears that the prisoner you apprehended last night is dead…" He trailed off.

"What happened? What could have happened? Last time I saw him he was being driven off to the station in perfectly good health with four armed men guarding him." His optimism that they were at last getting somewhere on the case plummeted, and his stomach felt as if someone had kicked him. It was difficult to take in after the high hopes of last night.

George said very formally, "I'm afraid I don't know the exact details, sir. I was just told to contact you and ask you to ring Sergeant Wallis for a detailed report of the incident."

Dazed and not understanding how anything could have happened, Derek rang Sergeant Wallis.

"He went absolutely berserk in the car. He severely injured two officers, who are now in hospital, and in the melee he was shot. It was only intended to wound him, naturally, but with all the bodies milling around, the bullet hit a vital artery and he died instantly. I'm very sorry, sir. If you'd like to inspect the body before the post mortem, then you can look through his clothes and possessions, which aren't very many…" He trailed off. "There'll be an official report on your desk later today, which will explain how this happened," he finally added.

"Thank you, Sergeant."

Derek sat feeling numb for a moment before he got out of bed. A sense of despair settled over him. Were there never going to be any answers to this problem? Were they going to win after all because he hadn't done enough? Should he have gone with them to the station and seen the man put into a cell? Could he have done any more?

He made himself some breakfast and drank two strong cups of coffee before he drove to the Armed Response Unit's premises. Security was tight and he had to show his identification several times before he was shown into Sergeant Wallis' office.

"I'm glad you could get here at such short notice, Chief Inspector Young."

"Tell me what happened," Derek said flatly.

"We put the prisoner in the front car, back seat left, with a policeman next to him on the right with his gun-hand free, in case he needed to use it. We followed in a convoy, which is standard procedure. We set off and had only gone about a mile when I could see some sort of struggle going on; there was a pair of legs in the air and the car was swerving from side to side. The car stopped and we pulled up right behind it. I rushed over and opened the passenger door. I could see that the policeman in the back was slumped over against the side of the car and the prisoner had his legs wrapped round the driver's neck, trying to strangle him. I grabbed the prisoner by the neck and started to pull him out of the car, but he wouldn't let go his grip on the driver, who by this time was almost throttled to death. The other officer tried to assist me but the door wasn't wide enough for both of us to get a grip on the prisoner, and taking a quick look round I realised that one officer was injured and the driver was nearly unconscious, so I pulled my gun with the intention of disabling him, but he sort of heaved himself up to finish off the driver and the shot went into his chest. We were able to drag him out of the car and on to the pavement. I called the paramedics, who came very quickly and tried to revive him, but he was pronounced dead at the scene. I'm very sorry, sir. I know what you were expecting to get from him and had he not moved like that, it would only have been a flesh wound and he would be alive now…" He trailed off miserably.

Derek asked about the two injured officers and was told that their injuries were quite serious but they should both make a complete recovery.

"We've lost the first positive lead," said Derek sadly.

"I'm sorry, sir," said Sergeant Wallis again, "but with one officer seriously injured and another being strangled to death, I had to do something. You weren't there, sir. His strength was phenomenal. He must've been on steroids or something. I could have shot him in both legs, but it still might not have stopped him strangling the driver, and I couldn't let that happen. As I said, my report will be on your desk later today."

They shook hands solemnly and Derek left, determined to interrogate his other prisoner. I must have a plan to make him give me all the information he has, he thought. He's got to know something of the organisation, enough to give us some facts we can follow up on.

After his disappointment, he racked his brains to think of a way of handling the forthcoming interview. In the end he decided on a painstaking method to wring the truth out of him. He went to the police station where Joseph Anatoby was being held and told the duty sergeant that he was going to interview the prisoner. He waited until he was told that the prisoner was in the interview room with a police officer, who was to remain while the interview took place.

Derek sat down and made a great fuss of rearranging his papers on the table. Immediately, Anatoby said, "I should have my solicitor here when you interview me."

Derek looked at him calmly. "And so you shall, but I'm not interviewing you at the moment. I'm not asking you any questions you might need guidance on; I just want to talk to you. We know you're connected to a terrorist group and we have evidence for that, as I told you when we first spoke. Last night, just before midnight, two men on a motorbike went to No. 29 Liverpool Road to kill the person you hired to make the threatening recordings for you. By that time, he was already in a safe house, quite a few miles away, but of course, the two men didn't know that or that armed police were waiting there to arrest them." Anatoby shifted on his chair, trying not to show interest. "One of them managed to get away, but the other one fell off the bike and we have him in custody. I think your associates will feel worried about that, because losing a man before the main event is the last thing they want; every man is needed to carry out their part of the plan. Now, if they tried to kill the actor, who knew nothing about them, what do you think they're going to do to you if we release you? What I don't understand is why you should want to be one of them anyway. You're a student with enough education to know that they're just indoctrinated psychopaths. Whatever they've told you, killers don't go to heaven, whatever religion they profess. If anything, they'd go to some kind of hell. Their cause is without reason or sense. But that aside, they cannot let you live because you've been caught and have been in custody for hours and they'll be determined to find out what you've told us. No matter how much you protest that you've said nothing, given nothing away, they'll not believe you and will use torture to obtain a confession. Then your body will be found floating in a canal or dumped on waste ground and even your own mother won't be able to identify you."

Anatoby was visibly agitated and shouted, "They won't do all that! I'm one of them now; they wouldn't. I'm loyal; they wouldn't."

"What difference would that make?" Derek said coolly. "They kill anyone who's no longer useful to them. You're just a young student who's completely westernised. You didn't go to a Muslim school from a very young age so you weren't brainwashed; you're just someone who's seen specially selected pictures of atrocities in Iraq and Afghanistan and was told how Muslim people are treated unfairly and persecuted. You were outraged at the unfairness of the situation. But this has nothing to do with reality; it's propaganda of the worst sort to fool young, naive people like you into believing in their cause. If you give us information to help us, we can eventually return you to the country of your choice."

"After what?"

"After we've arrested the people involved in the plot and the threat is no longer there."

"My lawyer will get me out of here soon. These things you're saying, they're just not true!"

Derek sighed and leaned back in his chair. "I'll give you an idea of what your future life will be like. I can arrest and charge you for terrorist acts, which means we could hold you for twenty-eight days for questioning. Then you'll go before the court, but it could be months before you make an appearance, depending on how busy they are before your case is reached. You'll be found guilty, because we have plenty of evidence and witnesses to convict you for what you've done. However, I have reason to believe that your organisation is on the point of carrying out a major atrocity, after which, if we're unable to halt their actions, you'll be deemed guilty as part of their organisation. Your sentence will be in the region of thirty years – you'll be about fifty when you come out of prison – there's no parole for terrorists – but I very much doubt you'd last that long: a young, good-looking man like you would be raped on a regular basis and you'll become some fat old lag's 'bitch'. Want me to continue?"

Joseph's expression of horror told Derek that this point had hit home. He muttered, "These things do not happen in British prisons; perhaps in America but not..." He fell silent.

Derek laughed. "Why not?"

"Because in British prisons the inmates have human rights and they can complain to their MPs if they're badly treated," he said eagerly.

"The warden and prison officers might know that, but the prisoners don't always stick to the rules and respect your human rights. After today you'll be put in prison on remand, so you'll be able to find out personally what sort of things happen." Derek paused for a moment to let his remarks sink in.

"Do I have an alternative?" Joseph asked looking petrified.

"That depends on what you can tell us."

"I wish to consult my lawyer."

"That would be a death wish; your lawyer would tell the terrorists that you were in custody and if you told him you were even considering telling us any details of their plans, you'd be eliminated very quickly, perhaps even tonight. It was your lawyer who told them you were here, which is why they sent two men to kill the actor. But we knew this and ensured he was taken to a safe place. However, I can't promise this in your case unless you tell us something worth knowing. I'd certainly not trust your lawyer, because he'll be working for them."

There was another period of silence. "I'll tell you what I know, but it's not all that much," Joseph said at last. "I'm a gopher; I fetch and carry and go for things, but they've never admitted me into their circle. They wouldn't trust me with anything big. I'm never included in their discussions. I've heard one or two things. It's going to be spectacular, whatever it is. At least forty people are waiting all over the UK to strike at the same time. There might be five or six top men, university graduates, trained in various skills like electronic engineering, mechanical and structural engineering. I kept my ears open because I didn't want to miss the big moment – some of the men are known for their leadership skills, and they're organising the whole thing."

"Do you know where they're hiding?"

"No, I've never been to where they live. They gave me a mobile phone and they text or ring me and tell me where to meet just one contact person, say somewhere deserted like the canal bank or a park."

"Do you every travel in any of their vehicles?"

"No, never. When we meet they're always on foot and they make me leave before they do so I don't see what direction they go in."

"How many of them have you met?"

"Just two."

"Could you help our sketch artist draw pictures of them?"

Joseph was suddenly very afraid, realising that he had now gone past the point of no return. He would be a wanted man for the rest of his life. "No, no." In a sudden panic, he refused to say any more. "What would you use sketches for?"

Grimly, Derek said, "I'd have them published in newspapers and displayed on TV."

"I can't do it. They'd know it was me. Have you tried that before, putting a sketch in the papers and on TV?"

"Yes, but without much success."

"In any case, they'll just change their appearance: a different hair style, grow a moustache or something; they even change the colour of their eyes with contact lenses and dye their hair. Well, that's what I've been told, anyway."

"So far, you've not told us anything we didn't already know. What we don't know is where the attack is going to take place, exactly when or how they're going to do it."

"I've told you, I don't know anything like that. Only a very small number of them would know and I'm sure the two men I've met don't know either. They're just foot soldiers. All I've been able to find out is that it's all been meticulously planned and that the people involved are very well trained and totally dedicated. They'd die before they betrayed their comrades!"

Where have I heard that one before, thought Derek?

"The attack is at a very advanced stage and one of my contacts hinted that it's something to do with your nuclear power stations, but that's just a guess."

"Would they not find that very difficult?"

"Well, you remember Chernobyl?"

Derek responded dismissively, "All our nuclear power stations have been modified since then, and I hardly think a rabble of terrorists could do much damage, either outside or even, should they manage to infiltrate a facility, inside!"

"Don't ask me what they're planning. All I know is they've a nuclear scientist in the group and I bet they'd worked something out. I overheard that on the phone a few weeks ago. Someone in the background said it, not my contact."

Derek changed his attitude to the prisoner and told him that they wanted his passport and if he sent it to them, he was free to go.

Joseph could hardly believe his ears. "You mean I'm a free man, I can go?"

"Yes. All you have to do is send your passport to us, but I'll just give you this warning. We've done nothing to publicise your arrest, but be very careful. I'm trusting you to post your passport, addressed to the police station here marked 'For the Duty Sergeant's Attention', but don't post it at the university; you have no idea how many students are sympathetic to the terrorists' cause. If we don't receive your passport at this police station, we'll have to come looking for you, and you'll be arrested again. I'm sure you won't want that. This is for your own protection, so keep a low profile, stay out of trouble and you'll be okay."

Joseph was amazed; he had imagined hours of captivity and possible violent treatment, but here was this policeman letting him go and trusting him to send in his passport! I'll never understand the British, he thought.

Derek ushered him out of the station and told the duty sergeant to enter 'released without charge' on his records.

Chapter 61

Derek rang for an appointment to see the Chief. His secretary told him to come right away.

He greeted her with, "You bring cheer to my heart."

"Yes, well, you could bring cheer to my heart if you brought me flowers or chocolates occasionally!" was the sour response.

"You know your husband would kill me if I did anything like that."

She sniffed and said, "You can go straight in!"

The Chief greeted him with the words, "And what harm have you done to my career now?"

"Settle down, Chief, and make yourself comfortable. I'm going to tell you a long story." He related the happenings of the previous night.

When he got to the part about the prisoner's attack on two armed policemen, the Chief shook his head in disbelief. "How can that happen to two armed men when the prisoner is handcuffed?"

"I think, sir, we could learn a lesson from the Americans here. They shackle their dangerous suspects, hands and feet, with a chain from the ankles to the wrists. This couldn't have happened if he'd been restrained like that."

The Chief was not impressed with this argument, stating that they could be charged with violating several of the prisoners' human rights and Amnesty International would be after their balls!

But Derek said coldly, "These terrorists aren't human."

"Be that as it may, we'd never be allowed to do that. So where are we now?"

Derek went on to tell him about the interview with the student, going into great detail, and finally he told the Chief of his release.

For a few moments the Chief was silent, tapping his fingers on his desk blotter. Then he said wryly, "I think that was probably a wise decision, but if you expect to get his passport in the post, you must be nuts! Still, you saved a lot of paperwork and trouble. Did you record the interview? I think you might have broken one or two little rules in the process."

"Ah, but you see I told him at the beginning of our little talk that I wasn't interviewing him; I was just going to have a little chat with him and wouldn't be asking him any questions which needed a lawyer's advice on how to answer. I've released him without charge, so there's no comeback. The information I gleaned was freely obtained."

"Do you think that threat to nuclear power stations is real?" asked the Chief.

"I hate to say it, but it falls in exactly with what we know so far, Chief. It would be a spectacular event for them, even bigger than Nine-Eleven. Apart from the number killed directly, many people would die lingering deaths from the fallout for possibly years to come. Some places like Harwell are right in the middle of a huge conurbation and London isn't far away. But we still don't know which one they're aiming for, but by putting a number of assault units within each power station, we stand a good chance of repelling an attack and arresting the terrorists."

"Surely their plans will be more sophisticated than that," said the Chief.

"They're relying on surprise attacks on unprepared targets, that is unless they're thinking of some sort of a rocket attack or an air raid."

"We could ban flights within a fifty-mile radius of all nuclear power stations," mused the Chief. "That should be fairly easy."

"Only if you gave an order to shoot down any unauthorised aircraft flying over the area, Chief. There's always some nitwit that'll stray into the area. I suppose we could get jet fighters on standby and they could patrol the areas, escorting any stray aircraft to a safe airstrip and forcing them to land, but I still think the attack, or attacks, is going to come from ground level. Unless a plane had a state-of-the-art guidance system, it would be hit-and-miss for a missile, but I wouldn't think they had access to either a plane or a missile. No, the more I think about it, the more I'm convinced it'll be a land attack."

"How soon?" queried the Chief.

"I'm sure it'll be in the next ten to fourteen days."

"Right, I'd better get in touch with the Home Secretary, brief him on this and get troops in position by next Monday." But his call was unsuccessful and he was told that the Home Secretary would ring back as soon as he was free. "Let's assume that we'll get our troops in place. What next?" the Chief asked.

"I think we'd just have to wait."

The Chief answered his phone on the first ring and Derek could just hear a voice saying, "Arthur Case here. What can I help you with, Chief?"

"We now know what the terrorists are aiming for, but unfortunately not exactly where."

Case hesitated a moment, fully aware of the importance of that remark. "What is their target?"

"One or more of our nuclear power stations."

"You *are* joking, I assume. This cannot be true; no one would be so irresponsibly stupid as to attack a nuclear power station. Think of the consequences, man! My mind goes back to Chernobyl and the effects it had, even in England. Tell me you're mistaken." He knew, however, that there was no way anyone would suggest this if it were not true. "So that's it," he continued, without waiting for a response. "What we've been dreading for years. What are your proposals to counteract it?"

"Chief Inspector Young, who has made every effort to uncover this information, suggests that in view of the comparatively few nuclear power facilities we have, we station experienced assault troops at each one of them."

"For how long?"

The Chief chose his words carefully. "At the moment, the information we have is that the attack will take place within the next two weeks."

"That accurate is it?"

The Chief detected a note of sarcasm in the voice, but he persevered. "I can only tell you what we feel sure is going to happen, but of course, sir, it's then up to you to give instructions as to how the situation should be handled."

Realising that he had been a little too impatient with the Chief, who was only informing him of a situation which beggared belief, he said, "How did you obtain this information? How reliable is it?"

"This is a very complex investigation and we managed to dig up very few facts. Suffice it to say that we managed to capture a terrorist sympathiser, who was helping them, but at a very unimportant low level. He knew very little, having been kept deliberately in the background, but after a very skilful interrogation, during which he was under the impression that he was just being given good advice, he admitted that about forty top-level men were being used, well-educated professional men, and it was hinted that one of them was a nuclear scientist. Now, they wouldn't use men like these to toss a few bombs; they wouldn't go to all that trouble to smuggle them into this country if something of a very important nature wasn't being planned. They would have been sent here with a very special objective in mind, at great expense, so an explosion at a nuclear power station would seem to be the most feasible explanation. This would cause a huge so-called dirty explosion, similar to the one at Chernobyl."

"I've a feeling that this information is coming from that Chief Inspector of yours; what's his name? Derek Young, isn't it? Okay, Chief; that number of men is going to take some organising. What number do you suggest? Forty per power station?"

"At least forty, as there may be forty of them, although it's possible they intend to strike all our nuclear facilities at the same time," said the Chief.

"Yes, but we're defending and they're attacking," said the Home Secretary, "and I seem to remember from my army service days that the attacking force has to have twice as many men as the defending force."

"There are so many factors to take into consideration here, one of which is that we mustn't lose this encounter. To lose would be catastrophic. It's not a war game we're playing."

"Very well, forty men per nuclear power station. You realise that with the war going on in Iraq and Afghanistan we have very few troops to spare?"

"I'm sure your colleagues would agree that going to war in Iran and Afghanistan is not as important and that leaving only a handful of troops to defend our vital national utility installations will not improve our ability to provide troops and provisions in the future. Innocent civilian lives are in great danger here, which is where our troops should be."

There was a pause before the Home Secretary said quietly, "You must feel very secure in your post to talk like that, Chief Constable!"

"Almost as secure as you are, Home Secretary. If the terrorists win this battle, I think my job will be more secure than yours."

"Don't forget; we're all on the same side! When is it you want these men in position, fully briefed and aware of all the possibilities?"

"By next Monday night."

"You'll have them."

Derek looked admiringly at the Chief. "You certainly didn't mince your words with him and stood your ground, despite his snide remarks."

The Chief sat back in his chair, breathing heavily. "I'm getting sick and tired of these wankers always telling you they can't do this and they can't do that. But don't worry; after what I said, you'll get your men. You don't think they'll attack all the nuclear power stations do you?"

Derek said wearily, "I don't think so, Chief, but it's a possibility, although the most vulnerable ones are Sellafield, the one in East Anglia and Harwell. They're the ones I'd pick, but they may go for the one we least expect, so we have to protect them all. I'll go back to my office and let George and Tony know what's going on and try to work out some sort of briefing for the CO of each army unit so that they understand what they're up against."

"Have you still got an up-to-date firearms license?" asked the Chief. "Maybe you'd better go and have a bit of target practice; you never know when it's going to come in useful. And by the way, I think you should consider being armed when you go out anywhere; you could well be a marked man now."

Derek wanted to laugh but thanked the Chief for his advice. At least somebody in authority cared whether he lived or died! "I do admire the way you stood up to the Home Secretary," he said.

"Ah, but will you still admire me when I'm standing outside the Jobcentre touting for a job? Goodbye and don't come back to my office until you have some good news!"

Chapter 62

When Derek returned to his office, Tony greeted him with the words, "So how was the holiday? Had good weather did you?"

Derek put his hand on his hip, pouted and said, "Sweetie, if you only knew what sort of day I've had..."

Tony grinned and told him to stop walking like that or he would have to arrest him! Derek told them in great detail what had been happening over the last forty-eight hours, only missing out some of the conversation between the Chief and the Home Secretary.

"Now for the sixty-four-thousand dollar question," said Tony. "Are you absolutely convinced they'll attack within the next two weeks?"

"I think they've been held up by something which is a key part of their operation, and I only wish I knew what it might be."

"Some kind of special weapon?" asked Tony.

"Well, yes, that might be it, or else a person who specialises in the nuclear construction part of a power station. It must be their Achilles' heel and they can't function without it."

George interrupted. "I've been thinking—"

"Always dangerous when George starts thinking," the other two chorused.

"Do you want to hear what I think or what?"

"Go ahead," Derek said.

"Well, it struck me that if you wanted details about how to construct one of those bombs or whatever, there must be any number of boffins at the university who'd be only too glad to enlighten you on their favourite subject. They think the police are a load of uneducated morons, so if you ask their advice, they'll be flattered. You'll find it a big help and it may help you to work out what it is these blokes are waiting for!"

Derek looked at Tony and they nodded in unison. "Don't ever stop thinking, George. You've played a blinder there; scored a try, so to speak. Now, which department do I need? Tony, can you set up an appointment for me with whoever's the best expert on nuclear fusion, without giving anything away about my reason for consulting an expert?"

Tony was on the phone for some time, contacting old friends, but eventually he got through to a Professor Stokowski's office, whose secretary informed him that the Professor had gone home but would be available in his office from nine to ten o'clock the next morning, before lectures. "It might be better if you met the Professor in the refectory; he's very particular about his coffee, and when he's had several cups he tends to be in a better mood, that is to answer questions about his latest project!"

Tony quickly told his boss the result of the conversation. "Apparently, Professor Stokowski has some new project he's working on, so I let his secretary think that's what you wanted to talk about. Tell you what, sir, I could take you in my car; it's easier to park and the university campus is very large and confusing. You could be wandering round for ages before you find the refectory, but I happen to know a short cut that would take us straight there. Besides, after what the Chief said, you might need a bodyguard!"

The next morning, Tony drove Derek to the university, found the shortcut, managed to squeeze his car into a minute parking space and led his boss through a short passageway to find the refectory. They selected a table and looked around at the other customers.

"Don't forget, sir, he likes his coffee black with plenty of sugar."

"Thank you, Tony. I'm not likely to forget something so important. Now look around and see if you can see him."

A tall, stooping man came towards them wearing an old-fashioned brown sports jacket with leather patches on the elbows, a washed-out looking checked shirt and baggy grey flannel trousers.

He nodded his head towards Derek and headed for the self-service counter, but Tony leapt up to head him off and buy the coffee before he could get in the queue.

"If you'd go and sit down with my boss over there, sir, I'll bring your coffee to you in a moment."

With precise intonation, showing that English was not his native language, the Professor introduced himself. "I'm Professor Jan Stokowski. I understand from my secretary that you wish to consult me about my new project. To whom am I speaking?"

Derek hesitated slightly before saying, "My name is Derek Young and this is my assistant Tony Bruce." It was a busy area and there was not much point in announcing he was a police inspector and encouraging every ear in the place to eavesdrop.

They sipped their coffee and the Professor murmured quietly, "How can I help you?"

"I understand you're an expert in nuclear physics and nuclear fusion, a subject I know very little about," explained Derek.

"That is my subject, yes," said the Professor, looking puzzled.

"There is a question which is worrying a certain number of government departments at the moment. You understand I'm speaking entirely off my own bat, but would it be possible for a number of people to break into a nuclear power station complex and create a situation similar to what happened at Chernobyl?"

"Is this a hypothetical question or is it a real possibility?"

"I'm afraid it's very much a real possibility, Professor," Derek affirmed.

"I think, Mr Derek Young, that you are perhaps employed by one of these worried government departments, although you have shown me no proof of this. But I will answer you as directly as I can. It might have been better to go to my office, but there is not sufficient time before my lecture starts, so this is what I can tell you. In theory it is quite possible. If you allow the fusion to go on unchecked, it will eventually become a huge atomic bomb. That is what happened at Chernobyl. It seems they were experimenting with the rods, misjudged the time and it exploded, at least that's the unofficial explanation."

"Could anyone do that in this country?"

"If you mean could it be achieved purposefully, if anyone was mad enough to do it, the answer is no. There have been many safety procedures introduced in these power stations worldwide since then, and this could never happen."

"So what you're saying is that all our nuclear power stations are a hundred per cent safe."

"Only a fool or a politician would ever say that," said the Professor. "What I mean is that control of the fusion process has been taken out of human hands and is controlled by computers with safety factors built in."

"So let me put it to you another way, posing the question from a different angle entirely. If I were a terrorist, could I get into a power station control room and make it explode like an atom bomb?"

The Professor considered Derek's question carefully; he was beginning to understand the consequences of his answers. He shrugged his shoulders slightly and said, "I'm not a construction expert, so although I know how the nuclear process works in power stations, I don't have the knowledge to say one could or could not do it. Of course, you would first have to seize control of the facility and hold it for several hours to enable some very clever people to accomplish their work."

"Let me take this a step further," said Derek, concentrating fiercely on what he knew would be the answer. "If I had say forty highly trained commandos, some experts like SAS men, could I take over a power station, cut off all communication with the outside world and let these clever people do their thing? Could they create an atomic explosion?"

"In theory," stressed the Professor, "they could do it, but they would all die!"

"It seems that some people are all too ready to die for their cause," said Derek sadly.

The Professor was outraged. "I cannot imagine any sane person thinking that their own deaths justified the killing of thousands of helpless people in an explosion and then the lingering deaths of thousands more from radiation poisoning."

"You forget, Professor, we're not talking about sane, rational people here. You only have to take Iraq as an example; Muslims are planting bombs to kill other Muslims just because they don't follow what they consider to be the true path, and where's the sense in that? It's like that silly saying: cutting off your nose to spite your face. There's no justification at all in killing someone because you disagree with the way he chooses to worship God."

The Professor was silent for a moment before saying, "What we have discussed is hypothetical, is it not?"

"Oh yes," Derek assured him. "Thank you for your time, Professor. I won't detain you any longer."

He and Tony shook hands with the puzzled Professor and went back to the car.

"Why did you say it was all hypothetical?" asked Tony.

"We don't want rumours to get out and for people to panic prematurely. Now I come to think about it, I should have asked him not to mention this to anyone."

"What do you think now, boss? Any more thoughts on how things are going?"

"As a matter of fact, this rather confirms what's going through my mind. Look at it like this: why would you bother to bring forty or more men into this country if you needed only a handful at most? If you planned to hit the fusion part of the nuclear power station, you don't need forty people. You might only need a couple of experienced missile-launching guys with two or three to support them. Dropping a bomb from the air is completely out of the question, so that only leaves you with some sort of assault-and-hold programme."

They drove on in silence.

At the office, George told them that the Chief had been on the phone and wanted to speak to Derek. With a slight sinking sensation in the region of his stomach, he rang and spoke to his secretary.

"I'll put you through," she said, "and don't you go upsetting him again!"

"Me?" Derek teased. "I have a very calming influence on him."

"Well, after your last visit, he was like a rhinoceros with toothache. It took me the rest of the day to smooth him down. I'm putting you through now."

"Derek," said the Chief.

"Yes, it's only me, your humble servant!"

"Humble? I like that! You're about the most arrogant chief inspector in the north of England and I don't know why I put up with you!"

"Oh, come on, Chief; I'm not that bad. Anyway, what can I do for you?"

"The Home Secretary has been on, nice as pie. I think I like it better when he's being nasty, then at least you can avoid the expected blows. But when he's being nice, it's completely out of character; you don't know what's coming next! Anyway, he assured me that all the places you wanted secure are secure."

"Chief, this is only Thursday and we didn't want them in place till next Monday."

"What are you complaining about? So you have them in place a bit early!"

Derek spoke without pausing to think. "If they're in place too early, every day and night they stay there without action, the less vigilant they'll become. They'll start thinking that this is just an exercise; it's not real. When the attack comes they might be caught by surprise and if that happens, even for a second, the terrorists could gain the upper hand."

"Well, there's nothing much we can do about that now," said the Chief. "And one other thing; Scotland's Home Defence people say they'll organise their own precautions and don't want any assistance from us!"

"Fine."

"Oh, and the Home Secretary says you're still in charge of co-ordinating the units for the whole investigation and organisation of the defence of England and Wales, but he also commented that 'with authority comes responsibility'. In other words, if anything goes wrong, you're stuck up shit creek, but if things go right, he'll say it's due to his flair in choosing the right people for the job."

"I don't give a damn."

"Well, that's all I have for you. Good luck."

"I'll see you in the queue at the Jobcentre."

"Can someone please explain to me what's going on?" wailed George plaintively. "You lost me a long way back!"

"It's simple, George. We, well, I really, think there's going to be an attack on one of our nuclear power stations. I'm the England and Wales co-ordinator for the defence of these installations. If the terrorists are beaten off or captured and killed before they can do any damage, the Home Secretary gets the credit. If it goes wrong, I get the blame. That's politics for you; always make sure there's someone below you to absorb the flak. If you ever reach the high echelons of management, George, just remember that! There's an old saying I seem to remember that says something like the higher in rank you get, the closer you are to the exit door, so it's a lot easier to push you out. Now, I must ring someone at Heathrow. Tony, can you get me Inspector Harris; he's in charge of Heathrow passport control. The number's somewhere on my desk."

Tony got straight through to Harris' office.

"Hello, Don. Derek Young here. I want your invaluable advice."

"Hi, Derek. What're you up to these days? Still picking your toes instead of having a bath!"

Derek pretended to be offended. "I've already had one bath this year, and as you well know, baths weaken your constitution."

"Oh, I thought it was sex that did that!"

"I wouldn't know about that, Don. Girls oop north wear iron knickers and it kind of blunts your instruments, if you know what I mean. Anyway, I didn't ring you to discuss politics."

"No, I somehow knew that, but I bet you're going to tell me something to make me feel really miserable, aren't you?"

"No, no. Why would I do a thing like that? It's just I thought I'd put you in the picture with regard to the latest situation concerning the terrorist threat we talked about a while back."

"I'm not involved in any of that. Down here, where it's civilised, we have MI5, MI6, Special Branch and an Anti-Terrorist Unit to deal with all that sort of thing. I'm a long way down the chain!"

"We don't have any of these highly professional people to work their magic in our neck of the woods. At this point there's just me. I thought I should tell you that we're expecting a terrorist attack on a nuclear power station."

Don was momentarily robbed of the power of speech, but eventually spluttered, "Are you having me on? You must be joking. What attack? Why haven't I been told and everybody warned about it? You have to be kidding!"

"No, I can assure you, as the Co-ordinator of Special Defences, or some title like that, that yours truly is in charge of protecting all nuclear installations in England and Wales. Scotland has declined our help and there are no nuclear power stations in Wales, so that leaves England. I have to emphasise that we don't yet know which one it's going to be, but in your area, Harwell is the most likely hit. You have got others, but Harwell is the best known."

"Hang on a minute," protested Don. "What are you raving on about? Why haven't I been told?"

"Quite frankly, I'm amazed you haven't been informed. If the terrorists were planning any escape, Heathrow would be a key area for them. They might catch a plane to any of the Arab countries and just disappear off the face of the earth!"

"Look, can you talk sense, please; I can't take it all in, you've lost me."

"Look, Don, I'm not sure how else to put it. I'll speak slowly. There's going to be a terrorist raid on one of England's nuclear power stations – got it so far?"

"I know what you're saying; what I don't understand is why you're telling me all this. Something may or may not happen, maybe at Harwell, maybe not, but I can't see the significance to me or my work here," said Don, puzzled.

"I was hoping you'd be my communication link in the south of England."

"What do you base this information on?"

"We've been chasing this gang for months now and a number of people have died in this country alone. If you include Germany,

Holland and Belgium, the number of deaths approaches fifty, nearly as many as were killed in the London bombings," Derek explained.

"But I don't see what this has to do with me or my job. We have over a thousand people in the Secret Service alone and for all I know, thousands more working undercover, so I say let them get on with it!"

"Okay, Don, thanks for your time. I don't think you're quite the man I'm looking for."

George looked over to him and said, "I take it he wasn't interested."

"No, the smug bastard is happy to leave it all to others."

"With that kind of attitude, he wouldn't have been any good to you anyway," Tony commented.

"Excuse me for saying this, boss," said George, "but do you think it was wise to tell him what you thought was going to happen? He's the sort of bloke who'll sit back and start to think about how it might affect him and then he'll go into a blind panic, running about, starting rumours. He might even do a bunk to get as far away as he can get from the UK. Just thought I'd mention it."

"You may be right, George, but there's not much I can do about it now. I guess I misjudged his character completely. I've tried to get someone in the south to keep me informed, someone with a common interest in keeping the peace, but now it'll have to be left to those who live and work there. Tony, can you get the Chief Constable of Cumbria on the phone?"

Derek was soon speaking to the Chief Constable of Cumbria, a man he didn't know personally.

"Good morning, sir. This is Chief Inspector Derek Young of the Manchester Police Department and I'm also the Anti-Terrorist Co-ordinator for England and Wales—"

He was cut short. "Yes, I've heard of you. Had a memo round the other day. What can I do for you, Chief Inspector?"

"Have you been informed, sir, about the possibility of an attack on the Sellafield nuclear installation?"

"Yes, I've been fully informed and we now have a unit of Marines patrolling the plant. However, I'd just like to point out to you that it's a huge complex and I'm not quite sure what forty Marines can do apart from token searches and remain on guard duty."

"Well, sir, the number of attackers is expected to amount to about the same number and at least the plant does have some extra security now. What I'm concerned with is that if the terrorists realise they're not succeeding in their mission and decide to run, we mustn't allow them to escape, because they would only regroup and try something else, perhaps at a later date."

"So you want us to be ready to block all the surrounding roads, is that it?"

"Yes, sir, that would be brilliant. If they can't use the roads, they're not going to get very far on foot!"

"Any idea of a possible date when this might happen?"

"We're fairly sure that this will happen within the next two weeks. I'm sorry, but we can't pin it down any closer. Our information is very sparse."

"Well, Chief Inspector, I suppose we'll have to make do with that. Keep me informed!" The phone went dead.

Derek then had a very unsatisfactory conversation with the Chief Constable of Suffolk and nearly threw the phone down after half an hour of listening to him going on about the things that could not be done: more policemen were needed; there was no money to pay them overtime; they were expecting a disaster before the disaster could happen.

"I don't know how some of these people ever make it to the top ranks," Derek bemoaned when he finally got off the phone. "All I got was a complaint that they couldn't possibly do it without more manpower. I can sympathise up to a point, but I'm afraid there's not a lot I can do about it. If he thinks the only way he can police his area is with a thousand more experienced constables and another billion pounds in the police budget, he's not making the most of his resources. Who wants a wanker like that in charge! Come on, lads, I think we've done all we can today. How about a quick pint!"

Chapter 63

The following morning, the phone was already ringing as Derek approached his desk. It was the Chief.

"Where have you been? I've been trying to reach you for half an hour."

"Good morning, Chief. Bad night, was it?"

"I've no time for chit-chat now. We've had a red van parked outside our building, left here some time during the night."

"Have you called the Bomb Squad to check it out?"

"Yes. We've cleared the immediate area, but I want you to come here. It's obviously been left by some of your friends. You can get in through the side door, so long as you don't go out in front."

"I'm on my way," said Derek, barging out of the office and nearly knocking George into next week.

"What on earth's up with you?" he asked.

"I'm in a hurry. There might be a bomb in a van parked outside police HQ and the Chief wants me there. Tell Tony when he comes in." He took the stairs two at a time.

He parked in a side street, just past the entrance, and edged his way to a corner of the building. Peering round the corner carefully, he saw the red van, innocuously and neatly parked close to the kerb. He made a note of its make and number and retreated to a safer area. He rang Tony and asked him to put the number through the police computer and made a note of the name, address and phone number of the owner. He rang the number. The man who answered seemed surprised that the police were ringing him up so early. He told Derek that he was a carpenter and that his van was parked just round the corner in a small lay-by. He hadn't used it the previous day, as he had been in his workshop.

Derek asked him to check on his van, knowing what the answer would be before he rang him back ten minutes later. His van had been stolen and what were the police going to do about it, he asked indignantly? Derek assured him that the police had found his van and hoped to be able to return it to him after they had carried out certain forensic tests in the hope of tracing the car thief or thieves.

When the Bomb Squad arrived, Derek showed them where to park.

"I'm Chief Inspector Young. Who's in charge of you lot?"

"Lieutenant Jack White at your service, sir," said the passenger, and gave him a quick salute. "Can you fill me in on the circumstances, please?"

How do they get to be so young, thought Derek. He looks as if he's hardly started shaving, yet he's in this dangerous situation and appears to be thriving on it. He indicated the red van parked further along the road in the cordoned-off area. "There you are; it's all yours. The only information I've been given is that it was parked here late last night or early this morning and everybody had the sense to leave it severely alone. Every non-essential person in the building has been evacuated and we were just waiting for you to turn up!"

"Right you are, Chief Inspector. Perhaps you would be kind enough to order everyone to switch off their mobile phones, as sometimes a signal to one of them will set the explosives off, that is if there's a bomb in it."

Lieutenant White got Robbie the robot out of their vehicle and carefully deployed him around the red van. Explosive materials were packed inside and could be clearly seen through the rear and front windows. But it was not possible to determine what sort of detonator was being used. Eventually, White said that the only way to see the detonator was to use a small charge to blow the back doors off their hinges, which, of course, was highly dangerous, as it carried the risk of triggering the explosives and blowing everything sky high with completely unknown consequences. Everyone waited, holding their breath, while a member of his team quickly attached a small charge to the door hinges and retired to await orders. A dull thud announced that the charge had gone off. The van doors hung drunkenly off the bodywork. Moments passed, but there was no further noise. When the smoke gradually filtered away, Robbie was once more deployed to look into the rear of the vehicle. The trigger for the bomb could then be seen. It was not a mobile phone or an alarm device but some sort of electronic trigger, which had Lieutenant White puzzled.

"I've not seen one of those before," he said. After examining it from every angle he was even more surprised.

They spent twenty minutes very carefully searching for another device, a booby trap or something similar hidden in the van, but could find nothing.

"Right," said Lieutenant White, "I'll have to confirm that there's nothing else there and disconnect the mechanism."

Adjusting his helmet and body armour, he strode over to the van and very carefully started his examination of the contents. The tension among the onlookers heightened; they didn't know whether to look and see him being blown up or not look and miss something.

Outside the tapes cordoning off the area, early morning workers were impatient to continue their journeys to their places of business, and were craning their necks to see what was happening.

After what seemed like an eternity, Lieutenant White turned round with a grin on his face. "As soon as we've got this baby on a loader, it can be taken away. Chief Inspector, come and look at this!"

Gingerly, Derek dipped under the tape and walked across to the van.

"Look at this," said the Lieutenant quietly and showed him what he had in his hand. "It's some kind of explosive trigger, but not one I've come across before. However, this was never going to trigger anything because one wire wasn't attached; it would never have ignited the explosives! I'm sending it to the lab to see what they can make of it."

"Perhaps it might be better if both the van and that device were taken to our forensic bods. You're quite sure it's safe? I wouldn't want to be blowing any of our lads sky-high with this."

"If you want convincing, I'll sit on top of it while you drive!"

"No thanks. I'll take your word for it."

Derek went to oversee the return of all those who had been evacuated and reassured the worried office staff that all was safe. Then he waited for the Chief to appear.

When the Chief found Derek he was keen to know the details.

"On the surface, it looks as though it was a completely amateur attempt to blow up part of the building, but it could also have been a deliberate attempt to divert us from their main event. We're setting up a squad to investigate the bomb, but the press, once they find out about it, will go to town in a big way," Derek explained, "so I suggest we try to keep it quiet and low key."

The Chief agreed and wondered if the forensic lab could come up with anything positive which Derek's team could work on.

"Whatever happened to the Alice Groves murder investigation?" asked Derek.

"It's still on-going."

"I'll let Hank Knowles take this on board to link this attempt to bomb HQ with the bomb outside their police station. They were just going through routine investigations, but this second attempt to bomb police property should keep them occupied for some time."

"When you've quite finished telling me how to do my job," said the Chief testily, "is there any other information you'd like to give me?"

Derek was by now immune to the undercurrent in the Chief's words and told him that he was worried about the attitude of the Chief Constable of Suffolk.

"Why?" asked the Chief. "Has he done something to upset you?"

"I asked him to be prepared to lay down roadblocks should an attack take place, in case the terrorists tried to make a run for it."

"So?"

"All I got was a litany of why he couldn't do this, plus a load of excuses."

"You have to remember that this attack might never take place; it's all very up in the air. But I know him from past experience and he's always a bit like that. Don't worry; when it comes to police work, he's very effective in his job. He'll do whatever's necessary in the end, once he realises the situation needs it. Can you tell me something?" the Chief went on. "Power stations occupy vast tracts of land; from the main gate to the reactor buildings could be a distance of two miles or more, so what damage could forty men do before they get to the real powerhouse, which is presumably well guarded and with top security?"

Derek groaned. "If I knew that, Chief, we could stop the whole thing now. When I asked the Professor about the possibilities, he said that only by being in command of the reactor for some time could the experts amongst them do something to cause it to explode. They might take hostages and threaten to execute them, which would give them time to work on the reactor. As I've said, I don't have a clue what they're going to try; I'm only interested in catching them before they can do it!"

"You do realise that if nothing happens we'll look like complete fools and no one will ever believe us again?"

"Never mind; we could always start a new career in security."

"That's not funny. You'd better leave my office now before I end up in tears."

Derek started to hum the seventies hit tune 'Big girls don't cry' and left the office before anything could be thrown at him.

Derek arrived home, took a shower and changed, wondering where Helen had got to. There was a knock on the front door and he went to open it, puzzled because he had left it on the latch. He flung the door open ready to grab her, but there were two young and pretty girls on his doorstep.

"It's a good job you didn't knock on the door five minutes ago or you'd have found me in the shower!" He was expecting a giggle, but the look on their faces didn't change; they looked very serious.

"We're calling to spread God's message," said the slightly taller of the two. "Would you like us to talk to you about renewing your faith in God?"

"And how long would that take?" asked Derek, wondering how quickly he could close the door.

"It'll take as long as you need us to convince you."

There's an answer to that, thought Derek, but I'm too much of a gentleman to say it. He was relieved to see Helen's car draw up in the drive. She came over to the three of them on the doorstep with an enquiring look on her face.

"You can say what you're thinking, sir," one of the girls was saying. "Unless you tell us what you're actually thinking, we'll not be able to explain to you how to achieve the light and understanding of faith in God when you're lost in the dark wilderness without Him." They hadn't noticed Helen standing behind them.

"Don't waste your time, you two," she told them. "He's a complete villain and quite beyond redemption. I should know; I'm his wife. You're both too young to know what I have to put up with!"

The two girls hesitated, clearly unsure about what they should do.

"Listen, you two," said Derek. "I'm a police inspector and you're far too pretty to be walking around alone, never mind knocking on people's doors. Sooner or later you'll get into trouble. You must get some men to walk with you, do you understand?"

They looked at each other and nodded before walking away down the drive.

"I don't know," said Helen. "I arrive home from work and find you accosting pretty young females. What am I going to do with you?"

"I'm just an old lecher," apologised Derek. "Are we eating in or out tonight?"

"I think it's time you bought me a decent meal, somewhere like … now let me think," pondered Helen.

"While you're thinking, shall I change into one of my many gentlemanly disguises: dinner jacket, white tie and tails, à la Fred Astaire, or—"

"No need to go that far; this is strictly 'en casuale' – that's French for casual, if you didn't know!"

"I speak French," said Derek. "How about 'can-can'?"

Helen looked at him solemnly and said, "I don't think 'can-can' is, strictly speaking, a French word!"

"Listen," said Derek happily, "if I say it's French, it's French, so there."

"Ooh, you are masterful tonight, Derek."

"Well, I have to assert myself sometimes. I've been far too lenient with you lately."

"Watch it, Constable, women rule, remember?"

"Yes, ma'am."

"That's better. You watch yourself or there'll be no hanky-panky tonight!"

Derek groaned. "Don't say that, even in jest. I've been working like crazy all week with just one thing on my mind."

After discussing the local restaurants, they decided on a Chinese one not far from the house that had recently re-opened under new management.

Derek told Helen that he had a present for her. He had had two house keys cut for her. "Keep them and you can come and go as you please. Just wait another two weeks and you can move in."

"An invitation no girl could refuse," she teased.

"I'm sorry; that didn't come out quite the way I meant it to," Derek apologised. "Let's go and eat."

On Sunday night, they sat comfortably on the settee surrounded by all the Sunday newspapers. Helen regarded Derek for a few moments and then said, "You've been quiet all day and you look a bit sad. Is anything the matter?"

Derek looked away. "Have you ever had a premonition that something is about to happen to you?" he asked.

"I'm far too down to earth to have fanciful ideas like that," she responded, trying to lighten his mood. "Are you trying to say that something's going to happen to you? You're beginning to worry me. What exactly do you mean?"

"Don't take any notice of me; I'm just being stupid." He gave her a lopsided grin. "All I know is that I love you and I couldn't bear to lose you now."

Chapter 64

On Monday morning, Helen and Derek drove off to their separate offices. Helen had been watching Derek carefully since their conversation the previous evening, but he seemed to have got over his slight depression. She kissed him goodbye, promising to ring him later on in the day.

In the office with Tony and George, Derek knew that they were all thinking the same thing. George put it into words. "Is it going to be this week?"

"I don't know, but it must be close," was Derek's response.

It was a frustrating day and it was difficult to concentrate on humdrum, ordinary tasks, waiting for a phone call, an item on the midday news, a story in the paper.

Derek was relieved to get home, have a shower and make a simple meal, which he ate while watching *News 24* until the endlessly repeated items made him switch off impatiently.

Deeply asleep, he suddenly woke to hear the bedside telephone shrilling. He looked at the clock. It was five to two. Who the hell would be ringing him at this ungodly hour unless it was Helen or some sort of emergency? He answered it irritably.

"This is Arthur Case, Home Secretary. Get dressed. You're going to Sizewell. The power station appears to be under attack. Don't ask me for any details, because at the moment I don't have any. Go to Manchester Airport where there'll be a police helicopter waiting to take you direct to the plant. You'll be fully briefed when you get there."

Derek tried to get his mind to wake up and he seized on the most obvious question he could think of. "Sir, what are the Marines doing about it?"

"It appears that the Ministry of Defence pulled them out on Saturday morning because their whole unit is due to fly to Afghanistan tomorrow. They were going to be replaced by a company of the Parachute Regiment from Colchester, and as far as I know, they're on their way there now."

"Bloody wonderful!"

"This isn't the time for recriminations; this is the time to act. You're in complete command of this operation. You have my authority to give any order you think fit. Now go!"

Only stopping to dress and to leave a note for Helen on the coffee table, he left for the airport. The helicopter was waiting for him and he climbed in next to the pilot, donning the ear protectors he was given. Two hours later, the helicopter landed in the middle of a road in front of the plant, near the gatehouse. He felt rather like a parcel being dumped in the middle of nowhere as the helicopter rose into the air to return to Manchester and left him standing there alone.

Lights were on in the gatehouse, but as he walked toward the door he saw the body of a policeman on the ground showing no sign of life. He knelt swiftly, hardly able to believe his eyes, and in the dim light saw several stab wounds. Cautiously, he approached the wall of the building and looked through the window. There was another policeman sprawled across a desk with his throat cut and there was a great deal of blood on the floor. He must have died instantly, thought Derek, his mind feeling quite detached from the horrible scene.

His mobile rang. The Chief said, "Where are you?"

As calmly as he could, he answered, "I'm standing by the gatehouse at Sizewell Nuclear Power Station looking at the bodies of two dead policemen – they've been stabbed to death."

"Who else is there?"

"I'm completely alone, so far as I know, and I'm just about to go in and flush out the terrorists single-handed."

"Derek, for heaven's sake keep calm; this is not the time to be funny!"

"Well, Chief, let's put it like this: it's either that or bursting into tears!"

"I was just about to tell you that the Home Secretary rang me because he didn't have your mobile number and I'm to tell you what's happened. The terrorists have taken over Plant A of the power complex – that's the first building to be put up on that site and appears to be the most vulnerable. Just as they were breaking into the control room, the shift supervisor managed to call the police, telling them that they were under attack. The message was passed to the Suffolk Chief Constable, who then rang the Home Secretary, telling him that his police force was not trained as assault troops and that he awaited instructions. Since then it appears that the terrorists are holding all key areas. When the Home Secretary managed to get in touch with them to try and negotiate, they told him they had a dirty atomic bomb ready to explode in the control room. When he pointed that out that they would all die in the resulting explosion, he was told that Allah would take care of his faithful followers who are fighting the infidel. He was told that there were forty or more commandos within the complex area and that any attempt at recapture it would lead to a disaster. The Home Secretary was reduced to pleading with the spokesman to negotiate and was told it might be a possibility later. The Home Secretary says you are his man on the ground and you'll have to make the decisions about the future conduct of this operation!"

"Thanks, Chief; the buck stops here. I've already had that made clear to me."

"Any idea how they bluffed their way in?"

"From where I'm standing, it looks as if they persuaded one of the guards on duty to unlock the gatehouse door and come outside, whereupon he was promptly stabbed. Forty men dressed in black, like commandos, would have been almost invisible on a moonless night like this and they'd have melted into the darkness to attack the control room, leaving behind one or two of their men to get into the gatehouse and slit the other guard's throat before he was even aware of the threat."

"Well," said the Chief in his most encouraging voice, "now for the good news. A company of Paras are on their way to you. They left Colchester Barracks at 2 a.m. and should be with you any time now."

"How are they travelling?"

"They left in a convoy of vehicles, but there should be no hold-ups; the roads will be pretty clear now."

"I think I can hear motor traffic not far away. Looks like they should be here any minute. I'd like you to ring the Chief Constable of Suffolk and inform him about the two dead policemen at the gatehouse. If they send an ambulance, tell them not to use their sirens; there's nothing anyone can do for them now. Goodbye now, Chief, I've got to go!"

The sound of army lorries grinding their gears got louder and they were soon visible. Derek waved the first vehicle to a stop and waited until someone got down from the cab.

"I'm Chief Inspector Derek Young, with the Home Secretary's full authority to take charge of this operation." He knew it sounded a bit pompous, but he also knew that he had to assert his authority immediately.

The officer looked him up and down before saying, "I'm Captain Horatio Benjamin Rodgers, known as Ben to my friends and enemies alike."

To break the ice, Derek said, "I only wish we were meeting in better circumstances. Just call me Derek, by the way. It's hardly the time to stand on our dignity and demand our full ranks and titles, is it? How many men have you brought? If they want to unload their gear and stretch their legs for a minute, I'll put you in the picture."

Captain Rodgers went over to the second lorry and spoke to his sergeant. "Tell the men to stand down and stretch their legs for a few minutes while Chief Inspector Young outlines what we're going to do." When he returned he said, "This gatehouse here, the lights are on; should we go in there where we can see better?"

"There are two dead men and a lot of blood in there," Derek told him. "I'm waiting for the bodies to be collected, but it could be some time before an ambulance arrives. It'll be getting light shortly, and I don't really have anything to show you as yet, so I'll just fill you in regarding the present situation. Somewhere between forty or fifty terrorists, probably dressed in black commando-raid style, have killed the two policemen on guard duty in the gatehouse. It appears that they then overcame the other security guards and infiltrated the control room of Plant A, which controls this whole complex, the most important part of the installation. They say they have a dirty bomb, which they'll detonate if we try to attack and regain control. I don't know if they do or don't have one of these bombs, but according to an expert at Manchester University, they probably propose to turn this plant into a kind of Chernobyl by letting someone with a good knowledge of nuclear physics work on the plant to force the rods into a meltdown situation and burn right through to the core. So all we have to do is recapture the control room before they get the chance to do this!"

"That easy, is it?" drawled Ben. "I might have known we'd be faced by something simple! Well within our capabilities; a walk in the park."

"Sarcasm will get you nowhere," said Derek. "I'll just fill you in with a bit of background info. The enemy leader, when speaking to the Home Secretary a short while ago, called his men commandos, and you can bet they're as good as. They're all young, extremely fit, very well armed with the latest weapons available and specially trained for this operation. It would appear that they've been planning this atrocity for a very long time. Finally, they're religious fanatics, brainwashed from a very early age and they're the sort of men who, even when mortally wounded, would shoot you in the back."

"You underestimate our men," Ben said. "They've done two tours in Afghanistan and they know how to fight terrorists and all the dirty tricks they try, even using women and children to hide explosives for them."

"This might be similar but not quite the same; your men are going to have to move through areas where the terrorists will be hiding. The territory is completely unknown to you, but they will already have familiarised themselves with it. We'll have to clear one small area at a time, then gradually clear the next space, and stop them contacting their leader and prevent him from setting off the bomb. So attack as soon as your men are ready.

"That's our job," said Ben. "Let's get on with it.

"Just one more thing to tell your men. We're not interested in taking prisoners and I don't want you to be part of the attack."

"Hey, wait a minute there. It's tradition in the Paras that the leader fights with his men."

"Well, I'm not a military man, but if you were wounded or killed, there'd be no one of your stature left to direct your men, so I want us to stay close but not participate in the fighting, even if that means leading your troops from behind. As it happens, I left in such a hurry I'm not even armed, so I'd be an awful responsibility. Who's second in command?"

"Sergeant Tom Oddy; 'Toddy' we usually call him. Look, you can't expect me to stand here at the gatehouse while my men are fighting wall to wall, corner to corner."

"No, you and I will move just behind the men, a sort of rearguard action, while they clear the area. Come on, it's nearly light now. We're wasting time. Let's get started by briefing your men what the task in front of them consists of and then it's all systems go."

Ben called his men together, introduced them to Derek and told them what the basic plan would be, explaining why he and Derek would be in the rear. "Sergeant Oddy will be my second in command and you will follow his orders explicitly, is that understood?"

The men nodded and moved into the compound with Derek and Ben close behind. It appeared that the power had not been turned off, as the compound was well lit. Despite trying to stay in the shadows, the terrorists had seen them and opened fire. Dodging the bullets as best they could, they passed the body of one of the terrorists. A close look showed bullet wounds to his chest. Derek pulled off the balaclava, but the face meant nothing to him.

They moved on stealthily, trying to check possible sniper positions overlooking their assault course, disguised by the light and shadows of the lamps. Another body. Ben checked that he was dead and nodded to Derek. They moved on, but the next body was that of a paratrooper who'd been shot through the head and had died instantly.

They had to leave the body in situ while the fighting was going on; body recovery would come at the end of the battle, win or lose.

The shooting intensified – short, sharp crackles of firing out of sight – but as yet Derek felt no feeling of being in danger. He had felt more threatened when he was driving with Helen, pursued by the three yobbos.

Ben checked the pulse of another body, a black-clad terrorist, and decided he was dead. He discovered a small radio in his hand.

"This one must have been a team leader of some sort, able to give orders over his radio." He switched it on and was about to say something when Derek snatched it from his hand and switched it off. "What was that for?" Ben hissed. "I was only going to say—"

"I know what you were going to say," whispered Derek. "You were about to announce 'This is Captain Horatio Benjamin Rodgers' and probably something about 'Surrender immediately or you'll all die'. Don't be stupid, man. You'd be signing your own death warrant. Do you think these are the only terrorists in the country? They'd make you a target of their revenge and sooner or later they'd make sure of your death. No names are to be used in radio communications; pass that on to your men."

Derek switched the radio on and said, "Ahmed to leader, Ahmed to leader, the battle is lost. I repeat, the battle is lost and we have many casualties." He switched the radio off and Ben looked at him in amazement.

"Do you think they'll believe you?"

"They'd expect us to say that," said Derek, "but if they hear it from one of their own men, it might be bad for their morale."

"How do you know if there's an Ahmed in their group?"

"I don't know for certain, but there's usually an Ahmed in that number of men; it's a very popular name and it's worth a try!"

"We find radios can distract you momentarily in the thick of a fight and we all know our objective in this one. We'll need to regroup when we reach the buildings. I'll send out some men to do a reconnaissance to find out the strength of the opposition and the best way in."

Keeping as low as possible to avoid being a target for the snipers, who seemed to be on top of the block, they discovered another paratrooper's body. He had been shot in the back, so it appeared that the gunman had let him go past his position and then shot him and fallen back to another stronghold.

Derek felt cold sweat on his face as he wondered if this was what he and Ben were exposed to. The hairs on the back of his neck stood up and he wished he were two hundred miles away in bed, preferably with Helen.

"Ben, have we walked past a sniper into a trap?" he said, trying to see into every shadowed corner.

"Just what I was thinking, but I reckon the one who did this will be under orders to retreat to a place where he can do more damage, not just pick up a couple of stragglers like us."

Derek tried to shake off his fear, and then realised that the firing had stopped. Was it possible that the men had stormed the building on Toddy's orders and captured the remaining terrorists? He knew that was really just a pipe dream.

"It looks like the enemy has left gaps in the deployment of their people, so my men aren't finding anyone," said Ben. "Perhaps they've all retreated into the control room for a final stand."

The fighting had been going on now for more than an hour and Derek was wondering how people could go on like this for hours, day after day. They had to be tough both physically and mentally to retain any sanity, but he supposed they got used to it – battle hardened. They say you can get used to anything.

An intensive bout of shooting shattered the short-lived silence. They were now near to the main building. Then there was a muffled explosion.

"Sounds as if they've blown the entrance doors to the main building and will be moving inside. Actually, I'm sorry to be missing all this," said Ben. "I think I'll join them and then I won't miss all the fun!"

Derek grabbed his arm before he could set off across the courtyard. "You're not going anywhere. If they've got a dirty nuclear device in that control room, now will be the time for them to set it off and we'll all die, so there's no need for you to get your knickers in a twist; you won't be missing anything!"

There was another quick burst of firing and then silence. They stood, transfixed, waiting for the sound that could kill them outright, or at least maim them, and they would have failed to avert Armageddon.

Derek realised that he was holding his breath. Into the silence came the incongruous sound of a bird trilling its song. Even the gunfire couldn't keep them quiet, he thought. Well, here goes. He nudged Ben and they approached the blown-out entrance doors carefully, glancing from left to right constantly, searching for any stray snipers. Inside the wrecked entrance they could see, at a quick count, at least fifteen bodies dressed in black as they hurried through a door with a sign on it which read 'Operation Control Room, authorised personnel only'. The door was slightly open and Ben pushed it very gently, revealing the bodies of three commandos. At the far side of the room were four men in white overalls, each bound to a chair, one with a bloodstained sleeve, obviously the nightshift on duty in the control room, together with Sergeant Oddy and three of his men.

Ben swiftly crossed the room to find out from Toddy what the present situation was. Derek asked for a knife and released the four prisoners, all the while looking around the huge room, wondering where their assailants were. The men were dazed and shocked; the bonds had constricted their circulation and the wounded man had a bullet in his upper arm. They were all in need of medical attention.

"Can you tell me what happened here?" Derek asked. "I'm Chief Inspector Young and the soldier in charge over there is Captain Rodgers. I'm here with the authority of the Home Secretary to investigate the circumstances. First, did they say they had a nuclear device they're going to explode?"

"Yes, Inspector," said a grey-haired man with 'Supervisor' on his overall. "It's over there!"

Derek turned to see a wooden box, one metre long, three quarters of a metre wide, and about the same in depth. It was open and the lid was lying at the side.

"Just give us a few minutes to get ourselves together," said the supervisor. "It's been a bit hairy round here tonight. Then I'll tell you what happened to us. Arthur here needs a bit of medical attention. Any chance of a large whisky?" he joked, holding out his hands to show their trembling.

"The Captain's got all that in hand," Derek replied. "Did they try to set it off or chicken out at the last moment?"

"Oh yes," said the supervisor in a matter-of-fact tone. "They did try to do something with it and there was a lot of what sounded like swearing, you know, in a foreign language, but nothing happened. Don't know what was wrong with it. Maybe it was a dud battery," he said with dour humour.

After the last few months when Derek's worst nightmare had been the exploding of a nuclear bomb on British soil, he didn't think it was possible to feel this much relief; he was light-headed with satisfaction. "Thank God it didn't go off," he said. "That's the first piece of luck we've had since we started tracking these people all those months ago. By the way, what's your name?"

"Stuart, Stuart Pierce."

"Is there anything your team should be doing at the moment to keep things ticking over?"

"It's mainly keeping an eye on those panels of instruments over there, reporting if anything fluctuates too much."

"Okay, I'd like you to tell me what happened, starting at the beginning of your shift last night."

"About ten o'clock we heard a commotion outside, a lot of shouting and then a small explosion. About a dozen men came running in shouting at us to get down or we'd all be shot. They were all dressed in black, you know, like in a James Bond film, and it looked as if they were armed with rifles. They also had side arms in their belts. Well, your blokes had been recalled or something – poor sods were going out to Afghanistan for another go at the rebels – and at first we thought it was some kind of an exercise to test the security of the plant, to keep us on our toes, that sort of thing. But we soon realised it was serious when they dragged us into the centre of the room and told us to lay there without moving and that if anyone disobeyed they'd be shot. Well, I couldn't see much, but it seemed to me they were trying to work out how to do something with the reactor, but nowadays there are so many fail-safe precautions installed in the machinery it's impossible to make them go wrong. There were four of them in charge, top dogs, leaders, and they had two other men to keep a watch on us. They kept trying to do something; they were drawing little diagrams of what looked like electric circuits and getting more and more worked up. They even came over and had the cheek to ask me if I knew how to make this plant go 'boom'. I ask you, the nerve. So I told 'em, there's no way you can do that and he just grinned and walked away. After that, they forced us to sit on those chairs and tied us to them. Not long after that we heard gunfire. They seemed to be quite surprised, as if they didn't expect that to happen. I think that early on they had a phone call from someone who seemed to be asking them what their demands were, because the leader replied in English. I heard him say that they had a dirty bomb here in the control room and if there were any attempt to recapture the plant, they'd explode it. One thing I did forget to tell you; when I first heard voices shouting outside I rang our local police station and said that I couldn't raise our security men in the gatehouse, and that something was going on, some kind of invasion and would they inform the authorities and send help. I only managed to say a few words before they broke into here. That's about all I can tell you. By the way," he added gruffly, "thanks for coming to our rescue. I don't think they'd have let us live much longer, the way they were carrying on."

"Thanks for explaining what went on here, Stuart. At this point I have some very urgent phone calls to make, but I'll get back to you in a few minutes."

Derek turned over the four dead terrorists and slowly peeled the balaclavas away from their faces. He didn't recognise the first two, but the third was the man in the passport photo that had been sent to him from Scotland Yard. "You should have stayed in Pakistan and not returned here a second time," he murmured.

Ben was standing at his side. "You know this man?" he asked.

"Only from a photograph. I guessed he'd entered the UK to take part in some atrocity, but we never managed to catch him. How are your men doing?"

"We're still sweeping the complex for any live enemy and picking up our dead and wounded."

"What are the figures?"

"So far, we've recovered five dead and six men wounded. I've called the ambulance service and they'll ferry my men to Ipswich Hospital."

"That's not the nearest."

"No, but it's the best equipped to deal with gunshot wounds."

"I've got to ring my Chief now and then we can all stand down and hand the place back to the resident staff."

"Does that ordinary looking box hold the dreaded dirty bomb?" laughed Ben, suddenly feeling light-headed with relief. "So why didn't it go up in a mushroom cloud?"

"It's a bit like 'M' in a James Bond film; it hasn't been perfected yet!"

"Ring your boss and let's see about getting that thing removed to a safe place where the boffins can get their hands on it, and welcome it, they will play with it for hours; then I'll buy you a long, stiff drink," said Ben cheerfully.

"That's the best offer I've had all day." Derek dialled the Chief's number. "Hi there, it's your long-lost son phoning to tell you he's still alive!"

"You sound happy," said the Chief. "Are you drunk?"

"No, but with any luck I soon will be. We've sorted out that little problem you and the Home Secretary gave me and I'm standing here in the middle of Plant A. Everything's running more or less normally and a lot of terrorists are no longer with us. In fact, to put it baldly, they're dead. The Paras, headed by Captain Horatio Benjamin Rodgers, have recaptured the plant, and their lousy bomb didn't go off, although they tried very hard to explode it. Everything's back to more or less normal and Ben and I are going to finish up here and go for a few stiff drinks, so you'll be getting my expenses claim form by the next post!"

"Will there be anywhere open this early in the morning?"

"We'll find somewhere."

Ben gathered his men together, checking that they had found no other terrorists, and left Toddy in charge of finalising the arrangements for the wounded.

The ambulances had arrived and the paramedics were treating the wounded and checking the unharmed civilians for shock. Derek shook hands with Stuart and left him to make arrangements for more staff to take over from them and then to report to management. Together with Ben, he walked out of the building into the daylight, although the plant lights had not been switched off.

"Back to your cosy police station now, is it?" queried Ben.

"That and writing hundreds of reports on every aspect of this investigation. I'll be lucky if I get to bed before the end of the month!"

"Stop exaggerating," laughed Ben as they passed the bodies of two terrorists not yet placed with the rest of the dead.

Suddenly, a shot rang out and Derek dropped to the ground. Ben saw a black-clad figure trying to balance on his elbow to aim another shot, this time at him. With a growl of fury, he kicked the gun out of his hand, drew his own pistol and shot the terrorist twice in the face.

Chapter 65

Helen arrived at her office as usual on Tuesday morning.

"Have you heard the latest?" asked her boss.

"No, I didn't catch the early news this morning. What's happened to get you all excited?"

"There's been a terrorist attempt to blow up Sizewell nuclear power plant. Not many details, but apparently the Paras from Colchester were called in, recaptured it and wiped out the whole of the terrorist group. They suffered some losses, but they're being a bit cagey about numbers." He carried on talking but Helen's mind was racing, wondering if Derek had been involved in any way. No, he couldn't have been; they said it was the Paras who recaptured the place. What would he be doing down on the east coast with an army unit from Colchester? No way. She decided to give him a ring at lunchtime and ask him if he missed all the excitement. But she felt uneasy and unable to concentrate all morning and went out of the office at lunchtime to make her call privately.

She rang Derek's number but a recorded voice said, 'Sorry, this number is unavailable at this time; please try later,' instead of Derek's usual cheerful message. Helen tried to persuade herself that he was probably asleep after being out on duty all night and decided to drive over after work to see him.

The day seemed interminably long and she couldn't concentrate; her mind constantly strayed from the work on her desk, and she made stupid mistakes. She longed for the clock to reach five-thirty, when she could reasonably expect to leave work.

At last she could put everything away and drive to Derek's house. She opened the front door and slipped inside. "Derek," she called, "it's me. Where are you hiding?"

The house was silent and empty. She checked upstairs; the bed was unmade and towels had been left scattered in the bathroom. Downstairs the kitchen light had been left on and an empty mug had been abandoned on the table, still half full of coffee.

Puzzled, she looked around. Normally he was very tidy, so he must have rushed off somewhere in a hurry, but where? And why hadn't he given her a quick call to set her mind at rest? Well, sod him, she thought. I'm going home if he can't even bother to ring me. Leaving everything as she had found it, she flounced out of the house, got in her car and drove home, highly indignant, although she wasn't quite sure what about.

She cooked herself a meal but found that she had no appetite. I'll warm it up later, she thought, when I'm a bit calmer, although what I'm getting upset about I don't know. I'll just have a small glass of wine and watch some television, or I could read a book. Once I've started to concentrate on something the time will soon pass! She took a sip of wine and looked at the clock; it was only five past seven. She walked into the kitchen and refilled her glass, switched the TV on and watched for ten minutes. Suddenly she was aware that she hadn't the slightest idea what they were talking about, and aware that she was listening for the phone, willing it to ring. He must be at home now, she thought. She tried his phone again, but the same recorded message was repeated. She discovered she was talking to herself, going over the puzzling events of the day. Where was he? Why didn't he ring? A tear found its way onto her cheek and trickled slowly down her face.

An hour later, she was still sitting in the same position, the glass of wine in her hand, watching a programme she couldn't remember. Her meal remained uneaten in the microwave. She drank the wine in one gulp, switched off the TV and went to bed, only to lie awake for most of the night until her weary brain finally let her sleep restlessly for a few hours.

She was up at six and forced herself to do a punishing exercise routine before showering. She nibbled at last night's uneaten meal before throwing the rest of it into the bin.

Once she was in the office, she felt slightly more cheerful and started work, but time dragged. At ten o'clock she said casually, "I really fancy a nice café latte."

"There's coffee here in the office," said her boss, slightly suspiciously.

"Oh yes, I know, but I'm just popping out to the Italian place next door to get a sandwich and a latte, just for a change. Anything I can get for you?"

"No thanks."

Once outside the office, she dialled Derek's number slowly and carefully, willing the machine to connect her to the voice she wanted to hear. But she was again told that the number was not available.

A thought came to her: if anyone knows where Derek is it must be the Chief. She rang his number, waiting impatiently for the Chief's secretary to answer in her pleasant voice. She meant to say that she was Derek's fiancée and ask the Chief to tell her if he was on some urgent assignment, but it came out as, "I must speak to the Chief. Where's Derek Young? I can't get in touch with him."

"Is anything the matter, dear? You sound very upset?" said the secretary. "I'm not aware of Chief Inspector Young's location at the present time. Wait one moment and I'll ask the Chief."

It seemed like hours later she heard the secretary say, "Miss Baker, I'm afraid the Chief is not aware of Chief Inspector Young's exact location, but…" She hesitated. "He was involved in some kind an operation at Sizewell. He rang the Chief to say everything had been completed smoothly and…" Again she hesitated. "But that's the last we heard from him. The Chief is trying to track him down for a full report on the matter. Unfortunately, no one seems to know his exact whereabouts and they're still trying to identify some of the fatalities, to inform next of kin and so forth."

Helen thought her heart had stopped beating but managed to reply, "There were casualties? How many? Are you saying that Derek was a casualty? How could he be a casualty? How could he have been involved in any fighting?" Helen found herself babbling.

Soothingly, the Chief's secretary said, "I think the best thing I can do is to put you through to the Chief; he's finished on the other line. He might have some new information."

When his secretary told him she had a slightly hysterical female on the line for him, the Chief winced and was tempted to put his phone down, pleading a broken connection. But he was made of sterner stuff and listened to what she had to say.

Helen explained that she had been trying to get in touch with Derek, but his mobile phone had a recorded message on it saying he wasn't available and she was sure something wasn't right.

The Chief knew this had to be handled delicately, so he said, "I'm as mystified as you are, but this is what I know. A group of terrorists mounted an attack on the Sizewell nuclear power station. Derek had volunteered himself to be the co-ordinator for England and Wales in the event of this kind of attack, and I was there with him, in the Home Secretary's office, when it was agreed. When the Home Secretary learned that the attack was taking place, he rang Derek at his home and told him there was a helicopter waiting for him at Manchester Airport to fly him to the combat zone and take charge of the situation. Derek rang me from inside the plant and told me he was inside the control room, and although there was still some fighting going on outside, the plant had been made safe. He was unable to say any more because it was an open line. However, he promised he'd give me a full report when he got back to Manchester, but in the meantime, he and the paratrooper commander, Captain Rodgers, were going for a drink. I've been unable to get any more information as to his whereabouts from the Suffolk police or the army commander, but I promise you that as soon as I know any details, so will you. Give your phone numbers to my secretary and we'll be in touch with you as soon as we find out anything, anything at all."

With that, Helen had to be satisfied, and she tried to concentrate on her work, knowing that at least someone else was trying to find news of Derek. She remembered that on Sunday night he had been very sad and asked her if she had ever had a premonition that something bad was going to happen to her. Had he been thinking along those lines? Was he worried that he was going to die? She shuddered at the thought. If he had been wounded in this attack, to which hospital would they have taken him?

She walked over to the wall map and studied Suffolk. There were quite a few smallish places, and any one of them could have a hospital, but men wounded during a battle might require a lot of specialist care, which would mean a big hospital. Somewhere like Ipswich.

She found the hospital's general enquiries number on their website and disappeared into the ladies' toilet to make the call.

A woman answered. "Can I help you?"

Helen asked if they had a patient by the name of Chief Inspector Derek Young.

"I'll make enquiries for you. Are you a relative of the patient?"

Helen lied, saying brightly, "Yes, I'm his wife."

"Hold on a moment." The moment turned into minutes until Helen thought she would scream at the delay. What was the difficulty in looking up a name on a list of patients, for heaven's sake? She heard a muttered conversation in the background and then the woman came back to her. "I'm sorry; there's no such person named on our list of admissions."

"What exactly does that mean?" said Helen, trying to prolong her hopes.

"If such person is not on our list, that person is not here, in this hospital," the woman said, carefully enunciating her words so that the simple person at the other end of the line would understand.

"Thank you," said Helen with a heavy heart.

Another endless day. When she finished work she decided to drive to Derek's house and found it exactly as she had left it the previous day. But when she came downstairs, she saw something that in her distracted state the day before she hadn't noticed. There was a sheet of paper on the coffee table in the lounge, the note Derek had scribbled before he left.

She sat down slowly and read the words: "My dear Helen, I wish I had time to kiss you goodbye. But that is not to be. I have to go and fight the bad guys. If I don't come back, please don't cry for me. Life on this planet is only a short intermission and I will be watching over you from a better place. We will meet again in heaven. I'll always love you. Derek."

Helen sat weeping quietly, thinking of two wasted lives. Morning found her depressed and puffy-eyed. At work, her boss asked anxiously what the matter was. He wondered if she had flu; she had been looking a bit under the weather lately, like death warmed up.

"Thanks," Helen responded acidly.

"I wasn't trying to be nasty," he protested. "It's just not like you. Perhaps you need a bit of a holiday. Why don't you take a few days off? There's nothing here that can't wait."

Just then her mobile rang. It was the Chief.

"Are you sitting down? I've got some good news for you! Chief Inspector Young is okay but he's been wounded. The specialist who's attending him says he'll make a full recovery—"

"Where is he?" Helen interrupted.

"Calm down, Sergeant Baker, I was just going to tell you. He's in a special unit at Manchester General Hospital. Go to the main entrance and ask at the desk for the Special Recovery Unit. You might need to identify yourself but they'll give you directions and then you can ring and tell me how he is. Got quite used to him popping in and out of my office, and my secretary always had a good word for him."

Helen turned to her boss. "I'll be taking two weeks' leave as from now," she said and gave him a smacking kiss before rushing out of the office.

She parked her car, hardly knowing how she had driven to the hospital, and rushed into the main entrance, searching for the enquiries desk. She followed their directions in a daze until, through the open doors of the ward, she saw Derek, propped up with pillows and looking very pale.

She felt almost embarrassed, sitting down next to his bed, but she couldn't prevent herself putting her hand on his, just to make sure he really was alive.

He opened his eyes. "The bastard shot me in the back; hadn't the courage to face me."

Typical, thought Helen. Trust a man to think of something stupid like that when all that matters is that he's here and alive! "You can tell me all the details when you're up and about."

"Thank you," said Derek. "I've only managed to save the world and win a victory for the Manchester Police; don't I even deserve a kiss?"

"Hold on a minute! Can't have your temperature going up too much, although it might bring a bit of colour to your cheeks."

"I lost a lot of blood, but luckily no vital organs were hit. It's just a case of my wound healing, some rest and relaxation and then I can start to show you who's boss once again!"

Derek was discharged a week later and Helen moved into his house. They were married two months later.

Chapter 66

Meanwhile, outside Islamabad in a desolate farmhouse in the deserted countryside, three men were sitting cross-legged on the carpeted floor. The man in the centre said regretfully, "It didn't go so well for us; none of our men escaped with their lives."

"But we have killed six of their soldiers and wounded many," said the man on the right.

"Forty-one of our warriors and six unbelievers dead is not something to fill Allah with joy," the man on the left said.

"I can hear a motorcycle approaching," said the man on the right. "Perhaps our leaders have decided to trust us with a new mission to bring glory and respect to our followers."

"We'll soon know," said the man in the centre as the engine stopped. "We had better welcome him." He got to his feet with some difficulty. As he reached the door, the engine stuttered into life and could be heard retreating the same way it had come. The man was standing near the door. "What is he playing at?" he said angrily.

Outside the motorcyclist was now over a hundred metres away from the house. He stopped and turned his head to look back, there was a huge explosion, when the dust settled, he could see a pile of rubble, that once was the house. He looked satisfied, turned his head and rode away.

When eventually, alerted by the cloud of smoke, the local officials arrived, they found the crumpled bodies of three old men. A cursory investigation concluded that they were probably terrorists priming a bomb when it went off, killing all three. Which was exactly what they deserved.